DEMOLITION ANGEL

ACKNOWLEDGMENTS

The author wishes to thank the following people for their help: Det. John Petievich, LAPD (retired); Det. Paul Bishop, LAPD; Det. Bob Nelson, Criminal Conspiracy Section, LAPD (retired); Lt. Mike DeCoudres, commanding officer, LAPD Bomb Squad; Sgt. Joe Pau, supervisor, LAPD Bomb Squad; Lt. Anthony Alba, LAPD Public Affairs; Special Agent Charles Hustmyer, ATF; Stephen B. Scheid, Explosives Specialist, ATF; Marc Scott Taylor, Technical Associates, Inc.; Steven B. Richlin, OD; Jane Bryson, Ph.D.; Angela Donahue, Ph.D., Behavioral Science Unit, LAPD; Patricia Crais; Celia Gleason; Clay Fourrier; Leslie Day; Tami Hoag; Gerald Petievich; Shawn Coyne; Steve Rubin; Gina Centrello; Aaron Priest; Norman Kurland; Emile Gladstone; Tricia Davey; Jonathan King; and Laurence Mark.

The explosives experts and bomb technicians with whom I spoke were justifiably concerned that this book neither be instructional, nor reveal the exact capabilities by which bomb techs ply their trade. To that end, I have changed certain facts and procedures and fictionalized others. Professionals knowledgeable in the field should note that the technical and procedural inaccuracies contained in this work are the author's responsibility, and his alone.

PROLOGUE

To be disrupted:

when the human body

is blown apart; as

by the pressure force

of a bomb.

—GRADWOHL'S LEGAL MEDICINE

CHARLIE RIGGIO STARED at the cardboard box sitting beside the Dumpster. It was a Jolly Green Giant box, with what appeared to be a crumpled brown paper bag sticking up through the top. The box was stamped GREEN BEANS. Neither Riggio nor the two uniformed officers with him approached closer than the corner of the strip mall there on Sunset Boulevard; they could see the box fine from where they were.

"How long has it been there?"

One of the Adam car officers, a Filipino named Ruiz, checked his watch.

"We got our dispatch about two hours ago. We been here since."

"Find anyone who saw how it got there?"

"Oh, no, dude. Nobody."

The other officer, a black guy named Mason, nodded.

"Ruiz is the one saw it. He went over and looked in the bag, the crazy Flip."

"So tell me what you saw."

"I told your sergeant."

"Tell *me*. I'm the sonofabitch who's gonna approach the damned thing."

Ruiz described seeing the capped ends of two galvanized pipes taped together with silver duct tape. The pipes were loosely wrapped in newspaper, Ruiz said, so he had only seen the ends.

Riggio considered that. They were standing in a strip mall on Sunset Boulevard in Silver Lake, an area that had seen increasing gang activity in recent months. Gangbangers would steal galvanized pipe from construction sites or dig up plastic PVC from some poor bastard's garden, then stuff them with bottle rocket powder or match heads. Riggio didn't know if the Green Giant box held an actual bomb or not, but he had to approach it as if it did. That's the way it was with bomb calls. Better than ninety-five percent turned out to be hairspray cans, some teenager's book bag, or, like his most recent call-out, two pounds of marijuana wrapped in Pampers. Only one out of a hundred was what the bomb techs called an "improvised munition."

A homemade bomb.

"You hear ticking or anything like that?"

"No."

"Smell anything burning?"

"Uh-uh."

"Did you open the bag to get a better look?"

"Hell, no."

"Did you move the box or anything?"

Ruiz smiled like Riggio was nuts.

"Dude, I saw those pipes and shit my pants. The only thing I moved was my *feet!*"

Mason laughed.

Riggio walked back to his vehicle. The Bomb Squad drove dark blue Suburbans, rigged with a light bar and crammed with all the tools of the bomb technician's trade, except for the robots. You wanted the robots, you had to call them out special, and he wasn't going to do that. The goddamned robot would just get bogged down in all the pot-holes around the box.

Riggio found his supervisor, Buck Daggett, instructing a uniformed sergeant to evacuate the area for a hundred yards in all directions. The fire department had already been called, and paramedics were on the way. Sunset Boulevard had been closed and traffic rerouted. All for something that might turn out to be some do-it-yourself plumber's cast-off drain trap.

"Hey, Buck, I'm ready to take a look at that thing."

"I want you in the suit."

"It's too hot. I'll use the chest protector for the first pass, then the suit if I have to bring out the de-armer."

All Riggio would be doing on the first pass was lugging out a portable X-ray to see inside the bag. If the contents appeared to be a bomb, he and Daggett would formulate a game plan and either de-arm the device or explode it in place.

"I want you in the suit, Charles. I got a feeling about this one."

"You've always got a feeling."

"I've also got the sergeant stripes. You're in the suit."

The armored suit weighed almost ninety pounds. Made of Kevlar plates and heavy Nomex batting, it covered every part of Riggio's body except his hands, which remained bare. A bomb tech needed the dexterity of unencumbered fingers.

When the suit was in place, Riggio took the Real Time RTR3 X-ray unit and lumbered toward the package. Walking in the suit was like walking with his body wrapped in wet quilts, only hotter. Three minutes in the armor, and sweat was already running into his eyes. To make it worse, a safety cable and hardwire dragged behind him, the hardwire connecting him to Daggett via a Telex communicator. A separate wire linked the Real Time to a computer in the Suburban's cargo bay. He felt like he was pulling a plow.

Daggett's voice came into Riggio's ear. "How you doing out there?"

"Sweating my ass off, thanks to you."

Riggio hated this part the most, approaching an object before he knew what it was. Every time was the same: Riggio thought of that unknown object as a living beast with a life and a mind. Like a sleeping pit bull. If he approached it carefully and made the right moves, everything would be fine. If he startled the dog, the damn thing would rip him apart.

Eighty-two slow-motion paces brought him to the box.

It was unremarkable except for a wet stain on one corner that looked like dog piss. The brown paper bag, crumpled and uneven, was open. Riggio peered into the bag without touching it. Leaning over was hard, and when he did, sweat dripped onto the Lexan faceplate like rain.

He saw the two pipes that Ruiz had described. The pipe caps appeared to be about two and a half inches in diameter and taped together, but nothing else about them was visible. They were loosely wrapped with newspaper, leaving only the ends exposed. Daggett said, "How's it look?"

"Like a couple of pipes. Stand by. I'll get us a picture."

Riggio placed the Real Time RTR3 on the ground at the base of the box, aimed for a side view, then turned on the unit. It provided the same type of translucent shadow image that security personnel see on airline baggage units, reproducing the image on two screens: one for Riggio on top of the RTR3 and another on the computer back at the Suburban.

Charlie Riggio smiled.

"Sonofabitch. We got one, Buck. We got us a bomb."

"I'm seeing it."

The two pipes were impenetrable shadows with what appeared

to be a spool of wire or fuse triangled between them. There didn't appear to be a timer or an initiator of a more sophisticated nature, leading Riggio to believe that the bomb was a garage project made by an enterprising local gangbanger. Low-tech, dirty, and not particularly difficult to de-arm.

"This one's going to be a piece of cake, Buck. I make a basic fuse of the light-it-and-run-like-hell variety."

"You be careful. Might be some kind of motion switch tucked away in there."

"I'm not gonna touch it, Buck. Jesus. Gimme some credit."

"Don't get cocky. Take the snaps and let's figure out what's what."

The procedure was to take a series of digital computer snaps of the device via the Real Time at forty-five-degree angles. When they had the device mapped, Riggio would fall back to the Suburban, where he and Daggett would decide how best to destroy or de-arm it.

Riggio shuffled around the box, aiming the Real Time over the different angles. He felt no fear as he did this because he knew what he was dealing with now and trusted he could beat it. Riggio had approached over forty-eight suspicious packages in his six years with the Bomb Squad; only nine had been actual explosive devices. None of those had ever detonated in a manner that he did not control.

"You're not talking to me, Charlie. You okay?"

"Just got to work around the potholes, Sarge. Almost done. Hey, you know what I'm having? I'm having a brainstorm."

"Stop. You'll hurt yourself."

"No, listen to this. You know those people on the infomercials who make all that money with the stupid shit they sell? We could sell these damned suits to fat people, see? You just wear it and you lose weight."

"Keep your damned head with that bomb, Riggio. How's your body temp?"

"I'm okay."

In truth, he was so hot that he felt dizzy, but he wanted to make sure he had good clean shots. He circled the box like a man in a space suit, getting front, side, and off angles, then pointed the Real Time straight down for a top view. That's when he saw a shadow that hadn't been visible in the side views.

"Buck, you see that? I think I got something."

"What?"

"Here in the overhead view. Take a snap."

A thin, hairlike shadow emerged from the side of one pipe and extended up through the spool. This wire wasn't attached to the others, which confused Riggio until a sudden, unexpected thought occurred to him: Maybe the spool was there only to hide this other wire.

In that moment, fear crackled through him and his bowels clenched. He called out to Buck Daggett, but the words did not form.

Riggio thought, *Oh, God.*

The bomb detonated at a rate of twenty-eight thousand feet per second, twenty-two times faster than a nine-millimeter bullet leaves the muzzle of a pistol. Heat flashed outward in a burst of white light hot enough to melt iron. The air pressure spiked from a normal fifteen pounds per square inch to twenty-two hundred pounds, shattering the iron pipes into jagged shrapnel that punched through the Kevlar suit like hyperfast bullets. The shock wave slammed into his body with an overpressure of three hundred thousand pounds, crushing his chest, rupturing his liver, spleen, and lungs, and separating his unprotected hands. Charlie Riggio was lifted fourteen feet into the air and thrown a distance of thirty-eight feet.

Even this close to the point of detonation, Riggio might have survived if this had been, as he first suspected, a garage bomb cooked up by a gangbanger with makeshift materials.

It wasn't.

Bits of tarmac and steel fell around him like bloody rain, long after Charlie Riggio was dead.

PART ONE

1

"TELL ME ABOUT the thumb. I know what you told me on the phone, but tell me everything now."

Starkey inhaled half an inch of cigarette, then flicked ash on the floor, not bothering with the ashtray. She did that every time she was annoyed with being here, which was always.

"Please use the ashtray, Carol."

"I missed."

"You didn't miss."

Detective-2 Carol Starkey took another deep pull on the cigarette, then crushed it out. When she first started seeing this therapist, Dana Williams wouldn't let her smoke during session. That was three years and four therapists ago. In the time Starkey was working her way through the second and third therapists, Dana had gone back to the smokes herself, and now didn't mind. Sometimes they both smoked and the goddamned room clouded up like the Imperial Valley capped by an inversion layer.

Starkey shrugged.

"No, I guess I didn't miss. I'm just pissed off, is all. It's been three years, and here I am back where I started."

"With me."

"Yeah. Like in three years I shouldn't be over this shit."

"So tell me what happened, Carol. Tell me about the little girl's thumb."

Starkey fired up another cigarette, then settled back to recall the little girl's thumb. Starkey was down to three packs a day. The progress should have made her feel better, but didn't.

"It was Fourth of July. This idiot down in Venice decides to make his own fireworks and give them away to the neighbors. A little girl ends up losing the thumb and index finger on her right hand, so we get the call from the emergency room."

"Who is 'we'?"

"Me and my partner that day, Beth Marzik."

"Another woman?"

"Yeah. There's two of us in CCS."

"Okay."

"By the time we get down there, the family's gone home, so we go to the house. The father's crying, saying how they found the finger, but not the thumb, and then he shows us these homemade firecrackers that are so damned big she's lucky she didn't lose the hand."

"He made them?"

"No, a guy in the neighborhood made them, but the father won't tell us. He says the man didn't mean any harm. I say, your daughter has been *maimed*, sir, other children are at *risk*, sir, but the guy won't cop. I ask the mother, but the guy says something in Spanish, and now she won't talk, either."

"Why won't they tell you?"

"People are assholes."

The world according to Carol Starkey, Detective-2 with LAPD's Criminal Conspiracy Section. Dana made a note of that in a leather-bound notebook, an act which Starkey never liked. The notes gave physical substance to her words, leaving Starkey feeling vulnerable because she thought of the notes as evidence.

Starkey had more of the cigarette, then shrugged and went on with it.

"These bombs are six inches long, right? We call'm Mexican Dynamite. So many of these things are going off, it sounds like the Academy pistol range, so Marzik and I start a door-to-door. But the neighbors are just like the father—no one's telling us anything, and I'm getting madder and madder. Marzik and I are walking back to the car when I look down and there's the thumb. I just looked down and there it was, this beautiful little thumb, so I scooped it up and brought it back to the family."

"On the phone, you told me you tried to make the father eat it."

"I grabbed his collar and pushed it into his mouth. I did that."

Dana shifted in her chair, Starkey reading from her body language that she was uncomfortable with the image. Starkey couldn't blame her.

"It's easy to understand why the family filed a complaint."

Starkey finished the cigarette and crushed it out.

"The family didn't complain."

"Then why—?"

"Marzik. I guess I scared Marzik. She had a talk with my lieutenant, and Kelso threatened to send me to the bank for an evaluation."

LAPD maintained its Behavorial Sciences Unit in the Far East Bank building on Broadway, in Chinatown. Most officers lived in abject fear of being ordered to the bank, correctly believing that it called into question their stability and ended any hope of career advancement. They had an expression for it: "Overdrawn on the career account."

"If I go to the bank, they'll never let me back on the Bomb Squad."

"And you keep asking to go back?"

"It's all I've wanted since I got out of the hospital."

Irritated now, Starkey stood and lit another cigarette. Dana studied her, which Starkey also didn't like. It made her feel watched, as if Dana was waiting for her to do or say something more that she could write down. It was a valid interview technique that Starkey used herself. If you said nothing, people felt compelled to fill the silence.

"The job is all I have left, damnit."

Starkey regretted the defensive edge in her voice and felt even more embarrassed when Dana again scribbled a note.

"So you told Lieutenant Kelso that you would seek help on your own?"

"Jesus, no. I kissed his ass to get out of it. I know I have a problem, Dana, but I'll get help in a way that doesn't fuck my career."

"Because of the thumb?"

Starkey stared at Dana Williams with the same flat eyes she would use on Internal Affairs.

"Because I'm falling apart."

Dana sighed, and a warmth came to her eyes that infuriated Starkey because she resented having to reveal herself in ways that made her feel vulnerable and weak. Carol Starkey did not do "weak" well, and never had.

"Carol, if you came back because you want me to fix you as if you were broken, I can't do that. Therapy isn't the same as setting a bone. It takes time."

"It's been three years. I should be over this by now."

"There's no 'should' here, Carol. Consider what happened to you. Consider what you survived."

"I've had enough with *considering* it. I've *considered* it for three fucking years."

A sharp pain began behind her eyes. Just from *considering* it.

"Why do you think you keep changing therapists, Carol?"

Starkey shook her head, then lied.

"I don't know."

"Are you still drinking?"

"I haven't had a drink in over a year."

"How's your sleep?"

"A couple of hours, then I'm wide awake."

"Is it the dream?"

Carol felt herself go cold.

"No."

"Anxiety attacks?"

Starkey was wondering how to answer when the pager clipped to her waist vibrated. She recognized the number as Kelso's cell phone, followed by 911, the code the detectives in the Criminal Conspiracy Section used when they wanted an immediate response.

"Shit, Dana. I've gotta get this."

"Would you like me to leave?"

"No. No, I'll just step out."

Starkey took her purse out into the waiting room, where a middle-aged woman seated on the couch briefly met her eyes, then averted her face.

"Sorry."

The woman nodded without looking.

Starkey dug through her purse for her cell phone, then punched the speed dial to return Kelso's page. She could tell he was in his car when he answered.

"It's me, Lieutenant. What's up?"

"Where are you?"

Starkey stared at the woman.

"I was looking for shoes."

"I didn't ask what you were doing, Starkey. I asked where you were."

She felt the flush of anger when he said it, and shame that she even gave a damn what he thought.

"The west side."

"All right. The bomb squad had a call-out, and, um, I'm on my way there now. Carol, we lost Charlie Riggio. He was killed at the scene."

Starkey's fingers went cold. Her scalp tingled. It was called "going core." The body's way of protecting itself by drawing the blood inward to minimize bleeding. A response left over from our animal pasts when the threat would involve talons and fangs and something that wanted to rip you apart. In Starkey's world, the threat often still did.

"Starkey?"

She turned away and lowered her voice so that the woman couldn't hear.

"Sorry, Lieutenant. Was it a bomb? Was it a device that went off?"

"I don't know the details yet, but, yes, there was an explosion."

Sweat leaked from her skin, and her stomach clenched. Uncontrolled explosions were rare. A Bomb Squad officer dying on the job was even more rare. The last time it had happened was three years ago.

"Anyway, I'm on my way there now. Ah, Starkey, I could put someone else on this, if you'd rather I did that."

"I'm up in the rotation, Lieutenant. It's my case."

"All right. I wanted to offer."

He gave her the location, then broke the connection. The woman on the couch was watching her as if she could read Starkey's pain. Starkey saw herself in the waiting room mirror, abruptly white beneath her tan. She felt herself breathing. Shallow, fast breaths.

Starkey put her phone away, then went back to tell Dana that she would have to end their session early.

"We've got a call-out, so I have to go. Ah, listen, I don't want you to turn in any of this to the insurance, okay? I'll pay out of my own pocket, like before."

"No one can get access to your insurance records, Carol. Not without your permission. You truly don't need to spend the money."

"I'd rather pay."

As Starkey wrote the check, Dana said, "You didn't finish the story. Did you catch the man who made the firecrackers?"

"The little girl's mother took us to a garage two blocks away where we found him with eight hundred pounds of smokeless gunpowder. Eight hundred pounds, and the whole place is reeking of gasoline because you know what this guy does for a living? He's a gardener. If that place had gone up, it would've taken out the whole goddamned block."

"My Lord."

Starkey handed over the check, then said her good-byes and started for the door. She stopped with her hand on the knob because she remembered something that she had intended to ask Dana.

"There's something about that guy I've been wondering about. Maybe you can shed some light."

"In what way?"

"This guy we arrested, he tells us he's been building fireworks his whole life. You know how we know it's true? He's only got three fingers on his left hand and two on his right. He's blown them off one by one."

Dana paled.

"I've arrested a dozen guys like that. We call them chronics. Why do they do that, Dana? What do you say about people like that who keep going back to the bombs?"

Now Dana took out a cigarette of her own and struck it. She blew out a fog of smoke and stared at Starkey before answering.

"I think they want to destroy themselves."

Starkey nodded.

"I'll call you to reschedule, Dana. Thanks."

Starkey went out to her car, keeping her head down as she passed the woman in the waiting room. She slid behind the wheel, but didn't start the engine. Instead, she opened her briefcase and took out a slim silver flask of gin. She took a long drink, then opened the door and threw up in the parking lot.

When she finished heaving, she put away the gin and ate a Tagamet.

Then, doing her best to get a grip on herself, Carol Starkey drove across town to a place exactly like the one where she had died.

Helicopters marked ground zero the way vultures circle roadkill, orbiting over the crime scene in layers like a cake. Starkey saw them just as the traffic locked down, half a mile from the incident site. She used her bubble flasher to edge into an Aamco station, left her car, and walked the remaining eight blocks.

A dozen radio units were on the scene, along with two Bomb Squad Suburbans and a growing army of media people. Kelso was standing near the forward Suburban with the Bomb Squad commander, Dick Leyton, and three of the day-shift bomb techs. Kelso was a short man with a droopy mustache, in a black-checked sport coat. Kelso noticed Starkey, and waved to catch her eye, but Starkey pretended she didn't see him.

Riggio's body lay in a heap in the parking lot, midway between the forward Suburban and the building. A coroner investigator was leaning against his van, watching an LAPD criminalist named John Chen work the body. Starkey didn't know the CI because she had never before worked a case where someone had died, but she knew Chen.

Starkey badged her way past the uniforms at the mouth of the parking lot. One of the uniforms, a younger guy she didn't know, said, "Man, that dude got the shit blown out of himself. I wouldn't go over there, I was you."

"You wouldn't?"

"Not if I had a choice."

Smoking at a crime scene was against LAPD policy, but Starkey fired up before crossing the parking lot to confront Charlie Riggio's body. Starkey had known him from her days on the squad, so she expected this to be hard. It was.

Riggio's helmet and chest protector had been stripped off by the paramedics who had worked to revive him. Shrapnel had cut through the suit, leaving bloody puckers across his chest and stomach that looked blue in the bright afternoon sun. A single hole had been punched in his face, just beneath the left eye. Starkey glanced over at the helmet and saw that the Lexan faceplate was shattered. They said that the Lexan could stop a bullet from a deer rifle. Then she looked back at his body and saw that his hands were missing.

Starkey ate a Tagamet, then turned away so that she wouldn't have to see the body.

"Hey, John. What do we have here?"

"Hey, Starkey. You got the lead on this one?"

"Yeah. Kelso said that Buck Daggett was out, but I don't see him."

"They sent him to the hospital. He's okay, but he's pretty shook. Leyton wanted him checked."

"Okay. So what did he say? You got anything I can use?"

Chen glanced back at the body, then pointed out the Dumpster.

"The device was over by that Dumpster. Buck says Riggio was over it with the Real Time when it went off."

Starkey followed his nod to a large piece of the Real Time portable X-ray that had been blown out into the street. She considered the Dumpster again, and guessed that the Real Time had been kicked more than forty yards. Riggio himself lay almost thirty yards from the Dumpster.

"Did Daggett or the medics pull him over here?"

Anytime there was an explosion, bomb techs were trained to expect a secondary device. She figured that Daggett would have pulled Riggio away from the Dumpster for that reason.

"You'd have to ask Daggett. I think this is where he fell."

"Jesus. We gotta be, what, thirty yards from the detonation point?"

"Buck said it was a helluva blast."

She guesstimated the distance again, then toed the body armor to examine the blast pattern. The suit looked as if twenty shotguns had been fired into it point-blank. She'd seen similar suit damage when "dirty" bombs had gone off with a lot of fire and shrapnel, but this bomb had pushed the shrap through twelve layers of armor and had thrown a man thirty yards. The energy released must have been enormous.

Chen took a plastic bag from his evidence kit, pulling the plastic tight to show her a piece of blackened metal about the size of a postage stamp.

"This is kind of interesting, too. It's a piece of the pipe frag I found stuck in his suit."

Starkey looked close. A squiggly line had been etched into the metal.

"What is that, an *S*?"

Chen shrugged.

"Or some kind of symbol. Remember that bomb they found in San Diego last year, the one with dicks drawn all over it?"

Starkey ignored him. Chen liked to talk. If he got going about a bomb with dicks on it, she would never get her work done.

"John, do me a favor and swab some of the samples tonight, okay?"

Chen went sulky.

"It's going to be really late when I finish here, Carol. I've got to work the Dumpster, and then there's going to be whatever you guys find in the sweep. It's going to take me two or three hours just to log everything."

They would search for pieces of the device everywhere within a hundred-yard radius, combing nearby rooftops, the faces of the apartment buildings and houses across the street, cars, the Dumpster, and the wall behind the Dumpster. They would search for anything and everything that might help them reconstruct the bomb or give them a clue to its origins.

"Don't whine, John. It's not cool."

"I'm just saying."

"How long does it take to cook through the gas chrom?"

The sulk became sullen and put-upon.

"Six hours."

Residue from the explosive would be present on any fragments of the bomb they found, as well as in the blast crater and on Riggio's suit. Chen would identify the substance by cooking it through a gas chromatograph, a process which took six hours. Starkey knew how long it would take when she asked, but asked anyway to make Chen feel guilty about it taking so long.

"Couldn't you swab a couple of samples first, just to start a chrom, then log everything after? An explosive with this kind of energy potential could really narrow down the field of guys I'm looking at, John. You could give me a head start here."

Chen hated to do anything that wasn't methodical and by the book, but he couldn't deny her point. He checked his watch, counting out the time.

"Let me see what time we finish here, okay? I'll try, but I can't guarantee anything."

"I gave up on guarantees a long time ago."

Buck Daggett's Suburban sat forty-eight paces from Riggio's body. Starkey counted as she walked.

Kelso and Leyton saw her coming and moved away from the others to meet her. Kelso's face was grim; Leyton's tense and professional. Leyton had been off shift when he'd gotten the call and had rushed over in jeans and a polo shirt.

Leyton smiled softly when their eyes met, and Starkey thought there was a sad quality to it. Leyton, the twelve-year commander of the Bomb Squad, had selected Carol Starkey for the squad, just as he'd selected Charlie Riggio and every other tech below the rank of sergeant-supervisor. He had sent her to the FBI's Bomb School in Alabama and had been her boss for three years. When she had been in the hospital, he had come every day after his shift to visit her, fifty-four consecutive days, and when she had fought to stay on the job, he had lobbied on her behalf. There wasn't anyone on the job she respected as much, or cared for as much.

Starkey said, "Dick, I want to walk the scene as soon as possible. Could we use as many of your people as you can get out?"

"Everyone not on duty is coming out. You've got us all."

She turned to Kelso.

"Lieutenant, I'd like to talk to these Rampart guys to see if we can't conscript some of their uniforms to help."

Kelso was frowning at her.

"I've already arranged it with their supervisor. You shouldn't be smoking here, Starkey."

"Sorry. I'd better go talk to him, then, and get things organized."

She made no move to put out her cigarette, and Kelso ignored the obvious rebellion.

"Before you do, you'll be working with Marzik and Santos on this."

Starkey felt another Tagamet craving.

"Does it have to be Marzik?"

"Yes, Starkey, it has to be Marzik. They're inbound now. And something else. Lieutenant Leyton says we might have a break here before we get started: 911 got a call on this."

She glanced at Leyton.

"Do we have a wit?"

"An Adam car took the call, but Buck told me they were responding to Emergency Services. If that's the case, then we should have a tape and an address."

That was a major break.

"Okay. I'll get on it. Thanks."

Kelso glanced toward the press again, frowning when he saw an LAPD media officer approaching them.

"I think we'd better go make a statement, Dick."

"Be right there."

Kelso scurried over to intercept the media officer while Leyton stayed with Starkey. They waited until the other man was gone, then Leyton considered her.

"How you doing, Carol?"

"I'm fine, Lieutenant. Kicking ass and taking names, like always. I'd still like to come back to the squad."

Leyton found it within himself to nod. They had weathered that pounding three years ago, and both of them knew that the LAPD Personnel Unit would never allow it.

"You were always a tough girl. But you were lucky, too."

"Sure. I shit luck in the morning."

"You shouldn't curse like that, Carol. It's not attractive."

"You're right, Boss. I'll straighten out as soon as I kick the smokes."

She smiled at him, and Leyton smiled back, because they both knew that she would do neither.

Starkey watched him walk away to join the press conference, then noticed Marzik and Santos talking to a uniformed sergeant amid a group of people outside one of the apartment buildings across the street. Marzik was looking over at her, but Starkey walked around to the front of the Suburban and examined it. The Suburban had faced the blast at about sixty-five yards away. The telex cables and security line that Riggio had pulled out with him still trailed from the rear of the Suburban to Riggio's armored suit, tangled now from the explosion.

The Suburban appeared undamaged, but on closer inspection she saw that the front right headlight was cracked. She squatted to look more closely. A piece of black metal shaped like the letter *E* was wedged in the glass. Starkey did not touch it. She stared until she recognized that it was part of a metal buckle from the straps that had held Riggio's armor suit. She sighed deep and long, then stood and looked back at his body.

The coroner's people were placing him into a body bag. John Chen had outlined the body's location on the tarmac with white chalk and now stood back, watching with an expression of profound disinterest.

Starkey wiped her palms on her hips and forced herself to take deep breaths, stretching her ribs and her lungs. Doing this hurt because of the scars. Marzik, still across the street, was waving. Santos looked over, maybe wondering why Starkey was just standing there.

Starkey waved back, the wave saying that she would join them in a moment.

The mall was a small strip of discount clothing shops, a used-book store, a dentist who advertised "family prices" in Spanish, and a Cuban restaurant, all of which had been evacuated before Riggio approached the bomb.

Starkey forced herself toward the restaurant, moving on legs that were suddenly weak, as if she'd found herself on a tightrope and the only way off was that singular door. Marzik was forgotten. Charlie Riggio was forgotten. Starkey felt nothing but her own hammering heart; and knew that if she lost control of it now, and of herself, she would certainly fall to her death.

When Starkey stepped into the restaurant, she began to shake with a rage beyond all hope of control. She had to grip the counter to keep her feet. If Leyton or Kelso walked in now, her career would be finished. Kelso would order her in to the bank for sure, she would be forced to retire with the medical, and all that would be left of Carol Starkey's life would be fear, and emptiness.

Starkey clawed open her purse for the silver flask, feeling the gin cut into her throat in the same moment she cursed her own weakness, and felt ashamed. She breathed deep, refusing to sit because she knew she would not be able to rise. She took a second long pull on the flask, and the shaking subsided.

Starkey fought down the memories and the fear, telling herself she was only doing what she needed to do and that everything would be all right. She was too tough for it. She would beat it. She would win.

After a while, she had herself together.

Starkey put away the flask, sprayed her mouth with Binaca, then went back out to the crime scene.

She was always a tough girl.

Starkey found the two Adam car officers, who gave her the log time of their original dispatch call. She used her cell phone to call the day manager at Emergency Services, identified herself, provided an approximate time, and requested a tape of the call as well as an address of origin. What most people didn't know was that all calls to 911 were automatically taped and recorded with the originating phone number and that phone number's address. It had to be this way because people in an emergency situation, especially when threatened or dying, couldn't be expected to provide their location. So the system took that into account and provided the address for them.

Starkey left her office number, and asked the manager to provide the information as quickly as she had it.

When Starkey was finished with Emergency Services, she walked across to the apartment buildings where Marzik and Santos were questioning the few residents who had been let back into the area. They saw her coming, and walked out to meet her by the street.

Jorge Santos was a short man with a quizzical expression who always looked as if he was trying to remember something that he'd forgotten. His name was pronounced "whore-hey," which had earned him the dubious nickname of Hooker. Beth Marzik was divorced, with two kids who stayed with her mother when she was on the job. She sold Amway products for the extra money, but she pushed it so hard that half the detectives at Spring Street would duck when they saw her approaching.

Starkey said, "Good news. Leyton says the call-out was responding to a 911."

Marzik smirked.

"This good citizen happen to leave a name?"

"I already put in a call to Emergency Services. They'll run the tapes and have something for us as soon as they can."

Marzik nudged Santos.

"Bet you a dollar to a blow job there's no name."

Santos darkened. He was a religious man, married with four children, and hated it when she talked like that.

Starkey interrupted her.

"I've gotta get the uniforms set up for the sweep. Dick says the Rampart detectives offered to help with the door-to-door."

Marzik frowned as if she didn't like that idea.

"Well, we're not going to get to most of these people tonight. What I'm hearing is that a lot of the people who were evacuated went to relatives or friends after the damned thing blew."

"You're getting a list of residents from the managers, right?"

"Yeah. So?"

Marzik looked suspicious. Her attitude made Starkey tired.

"Get the managers to pull the rental apps, too. They should be on file. Most of the rental applications I used to fill out wanted the name of a relative or somebody to vouch for you. That's probably where those people went."

"Shit, that'll take forever. I *used* to have a date tonight."

Santos's face grew longer than ever.

"I'll do it, Carol."

Starkey glanced toward the Dumpster, where Chen was now picking at something on the ground. She gestured back toward the apartment buildings behind them.

"Look, Beth, I'm not saying do everybody on the goddamned block. Just ask if they saw something. Ask if they're the one who called 911. If they say they didn't see anything, tell'm to think about it and we'll get back to them in the next few days."

Marzik still wasn't happy, but Starkey didn't give a damn.

She went back across the street to the Dumpster, leaving Marzik and Santos with the apartments. Chen was examining the wall behind the Dumpster for bomb fragments. Out in the parking lot, two of the Bomb Squad technicians were adjusting radial metal detectors that they would use when they walked the lawns out front of the surrounding apartment buildings. Two more off-duty bomb techs had arrived, and pretty soon everyone would be standing around with their thumbs up their asses, waiting for her to tell them what to do.

Starkey ignored all of them and went to the crater. It was about three feet across and one foot deep, the black tarmac scorched white by the heat. Starkey wanted to place her hand on the surface, but didn't because the explosive residue might be toxic.

She considered the chalk outline where Riggio's body had fallen, then paced it off. Almost forty paces. The energy to kick him this far must have been incredible.

Starkey impulsively stepped into Riggio's outline, standing exactly where his body had fallen, and gazed back at the crater.

She imagined a slow-motion flash that stretched through three years. She saw her own death as if it had been filmed and later shown to her on instant replay. Her shrink, Dana, had called these "manufactured memories." She had taken the facts as they had later been presented to her, imagined the rest, then saw the events as if she remembered them. Dana believed that this was her mind's way of trying to deal with what had happened, her mind's way of removing her from the actual event by letting her step outside the moment, her mind's way of giving the evil a face so that it could be dealt with.

Starkey sucked deep on the cigarette, then blew smoke angrily at the ground. If this was her mind's way of making peace with what had happened, it was doing a damned shitty job.

She went back across the street to find Marzik.

"Beth? I got another idea. Try to locate the people who own all these shops and see if anyone was threatened, or owed money, or whatever."

Marzik nodded, still squinting at her.

"Carol, what is that?"

"What is what?"

Marzik stepped closer and sniffed.

"Is that Binaca?"

Starkey glared at Marzik, then went back across the street and spent the rest of the evening helping the search team look for pieces of the bomb.

In the dream, she dies.

She opens her eyes on the hard-packed trailer-park earth as the paramedics work over her, their latex hands red with blood. The hum in her ears makes her think of a Mixmaster set to a slow speed. Above her, the thin branches of winter gum trees overlap in a delicate lace still swaying from the pressure wave. A paramedic pushes on her chest, trying to restart her heart. Another inserts a long needle. Cold silver paddles press to her flesh.

A thousand miles beyond the hum, a voice yells, "Clear!" Her body lurches from the jolt of current.

Starkey finds the strength to say his name.

"Sugar?"

She is never certain if she says his name or only thinks that she says it.

Her head lolls, and she sees him. David "Sugar" Boudreaux, a Cajun long out of Louisiana but still with the soft French accent that she finds so sexy. Her sergeant-supervisor. Her secret lover. The man to whom she's given her heart.

"Sugar?"

The faraway voices shout. "No pulse!" "Clear!" The horrible electric spasm.

She reaches toward Sugar, but he is too far away. It is not fair that he is so far. Two hearts that beat as one should not be so far apart. The distance saddens her.

"Shug?"

Two hearts that no longer beat.

The paramedics working on Sugar step away. He is gone.

Her body jolts again, but it does no good, and she is at peace with it.

She closes her eyes and feels herself rise through the branches into the sky, and all she knows is relief.

Starkey woke from the dream just after three that morning, knowing that sleep was beyond her. She lit a cigarette, then lay in the dark, smoking. She had finished at the crime scene just before midnight, but didn't get home until almost one. There, she showered, ate scrambled eggs, then drank a tumbler of Bombay Sapphire gin to knock herself out. Yet here she was, wide awake two hours later.

After another twenty minutes of blowing smoke at the ceiling, she got out of bed, then went through the house, turning on every light.

The bomb that took Starkey had been a package bomb delivered by a meth dealer to murder the family of an informant. It had been placed behind heavy bushes on the side of the informant's double-wide, which meant Sugar and Starkey couldn't use the robot to wheel in the X-ray or the de-armer. It was a dirty bomb, made of a paint can packed with smokeless powder and roofing tacks. Whoever had made the bomb was a mean sonofabitch who wanted to make sure he got the informant's three children.

Because of the bushes, Starkey and Sugar both had to work the bomb, Starkey holding aside the brush so that Sugar could get close with the Real Time. When two uniformed patrol officers had called in the suspicious package, they had reported that the package was ticking. It was such a cliché that Starkey and Sugar had burst out laughing, though they weren't laughing now because the package had stopped ticking. The Real Time showed them that the timer had malfunctioned; the builder had used a hand-wound alarm clock as his timing device, but for some inexplicable reason, the minute hand had frozen at one minute before reaching the lead that would detonate the bomb. It had just stopped.

Sugar made a joke of it.

"Guess he forgot to wind the damned thing."

She was grinning at his joke when the earthquake struck. An event every bomb tech working in Southern California feared. It would later be reported as 3.2 on the Richter scale, hardly noticeable to the average Angeleno, but the minute hand released, contact was made, and the bomb went off.

The old techs had always told Starkey that the suit would not save her from the frag, and they were right. Sugar saved her. He leaned in front of her just as the bomb went off, so his body caught most of the tacks. But the Real Time was blown out of his hands, and that's what got her. Two heavy, jagged pieces sliced through the suit, ripped along her right side, and dug a gaping furrow through her right breast. Sugar was knocked back into her, microseconds behind the Real Time. The force of him impacting into her felt as if she had been kicked by God. The shock was so enormous that her heart stopped.

For two minutes and forty seconds, Carol Starkey was dead.

Two teams of emergency medical personnel rushed forward even as pieces of the trailer and torn azalea bushes fell around them. The team that reached Starkey found her without a pulse, peeled away her suit, and injected epinephrine directly into her heart as they administered CPR. They worked for almost three minutes around the blood and gore that had been her chest and finally—heroically—restarted her heart.

Her heart had started again; Dave "Sugar" Boudreaux's had not.

Starkey sat at her dinette table, thinking about the dream, and Sugar, and smoking more cigarettes. Only three years, and the memories of Sugar were fading. It was harder to see his face, and harder still to hear his soft Cajun accent. More often than not, now, she returned to their pictures to refresh her memories and hated herself for having to do that. As if she was betraying him by forgetting. As if the permanence she had once felt about their passion and love had all been a lie told by someone else to a woman who no longer lived.

Everything had changed.

Starkey had started drinking almost as soon as she got out of the hospital. One of her shrinks—she thought it was number two—had said that her issue was survivor's guilt. Guilt that her heart had started, and Sugar's had not; guilt that she had lived, and he had not; guilt that, down deep, down in the center of herself where our secret creatures live, she was *thankful* that she had lived, even at the price of Sugar's life. Starkey had walked out of the therapist's office that day and never went back. She had gone to a cop bar called the Shortstop and drank until two Wilshire Division robbery detectives carried her out of the place.

Everything had changed.

Starkey pulled away from people. She grew cold. She protected herself with sarcasm and distance and the single-minded pursuit of her job until the job was all that she had. Another shrink—she thought it was number three—suggested that she had traded one armored suit for another, then asked if she thought she would ever be able to take it off.

Starkey did not return to answer.

Tired of thinking, Starkey finished her cigarette, then returned to her bedroom to shower. She pulled off her T-shirt and looked at herself with an absence of feeling.

The right half of her abdomen from her breast to her hip was rilled and cratered from the sixteen bits of metal that had punched into her. Two long furrows roped along her side following her lower ribs. Once tanned a walnut brown, her skin was now as white as a table plate because Starkey hadn't worn a bathing suit since it happened.

The worst of it was her breast. A two-inch piece of the Real Time had impacted on the front of her right breast just beneath the nipple, gouging out a furrow of tissue as it followed the line of her ribs before exiting her back. It had laid her open as if a river valley had been carved in her chest, and that is the way it healed. Her doctors had discussed removing the breast, but decided to save it. They had, but even after the reconstruction, it looked like a misshapen avocado. Her doctors had told her that further cosmetic surgeries could, in time, improve her appearance, but after four operations, Starkey had decided that enough was enough.

She had not been with another man since Sugar had left her bed that morning.

Starkey showered, dressed for the day, then called her office and found two messages.

"It's me, Starkey, John Chen. I got a pretty good swab from the blast crater. I'll set it up in the cooker, but that means I won't be out of here until after three. We should have the chrom around nine. Gimme a call. You owe me."

The Emergency Services manager had left the second message, saying that she'd duped the tape of the 911 call reporting the suspicious device.

"I left the tape at the security desk, so you can pick it up anytime you want. The call was placed from a pay phone on Sunset Boulevard at one-fourteen, that would be yesterday afternoon. I've got a street address here."

Starkey copied the information into a spiral casebook, then made a cup of instant coffee. She swallowed two Tagamet, then lit a cigarette before letting herself out into the sultry night air.

It was not quite five, and the world was quiet. A kid in a beat-up red hatchback was delivering the L.A. *Times*, weaving from side to side in the street as he tossed out the papers. An Alta-Dena dairy truck rumbled past.

Starkey decided to drive back to Silver Lake and walk the blast site again. It was better than listening to the silence in her still-beating heart.

Starkey parked in front of the Cuban restaurant next to a Rampart radio car watching over the scene. The mall's parking lot was otherwise deserted, except for three civilian vehicles that she remembered from the night before.

Starkey held up her badge before she got out.

"Hey, guys, everything okay?"

They were a male/female team, the male officer a skinny guy behind the wheel, the female short and chunky with mannish blonde hair. They were sipping minimart coffee that probably hadn't been hot for hours.

The female officer nodded.

"Yeah. We're good, Detective. You need something?"

"I've got the case. I'm gonna be walking around."

The female officer raised her eyebrows.

"We heard a bomb guy got creamed. That so?"

"Yeah."

"Bummer."

The male officer leaned past his partner.

"If you're gonna be here a few, you mind if we Code Seven? There's an In-'n-Out Burger a couple blocks over. We could bring you something."

His partner winked at Starkey.

"Weak bladder."

Starkey shrugged, secretly pleased to be rid of them.

"Take twenty, but you don't have to bring me anything. I won't be out of here before then."

As the radio car pulled away, Starkey clipped her pistol to her right hip, then crossed Sunset to look for the address that the Emergency Services manager had provided. She brought her Maglite, but didn't turn it on. The area was bright from surrounding security lights.

A pay phone was hanging on the side of a Guatemalan market directly across from the mall, but when Starkey compared it to the address, they didn't match. From the Guatemalan market, she could look back across Sunset at the Dumpster. She figured out which way the numbers ran and followed them to find the pay phone. It was housed in one of the old glass booths that Pac Bell was discontinuing, one block east on the side of a laundry, across the street from a flower shop.

Starkey copied the names of the laundry and flower shop into her notebook, then walked back to the first phone and checked to see if it worked. It did. She wondered why the person who called 911 hadn't done so from here. The Dumpster was in clear view, but wasn't from the other phone. Starkey thought that the caller might've been worried that whoever set the bomb could see them, but she decided not to worry about it until she heard the tape.

Starkey was walking back across Sunset when she saw a piece of bent metal in the street. It was about an inch long and twisted like a piece of bow tie pasta, one side rimed with gray residue. She had picked up nine similar pieces of metal the night before.

She brought it to her car, bagged it in one of the spare evidence bags she kept in the trunk, then walked around the side of the building to the Dumpster. Starkey guessed that the bomb hadn't been placed to damage the building, but wondered why it had been set beside the Dumpster. She knew that satisfying reasons for questions like this often couldn't be found. Twice during her time with the Bomb Squad, she had rolled out on devices left on the side of the freeway, far away from overpasses or exits or anything else they might harm. It was as if the assholes who built these things didn't know what else to do with them, so they just dropped them off on the side of the road.

Starkey walked the scene for another ten minutes and found one more small bit of metal. She was bagging it when the radio car returned to the lot, and the female officer got out with two cups.

"I know you said you didn't want anything, but we brought a coffee in case you changed your mind."

"That was nice. Thanks."

The female officer wanted to chat, but Starkey closed the trunk and told her she needed to get into the office. When the officer went back to her unit, Starkey walked around the far side of her own car and poured out the coffee. She was heading back to the driver's side when she decided to look over the civilian cars again.

Two of the cars had been pinged by bomb frag, the nearest of which had lost its rear window and suffered substantial damage. Parked closest to the blast, it belonged to the man who owned the bookshop. When the police let him back into the area, he had stared at his car, then kicked it and walked away without another word.

The third car, the one farthest away, was a '68 Impala with bad paint and peeling vinyl top. The side windows were down and the rear window had been replaced by cloudy plastic that was brittle with sun damage. She looked beneath it first, found nothing, and was walking around the front of the car when she saw a starburst crack on the windshield. She flashed the Maglite inside and saw a round piece of metal on the dash. It looked like a disk with a single fine wire protruding. Starkey glanced toward the Dumpster and saw it was possible that a piece of frag had come through the open windows to crack the windshield. She fished it out, examined it more closely with no idea what it might be, then dropped it into her pocket.

Starkey climbed back into her car without looking at the uniformed officers, then headed downtown to pick up the audiotape before reporting to her office. The sun was rising in the east, filling the sky with a great red fireball.

Mr. Red .

JOHN MICHAEL FOWLES leaned back on the bench across from the school, enjoying the sun and wondering if he had made the FBI's Ten Most Wanted List. Not an easy thing to do when they didn't know who you were, but he'd been leaving clues. He thought he might stop in a Kinko's later, or maybe the library, and use one of their computers to check the FBI's web page for the standings.

The sun made him smile. He raised his face to it, letting the warmth soak into him, letting its radiation brown his skin, marveling at the enormity of its exploding gases. That's the way he liked to think of it: one great monstrous explosion so large and bright that it could be seen from ninety-three million miles away, fueled so infinitely that it would take billions of years to consume itself, so fucking cool that the very fact of it spawned life here on this planet and would eventually consume that life when it gave a last flickering gasp and blew itself out billions of years from now.

John thought it would be seriously cool to build a bomb that big and set the sucker off. How cool it would be to see those first few nanoseconds of its birth. Way cool.

Thinking about it, John felt a hardening in his groin of a kind that had never been inspired by any living thing.

The voice said, "Are you Mr. Red?"

John opened his eyes. Even with his sunglasses, he had to shield his eyes. John flashed the big white teeth.

"I be him. Are you Mr. Karpov?"

Making like a Florida cracker talking street, even though John was neither from Florida, nor a cracker, nor the street. He enjoyed the misdirection.

"Yes."

Karpov was an overweight man in his fifties, with a heavily lined face and graying widow's peak. A Russian emigrant of dubious legality with several businesses in the area. He was clearly nervous, which John expected and enjoyed. Victor Karpov was a criminal.

John scooted to the side and patted the bench.

"Here. Sit. We'll talk."

Karpov dropped like a stone onto the bench. He clutched a nylon bag with both hands the way an older woman would hold a purse. In front, for protection.

Karpov said, "Thank you for doing this, sir. I have these awful problems that must be dealt with. These terrible enemies."

John put his hand on the bag, gently trying to pry it away.

"I know all about your problems, Mr. Karpov. We don't need to say another word about'm."

"Yes. Yes, well, thank you for agreeing to do this. Thank you."

"You don't have to thank me, Mr. Karpov, you surely don't."

John would have never even spoken to the man, let alone agreed to do what he was about to do and meet Karpov like this, if he had not thoroughly researched Victor Karpov. John's business was by referral only, and John had spoken with those who had referred him. Those men had in fact asked John's permission to suggest his name to Karpov, and were in a position to assure Karpov's character. John was big on character. He was big on secrecy, and covering one's ass. Which is why these people did not know him by his real name or know anything about him at all except for his trade. Through them, John knew the complete details of Karpov's problem, what would be required, and had already decided that he would take the job before their first contact.

That was how you stayed on the Most Wanted List, and out of prison.

"Leave go of the bag, Mr. Karpov."

Karpov let go of the bag as if it were stinging him.

John laughed, taking the bag into his own lap.

"You don't have to be nervous, Mr. Karpov. You're among friends here, believe you me. It don't get no friendlier than what I'm feeling for you right now. You know how friendly it gets?"

Karpov stared at him without comprehension.

"I think we're such good friends, me and you, that I'm not even gonna look in this bag until later. That's how such good friends we are. We're so fuckin' tight, you and me, that I know there is EXACTLY the right amount of cash in here, and I'm willing to bet your life on it. How's that for friendly?"

Karpov's eyes bulged large, and he swallowed.

"It is all there. It is exactly what you said, in fifties and twenties. Please count it now. Please count it so that you are satisfied."

John shook his head and dropped the sack onto the bench opposite Karpov.

"Nope. We'll just let this little scenario play out the way it will and hope you didn't count wrong."

Karpov reached across him for the sack.

"Please."

John laughed and pushed Karpov back.

"Don't you worry about it, Mr. Karpov. I'm just funnin' with you."

Funnin'. Like he was an idiot as well as a cracker.

"Here. I want to show you something."

He took a small tube from his pocket and held it out. It used to be a dime-store flashlight, the kind with a push-button switch in the end opposite the bulb. It wasn't a flashlight anymore.

"Go ahead and take it. The damned thing won't bite."

Karpov took it.

"What is this?"

John tipped his head toward the schoolyard across the street. It was lunchtime. The kids were running around, playing in the few minutes before they would have to troop back into class.

"Lookit those kids over there. I been watchin'm. Pretty little girls and boys. Man, look at how they're just running around, got all the energy in the world, all that free spirit and potential. You're that age, I guess everything's still possible, ain't it? Lookit that little boy in the blue shirt. Over there to the right, Karpov, Jesus, right there. Good-lookin' little fella, blond, freckles. Christ, bet the little sonofabitch could grow up fuckin' all the cheerleaders he wants, then be the goddamned President to boot. Shit like that can't happen over there where you're from, can it? But here, man, this is the fuckin' U.S. of A., and you can do any goddamned thing you want until they start tellin' you that you can't."

Karpov was staring at him, the tube in his hand forgotten.

"Right now, anything in that child's head is possible, and it'll stay possible till that fuckin' cheerleader calls him a pizzaface and her retarded fullback boyfriend beats the shit out of him for talking to his girl. Right now, that boy is happy, Mr. Karpov, just look at how happy, but all that is gonna end just as soon as he realizes all those hopes and dreams he has ain't never gonna work."

John slowly let his eyes drift to the tube.

"You could save that poor child all that grief, Mr. Karpov.

Somewhere very close to us there is a device. I have built that device, and placed it carefully, and you now control it."

Karpov looked at the tube. His expression was as milky as if he were holding a rattlesnake.

"If you press that little silver button, maybe you can save that child the pain he's gonna face. I'm not sayin' the device is over there in that school, but I'm sayin' maybe. Maybe that whole fuckin' play-ground would erupt in a beautiful red firestorm. Maybe those babies would be hit so hard by the pressure wave that all their shoes would just be left scattered on the ground, and the clothes and skin would scorch right off their bones. I ain't sayin' that, but there it is right there in that silver button. You can end that boy's pain. You have the power. You can turn the world to hell, you want, because you have the power right there in that little silver button. I have created it, and now I've given it to you. You. Right there in your hand."

Karpov stood and thrust the tube at John.

"I want no part of this. Take it. *Take it.*"

John slowly took the tube. He fingered the silver button.

"When I do what you want me to do, Mr. Karpov, people are gonna die. What's the fuckin' difference?"

"The money is all there. Every dollar. All of it."

Karpov walked away without another word. He crossed the street, walking so fast that his strides became a kind of hop, as if he expected the world around him to turn to flame.

John dropped the tube into the nylon bag with the money.

They never seemed to appreciate the gift he offered.

John settled back again, stretched his arms along the backrest to enjoy the sun and the sounds of the children playing. It was a beau-tiful day, and would grow even more beautiful when a second sun had risen.

After a while he got up and walked away to check the Most Wanted List. Last week he wasn't on it.

This week he hoped to be.

2

THE CRIMINAL CONSPIRACY Section where Starkey worked is housed on the fifth floor of an eight-story office building on Spring Street, just a few blocks from the LAPD's seat of power, Parker Center. LAPD's Fugitive Section and Internal Affairs Group are also housed there, on the fourth and sixth floors. The building is known to have the most congested parking of any building in city government, with the detectives on each floor having to wedge their cars together with barely enough room to open their doors. The officers who work there nicknamed the building "Code Three" because, if they had to respond to an actual emergency, they would make better time running out of the building on foot to grab a cab.

Starkey parked on the third floor after ten minutes of maneuvering, then climbed the steps to the fifth floor. She noticed Marzik watching her as soon as she walked in, and decided to see if Marzik wanted to make something of the Binaca. Starkey went over, stopping in Marzik's face.

"What?"

Marzik met her gaze without looking away.

"I got those rental apps, like you wanted. I figure most of those people will go home today, and we can talk to them first. If anyone doesn't show, we can use the apps to find them."

"Is there anything else?"

"Like what?"

"Like whatever you need to say?"

"I'm fine."

Starkey let it go. If Marzik confronted her about the drinking, she didn't know what she could do except lie.

"Okay. I've got the 911 call. Is Hooker in?"

"Yeah. I saw him."

"Let's listen to the tape, then I want to get over to Glendale. Chen's gonna have the chrom, and I want to see how they're coming with the reconstruction."

"They just started. How far could they be?"

"Far enough to know some of the components, Beth. We get some manufacturers, we get the chrom, we can get going here."

"We got all these interviews to do."

Marzik made her tired. It was a shitty way to start the day.

"You guys can start in with the interviews while I'm over there. Round up Jorge and come to the desk."

"I think he's in the crapper."

"Knock on the door, Beth. Jesus Christ."

Starkey borrowed a cassette player from the section sergeant, Leon Tooley, and brought it to her desk. Each CCS detective had a desk in a partitioned cubicle in the larger main room. There was the illusion of privacy, but the partitions were just low dividers, meaning that there was no real privacy. Everyone spoke in whispers unless they were showing off for Kelso, who spent most of his time hidden behind his office door. Rumor had it that he spent his day on the Internet, trading his stock portfolio.

Marzik and Santos showed up a few minutes later with coffee, Santos saying, "Did you see Kelso?"

"No. Should I?"

"He asked to see you this morning."

Starkey glanced at Marzik, but Marzik's face was unreadable.

"Well, Jesus, Jorge, nice of someone to tell me. Look, let's listen to this before I see him."

Santos and Marzik pulled up chairs as Starkey turned on the tape. The sound started with the Emergency Services operator, a black female, and was followed by a male voice with a heavy Spanish accent.

EMS:	**911. May I help you?**
CALLER:	**'aullu?**
EMS:	**911. May I help you, sir?**
CALLER:	**Eh . . . *se habla español?***
EMS:	**I can transfer you to a Spanish speaker.**
CALLER:	**Eh . . . no, is okay. Lissen, you better sen' a man to look here.**

Santos leaned forward and stopped the tape.

"What's that behind him?"

Starkey said, "It sounds like a truck or a bus. He's calling from a pay phone just off Sunset, a block east of the mall."

Marzik crossed her arms.

"Isn't there a pay phone right there outside that Cuban restaurant?"

"Yeah, and there's another across the street at that little food store, the Guatemalan place. But he walked down a block."

Santos looked at her.

"How do you know that?"

"EMS called back with the address. I walked the scene again this morning."

Marzik made a grunt, staring at the floor. Like only a loser without a life would do something like that.

Starkey started the tape again.

EMS:	Look at what, sir?
CALLER:	Eh . . . I look in dis box, and I tink dere's a bomb in dere.
EMS:	A bomb?
CALLER:	Dese pipes, see? I dunno. It made me scared.
EMS:	Could I have your name, sir?
CALLER:	Is by the trash dere, you know? The beeg can.
EMS:	I need your name, sir.
CALLER:	You better come see.

The line clicked when the man hung up. That was the end of the tape. Starkey turned off the machine.

Marzik frowned.

"If it's legit, why wouldn't he leave his name?"

Santos shrugged.

"You know how people are. Could be he's illegal. He's probably just some neighborhood guy, around there all the time."

Starkey scrounged for something to write on. The best she could do was a copy of *The Blue Line*, the LAPD's union newspaper. She drew a rough street map, showing the mall and the location of the phones.

"He says he looked in the bag. Okay. That means he's here at the mall. He says it scared him, seeing the pipes like that, so why not just use the phone right here outside the Cuban place or over here across the street? Why walk another block east?"

Marzik crossed her arms again. Every time Marzik didn't like something, she crossed her arms. Starkey could read her like the daily news.

"Maybe he wasn't sure it was a bomb, and then he wasn't sure he wanted to call. People have to talk themselves into things. Christ, sometimes I gotta talk myself into taking a shit."

Santos frowned at Marzik's mouth, then tapped the phone outside the laundry.

"If I found something I thought was a bomb, I'd want to get as far away from it as possible. I wouldn't want to stand next to it. Maybe he was scared it would explode."

Starkey considered that, and nodded. It made sense. She tossed *The Blue Line* into her wastebasket.

"Well, whatever. We've got the time of the call. Maybe someone around there saw something, and we can straighten this out."

Santos nodded.

"Okay. You want to do that while we get the apartment houses?"

"One of you guys swing past, okay, Hook? I've gotta meet Chen over in Glendale."

Starkey gave them the addresses, then went in to see Kelso. She walked in without knocking.

"Hooker said you wanted to see me."

Kelso jerked away from his computer and swiveled around to peer at her. He had stopped telling her not to barge in over a year ago.

"Would you close the door, please, Carol, then come sit down."

Starkey closed the door, then marched back across his office and stood at his desk. She was right about that cow Marzik. She didn't sit.

Kelso squirmed behind his desk because he wasn't sure how to come at what he wanted to say.

"I just want to make sure you're okay with this."

"With what, Barry?"

"You seemed just a little, ah, strained last night. And, ah, I just want to be sure you're okay with being the lead here."

"Are you replacing me?"

He began to rock, his body language revealing that that was exactly what he was thinking.

"Not at all, Carol. No. But this case strikes close to home with you, and we've had these, ah, episodes recently."

He let it hang as if he didn't know how to carry it further.

Starkey felt the shakes coming on, but fought them down. She was furious with Marzik and terrified that Kelso might reconsider ordering her to the bank.

"Did Marzik say that I was drinking?"

Kelso showed both palms.

"Let's leave Marzik out of this."

"You saw me at the crime scene, Barry. Did I act drunk or unprofessional to you?"

"That's not what I'm asking. You've been wound a little on the tight side, Carol. We both know that because we've talked about it. Last night you were confronted with a situation very similar to one that you yourself barely survived. Perhaps you were unnerved."

"You're talking about replacing me."

"I left our conversation last night thinking that I smelled gin. Did I?"

Starkey met his eyes.

"No, sir. You smelled Binaca. I ate Cuban for lunch, and I was blowing garlic all day. That's what you and Marzik smelled."

He showed his palms again.

"Let's leave Marzik out of this. Marzik didn't say anything to me."

Starkey knew he was lying. If Kelso had smelled gin on her breath, he would've said something at the scene. He was running with Marzik's complaint.

Starkey was very careful in how she stood. She knew he would be reading her body language the same way she read his. He would look for any sign of defensiveness.

Finally, he settled back, relieved that he'd said what he needed to say and had been the responsible commander.

"All right, Carol, this is your case. I just want you to know I'm here for you."

"I need to get over to Glendale, Lieutenant. The quicker I can get hard news on the bomb, the faster we can bag this puke."

Kelso leaned back, dismissing her.

"All right. If you need anything, you know I'm here. This is an important case, Carol. A human being died. More, an officer died, which makes it personal."

"It's personal to me and the guys on the Bomb Squad, Lieutenant. Believe it."

"I imagine it would be. Just take it easy, Carol, and we'll get through this all right."

Starkey went back into the squad room, looking for Marzik, but she and Santos had already left. She gathered her things, then wrestled her car out of the parking lot jockeying spots with a fat IAG detective named Marley. It took her almost fifteen minutes to get out of the building, and then she pulled to the curb, so angry at Marzik that her hands were shaking.

The flask of gin was beneath her seat, but Starkey didn't touch it. She thought about it, but she didn't touch it.

Starkey lit another cigarette, then drove like a bat out of hell, blowing smoke like a furnace.

It was only eight-thirty when Starkey pulled into the Glendale PD parking lot. Chen had said he'd have the chromatograph by nine, but Starkey figured that he'd built a fuck-up and paperwork cushion into that estimate.

She sat in her car smoking for five minutes before using her cell phone to call SID.

"John, it's Starkey. I'm out here in the lot. You have the results?"

"You're outside right now?"

"Affirmative. I'm on my way in to see Leyton."

Instead of giving her attitude or excuses, Chen said, "Give me two minutes and I'll be right down. You're gonna love this."

The LAPD Bomb Squad is based in a low-slung modern building adjacent to the Glendale police substation and piggybacked with the Scientific Investigation Division.

The building is built of red brick and snuggled behind a stand of rubber trees, most people would mistake it for a dental office, except that it is also snuggled behind a ten-foot fence topped with concertina wire. The parking lot is dotted with dark blue Bomb Squad Suburbans.

Starkey let herself into the Bomb Squad reception area and asked for Lieutenant Leyton. He'd stayed out with the others at the crime scene, walking the sweep like everyone else. Dark rings had set in around his eyes, making him look older than she'd ever seen him, even after Sugar Boudreaux died.

Starkey handed over the baggie.

"I walked the scene again this morning and found these. You got someone on the reconstruction yet?"

Leyton held up the baggie to look. All three bits would have to be logged into the evidence records, then tested to see if they were actually part of the device.

"Russ Daigle. He came in early to start sorting what we recovered last night."

"Chen's on his way down with the chrom. I was hoping to snatch whatever component manufacturers you have, so I can get rolling with this."

"Sure. Let's see what he has."

She followed Leyton down a long hall past the ready room and the sergeants' offices to the squad room. It didn't look like any other squad room in the department; it looked like a high school science lab, all small cramped desks and black Formica workbenches.

Every surface in the squad room was covered with de-armed bombs or bomb facsimiles, from pipe bombs and dynamite bombs to canister bombs and large military ordnance. An air-to-air missile hung from the ceiling. Trade journals and reference books cluttered any surface not sporting a bomb. FBI wanted posters were taped to the walls.

Russ Daigle was perched on a stool at one of the workbenches, sorting pieces of metal. Daigle was one of the squad's three sergeant-supervisors, and the man who had the most time on the squad. He was a short, athletic man with a thick gray mustache and blunt fingers. He was wearing latex gloves.

He glanced up when he heard them, nodding toward a smudged computer at the end of his workbench. It was covered with *Babylon 5* stickers.

"We got the snaps up. You wanna see?"

"You bet."

She moved behind him to see the monitor.

"End and side view. We got others, but these are the best. It's a classic goddamned pipe bomb. Betcha some turd built it in his garage."

The digital snapshots that Riggio had taken were displayed on the screen. They showed the two pipes as impenetrable black shadows neatly taped together with a spool of wire fixed to the cleft between them. All four pipe ends were capped. Starkey studied the images, comparing them to the bits of jagged black metal that were spread on white butcher's paper. One of the end caps was still intact, but the others were broken. Daigle had divided them by size and conformation, exactly the way you would the pieces in any other puzzle. He already had the major parts of all four caps separated and had made good progress with the tubes, but it was clear that forty or fifty percent of the pieces were still missing.

"What do we have, Sarge? Looks like typical galvanized iron pipe, two-inch diameter?"

He picked up a piece of end cap that showed a letter *V* cast into the iron.

"Yeah. See the *V*? Vanguard pipe company. Buy it anywhere in the country."

Starkey made note of it in her pad. She would compile a list of components and characteristics, and feed them through the National Law Enforcement Telecommunications System to the FBI's Bomb Data Center and the ATF's National Repository in Washington. The BDC and NR would search for signature matches with every bomb report in their systems.

Daigle ran his finger up under the edge of the cap, flaking off something brittle and white.

"See that? Plumber's joint tape. We got us a neat boy, here. Very precise. Even taped the joints. What does that tell you?"

Starkey knew that the old sergeant had already drawn a conclusion and was testing her. He'd done the same thing a hundred times when she was on the squad.

"You're plumbing your sink, you maybe want to tape the joints, but you sure as hell don't need to tape a bomb."

Daigle grinned, proud that she'd seen it.

"That's right. No reason to tape it, so maybe he does it out of habit, you know? Could be he's a plumber or a building contractor of some kind."

Another note for the feds.

"Both pipes are the same size, as near as I can measure from the snaps. He either cut or had'm cut to length, and he was particular. You see the tape shadow here, how careful he wrapped the tape? We got us a particular boy here, and he's good with his hands. Very precise."

Already Starkey was getting a picture of the builder. He might be a skilled tradesman or a machinist or a hobbiest who took pride in precision, like a model builder or woodworker.

"Did Chen show you the 5?"

"What 5?"

Daigle placed a piece of the tube frag under the glass. It was the *S* that Chen had pulled from Riggio's armor.

"It looks like an *S*."

Leyton said, "We're not sure what it is, an *S*, or a *5*, or some kind of symbol."

Daigle peered close at the glass.

"Whatever it is, he cut it in with a high-speed engraving tool."

Chen came in while they were discussing the snaps. Like the others, he looked as if he hadn't slept much, but he was excited when he handed Starkey the chrom results.

"I can tell you right now I'm cooking another sample to confirm, but the explosive was something called Modex Hybrid. He didn't buy this at the local hardware store."

They looked at him.

"The military uses it in artillery warheads and air-to-air missiles. We're talking about a burn rate of twenty-eight thousand feet per second."

Daigle grunted. The burn rate was a measure of how fast the explosive consumed itself and released energy. The more powerful the explosive, the faster the burn rate.

"TNT goes, what, twenty thousand feet per second?"

Starkey said, "Twenty, twenty-one, something like that."

Leyton nodded.

"If we're talking about a military explosive, that's good for us. It should narrow the field, Carol. We see who's missing some, then find out who had access."

Chen cleared his throat.

"Well, it won't be that simple. The chrom showed a lot of impurities in the chemical signature, so I phoned the manufacturer back in Pennsylvania. Modex comes in three forms: military grade, which is made under government contract, commercial grade, which is made for foreign export only—EPA won't let anyone use it here—and homegrown."

Daigle scowled.

"What's that mean, homegrown?"

"The company rep thought a kitchen chemist might've cooked up this batch. It's not that hard to do if you've got the components and the right pressure equipment. The guy says it's about as hard as cooking up a batch of crystal meth."

Starkey glanced over the chromatograph printout, but it didn't tell her what she wanted to know.

"Okay. If you can make the stuff by hand, I need the component list and the recipe."

"The rep's going to put it together and fax it. I asked him for manufacturers, too. As soon as I get'm, they're yours."

Starkey folded the page and put it with her notes. A unique explosive was a plus for the investigation, but she didn't like what it implied.

"If this stuff is a military explosive or needs some kind of high-end lab work, it changes my picture of the builder. We can't be talking about a guy who just wanted to see if he could do it. This is a serious bomb."

Leyton frowned and leaned against the bench.

"Not necessarily. If the Modex turns out to be stolen, that's true—a backyard nutcase wouldn't know how to get his hands on something like that. But if he made it himself, he could've pulled the formula off the Internet. Maybe he figured that using a more powerful explosive like this was part of the challenge."

Daigle crossed his arms, not liking it.

"Starkey's right about this being a serious bomb. So tell me this: Why does he build a device like this and just leave it by a Dumpster? There's gotta be more to it."

"We talked to every one of the shop owners, Sarge. Nobody says they were threatened. The bomb didn't damage the building."

Daigle scowled deeper.

"One of those fuckers is lying. You don't build a bomb this powerful just to play with yourself. You watch what I'm saying. One of those fuckers screwed somebody over and this thing is payback."

Starkey shrugged, thinking maybe Daigle was right as she studied the snaps.

"Sarge, I'm looking at this thing, but I don't see a detonator. No batteries. No power source. How did it go off?"

Daigle slid off the stool to stretch his back and tapped the picture on the screen.

"I got a theory. One pipe holds the explosive, the other the detonator. Look here."

He picked up two of the larger pieces of pipe, holding them for her and Leyton to see.

"See the white residue here on the inside of the curve?"

"Yeah. From when the explosive burned off."

"That's right. Now look at this other piece. Nothing in here. Clean. Makes me think maybe he had the detonator in this pipe, along with a battery or whatever."

"You think it was hooked to a timer?"

Daigle looked dubious.

"And the timer just happened to let go when Riggio was standing over it? I don't buy that for a second. We haven't found anything yet, but I'm thinking Riggio set off some kind of balance switch."

"Buck said Charlie never touched the package."

"Well, that's what Buck saw, but Charlie must've done something. Bombs don't just go off for no reason."

Everyone suddenly grew silent, and Daigle flushed. Starkey realized it was because of her, then she flushed, too.

"Jesus, Carol. I'm sorry. I didn't mean it that way."

"You've got nothing to be sorry for, Sarge. There was a reason. It's called an earthquake."

Starkey remembered the twisted disk she'd found, took it from the baggie, and showed it to the others.

"I found this at the crime scene this morning. I don't know if it came from the bomb, but there's a good chance. It could be part of the initiator."

Daigle put it under a magnifying glass for a closer look, chewing his lower lip, squinting and puzzled.

"Something electrical. Looks like we got a circuit board in here."

Chen crowded in and peered at it. He pulled on a pair of Daigle's gloves, then selected a narrow screwdriver and pried open the disk like a clamshell.

"Sonofabitch. I know what this is."

A single word was printed inside the disk, a word they all knew, that was so out of place it seemed absurd: MATTEL.

Chen put down the disk and stepped away. The others gathered closer for a better look, but Starkey was watching Chen. He looked stricken.

"What is it, John?"

"It's a radio receiver like they put in those remote-control cars for kids."

Now all of them stared at him because what John Chen was saying changed everything they'd been thinking about this bomb and the anonymity of its explosion.

"Charlie Riggio didn't set off this device, and it didn't just happen to explode. It was radio-controlled."

Starkey knew what he was saying at the same time as everyone else, but she was the one who said it.

"The lunatic who built this bomb was right there. He waited until Charlie was over the bomb, and then he set it off."

John Chen took another breath.

"Yes. He wanted to see someone die."

3

KELSO TASTED THE coffee he had just poured, making a face as if he'd sipped Drano.

"You really think the bastard triggered the device from the scene?"

Starkey showed him a fax she had received from a sales rep working for the radio control's manufacturer. It listed the receiver's performance specs and operating requirements.

"These little receivers operate on such low voltage that they're only tested out to sixty yards. The guy I spoke with gives us a ballpark maximum distance between transmitter and receiver of about a hundred yards. That's a line-of-sight distance, Barry. That puts our guy in open view."

"Okay. So what's your idea?"

"Every TV station in town had a helicopter overhead, broadcasting the scene. They had cameras on the ground, too. Maybe one of those tapes caught this mutt at the scene."

Kelso nodded, pleased.

"Okay, I like that. That's good thinking, Starkey. I'll talk to Media Relations. I don't see why there'd be a problem with that."

"One other thing. I had to split up Marzik and Hooker. Marzik is interviewing the residents, and Hooker is talking to the police and fire personnel who were at the scene. It would help if I could get more people to help with the field interviews."

He made the sour face again.

"Okay. I'll see what I can do."

Kelso started away, but turned back.

"You're still okay with this, right? You can handle it?"

Starkey felt herself flush.

"Asking for more bodies isn't a sign of weakness, Barry. We're making progress."

Kelso stared at her for a moment, then nodded.

"Yes. You are. I didn't mean to imply otherwise."

That surprised Starkey and pleased her.

"Did you talk with Sergeant Daggett yet?"

"No, sir."

"You should talk to him. Get him to thinking about the people he might've seen in that parking lot. When we get these tapes, you're going to want him to look at them."

When Kelso closed his door, Starkey went back to her cubicle with her stomach in knots. Daggett would be confused and angry. He would be shaken because of what happened; second-guessing every decision that he'd made, every action, and every movement. Starkey knew he would be feeling these things because she had felt them, too, and didn't want to revisit them.

Starkey sat in her cubicle for twenty minutes without moving, thinking about the flask in her purse and staring at Buck Daggett's address in her Rolodex. Finally, she couldn't stand it anymore and stalked down to her car.

Daggett lived in a cramped Mediterranean-style home in the San Gabriel Valley, identical with its beige stucco and tile roof to a hundred others in the low-cost housing development just east of Monterey Park. Starkey had been there once, for a Bomb Squad cookout three months before Sugar died. It wasn't much of a house. A sergeant-supervisor's pay would cover something nicer, but Starkey knew that Daggett had been divorced three times. The alimony and child support probably ate him alive.

Five minutes after she left the freeway, Starkey pulled into Daggett's drive and went to the door. A black ribbon had been tied to the knocker.

Daggett's fourth and current wife answered. She was twenty years younger than Buck and attractive, though today she seemed vague and distracted. Starkey showed her badge.

"Carol Starkey, Mrs. Daggett. I used to work with Buck on the squad. You and I have met, haven't we? I'm sorry, but I don't remember your name."

"Natalie."

"Natalie. Sure. Could I see Buck, please?"

"I had to stay home from work, you know? Buck's so upset."

"That's right, Natalie. It's terrible, isn't it? Now, is Buck home?"

Natalie Daggett led Starkey through the house to their backyard, where Buck was changing the oil in his Lawn-Boy. As soon as Starkey stepped out into the yard, Natalie vanished back into her house.

"Hey, Buck."

Daggett glanced up like he was surprised to see her, then scrambled to his feet. Just looking at him caused an ache in Starkey's chest.

He shrugged at the Lawn-Boy and seemed embarrassed.

"I'm trying to keep busy. I'd hug you, but I'm all sweaty."

"Busy is good, Buck. That's okay."

"You want a soda or something? Didn't Natalie offer you any-thing?"

He came over, wiping his hands on a greasy orange cloth that soiled his hands as much as cleaned them. It was hot in the tiny back-yard. Sweat dripped from his hair.

"I don't have much time. We're running short."

He nodded, disappointed, then opened a couple of lawn chairs that had been leaning against the house.

"I heard you caught the case. You doing okay over there on CCS?"

"I'd rather be back on the squad."

Daggett nodded without looking at her. She suddenly thought that if she was still on the squad it might've been her down in Silver Lake instead of Riggio. Maybe he was thinking that, too.

"Buck, I've got to ask you some questions about what hap-pened."

"I know that. Sure. Hey, I don't think I ever told you, but the guys in the squad are really proud you made the move to become a de-tective. That's real police work."

"Thanks, Buck. I appreciate that."

"What are you, a D-3 now?"

"A D-2. I don't have enough time in grade for the promotion."

Buck shrugged.

"You'll get there. Here you are with the lead, and only a D-2."

Starkey worried he might be wondering if she was up to the job. She liked Buck, and didn't want him to doubt her. She got enough doubt from Kelso.

"Anyone call you about the bomb? You hear about that?"

"No. Hear about what?"

He was searching her face, and it took all of her strength not to look away. He knew it was going to be bad. She could see the fear of it blossom in his eyes.

"What about the bomb, Carol?"

"It was detonated by remote control."

He stared at her without expression for a time, then shook his head, something like desperation edging into his voice.

"That can't be. Charlie made some good snaps with the Real Time. We didn't see a radio device. We didn't see *any* kind of detonator. If we'd seen anything like that, I would've yanked Charlie out of there. He would've come running."

"You couldn't have seen it, Buck. The power pack and initiator were inside one of the pipes. The explosive was in the other. Something called Modex Hybrid."

He blinked hard to hold back the tears, but they came anyway. Starkey felt her own eyes fill and put a hand on his arm.

"I'm okay."

She let go of his arm, thinking the two of them were a fine pair.

Buck cleared his throat, took a breath and let it out.

"Modex. That's military, right? I know that name."

"They use it in warheads. Almost ten thousand feet faster than TNT. But we're thinking maybe this batch was homemade."

"Jesus. You're sure about the remote? You're sure it was radio-controlled?"

"We found the receiver. The person who set it off was somewhere in the area. He could've set it off anytime he wanted, but he waited until Charlie was right over the bomb. We think he was watching."

He rubbed at his face and shook his head as if all of this was too much to bear.

She told him about the videotapes.

"Listen, Buck, I'm getting together the videos that the TV stations took. When we have everything together, I'd like you to come in and take a look. Maybe you'll see someone in the crowd."

"I don't know, Carol. My head was on the bomb. I was worried about Charlie's body temp and about getting good snaps. We thought we had some gangbanger over there, you know? A *pachuco* showing off for the homeboys. It was just a couple of goddamned pipes, for Christ's sake."

"It'll be another day or two before we get all the tapes. I want you to think about it, okay? Try to recall anyone or anything that stood out."

"Sure. I got nothing else to do. Dick made me take three days."

"It's good for you, Buck. Hey, you can take care of the weeds here in your yard. The place looks like shit."

Daggett grudged a wan smile, and the two of them fell into silence.

After a time, he said, "You know what they're making me do?"

"What?"

"I gotta go to the bank. Shit, I don't want to talk to those people."

Starkey didn't know what to say.

"They call it 'trauma counseling.' We got all these new rules now. You're in a shooting, you gotta go in. You get in a car wreck, you gotta go in. Now I guess I've got to tell some headshrinker what it feels like seeing my partner get blown to shit."

Starkey was still trying to think of something to say when she felt her pager vibrate. It was Marzik's number, followed by 911.

Starkey wanted to return the call, but she didn't want to leave Buck Daggett so quickly, or like this.

"Don't worry about the bank. It's not like you're being ordered in."

"I just don't want to talk to those people. What's there to say about something like this? What did *you* say?"

"Nothing, Buck. There's nothing to say. Just tell'm that. There's nothing to say. Listen, I've got to return this call. It's Marzik."

"Sure. I understand."

Daggett walked her out through the house and to the front door. His wife was nowhere around.

"Natalie's upset, too. I'm sorry she didn't offer you anything."

"Don't worry about it, Buck. I didn't want anything anyway."

"We were pretty tight, the three of us. She liked Charlie a lot."

"I'll call you about the videos. Think about it, okay?"

She was stepping through the door when Buck stopped her.

"Detective?"

She looked back at him, smiling at his use of her title.

"Thanks for not asking. You know what I mean? Everyone asks you how you are, and there's nothing to say to that, either."

"I know, Buck. It used to drive me crazy, everyone asking that."

"Yeah. Well, I guess we're a pretty small club, me and you."

Starkey nodded at him, and then Buck Daggett closed the door.

Starkey was paged a second time as she walked out to her car. This time it was Hooker. She called Marzik first because of the 911, using her cell phone as she sat in Daggett's drive.

Marzik got it on the first ring, as if she'd been waiting.

"Beth Marzik."

"It's Starkey. What's up?"

Marzik's voice was excited.

"I got something here, Starkey. I'm down by that flower shop, the one across from the phone? 911 gets the call from the phone at one-fourteen, right? Well, the owner's kid is out front, getting ready to deliver some flowers, and he sees a guy on the phone."

Starkey's pulse quickened.

"Tell me he saw a car, Beth. Say we've got a license plate."

"Carol, listen to this. It's even better. He said it was an Anglo guy."

"The caller was Latino."

"Listen to me, Starkey. This kid is solid. He's sitting in his truck, listening to the fuckin' Gipsy Kings while they load the flowers. He's there from a little after one to exactly one-twenty. I know he was there during the call because they logged his departure time. *He says it was a white guy.*"

Starkey tried not to let herself get excited, but it was hard.

Marzik said, "Why would a white guy pretend to be Latino unless it was the guy who set the bomb, Carol? If it was some white guy pretending to be Latino, then he was trying to hide, for Christ's sake. We could have an eye-wit to the fuckin' asshole who set the bomb."

Starkey saw the possibilities, too, but she knew that investigations often took turns that seemed to be sure things only to have them fall apart.

"Let's take it a step at a time, Beth. I think this is a good thing, and we're going to go with it, but let's not get ahead of ourselves. Your wit only thinks the guy he saw was Anglo. Maybe the guy was Anglo, but maybe he only looked Anglo to the kid. We'll just have to see."

"Okay. That's right. I know you're right, but the kid comes across solid. You need to come talk to him."

"Is he there now, Beth?"

"Well, for a while. He's got more deliveries to make and it's getting late."

"Okay. Keep him there. I'm coming down."

"I can't just keep him here. If they get an order, he's got to make the delivery."

"*Ask* him, Beth. Say pretty please."

"What do you want me to do, suck his dick?"

"Yeah. Try that."

Starkey broke the connection, then punched in Santos's number. When he answered, his voice was so soft that she could barely understand him.

"What are you whispering for?"

"Carol, is that you?"

"I can barely hear you. Speak up."

"I'm at the office. An agent from the ATF is here. He flew in from Washington this morning."

Starkey felt a burst of tension in her stomach and reached into her purse for a Tagamet.

"You're sure it's Washington? He didn't just drive over from the L.A. field office?"

She had submitted the preliminary bomb component information through the NLETS only yesterday. If this guy came from Washington, he must have hopped the first jet.

"He's from Washington, Carol. He went in there with Kelso, and now Kelso wants to see you. He's been asking for our reports. I think they're going to take over our case. Look, I've gotta go. I've been stalling, but Kelso wants me to give him what we have."

"Waitaminute, Jorge, did the guy say that? Did he *say* he wanted the case?"

"I've got to go, Carol. Kelso just stuck his head out. He's looking at me."

"Stall longer, Jorge. I'm coming in. Marzik turned up something good for us."

"From the looks of the guy in with Kelso, it's going to be something good for him."

Starkey ate a Tagamet, then drove back to Spring Street with her dash bubble flashing.

Starkey made it back to her office in twenty-five minutes. Santos caught her eye from the coffee machine and nodded toward Kelso's door. It was closed.

"Did you give him the reports?"

Her look made him cringe.

"What could I do, tell Kelso no?"

Starkey set her jaw and stalked to Kelso's door. She knocked hard three times, then opened the door without waiting.

Kelso gestured wearily toward her as he spoke to the man seated across from his desk.

"This is Detective Starkey. She comes in whenever she wants. Starkey, this is Special Agent Jack Pell from—"

"The ATF. I know. Is he taking over this case?"

Pell was leaning forward with elbows on knees as if he were about to leap forward. Starkey guessed him to be in his mid-thirties, but if he was older, it wouldn't have surprised her. He had pale skin and intense gray eyes. She tried to read the eyes, but couldn't; they seemed guarded.

Pell turned to Kelso without acknowledging her.

"I need a few more minutes with you, Lieutenant. Have her wait outside until we're ready."

Her. Like she wasn't standing there.

"Out, Starkey. We'll call you."

"This is my case, Lieutenant. It's *our* case. One of *our* people died."

"Wait outside, Detective. We'll call you when we want you."

Starkey waited outside his door, fuming. Santos started over, saw her scowl, and veered away. She was cursing Kelso for giving away the CCS investigation when her pager buzzed on her hip.

"Oh, shit. Marzik."

Starkey phoned Marzik from her cubicle.

"Carol, I'm standing here with this kid and he's got deliveries to make. Where in hell are you?"

Starkey kept her voice low, so the other detectives couldn't hear.

"Back at the office. The ATF is coming in."

"You're shitting me? What's happening?"

"All I know is that an agent is in there with Kelso now. Look, I'll talk with the kid when I'm done here. Tell him to make his damned deliveries."

"It's almost five, Carol. He's got deliveries, then he's going home. We can catch him tomorrow."

Starkey checked her watch and thought it through. She wanted to talk to the kid now because she knew that time was a witness's enemy; people forgot details, people grew confused, people had second thoughts about cooperating with the police. Starkey finally decided that she was getting ahead of herself and pressing too hard. She wouldn't help herself with this kid by making him wait around for another couple of hours.

"Okay, Beth. Set it up. Is he working tomorrow morning?"

Marzik told her to hang on. The kid must have been standing there with her.

"He's in at eight. His father owns the store."

"Okay. We'll get him tomorrow morning."

"Us or the ATF?"

"I'm about to find out."

Kelso stuck his head out, looking for her. Starkey put down the phone, wishing she'd used the time to eat more Tagamet. Sometimes she thought she should buy stock in that company.

When she reached Kelso, he whispered, "Just relax, Carol. He's here to help us."

"My ass he is."

Kelso closed the door behind them. Pell was still poised forward in the chair, so Starkey gave him her best scowl. Those damned gray eyes were the coldest eyes she'd ever seen, and she had to fight the urge to look away.

Kelso returned to his desk.

"Agent Pell flew in from D.C. this morning. The information you fed into the system raised some eyebrows back there."

Pell nodded.

"I don't have an interest in taking over your investigation, Detective. This is your town, not mine, but I do think I can help you. I flew out because we flagged some similarities between your bomb and some others we've seen."

"Like what?"

"The Modex is his explosive of choice: fast, sexy, and elite. He also likes to use this particular type of radio detonator, hiding it in one of the pipes so you can't see it with the X-ray."

"Who are we talking about?"

"If your guy is our guy, he uses the name Mr. Red. We don't know his true name."

Starkey glanced at Kelso, but his expression told her nothing. She figured he would be relieved to hand over the case to the feds, so he wouldn't have to worry about clearing it.

"What are we talking about here? Mr. *Red*? Is this guy some kind of serial bomber? Is he a terrorist? What?"

"No, Detective, this mutt isn't a terrorist. As far as we know, he doesn't care about politics or abortion or any of that. Over the past two years, we've had seven bombings that show Modex Hybrid and a radio-triggering device similar to the one used here. Because of the nature of the targets and the people involved, we believe that four of them were done for criminal profit. He blows up something or someone probably because he's being paid to do it. This is how he makes his money, Starkey, blowing up things. He's a hit man with a bomb. But he also has a hobby."

"I'm dying to know."

Kelso snapped, surprising the hell out of her.

"Shut up, goddamnit, and listen."

Starkey turned back to Pell, and the gray eyes were as depthless as stillwater pools. She found herself wondering why they might be so tired.

"He hunts bomb technicians, Starkey. He baits them, then he murders them. He's killed three so far, if we count your man, all with identical devices."

Starkey watched the gray eyes. They did not blink.

"That's insane."

"The profilers say it's a dominance game; I think he sees it as a competition. He makes bombs, bomb techs like you de-arm them, so he tries to beat you."

Starkey felt a chill; Pell clearly read it.

"I know what happened to you. I looked you up before I flew out."

Starkey felt invaded, and the invasion angered her. She wondered what he knew about her injuries and suddenly felt embarrassed that this man might know those things. She made her voice cool.

"Who and what I am is none of your business except for this: I am the lead investigator on this case."

Pell shrugged.

"You signed the NLETS request. I like to know who I'm dealing with."

Thinking about it now, Starkey had a recollection of reading an ATF flyer on an unknown suspect who might have been identified as Mr. Red. It was the kind of flyer that passed through their office on a routine basis, but bore little relevance, as the subject was operating in other parts of the country.

"I would have remembered this, Pell, some nut murdering bomb technicians. No one here has heard of this asshole."

Kelso shifted.

"They've kept that part of his activities on a need-to-know basis."

"We don't want copycats, Starkey. We've kept all the details of his M.O. and bomb designs classified except the components that we list through NLETS."

"So you're saying that your guy is our guy on the strength of a components list?"

"I'm not saying anything yet, but the Modex and the radio receiver are persuasive. The other design signatures are distinctive. And you have this letter you've found."

Starkey was confused.

"What letter? What are you talking about?"

Kelso said, "The number we found etched into the frag. The 5. Agent Pell thinks it might be the letter S."

"Why do you think it's a letter?"

Pell hesitated, leaving Starkey to wonder what he was thinking.

"We've found etchings in Mr. Red's work before. What I'll need to do is read your reports and compare your reconstruction with what we know. Then I'll make a determination whether or not your bomber is Mr. Red."

Starkey could see her case slipping away.

"Pardon me if I make up my own mind. But if you get to see mine, then I want to see yours. I want to compare whatever you have with what we find here."

Kelso showed his palms.

"Now, Starkey, we don't need to be adversaries here."

She wanted to kick him. That was just the kind of mealy-mouthed thing Kelso would say.

Pell gathered together a short stack of papers and gestured with them.

"That's not a problem, Detective. Lieutenant Kelso was kind

enough to share your case reports; I'll be happy to give you copies of mine. They're at my hotel now, but I'll get them to you."

Pell rolled the reports that Kelso had given him into a tube, then stood.

"I skimmed through these. They look pretty good, but I want to read them more carefully now."

Pell turned to Kelso and gestured with the reports.

"Could you set me up with a place to read these, Lieutenant? I'd like to cover as much ground this evening as I can before Detective Starkey and I get down to business."

Starkey blinked hard twice, then also faced Kelso.

"What does *that* mean? I've got my hands full with this investigation."

Kelso came around his desk to open the door.

"Just relax, Carol. We're all on the same side here."

As Pell walked past with the reports, he stopped beside Starkey, well into her personal space. She would have bet a thousand dollars that he did it on purpose.

"I won't bite, Detective. You don't have to be afraid of me."

"I'm not afraid of anything."

"I wish I could say the same."

Kelso called Santos to take care of Pell, then came back into his office and closed the door. He wasn't happy, but Starkey didn't give a damn. Her hands were shaking so badly that she put them in her pockets so that he wouldn't see.

"You couldn't have been any less helpful."

"I'm not here to be helpful. I'm here to find whoever killed Riggio, and now I've got to worry about the ATF second-guessing what I do and stealing my case."

"Try to remember that it's a team effort, Detective. It can't hurt to let him look. If he can't tie our bomb to his man, he'll go back to Washington and be out of our hair. If our bomber and his bomber are one and the same, we might be damned lucky to have his help. I've already spoken to Assistant Chief Morgan about this. He wants us to extend our full cooperation."

Starkey thought that was just like Kelso, call the brass and cover his ass.

"Marzik found a wit who might've seen our guy make the 911 call. He says that the person making the call was an Anglo guy."

That stopped Kelso, who fidgeted with his pencil as he considered it.

"I thought the caller was Hispanic."

"So did I."

Starkey didn't add anything more. She figured that even Kelso was smart enough to see the implication.

"Well, I guess you'd better see to it. Call me at home to tell me what develops."

"I was going to go see about it, Lieutenant, but I had to come meet Mr. Pell instead. Now it has to keep until tomorrow. The witness had plans."

Kelso looked disappointed.

"It couldn't be helped, then. See about it tomorrow and keep me informed. You're going to close this case, Starkey. I have every faith in that. So does the A-chief."

Starkey didn't answer. She wanted to get out of there, but Kelso looked nervous.

"You're doing okay with this, aren't you, Carol? You're okay?"

Kelso came around his desk again, getting close to her, as if he was trying to smell her breath.

"I'm fine."

"Good. Go home and get a good night's sleep. Rest is important to keep your mind sharp."

Starkey let herself out, hoping that she wouldn't see Pell when she left. It was after six when she pulled out into the downtown traffic, but she didn't head home. She turned her car west toward a bar called Barrigan's in the Wilshire Division.

Less than twelve hours ago, she had emptied her flask and promised herself that she would ease up on the drinking, but to hell with that. She ate two Tagamet and cursed her rotten luck that the ATF was involved.

Special Agent Jack Pell

Pell sat in a small white room not much bigger than a coffin to read the reports. He had been provided with the initial findings from the Bomb Squad, SID, and the autopsy of the deceased officer.

After reading them, he felt that LAPD's Scientific Investigation Division and Bomb Squad had done an excellent job of forensics and analysis, though he was disappointed that only a single letter—the S—had been recovered. Pell was certain there would be more, but had a high degree of confidence that the criminalist over there, Chen, would not have overlooked anything. Pell wasn't so certain about the Medical Examiner's office. An important step had not been noted in the autopsy protocol.

He brought the reports into the hall and found Santos waiting.

"Do you know if the medical examiner took a full X-ray of Riggio's body?"

"I don't know. If it's not in the protocol, they probably didn't do it."

"It's not, but it should be."

Pell paged open the autopsy protocol and found the attending medical examiner's name. Lee Richards.

"Is Starkey still here?"

"She's gone."

"I'd better see Lieutenant Kelso."

Twenty minutes later, after Kelso had made two phone calls to locate Richards, Santos drove Pell around behind the rear of the County-USC Medical Center to the Medical Examiner's building.

When Santos started to get out with him, Pell said, "Take five and grab a smoke."

"Don't smoke."

"You're not coming in there with me."

Pell could tell that Santos was bothered by that, but Pell didn't care.

"You think I wanna watch an M.E. dig around in a friend of mine? I'll grab a cup of coffee and wait in the lobby."

Pell couldn't object to that, so they crunched across the gravel toward the door.

Inside, Santos identified them to the security guard, then went for his coffee. Richards appeared a few minutes later, Pell following him into a cold tile X-ray room where they waited while two technicians wheeled in Riggio's body. The body was zipped into an opaque plastic bag. Pell and Richards stood silently as the technicians took the body from the bag and positioned it on the X-ray table. The great Y incision down the chest and abdomen that Richards had made during the autopsy was stitched closed, as were the wounds where the frags had done their worst damage.

Richards eyed the body as if he was assessing his work and liking it.

"The entry wounds were fairly obvious, as you can see. We took area X-rays wherever the entries appeared to be of a significant nature, and that's where we removed the fragments."

Pell said, "That's the problem. If you only look where you see an entry wound, you'll miss something. I've seen cases where shrapnel bounced off a pelvis and followed the femur down to a knee."

Richards looked dubious.

"I guess it's possible."

"I know it's possible. Where are his hands?"

Richards frowned.

"Hm?"

"Were his hands recovered?"

"Oh, yes. I examined them. I know I examined them."

Richards peered at the bony stubs of the wrists, then squinted at the technicians.

"Where are the goddamned hands?"

The technicians fished around in the bag and came out with the hands. Scorched from the heat flash and macerated by the pressure wave. Richards looked relieved.

"See? We've got the hands. It's all here."

Like he was proud of himself that all the body parts were accounted for.

Richards said, "What we'll do is look over the body with the scope first. We see anything, we'll mark it, okay? That'll be faster than screwing around with the X-ray."

"Fine."

"I don't like the X-ray. Even with all the shielding, I worry about the cancer."

"Fine."

Pell was given a pair of yellow goggles to wear. He felt nothing as he watched them wheel Riggio's body behind a chromatic fluoroscope. The fluoroscope looked like an opaque flat-screen television, but when Richards turned it on, it was suddenly transparent. As the body disappeared behind the screen, its flesh was no longer flesh but transparent lime Jell-O, the bones impenetrable green shadows. Richards adjusted the screen.

"Pretty cool, huh? This won't scramble your 'nads the way an X-ray will. No cancer."

At Richards's direction, the techs pushed the body slowly past the screen, revealing three sharply defined shadows below the knee, two in the left leg, one in the right, all smaller than a BB.

Richards said, "Sonofabitch, here you go. Right here."

Pell had expected to find even more, but the armored suit had done its work well. Only those fragments with a significant mass had carried enough inertia to punch through the Kevlar.

Richards peered at him.

"You want these?"

"I want it all, Doc."

Richards marked the spots on the body with a felt-tipped pen.

By the time they finished scanning the body, they had found eighteen metal fragments, only two of which had any real size: one, an inch-long piece of twisted metal that had lodged in Riggio's hip joint; the other, a half-inch rectangular fragment that Richards had overlooked when he'd removed a cluster of fragments from the soft tissue of Riggio's right shoulder.

As Richards removed them, the taller technician rinsed them of clotted blood and placed them in a glass tray. Pell inspected each bit of metal, but he found no etches or markings.

Finally, Richards turned off the light screen, and lifted his goggles.

"That's it."

Pell didn't say anything until the last of the fragments had been rinsed. It was the largest piece, and he wanted there to be something so badly that his heart was hammering, but when he examined it, he saw that there was nothing.

"Does any of this help, you think?"

Pell didn't answer.

"Agent?"

"I appreciate your staying, Doc. Thanks."

Richards peeled off his gloves to glance at his watch. It was a Mickey Mouse watch.

"We'll send these over to SID in the morning. We have to deliver them under seal to maintain the chain of evidence."

"I know. That'll be fine, thanks."

It wasn't fine and Pell didn't like it. A cold rage of frustration threatened to spill out of him.

Pell was already thinking that he was too late, that Mr. Red might have come and gone and be on to another city or maybe had never been here at all, when the taller technician mentioned the hands.

"Doc, you gonna scope the hands or should I bag this stuff and get out of here?"

Richards grunted like they might as well, then brought over the hands and placed them under the scope. Two bright green shadows were wedged among the metacarpal bones in the left hand.

"Shit. Looks like we missed a couple."

Richards removed them with the forceps, passing them to the tech, who rinsed them and put them with the others.

Pell inspected them as he had done the others, turning over both pieces without hope when he felt an adrenaline jolt of rage surge through his body.

The larger piece had six tiny letters etched into its surface, part of a sixth, and what he saw there stunned him. It wasn't what he expected. It wasn't anything that he had expected. His heart was beating so hard that it seemed to echo off the walls.

Behind him, Richards said, "Find anything?"

"No. Just more of the same stuff, Doc."

Pell palmed the shard with the letters and returned the remaining piece to the tray with the other recovered fragments. The lab technician did not notice that he had returned one piece and not two.

Richards must've read something in his eyes.

"Are you all right, Agent Pell? You need a drink of water or something?"

Pell put away those things he felt and carefully blanked his face.

"I'm fine, Doc. Thanks for your time."

Special Agent Jack Pell walked back into the outer hall, where the security guard stared at him with goldfish eyes.

"You looking for Santos?"

"Yeah."

"He took his coffee out to the car."

Pell turned toward the door and was halfway down the hall when crimson starbursts appeared in the air before him, followed by a sharp wave of nausea. The air around the starbursts darkened and was suddenly alive with wormy shapes that writhed and twisted.

Pell said, "Shit, not now. Not now."

Behind him, the guard said, "What?"

Pell remembered a bathroom. A men's room off the hall. He blinked hard against the darkening stars and shoved his way through the door. A cold sweat sprouted over his back and chest.

The dizziness hit him as he reached the sink, and then his stomach clenched and he barfed into the sink. The room felt as cold as a meat locker.

Closing his eyes didn't stop him from seeing the shapes. They floated in the air on a field of black, rising and twisting in slow motion as if filled with helium. He turned on the cold water and vomited again, spitting out the foul taste as he splashed water into his eyes. His stomach heaved a third time, and the nausea passed.

He heard voices in the hall and thought one of them might be Santos.

Pell clawed a towel from the rack, wet it with cold water, and staggered into the stall. When he straightened, his head spun.

He slumped onto the toilet and pressed the towel hard to his eyes, waiting.

He had done this before. He had done it many times and was scared because the time between bouts was shrinking. He knew what that meant, and it scared him more than anything in his life had ever scared him.

He sat on the floor, breathing through the wet towel until the floating monsters that haunted him vanished. When they were gone, he took out the piece of metal he had stolen and read the letters there, squinting to make his eyes work.

Pell hadn't told Kelso and Starkey everything about Mr. Red. He hadn't told them that Mr. Red didn't just kill random bomb techs. He chose his targets, usually senior techs with headline cases under their belts. He didn't kill just anyone; he killed only the very best.

When Pell learned of the S, he thought it would be from Charles. It wasn't.

Pell read the fragment again.

TARKEY

CRIME BOSS DIES IN FIERY BLAST
INNOCENTS DIE ALSO
By Lauren Beth
Exclusive to the Miami Herald

Diego "Sonny" Vega, the reputed chief enforcer of an organized Cubano crime empire, died early Thursday morning when a warehouse he owned was destroyed by a series of bomb blasts. The ex-

plosions occurred just after three A.M. It is not known whether Mr. Vega was intentionally murdered, or if his presence in the building was coincidental.

The industrial park warehouse was the site of a "knockoff" apparel operation, employing undocumented workers to manufacture counterfeit designer goods. Five of these workers were also killed, and nine others wounded.

Police spokesman Evelyn Melancon said, "Obviously, this was a sweatshop operation. We do not at this time know if Mr. Vega was the intended target, or if the warehouse itself was the target. We have no leads at this time as to who planted the bombs."

Arson investigators and bomb technicians from the Bureau of Alcohol, Tobacco, and Firearms are sifting through the rubble in an effort to—

John Michael Fowles was disappointed that the article was on page three, but decided not to show it. He was also pissed off that there was no mention of Mr. Red, nor of the fine work he had done in destroying the building. He folded the newspaper and handed it back to Angelo Rossi, the man who had put him in touch with Victor Karpov.

Rossi looked surprised when John returned the paper.

"There's more on the next page."

"It's just an article, Mr. Rossi. I'd rather be readin' the papers you got in that bag, if you know what I mean."

"Well, sure."

Rossi nervously handed over the bag with the money Karpov owed John. Karpov himself had refused to come meet John here at the library. He claimed illness, like a kid cutting class, but John knew the real reason: He was scared.

As before, John didn't bother to count it, or even open the bag. He put the money into his backpack, and lowered the pack to the floor. When John had told Rossi to meet him here in the periodicals section of the West Palm Beach Public Library, he had to explain what "periodicals" were.

John gave Rossi the cracker's hayseed grin as he leaned back against the reading table.

"Take it easy, Mr. Rossi. We're okay. You don't have an overdue book, do ya?"

Rossi glanced over his shoulder as if the book police were hot on his trail, clearly nervous and out of place. John wondered if the fat bastard had even been in a library except when he'd been sent there on high school detention.

"This is foolish, Red, meeting in a library like this. What kinda mook talks about shit like this in a library?"

"A mook like me, I guess. I like the order you find in a library, Angelo. It's the last place left where people behave with manners, don't you think?"

"Yeah. Whatever. Why'd you do your hair like that?"

"So people will remember it."

Rossi's eyes narrowed. John pictured rusty gears turning in Rossi's head, and had to bite his tongue to keep from laughing, though he knew Rossi to be a smart man.

"Don't you worry about it, partner. Mr. Red has his reasons."

"Oh, I get it. Mr. Red. The red hair."

"There you go."

Today, John's hair was cut way short and dyed a vivid red the colorist had called Promise of Passion. Contact lenses gave him green eyes. His sideburns were long and pointed, and he'd fit cotton wads into his lower cheeks to make his jaw appear more square. He was also wearing lifts that made him three inches taller.

If Rossi knew the real reason John had made himself up this way, the man would shit a Buick.

"Listen, my friends up in Jersey got another job I wanna talk to you about."

"Down here or up there?"

"We got a fuckass Cuban pirate knocking over our ganja boats down off Key West."

John shook his head before Rossi finished.

"No can do, Mr. Rossi. I'd like to oblige, but things are gonna be heating up for me around here now, so I've gotta split."

"Just listen a minute, okay, Red? What I'm talking about here won't take long at all. We just wanna kill a nigger, is all."

"So go shoot him. You done it before."

Rossi seemed agitated, and John wondered about that. He hadn't expected Rossi to pitch him another gig, and he was growing concerned with all the time he was wasting. He wanted Rossi to leave so that he could get on with his business. The real reason he had come to the library.

"Well, it's more than just walking up to some nigger and shooting him. I could get one'a these kids around here to do that. We wanna get him, his family, the whole damned nest of'm, you know. Kinda send a message, the way you're good at doing."

"Can't help you, Mr. Rossi. You had a job in another state, we could talk about it. But not here. I got some personal business I wanna take care of."

Rossi nervously glanced around again, then scooted his chair closer. He wasn't taking the hint to leave, which made John figure that he'd probably already told the Jersey people that Mr. Red would go along.

"Shit, the cops got nothing on you, and no way to connect you to that bastard Vega. You saw the paper. They don't know shit yet."

"Don't believe everything you read, Angelo. Now I got other stuff I need to do, so if you'll excuse me, get the fuck outta here."

In fact, John knew far more than Rossi or the press about what the blast investigators had gathered. At some time around eleven P.M. the night before, the Broward County Sheriff's laboratory had found his little calling card. They had entered their preliminary lab results and materials findings into the FBI's Bomb Data Center computer system. The BDC's computer had matched these findings with other known explosive devices that had been used around the country, and an alert had been kicked back to the sheriff and the local ATF office, as well as to the national FBI and ATF offices in Washington. John did not know, but he surmised, that while he and Angelo Rossi sat here in the coolness of the air-conditioned library, agents from the local ATF field office were scrambling to act on this information. Which was exactly what he wanted them to do.

"Look, Red, please. I'm telling you you can make a sweet buck here. How's twice what Karpov paid you sound?"

"Sorry, sir. Just can't."

"You got us over a barrel."

"Nah. I think *you*'re the one over a barrel, right? You shot off your mouth to those wops up north, and now you can't deliver."

Rossi glanced around again.

"Do me this as a favor, okay? I can give you everything you need to know about this nigger right now. Shit, I'll drive you there myself, you want."

"Nope. No niggers on the menu today. Now get the fuck outta here, okay?"

Rossi's nostrils flared and his hand slipped beneath his jacket. Ninety degrees and a hundred percent humidity, and this dumb guinea was wearing a sport coat like he just came out of a double bill of *Goodfellas*.

John rolled his eyes.

"Oh, please, Mr. Rossi. Let's not be small. What the fuck you think you're gonna do with that here in the library? Here in 'periodicals'? Jesus Christ, you're so dumb you think 'periodicals' is something a whore gets."

Rossi's jaw worked as if he was chewing gum.

John grinned wider, then let the smile fall away and leaned toward Angelo Rossi. He knew Rossi feared him. He knew Rossi was about to fear him more.

"Here's a tip, Angelo: Pretend that you dropped something on the floor and bend down to pick it up. When you're down there, you look up under the bottom of this table."

Rossi's eyes flickered.

"What you got down there?"

"You look, Angelo. You won't get bit."

John took the newspaper from the table and let it slip to the floor.

"You go on and look now, okay? You just look."

Rossi didn't bend down for the paper. Slowly, never taking his eyes from John, he slipped from the chair and squatted to the floor. When he rose again, Rossi's face was white.

"You crazy fuck."

"That might be, Angelo. Now you go on and kill your own damned nigger. Me and you will work together again another time."

Rossi showed his palms and backed away, bumping into two teenage girls who were trying to figure out how to use a reference computer.

When Rossi was gone, John considered the people at the surrounding tables. Mostly old people, reading newspapers and magazines. A group of preschool kids here on some kind of kindergarten field trip. A soft-looking man behind the research desk, reading a Dean Koontz novel. All of them just going along with their lives, oblivious.

John swung around to face the library's Internet research computer and tapped in the address for the FBI's web site: *www.fbi.gov.*

When the home page came up, he clicked on the Ten Most Wanted Fugitives icon and watched the page load.

Ten small pictures appeared, each with a link to its own page. John had checked the site before Rossi arrived, hoping to find his picture there. It wasn't then, and still wasn't.

A perfect example, John felt, of government inefficiency.

Disappointed, John went back to the home page, and clicked on the Unknown Suspects icon. Nine pictures appeared, three of which were artists' sketches. One of the sketches showed a studious young man with a balding pate, rim of brown hair, brown eyes, and dorky glasses. John had starved himself for two weeks before letting himself be seen that time, and the witnesses had certainly noticed: The sketch showed him to be gaunt and undernourished. He was also shown wearing a white button-down shirt and thin dark tie. It was a sketch that looked nothing like his true self, just as today he looked nothing like his true self.

He clicked on the sketch, which brought him to a page showing a brief (though inaccurate) description of himself, along with a catalog of the crimes he was suspected of committing. These charges included multiple counts of criminal bombing and murder. John was pleased to note that the feds considered him extremely dangerous, and that he used "sophisticated explosive devices for criminal gain." It wasn't as cool as being in the Top Ten, but it was better than getting piss on your shoe.

John felt that the FBI's refusal to include him in the Ten Most Wanted List was both cheesy and disrespectful. And lazy. The Top Ten was loaded with raghead terrorists, right-wing political kooks, and drug addicts who had murdered police officers. John had killed far more people than most of them. He believed himself to be the most dangerous man walking free in open daylight, and expected to be treated as such.

John guessed he would just have to up the stakes.

Beneath the table was a small device he had built for this library, specifically to be used as a message. It was simple, elegant, and, like every device he built, bore his signature. The local authorities would know within hours that Mr. Red had come to call.

"Excuse me. Are you finished using that?"

An older woman with a body like a squash stood behind him. She was holding a spiral notebook.

"You want to use the computer?"

"Yes. If you're finished with it."

John flashed the big grin, then scooped up his backpack and held the chair for her. Just before he stood, he reached beneath the table and turned on the timer.

"Yes, ma'am, I am. You sit right here. This chair's so comfy it'll make your butt smile."

The older woman laughed.

John left her there and walked out into the sun.

4

STARKEY WOKE THE next morning on the couch, her body
clenched into a fist. Her neck was stiff, and her mouth tasted as if it
were lined with sheep's wool seat covers. It was four-twenty in the
morning. She had gotten two hours' sleep.

Starkey felt disquieted by the dreams. A different quality had
been added. Pell. In her dreams, he chased her. She had run as hard
as she could, but her movements were sluggish and slow, while his
were not. Starkey didn't like that. In the dream, his fingers were bony
and sharp, like claws. She didn't like that, either. Starkey's dreams

had been a constant since her injury, but she found herself feeling resentful of this addition. It was bad enough that the sonofabitch was invading her investigation; she didn't need him in her nightmares.

Starkey lit a cigarette, then gimped into the kitchen, where she found a small amount of orange juice that didn't smell sour. She tried to remember the last time that she'd been to the market, but couldn't. The only things she bought in quantity were gin and cigarettes.

Starkey downed the juice, then a glass of water, then got herself together for the day. Breakfast was two aspirin and a Tagamet.

Marzik had left word on her voice mail that they could meet the wit, a kid named Lester Ybarra, at the flower shop when it opened at nine. By five-thirty, Starkey was at Spring Street, climbing the stairs to her office. Spring Street was quiet. Neither CCS, Fugitive Section, nor IAG maintained a night shift. Their commanders and sergeant-supervisors were on pagers. They, in turn, would contact the officers and detectives in their commands on an as-needed basis. Fugitive Section, by the nature of their work as manhunters, often started their days as early as three A.M. in order to bag their mutts in bed. But today the stairs were empty, and her steps echoed in the silent altar of the stairwell.

Starkey liked that.

She had once told Dana that she enjoyed being awake before everyone else because it gave her an edge, but that had been a lie. Starkey enjoyed the solitude because it was easier. No one intruded. No one stared behind her back, thinking that she was the one, the tech who'd been blown apart and stitched back together like Frankenstein's monster, the one who had lost her partner, the one who had escaped, the one who had died. Dana had called her on it, offering Starkey the truth by asking if Carol ever felt the weight of their stares or imagined that she could hear their thoughts. Starkey, of course, denied all of it, but she thought about it later and admitted that Dana was right. Solitude was a spell that freed her.

Starkey opened the CCS office, then put on the Mr. Coffee. As the coffee dripped, she went back to her desk. Like all the CCS detectives, she kept reference manuals and sourcebooks for explosives manufacturers, but, unlike the others, Starkey also had her texts and manuals from the FBI's Redstone Arsenal Bomb School, and the technical catalogs that she had collected during her days as a bomb technician.

Starkey brought a cup of coffee back to her desk, lit a fresh cigarette, then searched through her books.

Modex Hybrid was a trinary explosive used as a bursting charge in air-to-air missiles. Hot, fast, and dangerous. Trinary meant that it was a mixture of three primary explosives, combined together to form a compound more powerful and stable than any of the three alone. Starkey took out her case notebook and copied the components: RDX, TNT, ammonium picrate, powdered aluminum, wax, and calcium chloride. RDX, TNT, and ammonium picrate were high explosives. The powdered aluminum was used to enhance the power of the explosion. The wax and calcium chloride were used as stabilizers.

Chen had found contaminants in the Modex, and, after consulting with the manufacturer, had concluded that the Modex used in Riggio's bomb wasn't part of a government production. It was homemade, and therefore untraceable.

Starkey considered that, then searched through her books for information on the primary components.

TNT and ammonium picrate were available to the civilian population. You could get it damned near anywhere. RDX was different. Like the Modex, it was manufactured for the military only under government contract, but, unlike the Modex, it was too complicated to produce without industrial refining equipment. You couldn't cook up a batch in your microwave. This was the kind of break Starkey was hoping to find in her manuals. Someone could make Modex if they had the components, but they couldn't make the components. They would have to acquire the RDX, which meant that the RDX could be traced back to its source.

Starkey decided that this was a good angle to work.

She brought her notes to the NLETS computer, poured herself a fresh cup of coffee, then punched up a request form asking for matches with RDX. By the time she finished typing the form and entering the request, a few of the other detectives had begun to drift in for the start of the shift. The silence was gone. The spell was broken.

Starkey gathered her things and left.

Marzik was loading Amway products into her trunk when Starkey parked behind her outside the flower shop. Marzik carried the damned stuff everywhere and would make her pitch at the most inappropriate times, even when interviewing witnesses and, twice, when questioning potential suspects.

Starkey felt her stomach tighten. She had decided not to call Marzik on ratting her out to Kelso, but she now felt a wave of irritation.

They met on the sidewalk, Marzik saying, "Is the ATF going to take over the case?"

"He says no, but we'll see. Beth, tell me you weren't in there with the Amway."

Marzik slammed the trunk and looked annoyed.

"Why shouldn't I? They didn't mind. I made a good sale."

"Do me a favor and leave it in the trunk. I don't want to see that again on this case."

"Oh, for Christ's sake. I got two children to feed."

Starkey was going to say more when a short, thin Latino teenager stepped out of the flower shop and looked at Marzik. "Detective? My dad says I got to get going soon. We got morning deliveries."

Marzik introduced her to Lester Ybarra as the lead investigator on the case.

Starkey offered her hand. Lester's felt clammy from being inside the flower shop. He smelled of chemicals and baby's breath.

"Hi, Lester. I really appreciate your helping us out like this."

Lester glanced at Marzik, flashing a shy smile.

" 's no pro'lem."

Marzik said, "Lester saw someone using the phone across the street between one and one-fifteen the day the bomb went off, right, Lester?"

Lester nodded, and Marzik nodded with him.

"Can you describe that person to Detective Starkey?"

Lester glanced at Starkey, then snuck a quick peek back at Marzik. His eyes went to Marzik so much that Starkey figured he had probably developed a crush on her, which made Starkey wonder if he had fabricated parts of his story to impress her.

Starkey said, "Before we get to that, Lester, how about helping me set the scene, okay? So I can picture it?"

" 's no pro'lem."

"Your van was where? About here where my car is?"

"Yeah."

Starkey was parked directly outside the florist's front door in a red No Parking zone about fifteen feet from the corner.

"You always load the van out here in the street, bringing the flowers through the front door?"

"We got three vans. The other two was using the alley, so I had to be out here. I was supposed to leave by twelve-thirty, but we got this big order right when I was set to go. A funeral set, you know? Twelve sprays. We make a lotta money from funerals. My dad said I hadda wait, so I brought the van around front here."

"You were sitting in the van, waiting, or you were loading flowers?"

"When I saw the guy, I was sitting there behind the wheel. Nothing to do, you know? My sisters hadda make the sprays. So I was just sitting there in case the cops come and I hadda move."

Marzik said, "He was in the red zone."

Starkey nodded. Standing there listening, she had noticed that very few cars turned off Sunset onto the little side street. Lester would have an easy, unobstructed view of the pay phone hanging on the laundry across the street. She watched an older couple emerge from the laundry with a pink box and made a note to herself to mention it to Marzik.

"Okay, Lester, would you describe him for me? I know you described him for Detective Marzik, but now for me."

Starkey and Marzik locked eyes. They were getting down to it now. Whether the caller was Anglo or Latino.

Lester launched into his description, describing an Anglo man of medium height and build, wearing a faded blue baseball cap, sunglasses (probably Wayfarers), dark blue trousers, and a lighter blue work shirt. Lester's impression was that the man was wearing some kind of a uniform, such as a gas station attendant or bus driver. Starkey took notes, not reacting to Lester's statement that the caller was an Anglo. Lester had not heard the man's voice. He thought the guy had to be in his forties, but admitted to being a lousy judge of age. As Lester spoke, Starkey felt the pager at her hip vibrate and checked the number. Hooker.

When Lester finished, Starkey folded her pad on a finger.

"If you saw this guy again, you think you'd recognize him?"

Lester shrugged.

"I don't think so. Maybe. I didn't really look at him, you know? Just for a couple seconds."

"Did you see which way the man came from when he went to the phone?"

"I didn't notice."

"How about when he left? You see where he went?"

"I wasn't paying attention, you know? He was just some guy."

"He get out of or into a car?"

Lester shrugged.

Starkey put away the pad.

"Okay, Lester, I've got just one problem with this. We have reason to believe that the person making the call was Latino. You sure this guy was Anglo?"

"I'm pretty sure. His hair was light, you know? Not gray, but light."

Starkey and Marzik traded another look, neither as enthusiastic as they had been yesterday. "Pretty sure" was an equivocation.

"Light brown?"

"Yeah. A light brown. Kinda sandy."

Marzik frowned. "You could tell that with the cap?"

Lester touched his own ears.

"The part I could see down here, you know?"

That made sense to Starkey. She brought out the pad again and made another note. As she wrote, she had another thought.

"Okay. One more thing. Do you recall any identifying characteristics? A scar, maybe? A tattoo on his arm?"

"He was wearing long sleeves."

"He was wearing a long-sleeved shirt?"

"Yeah. That's why I couldn't see his arms. I remember it was greasy and old, like he'd been working on a car or something."

Starkey glanced at Marzik and found her staring. Marzik was clearly unhappy with Lester's uncertainty. When Starkey glanced back at Lester, he was watching Marzik.

"One last thing. You were out here, about, what? Fifteen minutes?"

"You keep sayin' that, one last thing. My old man's gonna kick my ass. I gotta go make these deliveries."

"I mean it this time, Lester. Just this last question. Anyone else make a call from that phone while you were out here?"

Starkey already knew that no other calls had been made from that phone. She wanted to see if he would lie about it to impress Marzik or to make himself more important.

"I didn't see anyone else. No."

Starkey put away her pad.

"Okay, Lester, thanks. I want you to come in with Detective Marzik and work with a sketch artist, see if we can't build a picture of this guy, okay?"

"That sounds pretty cool to me. My dad ain't gonna like it, though. He gonna raise hell."

"You go take care of your deliveries, and we'll square it with your father, maybe get you down there later this morning. Detective Marzik will buy you lunch."

Lester nodded his head like a collie.

"Okay. Sure."

Lester vanished into the flower shop, but Marzik and Starkey stayed on the sidewalk.

"Why'd you have to tell him that, for Christ's sake? I don't want to spend all day with him."

"Somebody has to be with him. You've set up the rapport."

"It's not going to do any good. You hear that, 'pretty sure'? The guy's wearing a cap, sunglasses, and a long-sleeved shirt on a day it's ninety-five fuckin' degrees. If it's our guy, he's wearing a goddamned disguise. If he's not, he's just some asshole."

Starkey felt the urge for more antacid.

"Why do you always have to be so negative?"

"I'm not being negative. I'm just stating what's obvious."

"Okay, then try this for obvious: *If* he's our guy, and *if* he's wearing the same clothes when he set off the bomb, and *if* he's on the news tape, the goddamned hat and sunglasses and long-sleeved shirt should make him easier to spot."

"Whatever. I'll go talk to the kid's father. He's a bastard."

Marzik stalked into the shop without another word. Starkey shook out a cigarette, lit it, and went to her car. She was so angry that she was trembling. First Pell, now this. She was trying to get past it because she had a job to do, and she knew the anger was getting in her way. She tried to remember some of the techniques that Dana had told her for setting aside her anger, but couldn't remember any of them. Three years in therapy, and she couldn't remember a goddamned thing.

Just as Marzik reappeared, Starkey was considering the people coming and going from the laundry, and how many of them passed the pay phone. She took a breath, calming herself.

"Beth, you talked to the people at the laundry, right?"

Marzik answered without looking at her. Sulking.

"I told you I did."

"Did you run the time and description by them? I'm thinking that one of their customers might've seen our guy."

Marzik pulled her pad from her purse, opened it to a list of names, then held it out with the same sulky indifference.

"I asked them for any customers they recalled between noon and two. I'm not stupid, Carol."

Starkey stared at Marzik, then dropped her cigarette and crushed it.

"Okay. I wasn't going to say anything about this, but I think you and I need to clear the air."

"About what? Your busting my balls about the Amway or because the kid isn't as solid as I thought he was?"

"You told Kelso that you thought I was drinking on the job."

Marzik went a bright crimson, confirming Starkey's suspicion.

"No, I didn't. Did Kelso say that?"

"Beth, this is hard enough. If you're going to lie to me, do me the kindness of not saying anything and just listen."

"I don't like being accused."

"If you don't want to work with me, let's go to Kelso and tell him we can't work together. I'll tell him it's mutual, and neither of us will lose points."

Marzik crossed her arms, then uncrossed them and squared herself in Starkey's face.

"If you want to talk about this straight-up, then let's get straight-up. Everyone on the squad knows you have a drinking problem. Jesus Christ, we can smell it. If you don't reek of gin, you're blowing Altoids to cover it."

Starkey felt herself redden and fought the urge to step away.

"Everybody feels sorry for you because of what happened. They set you up over here in CCS and took care to bring you along, but you know what? That shit doesn't cut any ice with me. No one set me up, and no one is looking out for me, and I got two kids to raise."

"No one's looking out for me."

Starkey felt as if she was suddenly on the spot, and defensive.

"My ass there isn't. Everybody knows that Dick Leyton used his clout at Parker to make Kelso take you, and he's *still* watching out for you. I've got these two kids to raise, and I gotta have this job. That job isn't babysitting you, and it sure as hell doesn't include taking a career fall to cover your bad habits."

"I'm not asking you to cover for me."

"Good, because I won't. I also won't ask off this case because this is the kind of case that leads to a promotion. If this thing about the guy being Anglo turns out to be real, I want the credit. I've been a D-2 for too damned long. I need the bump to D-3. I need the money. If you can't handle it, then *you* ask off, because I need the money."

Starkey felt her pager vibrate again, and, again, it was Hooker. She went into her car for her cell phone, thankful for the excuse, and berating herself for bringing up the business about the drinking. She knew that Marzik would deny ratting to Kelso, and as long as Marzik denied it, it was a no-winner. Now Marzik was openly hostile.

"Hook, it's me."

"You and Marzik get anything from the flower kid?"

"Marzik's going to bring him in to work with an artist. Can you get that set up?"

"Right away. Listen, we got the news tapes you wanted. From three of the stations, anyway. You want me to set up the room for us to watch?"

"It's the tape they shot from the helicopters over the parking lot?"

"Yeah. There are a lot of tapes here. You want me to set the room?"

Starkey flashed on the images trapped on the tape. She would see the bomb explode. She would see Charlie Riggio die.

"Set up the room, Jorge. I want the kid to look at them, too, but only after he's done with the artist, okay? I don't want him seeing the videos first, then describing someone he's seen just because he thinks they look suspicious."

"I'll get it set up."

"One more thing. What happened with Pell last night?"

"He didn't like something in the coroner's report. Kelso had me take him over there."

Starkey felt her stomach knot.

"What didn't he like?"

"The M.E. hadn't done a full body X-ray, so Pell made him do it."

"Jesus, Kelso's letting him work the case like he's local?"

"I can't talk, Carol. You know?"

"Did he find anything?"

"They found some more frag, but he said it didn't amount to very much."

Starkey felt herself breathe easier. Maybe Pell would lose interest and go back to Washington.

"Okay, arrange for the artist and lock down the room for the tapes. I'll be there in a few minutes."

She ended the call, then went back to Marzik. She had decided that she needed to smooth over things.

"Beth? We've got the videotape. Jorge's going to set up the artist for you. After that, how about you bring Lester back to watch the tapes? Maybe he'll pick out the hat man."

"Whatever."

"Look, I didn't mean to step on your toes about the laundry people. That was good thinking, getting the customer names."

"Thank you too much."

If that's the way she wanted it, Starkey thought, fine.

She got into her car and left Marzik waiting in the heat for Lester Ybarra.

Starkey intended to drive back to Spring Street, but as she passed the site where Riggio died, she slowed and turned into the parking lot.

Hearing that the videotapes had arrived had gotten her thinking. The remote-control manufacturer had told her that the maximum possible range for the transmitter was one hundred yards. Per Bomb Squad policy, the area had been cleared out to one hundred yards, which meant that whoever had the transmitter would have to be right at the edge of the boundary. Starkey thought that maybe the news tape would show the crowd where someone had been close enough to pull the trigger.

The parking lot had been released as a crime scene, and all of the shops except for the bookstore were once more open for business. Two young Latinos were painting the damaged wall, the Dumpster had been replaced, and the blast crater was now a black patch against gray tarmac. Life was moving on.

Starkey parked on the street, then walked over to the patch. She stared across Sunset Boulevard, trying to figure how far one hundred yards was, then looked south up the little side street past the apartment buildings, trying to gauge the distance. The sun beat down on her dark gray pants suit, making the fabric hot and uncomfortable. She took off her jacket and folded it across her arm. The painters stared at the pistol on her hip, so she unclipped it and held it in the fold of her jacket.

Starkey crossed Sunset at the light, then continued north past the Guatemalan market, counting paces until she reached one hundred and thirty. She figured this to be about a hundred yards. She was standing six parking meters north of Sunset Boulevard, about a car length north of a telephone pole. She noted the telephone pole in her casebook, figuring it would be easy to spot on the news video, then went back to the patch and counted the same number of paces south. She found herself beside a tall, spindly palm tree. With so many palms in the area, it would be hard to spot the right one. The apartment building across the street had a blue tile roof, so she noted that in her book. Starkey returned to ground zero twice more, counting paces east and west to fix obvious landmarks. When she was done, she lit a cigarette, then sat in her car, smoking.

She thought that somewhere within these boundaries the killer had watched, and waited, and murdered a man.

She wondered if he was the man that Lester Ybarra had described, if it was Pell's Mr. Red, or if it was someone else.

Hooker was sorting through the tapes in a cardboard box when Starkey reached CCS.

First thing he said was, "The ATF guy called."

"Pell called?"

"Yeah. I put it on your desk."

"Screw'm. Did you get Marzik set up with the sketch artist?"

"They don't have a computer free until later. She wanted me to ask if they can't come here and start on the tapes while they wait."

"No, I told her why not. I want the kid to describe who he saw before we show him any faces. Marzik knows better than that."

"I told her you'd say that. She wasn't happy about it."

"Marzik complains about everything."

Starkey saw a short stack of pink message slips as she dropped her purse into her file drawer. Chester Riggs, who was working out of Organized Crime, and Warren Perez, a D-3 in Rampart Bunco, were both returning her calls. Riggs and Perez were profiling the minimall shopkeepers to look for motives behind the bomb. Neither of them expected to find a link, and neither did Starkey. She didn't bother to read the message from Pell.

Starkey returned to Santos and fingered through the cassettes. They were in two sizes, big three-quarter-inch master tapes and half-inch VHS dubs that could be played on home machines.

Santos saw her frowning.

"These are only from three of the stations, Carol. We got more coming in. Man, it's hours. The running times are written on the outside, along with whether it's a close-up or the wide-angle."

Starkey turned the tapes so that she could see what he was talking about. The shortest tape showed a recorded time of seventy-four minutes. The longest, one hundred twenty-six minutes. Each tape was also marked CLOSE or WIDE.

"What does that mean, close or wide?"

"Some of the helicopters carry two cameras mounted on a swivel that pokes out the bottom of the nose, just like a couple of guns. Both cameras focus on the same thing, but one of the cameras is zoomed in close, and the other is pulled back for a wider field of view. They record both cameras up in the chopper and also back at the studio."

"I thought they show this stuff live."

"They do, but they record it at the same time. We've got both the wide shots and the close shots, so that means there's twice as much to watch."

Starkey was already thinking that the close shots wouldn't give her what she wanted. She pulled out the wide-angle VHS cassettes and brought them to her desk. She considered calling Buck Daggett, but decided that she should review the tapes first.

Behind her, Santos said, "I've got us set up in the TV room upstairs. We can go up as soon as I'm done."

Spring Street had one room that contained a television and VCR. CCS and Fugitive Section rarely needed or used it; much of the time it was used by IAG investigators watching spy tapes of other cops, and most of the time the VCR was vandalized because of that. Chewing gum, tobacco, and other substances were found jammed into the tape heads, even though the room was kept locked. Once, the hindquarters of a rat were found wedged in the machine. Cops were creative vandals.

"You sure the machine up there is working?"

"Yeah. I checked less than an hour ago."

Starkey considered the tapes. Three different views of Charlie Riggio being killed. Anytime there was a bomb call-out, the newspeople got word fast and swarmed the area with cameras. Camera crews and newspeople had been at the trailer park the day she and Sugar had rolled out. She suddenly recalled joking with Sugar about putting on a good show for the six o'clock. She had forgotten that moment until now.

Starkey took a cigarette from her purse and lit up.

"Carol! Do you want Kelso to send you home?"

She glanced over at Hooker, not understanding.

"The cigarette."

Starkey crushed it with her foot as she fanned the air. She felt herself flush.

"Didn't even realize I was doing it."

Hooker was watching her with an expression she read as concern.

Starkey felt a stab of fear that he might be wondering if she was drunk, so she went over to his desk and squatted beside him so that he could smell her breath. She wanted him to know that she wasn't blowing gin.

"I'm worried about this ATF guy, is all. Did he say anything last night when he finished with the medical examiner?"

"Nothing. I asked him if he found what he was looking for, but all he said was that they found some more frag."

"He didn't say anything else?"

"Nothing. He spent today over in Glendale, looking at the reconstruction."

Starkey went back to her desk, making a mental note to phone the medical examiner to see what they'd found and also to call John Chen. Whatever evidence was recovered would be sent to Chen for examination and documentation, though it might take several days to work its way through the system.

Hooker finished logging the tapes and put the box under his desk. Official LAPD filing. He waved one of the three-quarter-inch tapes.

"I'm done. We'd better get started unless you want to wait for Marzik."

Starkey's hands grew damp. She leaned back, her swivel chair squeaking.

"Jorge, look, I'd better return these calls. You start without me, okay?"

Hooker had spent a lot of time getting the tapes together. Now he was disappointed.

"I thought you wanted to see this. We've only got the room for a couple of hours."

"I'll watch them at home, Jorge. I've got these calls."

Her phone rang then. Starkey snatched it up like a life preserver.

"CCS. Starkey."

"Don't you return your calls?"

It was Pell.

"I've been busy. We've got a wit who might have seen the man who placed the 911 call."

"Let's meet somewhere. We need to discuss how we're going to handle the case."

"There is no 'we,' Pell. If my guy isn't your Mr. Red, then it doesn't matter to me. I still want to see what you have on the first seven bombings."

"I have the reports. I have something else, too, Starkey. Let's get together and talk about it. This is important."

She wanted to brush him off, but she knew that she would have to talk with him and decided to get it done. Starkey told him how to get to Barrigan's, then hung up.

Santos had been watching her. He came over with a handful of cassettes.

"Are the feds taking the case?"

"I don't know. He didn't say."

"I guess it's just a matter of time."

She looked at him. Santos shrugged and gestured with the tapes.

"I'm gonna go up. You sure you don't want to come?"

"I've got to meet Pell."

Starkey watched Santos walk away, embarrassed that she had not been able to look at them with him. She had been to the bomb site, she had seen Riggio's body, she had smelled the heat and the blast in the hot air. After that, her fear of seeing the tapes seemed inexplicable, though she understood it. Starkey wouldn't be seeing only Riggio on the tape; she would see herself, and Sugar. She had imagined the events of her own death a thousand times, but she had never seen tape of the actual event or even thought that the moments had been recorded until now: Joking with Sugar, the news crews watching with electronic eyes, tape reels spinning for the six o'clock news. Memories of those things had vanished with the explosion until now.

Starkey fingered the three cassettes, wondering if that tape of her own death still existed.

After a time, she told herself to stop thinking about it, gathered her things, and left to meet Pell.

Barrigan's was a narrow Irish bar in Wilshire Division that had catered to police detectives since 1954, when suits from the Homicide Bureau had held court with tales of blackjacking New York mobsters as they deplaned at LAX. The walls were covered with four-leaf clovers, each bearing the name and date of an officer who'd killed a man in the line of duty. Until only a handful of years ago, female police detectives were discouraged as customers, conventional wisdom being that the presence of female officers would discourage the emotionally dysfunctional secretaries and nurses who flocked to the bar eager to dispense sexual favors to any man with a badge. Though there was some truth to this, the female detectives replied, "Tough shit." The gender barrier was finally broken the night a Robbery-Homicide detective named Samantha Dolan shot it out toe-to-toe with two rape suspects, killing both. As is the custom after such incidents, a party was held for her at Barrigan's that same night. Dolan invited every female detective of her acquaintance, and the women decided they liked the place and would return. They informed the owner that they would be accorded proper service, else they'd have the good sisters over in the Department of Health close his ass down for health violations. That ended that. Starkey had never met Dolan, though she knew the story. Samantha Dolan had later been killed when she'd stepped through a doorway that had been booby-trapped with a double-barreled shotgun.

When Starkey entered Barrigan's late that afternoon, the bar was already lined with detectives. Starkey found a bench between a couple of Sex Crimes D-2s, struck up a fresh cigarette, and ordered a double Sapphire.

She was taking her first sip when Pell appeared beside her and put a heavy manila envelope on the bar.

"You always drink like that on the job?"

"It's none of your goddamned business what I do. But for the record, Special Agent, I'm off duty. I'm here as a favor to you."

The D-2 next to her glanced over, eyeing Pell. He tinkled the ice in the remains of his double scotch, offering Pell the opportunity to comment on his drink, too.

Starkey offered to buy Pell a drink, but Pell refused. He slid onto the bench next to her, uncomfortably close. Barrigan's didn't have stools; the bar was lined with little benches hooked to a brass rail that ran along the bottom of the bar, each wide enough for two people. Starkey hated the damn things because you couldn't move them, but that's the way it had been since 1954, and that's the way it was going to stay.

"Move away, Pell. You're too close."

He edged away.

"Enough? I could sit at another table if you like."

"You're fine where you are. I just don't like people too close."

Starkey immediately regretted saying it, feeling it revealed more of herself than she cared to share.

Pell tapped the manila envelope.

"These are the reports. I've got something else here, too."

He unfolded a sheet of paper and put it on the bar. Starkey saw that it was a newspaper article that he had printed off the net.

"This happened a few days ago. Read it."

BOMB HOAX CLEARS LIBRARY
By Lauren Beth
Miami Herald

The Dade County Regional Main Library was evacuated yesterday when library employees discovered what appeared to be a bomb.

When a loud siren began wailing, librarians found what they believed to be a pipe bomb fixed to the underside of a table.

After police evacuated the library, the Dade County Emergency Response Team recovered the device, which contained the siren, but no explosives. Police officials are calling the incident a hoax.

Starkey stopped reading.

"What is this?"

"We recovered an intact device in Miami. It's a clone of the bomb that killed Riggio."

Starkey didn't like the news about this Miami device. If the bombs were clones like Pell said, that would give him what he needed to jump the case. She knew what would happen then: The ATF would form a task force, which would spur the FBI to come sniffing around. The Sheriffs would want to get their piece of the action, so they would be included, and before the day was done, Starkey and her CCS team would be relegated to gofer chores like overnighting the evidence to the ATF lab up in San Francisco.

She pushed the article away.

"Okay. A hoax. If your boy Mr. Red is in Miami, why aren't you on a plane headed east?"

"Because he's here."

"It looks to me like he's in Miami."

Pell glanced at the D-2.

"Could we move to a table?"

Starkey led him to a remote corner table, taking the outside seat so that she could see the room. She figured that it would annoy him, having his back to the crowd.

"Okay, no one can hear you, Pell. We're free to be spies."

Pell's jaw flexed with irritation, which pleased her. She struck a fresh cigarette, blowing smoke past his shoulder.

"The Miami police didn't give the full story to the papers. It wasn't a hoax, Starkey, it was a message. An actual note. Words on paper. He's never done that before, and he's never done anything like this. That means we have a chance here."

"What did he say?"

"He said, 'Would the deaths of these people put me in the Top Ten?' "

Starkey didn't know what in the hell that meant.

"What does that mean?"

"He wants to be on the FBI's Ten Most Wanted List."

"You're kidding me."

"It's a symbol, Starkey. He's some underachieving nobody who resents being an asshole. He's not on the list because we don't know who the hell he is; no one makes that list unless we have an ID. We don't, so he's getting frustrated. He's taking chances he didn't take earlier. That means he's destabilizing."

Starkey's jaw felt like an iron clamp, but she understood why Pell was on it. When a perp changed his pattern, it was always good for the case. Any change gave you a different view of the man. If you could get enough views, pretty soon you had a clear picture.

"You said he's here. How do you know that? Did his message say that he was coming to Los Angeles?"

Pell didn't answer. He stared at her as if he was searching for something in her eyes, leaving her feeling naked and uncomfortable.

"What?"

"I didn't tell you and Kelso everything. When Mr. Red goes hunting, he does not hunt randomly. He picks his targets, usually senior people or a tech who's been in the news; he goes after the big dog. He wants to say he beats the best a Bomb Squad has to offer. It's the ego thing."

"That what he told you in his little note?"

"We know because he etches the target's name on the bomb casing. The first two techs he killed, we found their names in the frag during the reconstruction. Alan Brennert in Baltimore; Michael Cassutt in Philadelphia; both sergeant-supervisors who'd been involved in big cases."

Starkey didn't say anything. She drew a large 5 in the water rings on the table, then changed it to an S. She guessed it came from "Charles." Charlie Riggio wasn't exactly the big dog of the LAPD Bomb Squad, but she wasn't going to say that.

"Why are you telling me this here in a bar and not in Kelso's office?"

Now Pell glanced away. He seemed nervous about something.

"We try to keep that information on a need-to-know basis."

"Well, I'm honored, Pell. I sure as hell have a need to know, wouldn't you say?"

"Yes."

"Makes me wonder what else you might be holding back."

Pell glanced back sharply.

"As the lead, you could make statements to the press to help advance his destabilization. These aren't just little machines that he's building. These bombs are who he is, and he's meticulous about them. They are very precise, very exact. We know he takes pride in them. In his head, it could become a one-on-one game that keeps him in Los Angeles and gives us a better shot to nail him."

"Me versus him."

"Something like that. What do you say?"

Starkey didn't have to think about it.

"I'm in."

Pell sighed deeply, his shoulders sagging as he relaxed, as if he had been afraid that she wouldn't go along. She smiled to herself, thinking how little he knew.

"All right, Starkey. All right. We believe that he builds the bombs locally. He'll go into an area, acquire the things that he needs, and build the bomb there, so he doesn't have to transport anything, risking capture on the airlines. I put a list of the Modex components in with the reports. I want you to run a local check for people with access to RDX."

Even though Starkey was already running the search, it irritated her that he was giving instructions.

"Listen, Pell, if you want to run a search, do it yourself. You're not giving the orders here."

"It's important, Starkey."

"Then *you* do it!"

Pell glared at her, then seemed to reconsider. He showed his palms and relaxed.

"I guess you could look at it this way, Detective: If I do it, I'm taking over your case; if you do it, I'm only advising you. Which do you want it to be?"

Starkey looked smug.

"It's already happening, Pell. I punched it in today."

He nodded without expression and went on. She found herself irritated that he didn't acknowledge that she was ahead of him.

"Do we have a photograph of this guy? There must've been a security camera."

"There aren't any security cameras in the downtown branch, but I'll have a sketch by tomorrow. The wits described a white male in his twenties with bright red hair. We also have two other sketches from previous incidents. I can already tell you that all three look different. He changes his appearance when he lets himself be seen."

Starkey shrugged noncommittally. Lester had described an older man, nothing even close to young, but she decided not to mention Lester until they had the sketch.

"Whatever. I want a copy of all three of your sketches when you have them, and I want something else, too. I want to see the bomb."

"As soon as I get the report, you'll get the report."

"You didn't hear me. I want the bomb. I want it in my hands. I'm a bomb technician, Pell. I want to break it down myself, not just accept someone else's report. I want to compare it to the Silver Lake bomb and learn something. I know we can do this because I've traded comparative evidence with other cities before."

Pell seemed to consider her again, then nodded.

"Okay, Starkey, I think that's a good idea. But I think you should arrange it."

Starkey frowned, wondering if Pell was going to be deadwood.

"*Your* people have the damned thing. It would be easier for you to get it."

"The more I do, the more pressure I'll get from Washington to take over the case before the FBI comes in."

"Who's talking about the FBI? We're not dealing with a terrorist here. This is domestic."

"A terrorist is whoever the FBI says is a terrorist. You're worried about me coming in, I'm worried about the FBI. We all have something to worry about."

"Jesus Christ, Pell."

He showed his palms again, and she nodded.

"Okay. I'll do it myself."

Pell stood, then gave her a card.

"This is the motel where I'm staying. My pager number is on the back."

Starkey put it away without looking at it.

"Anything comes up, I'll give you a call."

Pell was staring at her.

"What?"

"Mr. Red is dangerous, Starkey. A guy like this in town, you don't want to be too drunk to react."

Starkey rattled the ice in her glass, then took a sip.

"I've already been dead once, Pell. Believe me, there are worse things."

Pell considered her another moment, Starkey thinking he wanted to say something, but then he left. She watched him until he stepped out of the bar into a wedge of blinding light and was gone. Pell had no fucking idea.

Starkey returned to her bench at the bar and ordered a refill. She was convinced that Pell knew more than he was saying.

The Sex Crimes dick leaned close.

"Fed?"

"Yeah."

"They're all pricks."

"We'll see."

Starkey spent most of the afternoon thinking about the tapes that waited in her car. Those tapes and what was on them were real. After a while, it was the weight of the tapes that pulled her from the bar. It was almost eight when she left Barrigan's and drove home.

Starkey's head hurt from the gin. She was hungry, but there was nothing to eat in her house and she didn't want to go out again. She put the tapes in her living room by the VCR, but decided to shower first, then read the reports.

She let the water beat into her neck and skull until it ran cold, then dressed in a black T-shirt and panties. She found a box of raisins, ate them standing at the kitchen sink. When she was finished, she poured a glass of milk, struck a fresh cigarette, and sat at the kitchen table to read.

The manila envelope contained seven ATF explosives profiles written at the ATF's National Laboratory Center in Rockville, Maryland. Each report contained an analysis of a device that was attributed to an unidentified suspect known only as Mr. Red, but each was heavily edited. Pages were missing, and several paragraphs in each report had been deleted.

Starkey grew angry at the deletions, but she found herself interested in the details that were present and read with clear focus. She took notes.

Every one of the devices had been built of twin pipe canisters capped and sealed with plumber's tape, one pipe containing the radio receiver (all receivers identified as being from the WayKool line of remote-control toy cars) and 9-volt battery, one the Modex Hybrid explosive. None of the reports mentioned the etched names that Pell had described. She thought that the deleted material probably referenced that.

When she finished with the reports, she went into her living room and stared at the tapes. She knew that she had been avoiding them, evidence that could potentially offer a breakthrough in her case. But even now, her stomach knotted at the thought of seeing them.

"Oh, goddamnit. This is stupid."

She went into the kitchen, poured herself a stiff gin, then loaded the first tape into the machine. She could have watched the tapes with Buck Daggett or Lester Ybarra, or with Marzik and Hooker, but she knew she had to see them alone. At least, this first time. She had to see them alone because she would be seeing things that none of the rest of them would see.

The image was a wide shot of the parking lot. The Bomb Squad Suburban was in place, the parking lot and the nearby streets cordoned off. The frame did not move, telling Starkey that the helicopter had been in a stationary hover. Riggio, already in the suit, was at the rear of the Suburban, talking with Daggett. Seeing them like that chilled her. Seeing Daggett pat Riggio's helmet, seeing Riggio turn and lumber toward the bomb was like watching Sugar.

"How you doin', cher? You gettin' a good air flow?"

"Got a windstorm in here. You?"

"Wrapped, strapped, and ready to rock. Let's put on a good show for the cameras."

They checked over each other's armor suit and cables. Sugar looked okay to her. She patted his helmet, and he patted hers. That always made her smile.

They started toward the trailer.

Starkey stopped the tape.

She took a breath, realizing only then that she had stopped breathing. She decided that her drink needed more lime, brought it into the kitchen, cut another slice, all the while knowing that she was simply avoiding the video.

She went back into the living room and restarted the tape.

Riggio and the Suburban were in the center of the screen. The bomb was a tiny cardboard square at the base of the Dumpster. The shot was framed too tightly on the parking lot to reveal any of the landmarks she had paced off that morning. The only figures visible were Riggio, Daggett, and a uniformed officer standing at the edge of the building in the bottom of the frame, peeking around the corner.

When Riggio started toward the bomb, the frame shifted, sliding above the minimall to reveal a small group of people standing between two apartment houses. Starkey focused on them, but they were too small and shadowed to tell if any wore long-sleeved shirts and baseball caps.

Starkey was cursing the tiny image when suddenly the frame shifted down, centering on Riggio and losing the people. The camera operator in the helicopter must have adjusted the shot, losing everything except the side of the mall, the bomb, and Riggio.

Riggio reached the bomb with the Real Time.

Starkey knew what was coming and tried to steel herself.

She had more of the drink, feeling her heart pound.

She glanced away and crushed out her cigarette.

When she looked at the screen again, Riggio was circling the box.

They were in the azaleas, wrestling the heavy branches aside so that Sugar could position the Real Time. Sugar looked for all the world like some kind of Star Trek *space invader with a ray gun. She had to twist her body to see him.*

Her eyes blurred as the white flash engulfed her. . . .

Starkey strained to see into the shadows and angles at the outer edge of the frame, between cars, on roofs, in garbage cans. She wondered if the bomber was somehow underground, peering out of a sewer drain or from the vent of a crawl space beneath a building. Riggio circled the bomb, examining it with the Real Time. She put herself in the killer's head and tried to see Riggio from the ground level. She imagined the radio control in her hand. What was he waiting for? Starkey felt anxious and wondered if the killer was growing frightened at the thought of murdering another human being, or excited. Starkey saw the switch as a TV remote, held in the killer's pocket. She saw his eyes on Riggio, unblinking. Riggio finished his circle, hesitated, then leaned over the box. In that moment, the killer pressed the switch and . . .

. . . the light hurled Charlie Riggio away like an imaginary man.

Starkey stopped the tape and closed her eyes, her fist clenched tight as if it was she who had clutched the switch and sent Charlie Riggio to hell.

She felt herself breathe. She felt her chest expand, her body fill with air. She gripped her glass with both hands and drank. She wiped at her eyes.

After a while, she pressed the "play" button and forced herself to watch the rest of the tape.

The pressure wave flashed across the tarmac, a ripple of dust and debris sucked up after it. The Dumpster rocked backwards into the wall. Smoke rose from the crater, drifting lazily in a swirl as Buck Daggett rushed forward to his partner and pulled off the helmet. An Emergency Services van screeched into the lot beside them, two paramedics rushing in to take over. Buck stood watching them.

Starkey was able to pick out the boundaries she had marked and several times found knots of people at the edge of the hundred-yard perimeter who were hidden behind cars or buildings. She froze the image each time, looking for long-sleeved males in blue baseball caps, but the resolution was too poor to be of much use.

She watched the other two tapes, drinking all the while. She examined the murky images as if willing them to clear, thinking that any of those shadowed faces might belong to the man or woman who had built and detonated the bomb.

Later that night, she rewound the tapes, turned off her television, and fell into a deep sleep there on her couch.

She is kicked away from the trailer by a burst of white light.

The paramedics insert their long needle.

She reaches for Sugar's hand as his helmet is pulled free.

His head lolls toward her.

It is Pell.

5

THE NEXT MORNING, Marzik walked through CCS like a shy student handing back test papers, passing out copies of the suspect likeness that had been created from Lester Ybarra's description. Kelso, the last to get one, scowled as if it were his daughter's failing exam.

"There's nothing here we can use. Your wit was a waste of time."

Marzik, clearly disappointed, was stung by Kelso's words.

"Well, it's not my fault. I don't think Lester really saw anything. Not the face, anyway."

Starkey was at her desk when Kelso approached with the picture. She kept her eyes averted, hoping that neither he nor Marzik would notice their redness. She was sure the gin was bleeding through her pores and tried not to blow in their faces when she commented on the likeness.

"It's a ghost."

Marzik nodded glumly, agreeing.

"Casper all the way."

The portrait showed a white male approximately forty years of age with a rectangular face hidden by dark glasses and a baseball cap. His nose was undistinguished in shape and size, as were his lips, ears, and jaw. It worked out that way more times than not. If a wit saw no identifying characteristics, the portrait ended up looking like every other person on the street. The detectives called them "ghosts" because there was nothing to see.

Kelso scowled at the portrait some more, then shook his head and sighed deeply. Starkey thought he was being an ass.

"It's nobody's fault, Barry. We're still interviewing people who were in the laundry at about the same time. The portrait is going to develop."

Marzik nodded, encouraged by Starkey's support, but Kelso didn't look impressed.

"I got a call from Assistant Chief Morgan last night. He asked how you were doing as the lead, Carol. He's going to want a report soon."

Starkey's head throbbed.

"I'll go see him whenever he wants. That's not a problem."

"He won't just want to look at you, Carol; he'll want *facts*, as in *progress*."

Starkey felt her temper starting to fray.

"What do you want me to do, Barry, pull the perp out of my ass?"

Kelso's jaw knotted and unwound like he was chewing marbles.

"That might help. He suggested that we could forestall the ATF taking over this case if we had something to show for our efforts. Think about it."

Kelso stalked away and disappeared into his office.

Starkey's head throbbed worse. She had gotten so drunk last night that she scared herself and had spent most of the morning worried that her drinking was finally out of hand. She woke angry and embarrassed that Pell had once more been in her dreams, though she dismissed it as a sign of stress. She had taken two aspirin and two Tagamet, then pressed into the office, hoping to find a kickback on the RDX. She hadn't. Now this.

Marzik said, "Kelso's a turd. Do you think he talks to us like that because we're women?"

"I don't know, Beth. Listen, don't sweat the picture. Pell has three other likenesses that he's going to deliver. We can show those to Lester. Maybe something will click."

Marzik didn't leave. Starkey was certain that she needed another breath mint, but wouldn't take one with Marzik standing over her.

"Even though Lester didn't get a face, he's solid on the cap and long-sleeved shirt."

"Okay."

"I've got him set up to come in this afternoon to look at the tapes. You see anything last night?"

Starkey leaned back to stay as far from Marzik as possible.

"Not on the wide shots. Everything is so murky you can't really see. I think we need to have them enhanced, see if that won't give us a better view."

"I could take care of that, you want."

"I already talked to Hooker about it. He's had tapes enhanced before when he was working Divisional Robbery over in Hollenbeck. Listen, I need to check the NLETS, okay? We'll talk later."

Marzik nodded, still not moving. She looked like she wanted to say something.

"What, Beth?"

"Carol, listen. I want to apologize for yesterday. I was a bitch."

"Forget it. Thanks for saying so, but it's okay."

"I felt bad all night and I wanted to apologize."

"Okay. Thanks. Thank you. Don't sweat the picture."

"Yeah. Kelso's such a turd."

Marzik took her portrait and went back to her desk. Starkey stared after her. Sometimes Marzik surprised her.

When Marzik wasn't looking, Starkey popped a fresh Altoid, then went for the coffee. When she checked the NLETS system on the way back to her desk, this time something was waiting.

Starkey had expected one or two hits on the RDX, but nothing like what she found.

The California State Sheriffs reported that Dallas Tennant, a thirty-two-year-old white male, was currently serving time in the California State Correctional Facility in Atascadero, a facility for prisoners receiving treatment for mental disorders. On three separate occasions two years ago, Tennant had exploded devices made with RDX. Starkey smiled when she saw it was three devices. RDX was rare; three devices meant that Tennant had had access to a lot of it. Starkey printed off the computer report, noting that the case had been made by a Sheriff's Bomb and Arson sergeant-investigator named Warren Mueller out of the Central Valley office in Bakersfield. Back at her desk, she looked up the phone number in her State Law Enforcement Directory, then called the Central Valley number, asking for the Bomb and Arson Unit.

"B and A. Hennessey."

"Warren Mueller, please."

"Yeah, he's here. Stand by."

When Mueller came on, Starkey identified herself as a Los Angeles police officer. Mueller had an easy male voice with a twang of the Central Valley at the edges. Starkey thought he had probably grown up downwind of one of the meatpacking plants up there.

"I'm calling about a perp you collared named Dallas Tennant."

"Oh, sure. He's enjoying a lease in Atascadero these days."

"That's right. Reason I'm calling is I got a kicker saying that he set off three devices using RDX. That's a lot of RDX."

"Three we know of, yeah. Coulda been more. He was buying stolen cars from some kids up here, hundred bucks, no questions, then driving'm out into the desert to blow'm up. He'd soak'm in gas first so they'd burn, you know? Crazy fool just wanted to see'm come apart, I guess. He blew up four or five trees, too, but he used TNT for that."

"It's the RDX that interests me. You know where he got it?"

"Well, he claimed that he bought a case of stolen antipersonnel mines from a guy he met at a bar. You believe that, I got some desert land up here I'll sell you. My guess is that he bought it off one of these meth-dealing biker assholes, but he never copped, so I couldn't tell you."

Starkey knew that the vast majority of bombings were the result of drug wars between rival methamphetamine dealers, many of whom were white bikers. Meth labs were chemical bombs waiting to happen. So when a meth dealer wanted to eliminate a rival, he often just blew apart his Airstream. Starkey had rolled out on almost a hundred meth labs when she was a bomb tech. Bomb Squad would roll even for a warrant service.

"So you think you could still have a guy up there with RDX to sell?"

"Well, that's possible, but you never know. We didn't have a suspect at the time, and we don't have one now. All we had was Dallas, blowing up his goddamned cars. The guy's your classic no-life, loner bomb crank. But the guy stood up, though, I'll give'm that. Wherever he got it, he didn't roll."

"Did he have any more RDX in his possession at the time of his arrest?"

"Never found any of his works. Said he made everything at home, but there was no evidence of it. He had this shithole apartment over here out past the meat plant, but we didn't find so much as a firecracker. We couldn't find any evidence of these mines he claimed to have bought, either."

Starkey considered that. Building bombs for bomb cranks like Dallas Tennant was a way of life. It was their passion, and they inevitably had a place where they built their bombs, in the same way that hobbiests had hobby rooms. Might be a closet or a room or a place in their garage, but they had a place to store their supplies and practice their craft. Such places were called "shops."

"Seems like he would've had a shop."

"Well, my personal feeling is that he was butt-buddies with the same guy sold him the RDX, and that guy packed up when Dallas was tagged, but like I say, that's just my feeling."

Starkey put that in her notes, but didn't think much of Mueller's theory. As Mueller had already pointed out, bomb cranks were introverted loners, usually with low self-esteem and feelings of inadequacy. They were often extremely shy and almost never had relationships with women. Sharing their toys didn't fit with the profile. Starkey suspected that if Tennant didn't cop to his shop, it was because he didn't want to lose his toys. Like all chronics, he would see explosions in his dreams, and probably spent much of every day fantasizing about the bombs he would build as soon as he was released.

Starkey closed her pad.

"Okay, Sergeant, I think that about does it. I appreciate your time."

"Anytime. Could I ask you something, Starkey?"

"I've asked you plenty."

He hesitated. She knew in that moment what was coming and felt her stomach knot.

"You being down there in L.A. and all, you the same Starkey got blown up?"

"Yeah. That was me. Listen, all I've got here is what the Sheriffs put out on the kicker. Could you fax your casework on Tennant to give me a little more?"

"This about that thing happened down there in Silver Lake?"

"Yes, sir."

"Sure. It's only a few pages. I can get to it right away."

"Thanks."

Starkey gave him the fax number and hung up before Mueller could say any more. It was always like that, even more so from the bomb techs and bomb investigators, from the people who lived so close to the edge but never looked over, in a kind of awe that she had.

Starkey refilled her coffee and brought it into the stairwell where she stood smoking with three Fugitive Section detectives. They were young, athletic guys with short hair and thick mustaches. They were still enthusiastic about the job and hadn't yet let themselves go, the way most cops did when they realized that the job was bureaucratic bullshit that served no purpose and did no good. These guys would bag their day at two in the afternoon, then head over to Chavez Ravine to work out at the Police Academy. Starkey could see it in their tight jeans and forearms. They smiled; she nodded back. They went on with their discussion without including her. They had made a collar that morning in Eagle Rock, a *veterano* gang member with a rep as a hard guy who was wanted for armed robbery and mayhem. The mayhem charge meant he'd bitten off a nose or an ear during one of the assaults. The three Fugitive cops had found him hiding under a blanket in a garage when they made the pinch. The tough *veterano* had pissed his pants so badly that they wouldn't put him in the car until they'd found a plastic trash bag for him to sit on. Starkey listened to the three young cops relive their story, then crushed out her cigarette and went back to the fax machine. Another cop story. One of thousands. They always ended well unless a cop took a bullet or got bagged in an unlawful act.

When Starkey got back to the fax machine, Mueller's casework was waiting in the tray.

Starkey read it back at her desk. Tennant had an arrest history of fire starting and explosives that went back to the age of eighteen and had twice received court-mandated psychiatric counseling. Starkey knew that the arrests had probably started even earlier, but weren't reflected in the case file because juvenile records were sealed. She also knew this because Mueller's notes indicated that Tennant was missing two fingers from his left hand, an explosives-related injury that occurred while he was a teenager.

Mueller's case involved interviewing a young car thief named Robert Castillo, who had stolen two of the three cars that Tennant destroyed, along with photographs of the demolished cars. Mueller had been summoned to the Bakersfield Puritan Hospital Emergency Room by patrol officers, where he found Castillo with a windshield wiper blade through his cheek. Castillo, having delivered a late-model Nissan Stanza to Tennant, had apparently stood too close when Tennant destroyed it, caught the blade through his face, and had been rushed to the hospital by his friends. Starkey read Mueller's interview notes several times before she caught something in the Castillo interview that reinforced her belief that Tennant still maintained his shop. She decided that she wanted to speak with him.

Starkey looked up the phone number for Atascadero, called, and asked for the law enforcement liaison officer. Police officers couldn't just walk in off the street to speak with prisoners; the prisoner had the right to have counsel present and could refuse to speak with you. Atascadero was a long way to drive just to be told to fuck off.

"You have an inmate up there named Dallas Tennant. I'm working an active case here in Los Angeles that he might have information relating to. Would you see if he'd talk to me without counsel?"

"Would you still want to see him if he demands counsel?"

"Yes. But if he wants to play it that way, I'll need the name of his attorney."

"All right."

She could tell by the way the man paused that he was writing. Soft music played behind him.

"When would you want to see him, Detective?"

Starkey glanced at the clock on the wall and thought about Pell. "Later today. Ah, say about two this afternoon."

"All right. He's going to want to know what it's about."

"The availability of an explosive called RDX."

The liaison officer took her number and told her he'd call back as soon as possible.

After she hung up, Starkey got a fresh cup of coffee, then went back to her desk, thinking about what to do. LAPD policy required detectives to always work in pairs, but Marzik had interviews and Hooker was going to see about the tape. Starkey thought about Pell. There was no reason to call him, no reason to tell him any of this until it was over and she had something to say.

She found his card in her purse and paged him.

Starkey completed the evidence transfer request, which she faxed to the ATF regional office in Miami, then waited for Pell in the lobby. The drive from downtown L.A. to Atascadero was going to be just over three hours. She had thought that Pell would want to drive, because men always wanted to drive, but he didn't. Instead, he said, "I'll use the time to read Tennant's case file, then we can work out a game plan."

There he was with the game plan again.

She gave him the report, then maneuvered out of the city and up the coast along the Ventura Freeway. He read without comment, seeming to take forever to get through the six pages. She found his silence irritating.

"How long is it going to take you to read that, Pell?"

"I'm reading it more than once. This is good stuff, Starkey. We can use this. Searching for the RDX paid off."

"I wanted to mention that to you. I want to make sure we don't get off on the wrong foot here."

Pell looked at her.

"What wrong foot?"

"I know you think you were advising me, but I don't need it. You come in, start telling me what to do and how to do it, and expect me to hop to it. It doesn't work that way."

"It was just a suggestion. You did it anyway."

"I just want to get things straight. Don't expect that I'll get coffee for you."

Pell stared at her, then glanced back at the pages.

"You spoke with the arresting officer?"

"Yeah. Mueller."

"Can I ask you to tell me what he said, or is that too much like asking you for a mocha?"

"I'm not trying to fight with you. I just wanted to set the ground rules."

She went through her conversation with Mueller, recounting pretty much everything that had been said. Pell stared at the passing scenery, so silent that she wondered if he was even listening. But when she finished, he glanced through the pages again, then shook his head.

"Mueller dropped the ball about Tennant not having a shop. According to this, Tennant was buying stolen cars to destroy them. Three cars, three explosions. The car thief—"

"Robert Castillo."

"Yeah, Castillo. Castillo said that Tennant had asked him to steal a fourth car. He wouldn't need another car if he didn't have more RDX to destroy it or knew how to get more."

Starkey's grip tightened on the wheel.

"That's what I figured."

Pell shrugged and put the pages aside.

It sounded so lame. That was exactly what Starkey had reasoned, and she wished that she had said it before Pell. Now it looked like he was the one who'd found the hole in Tennant's denials.

"You said you had a suspect likeness coming from Miami. Did you get it for me?"

"Yeah. That, and the first two we have."

He slipped them from his jacket and unfolded them for her.

"Can you see?"

"Yeah."

"There were enough people in the library to put together a pretty good composite. Our guy shows to be six feet, one-eighty or so, but he's probably wearing lifts and padding. The wits from the earlier sightings made him at five ten. He had a square jaw, bright red hair, sideburns. That doesn't square with the earlier sightings, either."

Starkey glanced at the three sheets as she drove. Pell was right, none of the three looked very much alike, and none of them looked like the man Lester Ybarra described. The Miami likeness was as Pell said, the second likeness showed a balding, professorial-looking man with glasses, and the third, which was the first description that the feds had, showed a much heavier man with woolly Rasta braids, sunglasses, and a beard.

She handed them back to Pell.

"This last one looks like you in drag, Pell."

Pell put the sheets away.

"What about your guy? He match any of these?"

Starkey told him to open her briefcase, which was on the backseat. When Pell had it, he shook his head.

"How old is this guy supposed to be?"

"Forty, but our wit isn't dependable."

"So he might've made himself up to look older."

"Maybe. If we're talking about the same guy."

"Mr. Red is in his late twenties, early thirties. That's about all we know for sure. That, and him being white. He lets himself be seen, Starkey. He changes his look to fuck with us. That's how he gets off, fucking with us."

After that, they drove in silence for a while, Starkey thinking about how she was going to approach Tennant. She happened to glance over and found Pell staring at her.

"What?"

"You said you had gotten videotapes from the Silver Lake event. Did you look at them yet?"

Starkey put her eyes on the road. They had passed Santa Barbara; the freeway was curving inland toward Santa Maria.

"Yeah. I looked at them last night."

"Anything?"

Starkey shrugged.

"I've gotta have them enhanced."

"That must've been hard for you."

"What?"

"Looking at what happened. It must've been hard. It would be for me."

Pell met her eyes, then went back to staring out the window. She thought he might be pitying her and felt herself flush with anger.

"Pell, one more thing."

"What?"

"When we get there with Tennant, it's my show. I'm the lead here."

Pell nodded without expression, without looking at her.

"I'm just along for the ride."

Starkey drove the remaining two hours in silence, pissed off that she had invited him along.

The Atascadero Minimum Security Correctional Facility was a village of brown brick buildings set in the broad open expanse of what used to be almond groves in the arid ranchland south of Paso Robles. There were no walls, no guard towers; just a ten-foot chain-link fence and a single front gate with two bored guards who had to slide a motorized gate out of the way.

Atascadero was used to house nonviolent felons who the court deemed unsuitable for the general prison population: ex-police officers, white-collar criminals convicted of one-shot paper crimes, and vacationing celebrities who'd wrung out the eight or nine chances the courts inevitably gave them on drug charges. No one ever got knifed or gang-raped at Atascadero, though the inmates did have to maintain a three-acre truck garden. The worst that could happen was heatstroke.

Starkey said, "They're going to make us check our guns. Be faster with the paperwork if we leave'm in the car."

"You going to leave yours?"

"It's already in my briefcase. I never carry the damned thing."

Pell glanced over, then pulled an enormous Smith 10mm autoloader and slipped it under the seat.

"Jesus, Pell, why do you need a monster like that?"

"No one gets a second shot."

Starkey badged the gate guards, who directed her to the reception area. They left the car in a small, unshaded parking lot, then went inside to find the law enforcement liaison officer, a man named Larry Olsen, waiting for them.

"Detective Starkey?"

"Carol Starkey. This is Special Agent Pell, with the ATF. Thanks for setting this up."

Olsen asked for identification and had them sign the log. He was a bored man who walked as if his legs hurt. He led them out the rear through double glass doors and along a walk toward another building. From back here, Starkey could see the truck garden and two basketball courts. Several inmates were playing basketball with their shirts off, laughing and enjoying themselves. They missed easy shots and handled the ball poorly. All of them except one were white.

Olsen said, "I should tell you that Tennant is currently being medicated. These are court-mandated therapies. Xanax for anxiety and Anafranil to help regulate his obsessive-compulsive disorder. He's required to take them."

"Is that going to give us a problem with him agreeing to have no lawyer present?"

"Not at all. They don't affect his judgment, just his compulsions. He was off the meds for a while, but we had a problem recently and had to resume the treatment."

Pell said, "What kind of problem?"

"Tennant used cleaning products and some iodine he stole from the infirmary to create an explosive. He lost his left thumb."

Pell shook his head.

"What an asshole."

"Well, this is a minimum-security installation, you know. The inmates have a great deal of freedom."

Dallas Tennant was an overweight man with pale skin and large eyes. He was sitting at a clean Formica table that had been pushed against the wall, but stood when Olsen showed them into the interview room. His left hand was bandaged, strangely narrow without its thumb. Tennant's eyes locked on Starkey and stayed there. He barely glanced at Pell. The index and middle fingers of his right hand were missing at the second joint, the caps of scar old and worn. This was the injury that Starkey had read about in Mueller's case file.

Tennant said, "Hello, Mr. Olsen. Is this Detective Starkey?"

Olsen introduced them, Tennant offering his hand, but neither Starkey nor Pell taking it. You never shook their hand. Shaking hands put you on an equal basis, and you weren't equals. They were in prison; you weren't. They were weak; you were strong. Starkey had learned that it was a game of power when she was still in uniform. Assholes in prison thought of a friend as someone it was easy to manipulate.

Olsen put his clipboard on the table and opened a felt-tipped pen.

"Tennant, this form says that you have been advised of your right to have an attorney present for this interview, but that you have declined that right. You have to sign it here on this line, and I will witness."

As Tennant signed the forms, Starkey noticed a thick plastic book on the corner of the table. Two screw-thread hasps kept it fastened at the spine; the cover was of a tropical island at sunset with script letters that read *My Happy Memories*. It was the kind of inexpensive photo album you could buy at any dime store.

When Starkey glanced up, Tennant was staring at her. He smiled shyly.

"That's my book."

Olsen tapped the form.

"Your signature right here, Detective."

Starkey forced her eyes away from Tennant and signed. Olsen signed beneath her signature, dated the page, then explained that a guard would be outside the room to remove Tennant when they were finished. After that, he left.

Starkey directed Tennant where to sit. She wanted to be across from him, and she wanted Pell at his side so that Tennant would have to look at one or the other, but not both. Tennant slid his scrapbook across the table when he changed seats to keep it near him.

"First off, Dallas, I want to tell you that we're not investigating you. We're not looking to bring charges against you. We're going to overlook any crimes you admit to, as long as they don't include crimes against persons."

Tennant nodded.

"There won't be any of that. I never hurt anyone."

"Fine. Then let's get started."

"Can I show you something first? I think it might help you."

"Let's not get sidetracked, Dallas. Let's stay with the reason we're here."

He turned his book for her to see, ignoring her objection.

"It won't take long, and it's very important to me. I wasn't going to see you at first, but then I remembered your name."

He had marked a place in the book with a strip of toilet tissue. He opened to the marked page.

The newspaper clip was yellow from being smothered by the plastic for three years, but the below-the-fold two-column headline was still readable. Starkey felt her skin grow cold.

OFFICER KILLED IN BOMB BLAST; SECOND OFFICER CRITICAL

It was an L.A. *Times* article about the trailer park bombing that had killed Sugar and wounded Starkey. Above the headline was a grainy black-and-white picture that showed the two EMP teams, one team working on Sugar, the other on Starkey, as firefighters hosed the flaming trailer behind them. She had never read the article or the three follow-up articles that followed. A friend of Starkey's named Marion Tyson had saved them and had brought them to Starkey in the week after her release from the hospital. Starkey had thrown them away and had never spoken to Marion Tyson again.

Starkey took a moment to make sure her voice would not waver, that she wouldn't give away her feelings.

"Are all the articles in this book bomb-related?"

Tennant flipped the pages for her to see, revealing flashes of death and devastated buildings, crumpled cars, and medical text photographs of severed limbs and disrupted bodies.

"I've collected these since I was a child. I wasn't going to talk to you, but then I remembered who you are. I remember watching the news the day you were killed, and what an impression that made on me. I was hoping I could get you to autograph it."

Before she could respond, Pell reached across the table and closed the book.

"Not today, you piece of shit."

Pell pulled the book close and laid his arm across it.

"Today, you're going to tell us where you got the RDX."

"That's mine. You can't take that. Mr. Olsen will make you give it back."

Starkey was inwardly livid with Pell for intruding, but she kept her manner calm. The change in Pell was dramatic; in the car, he'd seemed distant and thoughtful; this Pell was poised in his chair like a leopard anxious to pounce.

"I'm not going to sign your book, Dallas. Maybe if you tell us where you got the RDX and how we could get some, maybe then I might sign it. But not now."

"I want my book. Mr. Olsen is going to make you give it back."

"Give it back, Pell."

Starkey eased the book away from Pell and slid it across the table. Tennant pulled the book close again and covered it with his hands.

"You won't sign it?"

"Maybe if you help us."

"I bought some mines from a man I didn't know. Raytheons. I don't remember the model number."

"How many mines?"

He had told Mueller that he'd bought a case, which, she knew because she had phoned Raytheon, contained six mines.

"A case. There were six in the case."

Starkey smiled; Tennant smiled back at her.

Pell said, "What was this man's name?"

"Clint Eastwood. I know, I know, but that was how he identified himself."

Starkey took out a cigarette and lit up.

"How could we find Clint?"

"I don't know."

"How did *you* find Clint?"

"You're not supposed to smoke in here."

"Mr. Olsen gave me special permission. How did you find Clint? If we let you out today and you wanted more RDX, how would you reach him?"

"I met him in a bar. That's all there was to it. Like I told them when they arrested me. He had a case of antipersonnel mines, I bought it, and then he was gone. I didn't want *mines*; I mean, I wasn't going to put them out in a field and watch cows walk on them or anything. I bought them to scavenge the RDX."

Starkey believed that Tennant was telling the truth about salvaging his RDX from stolen mines; high-order explosives were almost always acquired that way, from mortar shells or hand grenades or other military gear. But she also believed that his source wasn't some nameless yahoo in a roadhouse. Bomb cranks like Tennant were low self-esteem loners; you wouldn't find "Plays well with others" on his report cards. Starkey knew that, as with arsonists, Tennant's obsession with explosives was a sublimated sexuality. He would be awkward with women, sexually inexperienced in the normal sense, and find his release in a large pornography collection devoted to deviant practices such as sadomasochism and torture. He would avoid face-to-face confrontations of any kind. He would lurk in hobby shops like the one where he had been employed and swap meets; he would be far too afraid to connect in a biker bar. Starkey decided to change her approach and come at him from a different direction. She took out the photographs of the three cars and the interview pages from Mueller's case file. The same things that Pell had read and understood on the drive up.

"All right, Dallas. I can buy that. Now tell me this, how much RDX do you have left?"

Tennant hesitated, and Starkey knew that Mueller had never asked that.

"I don't have any left. I used it all."

"Sure you do, Dallas. You only blew up three cars. I can look at these pictures and tell that you didn't use all the RDX. We can calculate things like that, you know? Start with the damage, then work backwards to estimate the amount of the charge. It's called an energy comparison."

Tennant blinked his eyes blandly.

"That's all I had."

"You bought the cars from a young man named Robert Castillo. Mr. Castillo said that you asked him for a fourth car. Why would you need a fourth car if you only had enough pop for three?"

Tennant wet his lips and made the shy smile. He shrugged.

"I had some dynamite. You soak the interior with enough gasoline, they go fine even with the dynamite. Not as good as with the RDX, but that's special."

Starkey knew he was lying, and Tennant knew she knew. He averted his eyes and shrugged.

"I'm sorry. There's nothing to say."

"Sure there is. Tell us where we can find your shop."

Starkey was certain that if they could find his shop, they would find evidence that would lead to his source of the RDX or to other people with similar sources.

"I didn't have a shop. I kept everything in the trunk of my car."

"Nothing was found in the trunk of your car except a few clips and wire."

"They kept asking me about that, but there was nothing to say. I'm a very neat person. They even offered to reduce my time and give me outpatient status, but I had nothing to trade. Don't you think I would have made a deal if I could?"

Pell leaned forward and put his hands close to Tennant's book.

"I think you jerk off every night about using the rest of your stuff when you get out of here, but you're here on a mental. That's a one-way ride until the headshrinkers decide that you're sane, which figures to be never. Does a sane man blow off his own thumb?"

Tennant flushed.

"It was an accident."

"I represent the United States Government. Detective Starkey here represents the Los Angeles Police Department. Together, with a little cooperation from you, we might be able to help get your time reduced. Then you won't have to mess around popping off fingers with window cleaner, you can go for the whole hand, maybe even an arm."

Starkey stared at Tennant, waiting.

"I never hurt anybody. It's not fair they keep me here."

"Tell that to the kid with the windshield wiper through his face."

Starkey could see that Tennant was thinking. She didn't want to give him much time, so she stepped in, trying to appear sympathetic.

"That's right, Dallas. You didn't intend to hurt that boy, you even tried in your own way to keep him safe."

"I told him to take cover. Some people just won't listen."

"I believe that, Dallas, but the thing is, you see, this is why we're here, we've got someone out there who doesn't care about people the way you do. This person is trying to hurt people."

Tennant nodded.

"You're here because of the officer who was killed. Officer Riggio."

"How do you know about Riggio?"

"We have television here, and the Internet. Several of the inmates are wealthy people, bankers and lawyers. If you have to be in prison, this is the place to be."

Pell snorted.

"Officer Riggio was killed with RDX?"

"RDX was a component. The charge was something called Modex Hybrid."

Tennant leaned back and laced his fingers. The missing thumb must have hurt because he winced and drew back his hand.

"Did Mr. Red set that bomb?"

Pell came out of his chair so suddenly that Starkey jumped.

"How do you know about Mr. Red?"

Tennant glanced nervously from Starkey to Pell.

"I don't, really. People gossip. People share news, and lies. I don't even know that Mr. Red is real."

Pell reached across the table and gripped Tennant's wrist above his bandaged hand.

"Who, Tennant? Who's talking about Mr. Red?"

Starkey was growing uncomfortable with Pell's manner. She was willing to let him play bad guy to her good guy, but she didn't like it that he was touching Tennant, and she didn't like the intensity she saw in his eyes.

"Pell."

"What do they say, Tennant?"

Tennant's eyes grew larger and he tried to twist away.

"Nothing. He's a myth, he's someone who makes wonderful elegant explosions."

"He *kills* people, you sick fuck."

Starkey pushed out of her chair.

"Leave go of him, Pell."

Pell's face was bright with anger. He didn't leave go.

"He knows that Red uses Modex, Starkey. We've never released that information to the public. How does he know?"

Pell gripped Tennant's bandaged hand. Tennant went white and gasped.

"Tell me, you sonofabitch. How do you know about Mr. Red? What do you know about him?"

Starkey shoved Pell hard, trying to move him away, but couldn't. She was terrified that the guard would hear and burst in.

"Damnit, Pell, leave go! Step away from him!"

Tennant slapped at Pell without effect, then fell backward out of the chair.

"They talk about him on Claudius. That's how I know! They talk about the bombs he builds, and what he's like, and why he's doing these things. I saw it on Claudius."

"Who the fuck is Claudius?"

"Goddamn you, Pell. Get back."

Starkey shoved at Pell again, and this time he moved. It was like pushing a house.

Pell was breathing hard, but he seemed in control again. He stared at Tennant in a way that Starkey read with certainty that if Pell had his gun, he would be holding it to the man's head.

"Tell me about Claudius. Tell me how you know about Mr. Red."

Tennant whimpered from the floor, cradling his hand.

"It's an Internet site. There's a chat room for people . . . like me. We talk about bombs and the different bombers and things like that. They say that Mr. Red even lurks there, reading what they say about him."

Starkey turned away from Pell, staring at Tennant.

"Have you had contact with Mr. Red?"

"No. I don't know. It's just a rumor, or maybe it isn't. I don't know. If he's there, he uses a different name. All I'm saying is what the others say. They said the Unabomber used to come around, too, but I don't know if that was true."

Starkey helped Tennant to his feet and put him in the chair. A red flower blossomed on the bandage; his wound was seeping.

"You okay, Tennant? You all right?"

"It hurts. Goddamn, it hurts. You bastard."

"You want me to get the guard? You want the doctor?"

Tennant glanced at her and picked up his book with his good hand.

"I want you to sign."

Starkey signed Tennant's book, and then she called the guard and got Pell out of there. Tennant seemed fine when they left, but she wasn't sure what he might say once they were gone.

Pell moved like an automaton, stalking out ahead of her, stiff with tension. Starkey had to walk hard to keep up, growing angrier and angrier. Her face felt like a ceramic mask, so brittle that if he stopped walking before they reached the car, it might shatter and, with it, her control.

She wanted to kill him.

When they reached the parking lot, Starkey followed him to his side of the car and shoved him again. She caught him from behind, and this time he wasn't ready. He stumbled into the fender.

"You crazy bastard, what was that all about? Do you *know* what you did in there? Do you *know* what kind of trouble we could be in?"

If she had her Asp from her uniform days, she would happily beat him stupid.

Pell glared at her darkly.

"He gave us something, Starkey. This Claudius thing."

"I don't give a *shit* what he gave us! You touched a prisoner in there! You tortured him! If he files a complaint, it's over for me. I don't know about the motherfucking ATF, but let me tell you something, Pell, *LAPD will have my hide on the barn!* That was wrong, what you did in there. That was *wrong*."

She was so angry that she wanted to throttle him. All he did was stand there, and that made her feel even angrier.

Pell took a deep breath, spread his hands, and looked away as if whatever had driven him inside was leaching away.

"I'm sorry."

"Oh, that's great, Pell, thanks. You're sorry."

She walked away from him, shaking her head. She could still feel last night's drunk, and suddenly she realized that she was already thinking about getting there again, blasting back a couple of quick shots to kill the knots in her neck. She was so damned angry that she didn't trust herself to speak.

That's when Pell said, "Starkey."

Starkey turned back just in time to see Pell stagger against the car. He caught himself on the fender, then collapsed to one knee.

Starkey ran to him.

"Pell, what's wrong?"

He was as pale as milk. He closed his eyes, hanging his head like a tired dog. Starkey thought he was having a heart attack.

"I'm going to get someone. You hang on, okay?"

Pell caught her arm, holding tight.

"Wait."

His eyes were clenched shut. He opened them, blinked, then closed them again. His grip on her was so strong that it hurt.

"I'm okay, Starkey. I get these pains sometimes. It's a migraine, that's all. Like that."

He wasn't letting go of her.

"You look like shit, Pell. I'd better get someone. Please."

"Just give me a minute."

He closed his eyes, taking deep breaths. Starkey had the frantic thought that he was dying right here in the damned parking lot.

"Pell?"

"I'm okay."

"Let go of me, Pell, or I might have to smack you again."

He held her with a grip like pliers, but when she said it, his face softened, and he let go. Color began to return to his face.

"Sorry. I didn't mean to hurt you."

He looked at her then. She was very close to him. His closeness embarrassed her, and she scooted away.

"Let me just sit here for a second. They can't see us, right?"

She had to stand to peer over the car at the reception building.

"Not unless they can see through the car. If they saw what happened, they probably think we're down here making out."

Starkey flushed, surprised that she'd said something like that. Pell seemed not to notice.

"I'm okay now. I can get up."

"You don't look okay. Just sit here for a minute."

"I'm okay."

He stood, balancing himself against the car, then used the door for support as he climbed in. By the time she went around the other side and got behind the wheel, he had more color.

"Are you okay?"

"Close enough. Let's go."

"You really fucked us up in there."

"I didn't fuck us up. He gave us Claudius. That's something we didn't have before."

"If he files a complaint, you can use that to explain to Internal Affairs why they shouldn't bring me up on charges."

Pell reached across the seat and touched her thigh. His expression surprised her; his eyes were deepened with regret.

"I'm sorry. If he files a complaint, I'll take the bullet. It wasn't you in there, Starkey, it was me. I'll tell them that. Just drive, would you, please? That isn't an order; it's a request. It's a long ride home."

She stared at him a moment longer, then she started the car and pulled away, her leg feeling the weight of his hand as if it were still there.

6

IT WAS AFTER seven when Starkey let Pell off at the curb outside Spring Street. The summer sun was still high in the west, resting on the crown of a palm. Soon, the sky would purple.

Starkey struck a fresh cigarette, then turned into the traffic. Hooker and Marzik had long since gone home. Even Kelso was gone, probably eating dinner about now. Starkey passed an In-'n-Out Burger, her stomach clenching at the thought of food. She hadn't eaten anything since breakfast, so she made do with a couple of antacids.

In the long silence coming back to L.A., Starkey had decided that Pell was dangerous to her case and to her chances of reclaiming her career. If Tennant filed a complaint or squawked to his attorney, she was done. Olsen might be on the phone with Kelso right now; Kelso might be filing for an IAG investigation. A lot could happen in three hours.

Starkey flicked her cigarette out the window, hard. Trading her job for this Claudius thing seemed like a sour deal. The only way Starkey could protect herself was to report Pell and file an officer complaint. She could call Kelso at home and explain what happened. Tomorrow morning, he would walk her up to IAG, where she would be interviewed by a lieutenant, who would then phone Olsen and ask him to interview Tennant. By midafternoon, the lines between Spring Street and the ATF field office would burn. Washington would jerk Pell from the case, and her own ass would be covered. Then, if Tennant squawked, Starkey would be clear. She would have acted accordingly and by the book. She would be safe.

Starkey lit a second cigarette, thankful for the slow pace of the traffic. Around her, cars pulsed from parking garages like the life bleeding from a corpse. Going to Kelso was not an acceptable option. Even thinking about it made her feel cheesy and low.

She couldn't get Pell out of her head.

Starkey didn't know anything about migraine headaches, but what had happened in the parking lot had scared her even more than Pell losing control with Tennant. She fretted that beating the hell out of suspects was Pell's ATF way of doing things, and that meant he would do it again, placing her in even greater legal jeopardy. She was certain that he was hiding something. She had enough secrets of her own to know that people didn't hide strengths; they guarded their weaknesses. Now she feared Pell's. The bomb investigators that she had known were all detail people; they moved slowly and methodically because they built puzzles often made of many small pieces over investigations that lasted weeks, and often months. Pell didn't act like a bomb investigator. His manner was predatory and fast, his actions with Tennant extreme and violent. Even his gun didn't fit the profile, that big ass Smith 10.

She drove home, feeling as if she was in a weakened position and angry because of it. She thought about calling Pell at his hotel and raising more hell, but knew that would do no good. She could either call Kelso or move on; anything else was just jerking off.

At home, Starkey filled her tub with hot water for a bath, then poured a stiff gin and brought it to her bedroom where she took off her clothes.

Naked, she stood at the foot of her bed, listening to the water splash, sipping the gin. She was intensely aware of the mirror on the closet. It was behind her, almost as if it were waiting. She took a big slug of the drink, then turned and looked at herself. She saw the scars. She saw the craters and rills and valleys, the discolorations and the pinhole stitching. She looked at her thigh, and saw the print of his hand as clearly as if she bore a brand.

Starkey sighed deeply and turned away.

"You must be out of your goddamned mind."

She finished the drink in a long series of gulps, stalked into the bath, and let the heat consume her.

7

"TELL ME ABOUT Pell."

"He's a fed with the ATF. That's Alcohol, Tobacco, and Firearms."

"I know."

"If you knew, why did you ask?"

"I meant I know what the acronym stands for, that ATF is the Bureau of Alcohol, Tobacco, and Firearms. You seem irritable today, Carol."

"How inconsiderate of me. I must have forgotten to take my daily dose of mellow."

Starkey was annoyed with herself for mentioning Pell to Dana. On the drive to Santa Monica, she had mapped out what she wanted to talk about in today's session, which had not included Pell, yet Pell was the first damned thing that popped from her mouth.

"I put myself at risk for this guy, and I don't even know him."

"Why did you do that?"

"I don't know."

"If you had to guess."

"Nobody likes a rat."

"But he violated the law, Carol. You said so yourself. He laid hands on this prisoner, and now you are in jeopardy for not reporting him. You clearly don't approve of what he did, yet you are conflicted about what to do."

Starkey lost track of Dana's voice. She stood at the window, watching the traffic on Santa Monica Boulevard, smoking. A cluster of women waited at the crosswalk below, anxiously watching their bus idle on the other side of six lanes of bumper-to-bumper morning rush hour traffic. From their squat Central American builds and plastic shopping bags, Starkey made them for housekeepers on their way to work in the exclusive homes north of Montana. When the light changed, the bus began to rumble away. The women panicked, charging across the street even as cars continued through the red. Horns blew, a black Nissan swerving, almost nailing two of the women, who never once looked at the car as it passed. They ignored it in their need to catch the bus, giving themselves up to chance. Starkey knew she could never do that.

"Carol?"

Starkey didn't want to talk about Pell anymore or watch a bunch of women with nothing more on their minds than catching a god-damned bus.

She went back to her seat and crushed out her cigarette.

"I want to ask you a question."

"All right."

"I'm not sure if I want to do this or not."

"Do what, Carol? Ask me the question?"

"No, do what I'm about to tell you about. I got these tapes of what happened to Charlie Riggio, the news video that the TV stations took. You know what I realized? The TV station has tapes of me, too. They have videotape of what happened to me and Sugar. Now I can't stop thinking about it, that it's out there right now, trapped on a tape, and I could see it."

Dana wrote something on her pad.

"When and if you decide that you're ready for something like that, I think it would be a good idea."

Starkey's stomach went cold. Part of her had wanted Dana's permission; part of her had wanted to be let off the hook.

"I don't know."

Dana put her pad aside. Starkey didn't know whether to be frightened by that or not. She had never known Dana to put aside the pad.

"How long have you had the dreams, now, Carol?"

"Almost three years."

"So you see Sugar's death, and your own, almost every night for three years. I had a thought about this the other day. I don't know if it's right or not, but I want to share it with you."

Starkey eyed her suspiciously. She hated the word "share."

"Do you know what a perception illusion is?"

"No."

"It's a drawing. You look at it, and you see a vase. But if you look at it with a different mind-set, you see two women facing each other. It's like a picture hidden within a picture. Which you see depends upon the perceptions and predispositions you bring to the viewing. When a person looks at a picture over and over again, maybe they're trying to find that hidden picture. They keep looking, hoping that they'll see it, but they can't."

Starkey thought this was all bullshit.

"You're saying that I'm having the dream because I'm trying to make sense of what happened?"

"I don't know. What do you think?"

"I think that if you don't know, I sure as hell don't. You're the one with a Ph.D."

"Fair enough. Okay, the Ph.D. suggests that we have to deal with the past in order to heal the present."

"I do that. I try to do that. Christ, I think about that goddamned day so much I'm sick of it." Starkey raised a hand. "And, yes, I know that thinking about it isn't the same as dealing with it."

"I wasn't going to say that."

"Right."

"This isn't a criticism, Carol. It's an exploration."

"Whatever."

"Let's get back to the perception illusion. The notion I had is that your dream is the first picture. You return to it because you haven't found the second picture, the hidden picture. You can only see the vase. You're looking for the two women, you suspect that they're there, but you haven't been able to find them. It occurred to me that maybe this is because what you're seeing isn't what really happened. It's what you imagined happening."

Starkey felt her irritation turning to anger.

"Of course it's what I imagined. I was fucking dead, for Christ's sake."

"The tape would show what really happened."

Starkey drew a deep breath.

"Then, if there are two women to be found, you might be able to find them. Maybe what you would discover is that there is only the vase. Whichever you find, maybe that knowledge would help you put this behind you."

Starkey looked past Dana to the window again. She pushed to her feet and went back to the window.

"Please come back to your seat."

Starkey shook out a cigarette, lit up. Dana wasn't looking at her. Dana faced the empty seat as if Starkey were still there.

"Carol, please come back to your seat."

Starkey blew out a huge screen of smoke. She sucked deep, filled the air with more.

"I'm okay over here."

"Have you realized that whenever we come to something that you don't want to hear or that you want to avoid, you escape through that window?"

Starkey stalked back to the chair.

"The dream changed."

"How so?"

Starkey crossed her legs, realized what she was doing, uncrossed them.

"Pell was in the dream. They took off Sugar's helmet, and it was that bastard Pell."

Dana nodded.

"You're attracted to him."

"Oh, for Christ's sake."

"Are you?"

"I don't know."

"A little while ago, you told me that he scared you. Maybe this is the true reason why."

"The two faces?"

"Yes. The hidden picture."

Starkey tried to make a joke of it.

"Maybe I'm just a freak who likes to put herself at risk. Why else would I work the Bomb Squad?"

"You haven't seen anyone since it happened?"

Starkey felt herself flush. She averted her eyes, hoping she looked thoughtful instead of sick to her stomach with fear.

"No. No one."

"Are you going to act on this attraction?"

"I don't know."

They sat quietly until Dana glanced at her clock.

"Looks like our time is almost up. I'd like to leave you with something else to think about for next time."

"Like I don't have enough?"

Dana smiled as she picked up the pad, laying it across her legs as if she was already considering the notes she would write.

"You made a joke about working on the Bomb Squad because you enjoyed the risk. I remember something that you said when we were first seeing each other. I had said that being a bomb technician seemed like a very dangerous profession."

"Yeah?"

Starkey didn't remember.

"You told me that it wasn't. You told me that you never thought of bombs as dangerous, that a bomb was just a puzzle that you had to solve, all neat and contained and predictable. I think you feel safe with bombs, Carol. It's people who scare you. Do you think that's why you enjoyed the Bomb Squad so much?"

Starkey glanced at the clock.

"Looks like you were right. Time's up."

After leaving Dana, Starkey worked her way through the crosstown traffic toward Spring Street with a growing sense of inevitability. She told herself it was resolve, but she knew it was as much about resolve as a drunk falling down stairs. He was going to hit the bottom whether he resolved to or not. She was on the stairs. She was falling. She was going to see herself die.

By the time Starkey reached CCS, she felt numb and fuzzy, as if she were a ghost come back to haunt a house, but was now separate from it, unseen and weightless.

Across the squad room, Hooker was screwing around with the coffee machine. She watched him, thinking that Hooker had the phone numbers for the TV news departments. She told herself to get the numbers, start calling, and find the goddamned tapes of herself. Do it *now*, before she chickened out.

She marched to the coffee machine.

"Jorge, did you set it up to have those tapes enhanced?"

"Yeah. I told you I'd take care of it, remember?"

"Mm. I just wanted to be sure."

"It's a postproduction company in Hollywood that the department uses. We should have them in two or three days."

"Right. I remember. Listen, did we get any of those tapes from channel eight?"

"Yeah. You took one of them home, Carol. Don't you remember?"

"For Christ's sake, Jorge, I took a shitload of tapes home. Can I remember where they all came from?"

Hooker was staring at her.

"No. I guess not."

"Who'd you talk to over there at channel eight? To get the tapes?"

"Sue Borman. She's the news director."

"Lemme have her phone, okay? Something I want to ask her about."

"Maybe I can help. What do you want to know?"

Nothing was easy. He couldn't just say, sure, and go get the goddamned number.

"I want to talk to her about the tapes, Jorge. Now, could I please have her number?"

Starkey followed Hooker back to his desk for the number, then went directly to her phone where she called channel eight. She punched the number mechanically, without thought of what she would say or how she would say it. She didn't want to think. She didn't want to give herself time to not do it.

Channel eight was the only television station that she recalled at the trailer park. She knew that others had been there, but she did not remember which others and didn't want to call around, asking. Channel eight she remembered because of their station ID letters. KROK. The bomb techs used to call the KROK remote vehicle the shitmobile.

"This is Detective Carol Starkey with LAPD. I'd like Sue Borman, please."

When Borman came on, she sounded harried. Starkey guessed that probably went with the job.

"We sent tapes over there. Is everything all right with them? You don't have a playback problem, do you?"

"No, ma'am. The tapes are fine. We appreciate your cooperation. I'm calling about another set of tapes."

"What you got are the only tapes we have. We sent you everything."

"These are older tapes. They'd probably be in your library. Three years ago, an officer was killed at a trailer park in Chatsworth, and another officer was injured. Do you remember that?"

"No. Was that another bomb thing?"

Starkey closed her eyes.

"Yes. It was a bomb thing."

"Waitaminute. It wasn't just one guy; both guys were killed, but they brought back one of them at the scene, right?"

"That's the one."

"I was a news writer back then. I think I wrote the story."

"It's been three years. Maybe you don't keep the tapes."

"We keep everything. Listen, what did you say your name is?"

"Detective Starkey."

"You're not who I talked to about the Silver Lake thing, right?"

"No, that was Detective Santos."

"Okay, what I'll have to do is check our library. I'll do that and get back to you. Gimme the date of the incident and your phone number."

Starkey gave her the date and phone number.

"You want the tape if we have it?"

"Yes, ma'am."

"Is this connected to what happened in Silver Lake?"

Starkey didn't want to tell this woman that she was one of the officers on the tape.

"We don't believe that they're connected, but we're checking. It's just something we have to follow up."

"If there's a story here, I want in."

"If there's a story, you can have it."

"What did you say your name was?"

"Starkey."

"I'll get back to you."

Starkey was shaking when she put down the phone. She put her hands flat on the desk and tried to still them. She couldn't. She thought she should feel elated or proud of herself for taking this step, but all she felt was sick to her stomach.

She dry-swallowed a Tagamet and was waiting for the nausea to pass when Pell called.

"Can you talk?"

"Yes, I can talk."

"I wanted to apologize again about yesterday, up there with Tennant. I hope that what happened hasn't created a problem for you."

"I haven't been marched upstairs to Internal Affairs yet, if that's what you mean. Tennant could still change his mind and destroy my career, but so far I'm safe."

"Did you report me?"

"Not my style, babe. Forget it."

"Okay. Well, like I said yesterday, if it comes to that, I'll take the hits."

She felt herself flush with an anger that seemed more aimed at herself than him.

"You can't take the hits, Pell. I guess you're being noble or something, but I'm fucked for not reporting you whether you take the hits or not. That's the way it works here on the local level."

"Okay. Listen, there's another reason I called. I've got someone who can help us with this Claudius thing."

"What do you mean?"

"If it's true what Tennant said, that Mr. Red goes there, I'm thinking we can use that. The ATF has a guy at Cal Tech who knows about this stuff. I've set it up, if you're game."

"You're damn right I am."

"Great. Can you pick me up?"

The card from Pell's hotel was on her desk. She looked at it and saw that he was staying in Culver City near LAX. A place called the Islander Palms.

"You mean you want me to come get you? Why don't we just meet there? You're way the hell in the wrong direction."

"I'm having trouble with my damned rental car. If you don't want to pick me up, I'll take a cab."

"Take it easy, Pell. I'll see you in twenty minutes."

The Islander Palms was a low-slung motel just off Pico Boulevard, a couple of blocks west of the old MGM Studio. It was two floors, with neon palm trees on a large sign overlooking the parking lot, sea-green trim, and an ugly stucco exterior. Starkey was surprised that Pell was staying in such a dump and thought he'd probably picked it out of a low-end tour book. It was the kind of place that screamed "family rates."

Pell stepped out of the lobby when she turned into the parking lot. He looked pale and tired. The dark rings under his eyes made her think that the trouble wasn't with his car; he was probably still shaken from whatever had rocked him up at Atascadero.

He got in without waiting for her to shut the engine.

"Jesus, Pell, is the ATF on a budget? LAPD would put me up in a better place than this."

"I'll call the director and tell him you said to shape up. You know how to get there?"

"I was born in L.A. I got freeways in my blood."

As they drove back across the city, Pell explained that they were meeting a man named Donald Bergen, who was a graduate student in physics. Bergen was one of several computer experts employed by the government to identify and monitor potential presidential assassins, militia cranks, pedophiles, terrorists, and others who used the Internet as a source of communication, planning, and execution of illegal activity. This was a gray area of law enforcement, and getting darker every day. The Internet wasn't the U.S. Postal Service, and chat rooms weren't private phone calls, yet law enforcement agencies were increasingly limited as to what they could and could not do on the Internet.

"Is this guy some kind of spook?"

"He's just a guy. Do me a favor, okay, and don't ask him about what he does, and don't tell him too much about what we're doing. It's better that way."

"Listen, I'm telling you right now that I'm not going to do anything that's illegal."

"This isn't illegal. Bergen knows why we're coming, and he knows about Claudius. His job is to get us there. After that, it's up to us."

Starkey considered Pell, but didn't say any more. If Bergen and Claudius could help close her case, then that's what she wanted.

Twenty minutes later, they found a spot in visitors' parking and entered the Cal Tech campus. Even though Starkey had spent her life in L.A., she'd never been there. It was pretty; earth-colored buildings nestled in the flats of Pasadena. They passed young men and women who looked normal, but, she thought, were probably geniuses. Not many of the kids here would choose to be cops. Starkey thought that if she were smarter, neither would she.

They found the Computer Sciences building, went down a flight of stairs, and walked along a sterile hall until they found Bergen's office. The man who opened the door was short and hugely muscular, like a bodybuilder. He smelled, faintly, of body odor.

"Are you Jack Pell?"

"That's right. Mr. Bergen?"

Bergen peered at Starkey.

"Who's she?"

Starkey badged him, already irritated.

"*She* is Detective Carol Starkey, LAPD."

Bergen looked back at Pell, suspicious.

"Jerry didn't say anything about this. What's the deal with her?"

"We're a matched set, Bergen. That's all you need to know. Now open the door."

Bergen leaned out to see if anyone else was in the hall, then let them in, locking the door after them. Starkey smelled marijuana.

"You can call me Donnie. I'm all set up for you."

Bergen's office was cluttered with books, software manuals, computers, and pinups of female bodybuilders. Bergen told them to sit where two chairs had been set up in front of a slim laptop computer. Starkey was uncomfortable, sitting so close to Pell that their arms touched, but there wasn't room to move away. Bergen pulled up a tiny swivel chair to sit on the other side of Pell, the three of them hunched in front of the small computer as if it were a window into another world.

"This isn't going to take long. It was pretty easy, compared to some of the stuff I do for you guys. But I'm kinda curious about something."

Starkey noted that Bergen talked to Pell without looking at her. She thought that he was probably uncomfortable around women.

Pell said, "What's that?"

"When I get jobs like this, I file a voucher back through Jerry, but this time he said leave it alone."

"We'll talk about that later, Donnie. That isn't Detective Starkey's concern."

Bergen turned a vivid red.

"Okay. Sure. Whatever you say."

"Show us about Claudius, Donnie."

"Okay. Sure. What do you want to know?"

"Show us how to find Claudius."

"It's already found. I was there this morning."

Bergen, who was sitting on the far side of the Pell, as far from Starkey as he could get, reached over and punched several computer keys.

"First thing I did was run a search for web sites about bombs, explosives, improvised munitions, mass destruction, things like that. There are hundreds of them."

As Starkey watched, the screen filled with the home page of something called GRAVEDIGGER, showing a skull with atomic bomb mushroom clouds in the eye sockets. Bergen explained that it was built and maintained by a hobbiest in Minnesota and was perfectly legal.

"A lot of the more elaborate sites have message boards so people can post notes to each other or get together in a chat room so they can talk in real time. Do you know how we run the assassination scans?"

Starkey said, "Donnie?"

Bergen cleared his throat, glancing at her quickly before looking away.

"Yes, ma'am?"

"You don't have to ma'am me. But I want you to talk to me, too, okay? I'm not going to bust you for smoking pot or whatever it is you're worried about, okay?"

"I wasn't smoking pot."

"Just talk to me, too. I have no idea how you run the assassination scans. I don't even know what assassination scans are."

Pell said, "Maybe we shouldn't get into this."

Bergen turned red again.

"Sorry."

"Just tell us how you found Claudius and bring us there."

Bergen twisted around to point out a stack of bright blue Power-Macs wired together on a metal frame.

"What you do is search for word combinations. Say your combination is President, White House, and kill. I've got software that floats on forty service providers, constantly searching for that combination of words on message boards, newsgroups, and in chat rooms. If the combination shows up, the software copies the exchange and the e-mail addresses of the people involved. What I did was task the software with looking for the word 'Claudius,' along with a few others, and this is what we found. It's as easy as keeping the world safe for democracy."

Bergen clicked another button, and a new page appeared. His chest swelled expansively.

"You can run but you can't hide, motherfuckers. That's Claudius."

It was a face with a head of flames. The face was tortured, as if in great pain. Starkey thought it looked Roman. Along the left side was a navigation bar that showed different topics: HOW TO, THE PROS, MILITARY, GALLERY, LINKS, MOST WANTED, and several others.

Starkey leaned toward the screen.

"What are all these things?"

"Pages within pages. The gallery is pictures of blast victims. It's pretty gruesome. The how-to pages have articles about bomb construction and a message board where these a-holes can talk about it with each other. Here, let's take a tour."

Bergen used a mouse control to click them through a tour of hell. Starkey watched diagrams of improvised munitions flick past on the screen, saw articles on substituting common household products for their chemical counterparts in order to create explosives. The gallery contained photographs of destroyed buildings and vehicles, medical text pictures of people that had been killed by explosive blasts, endless shots of third-world people missing feet and legs from land mines, and photos of animals that had been blown apart in wound research studies.

Starkey had to look away.

"These people are fucking nuts. This is disgusting."

"But legal. First Amendment, babe. And if you read close, you'll note that nothing posted on these pages, which we call public pages, is legally actionable. No one is admitting to crimes or to buying and selling illegal items. They're just hobbiests. Ha."

Pell said, "We're looking for someone who calls himself Mr. Red. They talk about him here. We were told that he might even visit himself."

Bergen was nodding again before Pell finished, letting them know that he was still ahead of them. He checked his watch, then glanced over at a large desktop Macintosh.

"Well, if he's been here since eleven-oh-four last night, he's calling himself something else. I'm charting the sign-ons."

He swiveled back to the laptop and used the mouse control to open the message boards.

"As far as people posting about him, you got a lot of that. A bunch of these freaks think he's a fucking hero. Red, and these other assholes. We've got discussion threads here about the Unabomber; that guy out in California they called the IRS Bomber, Dean Harvey Hicks; that asshole down south who was trying to kill judges and lawyers; those Oklahoma pricks; and a *ton* of stuff about Mr. Red."

Starkey said, "Show us."

Bergen punched up a thread devoted to Mr. Red, explaining that a thread was a string of messages posted on a particular bulletin board and how she could move sequentially from message to message to follow the exchange.

She said, "Where do I start?"

"Start anywhere. It won't matter. The thread goes on forever."

Starkey chose a message at random and opened it.

SUBJECT: **Re: Truth or Consequences**
FROM: **BOOMER|**
MESSAGE-ID: *>187765.34 @ zipp<*

>> . . . that the Unabomber did his thing for so many years without being caught proves his superiority . . . <<

Kaczynski was lucky. His devices were simple, crude, and embarrassing. If you want elegance, look to Mr. Red.

The Boomster
(often mistaken, but never wrong)

Starkey opened the next message of the thread.

SUBJECT: **Re: Truth or Consequences**
FROM: **JYMBO4**
MESSAGE-ID: *>222589.16 @ nomad<*

>>If you want elegance, look to Mr. Red.<<

What elegance, Boom? So he uses a schmantzy goo like Modex, and nobody knows who he is. The Unabomber

**wasn't identified for seventeen frigging years. Red's
only been around for two. Let's see if he's smart enough
to stay uncaught.**

**But I do have to admit that his nonpolitical nature
appeals to me. Ragheads and terrorists give bombers
a bad name . . . ha! I dig it that he's a straight-ahead
asskicker.**

**Rock on,
J**

Starkey looked at Pell.

"None of these people should be allowed to breed."

Pell laughed.

"Don't worry about that, Starkey. I'd guess most of these people have never had a date."

Starkey glanced at Bergen.

"That's what they do here, they leave messages back and forth like this?"

"Yeah. That's why they call it a message board. But these guys are the lightweights. No one here is gonna admit to anything criminal. If you want the real kooks, you've got to go to the chat room. See, most anyone can get where we are now if you know where to look, but the chat room here is different. You can't just sign on, you know, like, knock, knock, here I am. You've got to be invited."

"How did you get invited?"

Bergen looked smug.

"I didn't need an invitation; I broke in. But normal people need what's called a hot ticket, that's special software that someone has to send to you via e-mail. It's like a key to get in. These guys want to talk about things they can be arrested for, so they want their privacy. They know that I'm out here, man, the guys like me. But they think they're safe in the chat room."

Bergen hit more keys, after which a window on the screen opened, showing two names having a conversation, ALPHK1 and

22TIDAL. They weren't discussing bombs, or explosives, or anything even remotely related; they were discussing a popular television series.

Pell said, "They're talking about a goddamned actress."

"They can talk about anything they want in a chat room. It's real time. They're having a conversation just like we are, only they're typing it. These guys could be anywhere on the planet."

Starkey watched their exchange with a sense that she was peeking through a window into another world.

"Can they see us?"

"Nope, not now. We are cloaked, man, absolutely invisible. There are no walls on the Internet, no walls at all when I am at play."

Bergen laughed again, and Starkey thought he was probably as crazy as the loons they were watching.

Pell sighed deeply, then nodded at her.

"I can see him here, Starkey. These people would appeal to his ego. He would come here, read all this crap about how great he is, it's just the kind of thing a guy like this would do. We can reach him here."

Starkey was swept by the realization that any of these people could be Mr. Red himself.

She looked past Pell to Bergen.

"We can leave messages here if we have a screen name?"

"Sure. Post messages, come here into the chat room, anything you want if I set you up for it. That's why we're here, right?"

She looked at Pell, and Pell nodded.

"That's what we want."

"No problemo. Let's get to it, and you can get on your way."

Pell

They chose the name HOTLOAD. Pell thought it was silly, but, as they sat there working, he decided that there was a subliminal sexuality to it that could work for them.

He watched Starkey out the corner of his eye, admiring her intensity. Bergen's office was small and cramped; barely big enough for the three of them to fit in front of the computer. Bergen smelled so bad that Pell kept leaning away from him into Starkey. Every time Pell touched her, Starkey shrank away. Once, when their thighs touched, he thought she was going to fall out of her chair.

Pell wondered about that, thinking that maybe she had an aversion to men or hated being touched, but he decided that this was unlikely. When he'd had the damned spell in Atascadero, she had expressed a surprising warmth that he'd found moving . . . even as she chewed his ass about Tennant.

"Earth to Pell."

Starkey and Bergen were both staring at him. He realized that he hadn't been paying attention, that he had been thinking about Starkey.

"Sorry."

"Well, Jesus Christ, Pell, pay attention. I don't want to spend the night here."

Bergen showed them how to use the little computer, how to turn it on and off, and set them up with an Internet address through an anonymous provider owned and operated by the government. Then he showed them how to get to Claudius once they had accessed the Internet. They talked over how to proceed and decided to do something that Bergen called "trolling." Writing as Hotload, they posted three messages about Mr. Red on the message boards: two affirming Hotload's status as a fan and one reporting a rumor that Mr. Red had struck again in Los Angeles, asking if anyone knew if this was true. Bergen explained that the idea was to provoke a response and establish a presence on the boards.

When they finished, Pell told Bergen that he would be back in a few minutes, then walked Starkey out.

Starkey said, "Why do you have to go back?"

"ATF business. Don't worry about it."

"Oh, fuck yourself, Pell. Jesus."

"This annoyance? Is it perpetual with you?"

Starkey frowned without answering. She shook out a cigarette and lit up. Pell thought about all the smoking and drinking, wondering if she had always been this way or if this Starkey had been born that day in the trailer park. Like the tough talk and bad attitude. Sometimes, as he drove around the city or lay in his shitty hotel room, Pell wanted to ask her those things, but knew it wouldn't be appropriate. He knew too damned much for his own good, such as how something like the trailer park could change a person, like if your inside was weak, you covered it with a hard outside. He forced himself to stop thinking these things.

She waved the cigarette like she wasn't happy with the way it was lit, then stared past him.

"I've got to get back to Spring Street. I'm supposed to go out with Marzik, looking for people who saw our guy."

"You take the computer. We can get together at your place later to see if anyone responded."

She glanced at him, then shrugged.

"Sure. We can do it at my place. I'll wait in the car."

Pell watched Starkey walk away until she was gone, then went back to Bergen's office. He knocked again, and Bergen peered past him down the hall just like before, making sure that the coast was clear. Pell hated dealing with people like this.

When the door was closed, Bergen said, "I hope I didn't say anything wrong in front of her."

Pell took out an envelope containing twelve hundred dollars, then watched as Bergen counted it.

"Twelve hundred. That's fine. This is the first time you guys have paid me in cash. Usually I file a voucher, but this time Jerry said to leave it alone."

"If Jerry said to leave it alone, you should leave it alone."

Bergen shrugged, nervous.

"Right. You want a receipt?"

"What I want is a second computer."

Bergen stared at him.

"You want another one? Just like the one I gave you?"

"Yes. Set up so I can reach Claudius."

"What do you need a second one for?"

Pell stepped closer, met Bergen's eyes in a way that made the muscular man flinch.

"Can you fix me up with a second computer or not?"

"It's another twelve hundred."

"I'll come back later. Alone."

8

AFTER STARKEY DROPPED Pell back at his motel, she and Marzik spent the afternoon interviewing customers of the Silver Lake laundry with no success. No one recalled seeing a man in a baseball cap and long-sleeved shirt making a call. Starkey dreaded reporting to Kelso that the suspect likeness would remain unresolved.

At the end of the day, they swung past the flower shop to show Lester Ybarra the three likenesses that Starkey had gotten from Pell.

Lester considered the three pictures, then shook his head.

"They look like three different guys."

"They're the same guy wearing disguises."

"Maybe the guy I saw was wearing a disguise, too, but he looked older than these guys."

Marzik asked to bum one of Starkey's Tagamet.

Starkey drove home that night determined to give herself a break from the gin. She made a large pitcher of iced tea. She sipped it as she tried to watch television, but spent most of the evening thinking about Pell. She tried to focus on the investigation instead, but her thoughts kept returning to Pell and their earliest conversation that day, Pell saying that he would take the bullets if Tennant filed the charge, Pell saying he would take the hits.

Starkey shut the lights, went to bed, but couldn't sleep. Not even her usual pathetic two hours.

Finally, she took Sugar's picture from her dresser, brought it into the living room, and sat with it, waiting for the night to end.

One man had already taken the hits for her. She would never allow another man to do that again.

At ten minutes after nine the next morning, Buck Daggett called her at Spring Street.

"Ah, Carol, I don't want to be a pest, but I was wondering if you've had any breaks."

Starkey felt a wave of guilt. She knew what it was like to be in Buck's position, feeling that you were on the outside of something so devastating. She had felt that way after the trailer park. She still did.

"Not really, Buck. I'm sorry."

"I was just wondering, you know?"

"I know. Listen, I should call to keep you up on this. I've just been so busy."

"I heard they found some writing in the frag. What's that about?"

"We're not sure what we found. It's either a 5 or an S but, yeah, it was cut into the body of the pipe."

Starkey wasn't sure how much she should tell him about Mr. Red, so she let it go at that.

Buck hesitated.

"A 5 or an S? What in hell is that, part of a message?"

Starkey wanted to change the subject.

"I don't know, Buck. If anything develops, I'll let you know."

Santos waved at her, pointing at the phone. A second line light was blinking.

"Listen, Buck, I got a call. As soon as we get anything, I'll call."

"Okay, Carol. I'm not nagging or anything."

"I know. I'll see you later."

Starkey thought he sounded disappointed, and felt all the more guilty for avoiding him.

The second call was John Chen.

"We got an evidence transfer here in your name from the ATF lab in Rockville."

"Is it bomb components from Miami?"

"Yeah. You should've told me it was coming, Starkey. I don't like stuff just showing up like this. I got court today, and now I have to take care of all this chain of evidence paperwork. I've gotta be at court by eleven."

Starkey glanced at her watch.

"I'll be there before you leave. I want to look at it."

To maintain the chain of evidence, Chen or another of the criminalists would have to personally log over the components into Starkey's possession.

"I've got court, Carol. Make it later today or tomorrow."

He got this whiny quality to his voice that annoyed the hell out of her.

"I'm leaving now, John. I'll be there in twenty minutes."

She was on her way out when Kelso's door opened, and she remembered Tennant. For a few brief minutes, she had forgotten Atascadero.

"Starkey!"

Kelso steamed across the squad room, carrying a coffee cup that read WORLD'S SEXIEST LOVER. Starkey watched him without expression, thinking, fuck it, if Olsen had made the call filing a complaint, it was too late to worry about it.

"Assistant Chief Morgan wants to have a meeting this afternoon. One o'clock in my office."

Starkey felt the ground fall away beneath her.

"About what?"

"What do you think, Detective? He wants to know what we're doing down here about Riggio. Dick Leyton will be here, too. You will advise them on the status of the investigation, and I hope to hell you have something to say."

Starkey felt her panic ease; apparently, no one was complaining to Internal Affairs.

Kelso spread his hands.

"So? Would you care to give me a preview?"

Starkey told him about Claudius, explaining that Tennant had learned about Mr. Red there, and that she felt it was a possible source of information.

Kelso listened, somewhat mollified.

"Well, that's something, I guess. At least it looks like we're doing something."

"We *are* doing something, Barry."

Even with nothing to drink, he made her head throb.

Starkey was still shaking when she left CCS, hoping to reach Chen before he left for court. She did, catching him coming down the stairs with a sport coat draped over his arm. He wasn't happy to see her.

"I told you I had court, and you said you'd be here in twenty minutes."

"Just get me squared away, then you can leave me to it."

She preferred being alone when she worked. It would be easier to concentrate if Chen wasn't watching over her shoulder, being male and offering his help.

Chen grumped about it, but turned and two-stepped the stairs, bringing her back along the hall and into the lab. Two techs were eating sandwiches between plastic bags containing what appeared to be human body parts. The smell of preservative was strong.

Chen said, "They sent two devices, Starkey. It isn't just the library device like you said."

That surprised her.

"All I expected was the library device."

"We got that, but we also got the frag from a detonation they had down there. The reports say they're pretty much the same design, only one was really a bomb and the other wasn't."

Starkey recalled what Pell had told her about a sweatshop bombing, which was described in one of the seven reports he had provided. She had already read the Dade County report on that device and thought that having it might prove useful.

Chen led her to a corner of the lab where two white boxes rested on the black lab table. Both boxes had been opened.

Chen said, "Everything's bagged, tagged, and logged. You've gotta sign here, then the ATF says you're clear to do whatever you want, up to and including destructive testing."

Destructive testing was sometimes necessary to separate components or obtain samples. Starkey didn't anticipate having to do that and would refer to those results that the Miami authorities had found.

Starkey signed four federal evidence forms where Chen indicated, then gave them back to him.

"Okay. Can I work here at your table?"

"Just try not to make a mess. I know where everything is, so put it back in its proper place. I hate when people move things."

"I won't move anything."

"You want me to tell Russ Daigle you're up here? He'll probably want to see this."

"I'd rather work the bomb by myself, John. I'll get him when I'm done."

When Chen was finally gone, Starkey took a breath, closed her eyes, and felt the tension melting away with the glacial slowness of ice becoming water. This was the part of the job that she loved, and had always loved. This was her secret. When she touched the bomb, when she had its pieces in her hands, when they pressed into the flesh of her fingers and palms, she was part of it. It had been that way since her first training exercise at the Redstone Arsenal Bomb School. The bomb was a puzzle. She became a piece in a larger whole that she was able to see in ways that others couldn't. Maybe Dana was right. For the first time in three years, she was alone with a bomb, and she felt at rest.

Starkey pulled on a pair of vinyl gloves.

The ATF had sent both devices along with their respective reports, one each from the Dade County Bomb Squad and the ATF's National Laboratory Center in Rockville, Maryland. Starkey put the reports aside. She wanted to come at the material with a fresh eye and draw her own conclusions. She would read their reports later to compare the conclusions of the bomb techs in Maryland and Miami with her own.

The exploded device was the usual scorched and twisted frag, the fragments in twenty-eight Ziploc bags, each bag labeled with a case number, an evidence number, and description.

#3B12:104/galvanized pipe
#3B12:028/detonator end plug
#3B12:062-081/assorted pipe

Starkey glanced at the contents of each without opening the bags because she saw no need; her interest was in the intact device. The largest fragment was a twisted, four-inch piece of pipe that flattened into a perfect rectangle, its edges as perfect as if they had been cut with a machinist's tool. Explosions could do that, changing the shape of things in unexpected and surprising ways, ways that often made no sense because every distortion was not only the result of the explosive, but was also predicted by the inner stresses of the material being changed.

She returned the bags to their box, pushed that box aside. The second box contained the disassembled parts of the device that had been recovered from the library. She laid these bags out on the bench, organizing them by components. One bag contained the siren that had sounded to draw attention, another the timer, another the siren's battery pack. The siren had been crushed and two of three AA batteries ruptured when Dade County de-armed the device with its water cannon. Starkey thought she would not have recognized the siren if the bag hadn't been labeled.

When the bomb components were laid out, Starkey opened the bags.

The two galvanized pipe cylinders had been blown open like blooming flowers, but were otherwise intact. The duct tape that had joined the pipes had been scissored, but was still in place. The scent of the glue that Dade County had used in their attempt to bring up fingerprints still clung to the metal. Starkey knew that the Dade County forensics team would have expected to find print fragments, even though they might not have belonged to Mr. Red. Salespeople, store clerks, the person who rang up the sale. But nothing had been found. Mr. Red had cleaned the components, leaving nothing to chance.

Starkey assembled the pieces with little effort. Some of the pieces would no longer fit together because they were misshapen by the de-armer, but Starkey had everything close enough. Outwardly, the only difference between this device and the one that had killed Charlie Riggio was the addition of the timer. Red had placed the device, then, when he was ready, pressed the switch to start the countdown. She guessed by the looks of it that the timer was probably good for an hour, counting down from sixty minutes. The police report, if it was thorough, would have constructed a timeline built from witness reports to try to establish how long between the time Red was last seen near the table and the siren going off. This didn't interest Starkey.

She placed her hands on the components, feeling the substance of them. The gloves hid much of the texture, but she kept them on. These were the same pieces of metal and wire and tape that Mr. Red had touched. He had acquired the raw components, cut them, shaped them, and fitted them together. The heat of his body had warmed them.

His breath had settled over them like smoke. Oils from his skin stained them with unseeable shadows. Starkey knew that you could learn much about a person by the way they kept their car and their home, by the way they ordered the events of their life or covered canvas with paint. The bomb was a reflection of the person who built it, as individual as their face or their fingerprints. Starkey saw more than pipe and wire; she saw the loops, arches, and whorl patterns of his personality.

Mr. Red was proud of his work to the point of arrogance. He was meticulous, even obsessive. His person would be neat, as would his home. He would be short-tempered and impatient, though he might hide these things from other people, often by pretending to be someone else. He would be a coward. He would only let out his rage through the perfect devices that he constructed. He would see the devices as himself, as the self he wished to be—powerful, unstoppable. He was a creature of habit because the structure of it gave him comfort.

Starkey examined the wiring, noting that where the wires were joined, each had been connected with a bullet connector of a type available in any hobby store. The connector sleeves were red. The wires were red. He wanted people to see him. He wanted people to know. He was desperate for the attention.

Starkey put the bullet connectors under a magnifying glass and used tweezers to remove the clips. She found that the wire was looped around the connector three times in a counterclockwise direction. Every wire. No bullet connectors from Riggio's bomb had been found, so she had nothing to compare it with. She shook her head at Mr. Red's preciseness. Every wire, three times, counterclockwise. The structure gave him comfort.

Starkey examined the threads cut into the pipe ends and the white plastic plumber's tape that had been peeled away. Starkey hadn't removed the tape from Riggio's bomb because she hadn't thought it necessary, but now she realized that this was a mistake. The plumber's tape was a completely unnecessary part of the bomb, and therefore potentially the most revealing. It occurred to Starkey that if Mr. Red liked to write messages, he might write them on the tape, which had started out as a clean white surface.

She examined the tape fragments that the ATF people had stripped, but found nothing. The tape, designed to be crushed to make the pipe joint airtight, had been shredded when it was removed. Even if something had been written there, she couldn't have found it.

Deciding to examine the tape from the remaining joints, Starkey brought the pipes to a vise at the end of Chen's bench. She fit rubber pads on the vise jaws so that the pipe wouldn't be marred, then used a special wrench with a rubber mouth to unscrew the end cap. It wasn't particularly tight and didn't take much effort.

The plumber's tape was cut deep into the threads. She brought the magnifying glass over and, using a needle as a probe, worked around the root of the threads until she found the end of the tape. Working this close made her eyes hurt. Starkey leaned away, rubbing her eyes with the back of her wrist. She noticed the black tech smiling at her, gesturing with her own reading glasses. Starkey laughed. That would come soon enough.

Starkey worked the tape for almost twenty minutes before she got it free. She found no writing or marks of any kind. She switched the pipes in the vise, then went to work on the second tape. This one didn't take as long. Ten minutes later, Starkey was unpeeling the tape when she realized that both joints had been wrapped the same way. Mr. Red had pressed the tape onto the top of the pipe, then wrapped away from himself, winding the tape over and down and around before bringing it under the pipe and back up again. Clockwise. Just as he had wound the wire to the bullet clips the same way every time, he had wrapped the plumber's tape to the threads the same way every time. Starkey wondered why.

Starkey's eyes were killing her, and the beginnings of a headache pulsed behind her forehead. She peeled off the gloves, got a cigarette, and went out to the parking lot. She leaned against one of the blue Bomb Squad Suburbans, smoking. She stared at the red brick garages at the back of the facility where bomb techs practiced aiming and firing the de-armer. She remembered the first time she had fired the de-armer, which was nothing more than a twelve-gauge water cannon. The noise had scared the hell out of her.

Mr. Red thought about his bombs and built them carefully. She suspected that he had a reason for wrapping the tape clockwise around the pipe threads. It bothered her that she didn't see it. If he saw a reason that she couldn't see, it meant he was better than her, and Starkey could not accept that. She flicked away her cigarette, pretended to hold the pipe and wrap it. She closed her eyes and pretended to screw on the end cap. When she opened her eyes, two uniformed officers heading out to their cars were laughing at her. Starkey flipped them off. The third time she assembled her imaginary pipe, she saw the reason. He wrapped the tape clockwise so that when he screwed on the end cap—also clockwise—the tape would not unwind and bunch. If everything went clockwise, the cap would screw on more easily. It was a small thing, but Starkey felt a jolt of fierce pride like nothing she had known in a long time. She was beginning to see how his mind worked, and that meant she could beat him.

Starkey went back inside, wanting to check the taping on the sweatshop bomb, but found only a fragment of an end cap. There would be a sample of joint tape in the threads, but not enough to tell her the direction of the winding. She went downstairs to the Bomb Squad, looking for Russ Daigle. He was in the sergeants' bay, eating a liverwurst sandwich. He smiled when he saw her.

"Hey, Starkey. What are you doing here?"

"Upstairs with Chen. Listen, we got an end cap off Riggio's bomb, right?"

He took down his feet and swallowed as he nodded.

"Yep. Got one intact and a piece of another. I showed you the joint tape, remember?"

"You mind if I take apart the one that's intact?"

"You mean you want to unscrew it?"

"Yeah. I want to look at the tape."

"You can do whatever you want with it, but that's going to be hard."

He brought her out to his workbench where the pieces of the

Silver Lake bomb were locked in a cabinet. Once Chen had released them, they were Daigle's to use in the reconstruction.

"See here? The pipe is still mated to the cap, but they bulged from the pressure so you can't unscrew them."

Starkey saw what he meant and felt her hopes sag. The pipe wasn't round; it had been distorted by gas pressure into the shape of an egg. There was no way to unscrew it.

"Can I take it upstairs and play with it?"

Daigle shrugged.

"Knock yourself out."

Starkey brought the cap upstairs, fit it into the vise, then used a high-speed saw to cut it in half. She used a steel pick to pry the inner pipe halves away from the outer cap halves, then fitted the two inner pipe halves together again in the vise. Daigle would probably be irritated because she had cut the cap, but she couldn't think of another way to reach the tape.

It took Starkey almost forty minutes to find the end of the tape, working with one eye on the clock and a growing frustration. Later, she realized that it took so long because she thought it would be wrapped overhand like the tape on the Miami device. It wasn't. The tape on this joint had been wrapped underhand.

Counterclockwise, not clockwise.

Starkey stepped away from the bench.

"Jesus."

She flipped through the report that had been sent from Rockville and found that it had been written by a criminalist named Janice Brockwell. She checked the time again. Three hours later in D.C. meant that everyone back there should have returned from lunch, but not yet left for the day. Starkey searched through the lab until she found a phone, called the ATF's National Laboratory, and asked for Brockwell.

When Janice Brockwell came on, Starkey identified herself and gave the case number of the Miami hoax device.

"Oh, yeah, I just sent that out to you."

"That's right. I have it here now."

"How can I help you?"

"Are you familiar with the first seven devices?"

"The Mr. Red bombs?"

"That's right. I read those reports, but don't remember seeing anything about the tape on the pipe joints."

Starkey explained what she had found on the library device.

"You were able to unwrap the tape?"

Starkey could hear the stiffness in Brockwell's voice. She felt that Starkey was criticizing her.

"I unscrewed one of the end caps, and the tape darn near unwrapped itself. That got me to thinking about it, so I worked the other loose. Then I started wondering about the caps on the other bombs."

Starkey waited, hoping her lie would soften the sting.

The defensiveness in Brockwell's voice eased.

"That's a pretty cool notion, Starkey. I don't think we paid attention to the tape."

"Could you do me a favor and check? I want to know if they match."

"You say they're clockwise, right?"

"Yeah. Both windings were clockwise. I want to see if the others match."

"I don't know how many intact end caps we have."

Starkey didn't say anything. She let Brockwell work it through.

"Tell you what, Starkey. Let me look into it. I'll get back to you, okay?"

Starkey gave Brockwell her number, then returned the bomb components to their boxes and locked them beneath Chen's bench.

Starkey arrived back at Spring Street with ten minutes to spare. She was harried by the rush to get back, so she stopped on the stairs, smoking half a cigarette to give herself a chance to calm down. When she had herself composed, she went up and found Marzik and Hooker in the squad room. Marzik arched her eyebrows.

"We thought you were blowing off the meeting."

"I was at Glendale."

She decided that she didn't have time to tell them about the Miami bomb. They could hear it when she went over it for Kelso.

"Is Morgan here yet?"

"In there with Kelso. Dick Leyton's in there, too."

"Why are you guys still out here?"

Marzik looked miffed.

"Kelso asked us not to attend."

"You're kidding."

"The prick. He probably thinks his office will look smaller with too many bodies in there."

Starkey thought Marzik's guess was probably true. She saw that she still had a minute, so she asked Marzik and Santos if they had anything new. Marzik reported that the Silver Lake interviews were still a bust, but Santos had spoken with the postproduction facility and had some good news.

He said, "Between all the tapes, we've got pretty much of a three-hundred-sixty-degree view of the area around the parking lot. If our caller is there, we should be able to see him."

"When can we have the tape?"

"Day after tomorrow at the latest. We're going to have to go see the tape on their machine for the best possible clarity, but they say it's looking pretty good."

"Okay. That's something."

Marzik came closer to her, glancing around to make sure no one could overhear.

"I want to warn you about something."

"You're always hearing these things you warn me about."

"I'm just telling you what I heard, all right? Morgan's thinking about turning over the investigation to Robbery-Homicide."

"You're shitting me."

"It makes sense, doesn't it? A man died. It's a murder. You have Homicide investigate. Look, I'm just telling you what I heard, is all. I don't want to lose this investigation any more than you."

Starkey could tell by Santos's expression that he took it seriously, too.

"Okay, Beth. Thanks."

Starkey checked her watch again. All this time she'd been worried about losing the case to a federal task force, and now this. She decided not to think about it because there was nothing that she could say. She would either convince Morgan that she was on top of the case or she wouldn't. She popped an Altoid and a Tagamet, then steeled herself and knocked on Kelso's door exactly at one o'clock.

Kelso answered with his smarmiest smile, putting on a show for the A-chief. Dick Leyton smiled as he greeted her.

"Hi, Carol. How you doing?"

"Fine, Lieutenant. Thanks."

Her palms were wet when she shook his hand. He held on to her an extra moment, giving her hand a squeeze to show his support.

Kelso introduced her to Assistant Chief of Police Christopher Morgan, an intense, slender man sporting a charcoal suit. Like most officers, Starkey had never met Morgan, or any of the other six assistant chiefs, though she knew them by reputation. Morgan was reputed to be a demanding executive who micromanaged his domain with a violent temper. He had run in twelve consecutive Los Angeles City Marathons, and he demanded that his staff run, also. None of them smoked, drank, or were overweight. Like Morgan, all of them were immaculately groomed, wore charcoal suits, and, outside the office, identical military-issue sunglasses. Officers in the lower ranks called Morgan and his staff the Men in Black.

Morgan shook her hand without emotion, bypassing pleasantries by asking her to bring him up to date.

Leyton said, "Carol, why don't you start by describing the device, since your investigation stems from there?"

Starkey briefed Morgan on the Silver Lake bomb's configuration, how it had been detonated, and how they knew that the builder had been on the scene within one hundred yards. She used these descriptions to brief him on Mr. Red. When she was explaining his use of radio detonation and why they believed he had been within one hundred yards of the bomb, Morgan interrupted.

"The TV stations can help you with that. They can provide videotape."

Starkey told him that she had already acquired the tapes and was currently having them enhanced. Morgan seemed pleased with that, though it was hard to tell because his expression never changed.

It took her less than five minutes to describe everything that had been done, including their development of Claudius as a possible source of information about RDX and Mr. Red. All in all, she felt that she had done a pretty good job.

"This bomb couldn't have been placed in Silver Lake as a threat to one of the businesses there?"

"No, sir. Detectives from the OC Bureau and Rampart did background checks on all the businesses in the mall, and the people who work in them. Nothing like that came up. No one was threatened, and, so far, no one has taken credit for the bombing."

"So what's the line of your investigation?"

"The components. Modex Hybrid is an elite explosive, but it's not complicated to make if you have the components. TNT and ammonium picrate are easy to come by, but RDX is rare. The idea now is to use the RDX as a way to backtrack to whoever built the bomb."

Morgan seemed to consider her.

"What does that mean, 'whoever'? I thought it was understood that Mr. Red built the bomb."

"Well, we're working under the assumption that he did, but we also have to consider that it might have been built by someone else, too."

Dick Leyton shifted on the couch, and Kelso frowned.

"What are you talking about, Starkey?"

Starkey described comparing the joint tape from both end caps of the Miami device and the surviving end cap from the Silver Lake device.

"Each of the bombs that has been linked to Mr. Red has been designed and constructed the same way. Even the way he binds the wire to the bullet connectors, three clockwise twists. Same way every time. He's a craftsman, he probably even thinks of himself as an artist. There's something different about the Silver Lake bomb. It's small, but people like this are creatures of habit."

Dick Leyton appeared thoughtful.

"Was that noted in the seven earlier bombs?"

"I called Rockville and asked about it. No one thought to check the direction of the wrapping before."

Morgan crossed his arms.

"But you did?"

Starkey met his eyes.

"You have to check everything, Chief. That's the way it works. I'm not saying we have a copycat; the security around the Mr. Red investigation has been tight. All I'm saying is that I found this difference. That bears consideration."

Starkey wished that she'd never brought it up. Morgan was frowning, and Kelso looked irritated. She felt like she was digging a hole for herself. Dick Leyton was the only one in the room who seemed interested.

"Carol, if this were the work of a copycat, how would that affect your investigation?"

"It expands. If you assume that this bomb wasn't built by Mr. Red, you have to ask who *did* build it? Who knows enough about Mr. Red to duplicate his bombs, and how would they get the components? Then you start to wonder, why? *Why* copycat Mr. Red? Why kill a bomb tech, or anyone else, especially if you're not taking credit for it?"

Morgan heard her out, his face an impenetrable mask. When she was done, he glanced at his watch, then at Kelso.

"This sounds like a Homicide investigation. Barry, I'm thinking we should let Robbery-Homicide take over. They have the experience."

There it was. Even with Marzik's warning, Starkey's breath caught. They were going to lose the case to the Homicide Bureau.

Kelso wasn't happy with that.

"Well, I don't know, Chief."

Dick Leyton said, "Chief, I think that would be a mistake."

His statement surprised her.

Leyton spread his hands reasonably, looking for all the world like the calm, assured professional.

"The way to get to this guy is through a bomb investigation. Following the RDX, just as Detective Starkey is doing. It takes a bomb investigator to do that, not a homicide cop. Starkey's doing a good job with that. As for this difference she's found, we have to recognize it, but not get carried away with it. Serial offenders like Mr. Red undergo evolutions. Yes, they're creatures of habit, but they also learn, and they change. We can't know what's in his mind."

Starkey stared at him, feeling a warmth that embarrassed her.

Morgan seemed thoughtful, then checked his watch again and nodded.

"All right. We've got a cop killer out there, Detective Starkey."

"Yes, sir. We're going to find him. I am going to clear this case."

"I hope so. Those are all fine questions you raise. I'm sure you could spend a very long time finding answers for them. But, considering what we know, it seems like a long shot. Long shots are enormous time wasters. All the evidence seems to point to Mr. Red."

"The tape was just something that didn't fit, that's all."

Her voice came out defensive and whiny. Starkey hated herself for saying it.

Morgan glanced at Kelso.

"Well, as long as we don't get sidetracked chasing theories that don't pan out. That's my advice to you, Detective. Listen to Lieutenant Leyton. Keep your investigation moving forward. Investigations are like sharks. If they stop moving forward, they sink."

Kelso nodded.

"It will move forward, Chief. We're going to lock down this sonofabitch. We're going to get Mr. Red."

Morgan thanked everyone for the fine jobs they were doing, then glanced at his watch again and left. Dick Leyton winked at her, then followed Morgan out. Starkey wanted to run after him and kiss him, but Kelso stopped her.

Kelso waited until Morgan and Leyton were gone, then closed the door.

"Carol, forget this copycat business. You were doing fine until you said that. It sounds like nonsense."

"It was only an *observation*, Barry. Did you want me to ignore it?"

"It made you sound like an amateur."

Southern Comfort

JOHN MICHAEL FOWLES bought the 1969 Chevelle SS 396 from a place called Dago Red's Used Cars in Metairie, Louisiana. The SS 396 sported a jacked-up rear end, big-assed Goodyear radials with raised letters, and rust rot along the fenders and rocker panels. The rust rot was extra; John bought it because the damned thing was red. A red car from Dago Red's for Mr. Red. John Michael Fowles thought that was a riot.

He used the Miami money, paying cash with a false Louisiana driver's license that gave his name as Clare Fontenot, then drove to a nearby mall where he bought new clothes and a brand-new Apple iBook, also for cash. He got the one colored tangerine.

He drove across Lake Pontchartrain to Slidell, Louisiana, where he ate lunch at a diner called Irma's Qwik Stop. He had seafood gumbo, but didn't like it. The shrimp were small and shriveled because they'd been simmering all day. This was the first time John Michael Fowles had been to Louisiana. He didn't think much of the place. It was as humid as Florida, but not nearly so pretty. Most of the people were fat and looked retarded. Too much deep-fried food.

Irma's Qwik Stop was across a narrow two-lane road from a titty bar called Irma's Club Parisienne. John was going to meet a man there at eight that night who called himself Peter Willy, Peter Willy being a play on Willy Peter, military slang for white phosphorous explosive. Peter Willy claimed to have four Claymore antipersonnel mines to sell. If this was true, John would buy the mines for one thousand dollars each in order to recover the half pound of RDX housed in them. RDX, which he needed for the Modex Hybrid he used in his bombs, was harder than hell to find, so it was worth the effort to come to Louisiana for it, even though Peter Willy was probably full of shit.

John had "met" Peter Willy, as with many of his contacts, in an Internet chat room. Peter Willy purported to be a death-dealing ex-Ranger and former biker who now worked the offshore oil platforms for Exxon, two weeks on, two weeks off, and occasionally spent his off time hiring out as a mercenary in South America. John knew this was bullshit. Using what was known as a "Creeper" program, John had backtraced Peter Willy's screen name to an Earthlink member named George Parsons and to the Visa card number with which Parsons paid for his account. Once John had the Visa number, it was easy to establish Parsons's true identity as an FAA flight controller employed at New Orleans International Airport. Parsons was married with three daughters, had never been convicted of a crime, and was not a veteran of military service, let alone being a death-dealing ex-Ranger and part-time mercenary. Maybe he would show tonight, but maybe he wouldn't. People like Peter Willy often chickened out. Big talk on the net, but short of action in the real world. This, John knew, is what separated the predators from the prey.

John sat in the diner, sipping iced tea until six women rose from a corner booth and left. The alpha female, a busted-out Clairol blonde with cratered skin and an ass as wide as a mobile home, had put the bill on her charge card. Now, as they herded out, John ambled past their table. He made sure that no one was looking, then palmed the credit card slip and tucked it into his pocket.

As it was only a little after two in the afternoon, John had time to kill and was curious to learn what the ATF had made of his little love letter in the Broward County Library. John had been moving steadily since then, working Claudius to locate a new source of RDX, but was now anxious to read the alerts that had been written about him in the ATF and FBI bulletins. He knew that his little stunt at the library would not place him on the Ten Most Wanted List, but he expected that field offices around the country would be buzzing with alerts. Reading them gave him a serious boner.

John laughed at the absurdity.

Sometimes he was so goddamned bizarre that he amazed himself.

John paid for his meal without leaving a tip (the crappy shrimp), saddled up the big 396, and rumbled down the road back to the Blue Bayou Motel, where he had acquired a room for twenty-two dollars. Once in his room, John plugged the new iBook into the phone line and dialed up AOL. Typically, he would sign on to Claudius to read what the geeps posted about him, and sometimes he would even pretend to be someone else, dropping hints about Mr. Red and enjoying his mythic status. John ate that stuff up: John Michael Fowles, Urban Legend, Rock God. But not tonight. Using the Visa card slip and the Clairol blonde's name, he joined AOL, signed on to the Internet, then typed in the URL address for a web site he maintained under the name Kip Russell. The web site, housed in a server in Rochester, Minnesota, was identified by a number only and had never been listed on any search engine. It could not be found on Yahoo!, AltaVista, Hot-

Bot, Internet Explorer, or anything else. John's web site was a storage facility for software.

John Michael Fowles traveled light. He moved often, abandoned those possessions and identities by which he could be tracked, and often carried no more than a bag of cash. He was without bank accounts, credit cards (except those he stole or bought for temporary use), and real property. Wherever he relocated, he acquired the things he needed, paid cash, then abandoned them when he moved. One of the things he often needed but never carried was software. His software was indispensable.

Before John built bombs, he wrote software. He hacked computer systems, networked with other hackers, and was as deeply into that world and its ways as he was into explosives. He wasn't as good at it as he was with explosives, but he was good enough. The software that waited for him in Rochester was how he was able to run background checks on doofballs like Peter Willy, and how he knew what the feds knew about Mr. Red. With the software that rested in Rochester, he could open doors into credit card companies and banks, telephone systems and the National Law Enforcement Telecommunications System, including the FBI's Bomb Data Center, the ATF's National Repository, and some branches of the Defense Department, which he often scanned for reports of munitions thefts.

When John had accessed his web site, he downloaded an assault program named OSCAR and a clone program named PEEWEE. The downloading took about ten minutes, after which John hand-dialed the phone number for a branch of Bank of America in Kalamazoo, Michigan, and used OSCAR to hack into their system. PEEWEE piggybacked on OSCAR and, once in the B of A system, cloned itself into a free entity that existed only within the B of A branch in Kalamazoo. PEEWEE, from Kalamazoo, then dialed into the ATF's National Repository. As expected, PEEWEE was stopped at a gate that demanded a coded password. PEEWEE then imported OSCAR to assault the gate. Start to finish, the process took two minutes and twelve seconds, whereupon John Michael Fowles, also known as Mr. Red, had access to everything within the government's database of information on bombs and bombers.

John smiled to himself as he always did, and said, "Piece a' fuckin' cake."

The most recent entry was from Los Angeles, which surprised John. It should have been from Miami, but it wasn't.

John Michael Fowles had not been to Los Angeles in almost two years.

John stared at the entry for several seconds, curious, then opened the file. He skimmed the summary remarks, learning that an LAPD bomb technician named Charles Riggio had died in a Silver Lake parking lot. John scanned the summary, the last lines of which hit him with all the impact of a nuclear device.

. . . analysis finds residue of the trinary explosive Modex Hybrid . . . Initial evidence suggests that the perpetrator is the anonymous bomber known as "Mr. Red."

John walked across the room, leaned against the wall and stared at nothing. He was breathing harder now, his back clammy. He stalked back to the iBook.

John's eye zoomed into the components of the bomb until they filled his screen.

MODEX HYBRID

He wondered for a crazy, insane moment if he had built the bomb and somehow forgotten it, laughed aloud at that, then threw the iBook across the room as hard as he could, gouging a three-inch rent in the wall and shattering the plastic case.

John shouted, "You MOTHERFUCKER!"

John Michael Fowles grabbed his bag of cash and ran out of the motel. Peter Willy would have a long night at the titty bar, waiting for someone who would not show. John barrel-assed the big red SS 396 along the edge of the lake, pushing the gas-guzzling engine hard and making the fat, low-class tires squeal. He stopped on the side of the causeway long enough to throw the iBook into the water, then drove like a motherfucker all the way back to the airport. He put the car in long-term parking, wiped down the interior and doors to remove his fingerprints, then paid cash for a one-way ticket to Los Angeles.

No one knew better than John Michael Fowles what it took to make Modex Hybrid or how to find those things within the bomb community.

John Michael Fowles had resources, and he had clues.

Somebody had stolen his work, which meant someone was trying to horn in on his glory.

John Michael Fowles was not going to tolerate that.

He was going out there to get the sonofabitch.

PART TWO

I Luv L.A.

JOHN MICHAEL FOWLES got off the plane with twenty-six thousand dollars, three driver's licenses, and four credit cards, two of which matched with names on the licenses. He also had the phone number of a twenty-eight-year-old flight attendant with dimples deep enough to swallow you and a tan warmer than a golden sunset. She lived in Manhattan Beach. Her name was Penny.

Just being in Los Angeles made John smile.

He loved the dry sunny weather, the palm trees, the good-looking babes in their skimpy clothes, the cool people, the slick cars, the hunger for wealth, the asshole movie stars, that the whole damned place was so big and flat and spread to hell, the La Brea Tar Pits, hot dog stands that looked like hot dogs, that big-ass Hollywood sign spread across that friggin' mountain, earthquakes and firestorms, the funky clubs on the Sunset Strip, sushi, the caramel tans, Mexicans, the tour buses filled with people from Iowa, the glittering swimming pools, the ocean, Arnold Schwarzenegger, the G's with their forties, and Disneyland.

It was a great place for devastation.

First thing he did was rent a convertible from Hertz, strip off his shirt, slip on his shades, and cruise up Sepulveda Boulevard, looking good. He was past his mad now, over his snit; now was the time for cold calculation and furious vengeance. Mr. Red had arrived.

John dropped the shitkicker persona and went black. He loved white guys who acted black. M&Ms. Light on the outside, dark on the inside. *Yo, G, 'sup?* L.A. was the perfect place for this. Everyone was always pretending to be something they weren't.

John bought oversized clothes from a secondhand shop two blocks up from the beach in Venice, a new iBook, and the other things he needed, then took a room at a small motel called the Flamingo Arms. It smelled of foreigners. John shaved his head, draped himself with faux gold chains, then signed on to the Internet. This time he didn't bother with cracking into the NLETS system. He searched for news stories on the Silver Lake bomb, finding three pieces. The first two articles contained pretty much the same thing: the LAPD Bomb Squad had rolled out to investigate a suspicious package, whereupon Officer Charles Riggio, thirty-four, a nine-year veteran of the squad, was killed when the package exploded. None of the news stories gave details of the device, though the detective leading the investigation, a woman named Carol Starkey, was quoted as attributing the bomb, "a crude, poorly made device," to "an infantile personality." John laughed when he read that. He knew that the ATF suspected him, and that, therefore, LAPD suspected him, also.

John said, "The dumb bitch is trying to play me."

John was especially intrigued by the third story, a sidebar article on Starkey herself, who had once been a bomb tech until she had been caught in an explosion. The article said that Starkey had actually died, but had been revived at the scene. John was fascinated by that. There was a photograph of Starkey and some other cops at the scene, but the picture was small and the resolution was poor. John stared at Starkey, trying to see through the murk, and touched the screen.

"Well."

In the final paragraph, Starkey vowed to find the person or persons responsible for Riggio's death.

John smiled at that one.

"Not if I find the motherfucker first."

John dumped the news stories and went to his web site in Rochester for the list of phone numbers, e-mail addresses, and other things he often needed but didn't carry. He copied the phone number of a man he knew as Clarence Jester, who lived in Venice. Jester owned a small pawnshop as his primary occupation, but was an arsonist. Now in his late fifties, Jester had once served twelve years of federal time for starting fires and was an on-again, off-again psychiatric patient. His hobby was adopting dogs from the pound, dousing them with gasoline, and watching them burn. In the past, John had found him an excellent source of information about those in the bomb community.

"Clarence. It's LeRoy Abramowicz, my man. I'm in L.A."

"Yeah?"

Clarence Jester spoke with the careful hesitancy of a paranoid, which he was.

"Thought I might swing by and do a little business. That cool?"

"I guess."

Anxious to get going, but hungry, John scarfed a Big Kahuna burger on the way, ambling into Clarence Jester's pawnshop a few minutes later.

Jester was a small, nervous man, with badly thinning hair. He would not shake hands, explaining that he had a thing about germs.

"Hey, Clarence. Let's go for a walk."

Clarence, ready for him, closed the shop without a word.

Outside, Clarence eyed him carefully.

"You look different."

"I went black. Everybody's doing it."

"Mm."

Business was always done outside, John knowing that Clarence would be more than happy to trade customers for prison time. Twice before, John had bought ammonium picrate from Jester. In addition to being an arsonist, Jester bought and sold explosives, extreme pornography, and the occasional automatic assault weapon. John knew that whoever duplicated his bomb would have to mix their own Modex Hybrid, which meant they would have had to acquire RDX.

"Clarence, I'm looking for a little RDX. You help me with that?"

"Ha."

"What's the 'ha' mean, my man?"

"You don't sound black. You sound like a white man trying to talk nigger."

"Stay with the RDX, Clarence. Do me that courtesy."

"Nobody has RDX. I see some RDX once every couple of years, that's it. I got some TNT and PETN, though. That PETN will blow your ass off."

Clarence brushed his fingers across his mouth as he said it, mumbling his words. He probably thought John was wired.

"Gotta be RDX."

"I can't help you with that."

"That's you. There's gotta be someone else. Hell, you're not living in Buttcrack. This is L.A. You got everydamnthing out here."

A girl in a Day-Glo green bikini bladed past, her ears wrapped in headphones. She had a tattoo of a sun rising out of her pants and a yellow cocker spaniel on a leash. John noticed that Clarence watched the dog.

"Just point the way, Clarence. I find what I'm looking for, I'll kick back a finder's fee to you. I won't leave you cold."

The dog disappeared around a corner.

"The RDX is ringing a bell."

"There you go."

"Don't get excited just yet. When I say it's hard to find, I mean it's hard to find. Just a few years ago, there was a fellow up north who got busted for blowing up cars. He was using RDX. I can maybe put you in touch with him."

John began to feel jazzed. Connections lead to connections.

"A customer of yours?"

"He didn't get the RDX from me, I'll tell you that."

Clarence proceeded to tell him about a man named Dallas Tennant, who was now serving time. John stopped him when he got to the part about prison, irritated.

"Hold on. What in hell good does it do me if he's in the goddamn prison?"

"You can talk to him on Claudius."

"In prison?"

"Like that means shit. You wouldn't believe the stuff I did when I was in prison. Listen, somehow this guy turned enough RDX to blow up three cars. If he can't help you, maybe he can put you with someone who can."

His irritation lifted, and John began to feel jazzed again. This was the way he knew it had to be, all the way out from New Orleans. He wondered if Detective Starkey was smart enough to backtrack the RDX. And if their paths would cross.

"Do you know Mr. Tennant's screen name?"

"Got it back in my computer. You know how to get on Claudius?"

"I know."

John clapped Jester on the back, just to see him flinch.

"Thanks, Clarence."

"Don't touch me. I don't like that."

"Sorry."

"Hey, you heard the big rumor we got out here?"

"No. What rumor?"

"Mr. Red came to town. They're saying he blew up some cop in Silver Lake."

His mood ruined, John clapped Clarence Jester on the back again.

Atascadero

WHEN THE LAST of the inmates had left the library, Dallas Tennant gathered the magazines and books from the tables, stacking them on his cart. The library wasn't very big, only six tables, but the reading selection was current and varied. Several of the inmates at Atascadero were millionaires who had arranged for generous donations of books so that they would have something to read. The Atascadero library was the envy of the California State Prison system.

Mr. Riley, the civilian employee who managed the library, turned out the light in his office. He was a retired high school history teacher.

"Are you almost done here, Dallas?"

"I just have to put these away, then dust the stacks. It won't take long."

Mr. Riley hesitated in his door. He was never comfortable leaving the inmate employees unattended, though there was nothing in the rules against it.

"Well, maybe I should stay."

Dallas smiled pleasantly. Earlier, Dallas had overheard Mr. Riley say that his son and daughter-in-law were coming for dinner, so he knew that Riley was anxious to leave.

"Oh, that's all right, Mr. Riley. We got that box of new books today. I thought I would enter them into the computer tonight so I'd have more time to restack the shelves tomorrow. That might keep me here later than I thought."

"Well, as long as the door is closed by nine. You have to be at the infirmary by nine or they'll come looking for you."

Inmates at Atascadero had enormous freedom, but there was still oversight. Dallas, for example, could work late at the library, but was required to stop by the infirmary for his nightly meds. If he didn't report there by nine P.M., the nurse would notify the duty guard, who would set about finding him.

"I know, sir. I will. Would you tell the guard that I'll be in your office, please, just in case he walks by and sees me in there?"

"I will. You have a good evening, Dallas."

"You too, sir."

Not wanting to linger, Mr. Riley left, thanking Dallas for his good work just as he thanked him every evening.

Dallas Tennant was a good boy. Always had been and still was, even in Atascadero. He was polite, well-mannered, and even-tempered. He was also a bright boy, way bright enough not only to mix chemicals and construct intricate devices, but also to manipulate others.

As soon as Dallas arrived at Atascadero, he had arranged for a job in the kitchen, which not only gave him access to things like baking soda and match heads, but also gave him an unlimited supply of snack foods. He was then able to trade the snacks with inmates work-ing in Janitorial Services for certain cleaning products, which, when combined with things pilfered from the kitchen, created dandy little explosives.

His little accident and the loss of his thumb had ruined that, getting him banned from any area containing chemical supplies, but this library job was almost as good for a different kind of access.

The ironic part of being banned from kitchen and cleaning duty was that Dallas did not create that particular explosive from supplies found within the prison. He had traded for that explosive with some-one from the outside.

Dallas still smiled, thinking about it, even with the loss of his thumb. Some things were worth a small sacrifice.

Dallas cleared the remainder of the magazines and books, but didn't take the time to put them in their proper places. He stepped out into the hall, making sure that Mr. Riley was gone, then checked the time. A guard would be along in about twenty minutes to see if Dallas was where he was supposed to be. Dallas went into Riley's office, broke out the box of books that the guard would be expecting to see, then recovered the software diskette that he kept hidden behind Riley's file cabinet. Though Atascadero was a modern facility and was linked to the California prison system via the Internet, no computer that prisoners could access was supposed to have Internet software in-stalled; that was reserved for secure office machines and the comput-ers belonging to the administrators.

Dallas had acquired his own software, arranging for his attorney to pay his monthly service charges from his rental income.

He loaded the software onto Riley's hard drive, connected the modem to the phone line, and signed on. When he was finished for the evening, he would un-install, and Mr. Riley would be none the wiser.

In moments, Dallas Tennant was home again.

Claudius.

It was the one place where Tennant felt comfortable, an anony-mous world where he was not judged or ridiculed, but embraced as one of a like tribe. His only friends were there, other anonymous screen names with whom he shared posts in the public areas and often chatted in the secret chat room. His instant-messaging list showed several who were currently signed on: ACDRUSH, who loved to post intricate chemical formulas that were, Tennant believed, always wrong; MEYER2, who shared Tennant's admiration for Mr. Red; RAT-BOY, who had written a fourteen-page treatise on how the Oklahoma City bomb could have generated forty percent more explosive force with a few small enhancements; and DEDTED, who believed that Theodore Kaczynski was not the Unabomber.

Tennant posted under the name BOOMER.

Careful to keep an eye out for the guard, he scanned a message board thread that he had created about Mr. Red's appearance in Los Angeles. He was writing an addition when a messaging window appeared on his screen.

WILL YOU ACCEPT A MESSAGE FROM NEO?

Tennant did not know a "Neo," but was curious. He clicked the button to accept, and the instant-messaging window opened.

NEO: **You don't know me, but I know you.**

Tennant glanced toward the hall again, nervous because he knew that the guard was due soon, and his time on-line was short. He typed a response.

BOOMER: Who are you?

Neo's response came back quickly.

NEO: **Someone who admires your use of RDX. I want to discuss it.**

Tennant, like all habitués of Claudius, was aware that law enforcement agents often trolled to entrap people into saying something incriminating. He was careful never to post anything incriminating outside of the secure chat area.

BOOMER: **Good night.**
NEO: **Wait! You want to meet me, Dallas. I am giving you an opportunity tonight that others only dream about.**

Tennant felt a flush of fear at the use of his true name.

BOOMER: **How do you know my name?**
NEO: **I know many things.**
BOOMER: **You think highly of yourself.**
NEO: ***You*** **think highly of me, Dallas. You have written many posts about me. Come to the chat room.**

Tennant hesitated. This changed things. If Neo had a key to the chat room, then someone had vouched for him. He was as safe as safe could be in this uncertain world.

BOOMER: **You have a key?**
NEO: **I do. I am in the chat room now. Waiting.**

Tennant used his own key and opened the chat room window. It was empty except for Neo.

BOOMER: **Who are you?**
NEO: **I am Mr. Red. You have something that I want, Dallas. Information.**

Tennant stared at the name . . . incredulous . . . disbelieving . . . hopeful.
Then he typed:

BOOMER: **What do you have to trade?**

9

AS SOON AS Starkey walked through her door that night, she regretted agreeing to let Pell come to her home. She scooped magazines and newspapers off the floor, policed up a Chinese food carton, and fretted that the air smelled. She tried to remember the last time that she had cleaned the kitchen and the bathroom, but couldn't. There was nothing in the house to drink except gin, tonic, and tap water. You could write your name in the dust on top of the television. She grabbed a fast shower, dressing in jeans and a black T-shirt, then made a half-hearted attempt to make her house presentable. The last guest that

she'd had was Dick Leyton, almost a year ago. He'd stopped by to
catch up with her, and stayed for a drink.

*You really should get a life, Starkey. Maybe they sell'm at the
Best Buy.*

Whatever Kelso thought, Starkey had a good feeling about the
investigation. Having her hands on the Miami bomb had been good for
her; it was concrete and real and had led to her learning something
new, something she would not have otherwise known, about the Silver
Lake bomb. Maybe Kelso and the others couldn't see it, but Starkey
was a bomb tech; she believed that the pieces added up, and now she
had another piece. She was anxious to see if Claudius would yield
anything useful, and was encouraged by Hooker's report from the postproduction facility. She also felt that there was more to be had from
Dallas Tennant.

Starkey set up the laptop on her dining room table, figuring that
was the best place for them to work. She had plugged it in and turned
it on when she heard Pell's car turn into her drive.

When she opened the door, he was carrying a pizza and a white
bag.

"It's the dinner hour, so I thought I would bring something. I've
got a pizza here and an antipasto. I hope you didn't make something."

"Crap. I've got a duck baking."

"I guess I should've called."

"Pell, I'm joking. My usual dinner is a can of tuna fish and
some tortilla chips. This will be great."

She brought the food into the kitchen, feeling doubly embarrassed that there was nothing to drink. She wasn't even sure she had
clean dishes.

"You don't drink gin and tonic, do you?"

"Maybe some tonic without the gin. Where's the computer?"

"It's on the table in the dining room, through there. You want to
eat first?"

"We can eat while we work."

Starkey thought he was probably anxious to leave. She found
that her glasses were spotted and hoped he wouldn't notice. She filled

two glasses with ice and tonic. She felt a fierce urge to add gin to her glass, but resisted.

When she turned to hand him the glass, he was watching her.

"I didn't know what you liked, so I got half veggie, half pepperoni and sausage."

"Either way is fine, but thanks. That was thoughtful."

Just hearing the words come out made her groan to herself. The two of them sounded like a couple of social misfits on an awkward first date. She reminded herself that this was work, not a date. She didn't date. She still needed to go to Best Buy to pick out a life.

As she got out plates and silverware, she considered telling him what she had learned about the joint tape, but she decided against it. She would wait until she heard from Janice Brockwell. She told herself that then she would know whether or not she had something, but part of her didn't want Pell to dismiss her discovery out of hand the way Kelso had.

They divided the antipasto and pizza, then brought their plates and glasses into the dining room. They put two chairs together, just like in Bergen's office, then Starkey signed on to Claudius. She sat with an uncomfortable awareness of Pell's proximity, then edged her chair away.

"Maybe we should eat first. So we don't get grease on the keys."

"Let's not worry about the keys. I want to see if anyone responded."

Starkey shifted her chair next to him again, and they opened the door into Claudius.

With Bergen, they had posted three messages, two expressing enthusiastic admiration for Mr. Red, one asking if the rumor that Mr. Red had struck again in Los Angeles was true. This last message had drawn several responses, one of which reproduced a story from the *Los Angeles Times*, but most of which doubted Mr. Red's appearance, citing his recent criminal blast in Miami and growing status as "Urban Legend." One poster compared Mr. Red to Elvis, suggesting that pretty soon he was going to be seen working in every Denny's in America.

Starkey used the mouse control to advance from message to message, reading, waiting for Pell's grunt, then clicking to the next message. As she concentrated on the bizarre nature of the posts, her awareness of Pell lessened until he reached across her and abruptly took the mouse.

"Hang on. I want to read the last one again."

In the moment when his hand covered hers, she drew away from him as if she'd received an electrical charge, then felt herself flush with embarrassment. She covered it by taking back the mouse and asking a question.

"What did you see?"

"Read it."

SUBJECT: **Re: Truth or Consequences**
FROM: **AM7TAL**
MESSAGE-ID: >9777721.04 @ selfnet<

>>truth to the rumor?<<

My sources inform me that The Man recently laid waste in south Florida, and that is confirmed. History tells us that he waits a while between gigs. The practical reality is that nobody shits Modex in the morning. Anybody got some for sale?

Ha ha. Just kidding, federal motherfuckers!

Am7

Starkey reread the message.

"You think he's Mr. Red?"

"No. He's making the joke about buying Modex, but Mr. Red mixes his own. Red wouldn't expect to buy it, he would buy the components. What if we post back to this guy, making a joke of our own, saying something like we don't have any Modex, but we could probably help him out with some RDX?"

"Throw bait on the water."

"For him, and anyone else reading this stuff."

Pell turned the keyboard and shifted in his seat. His knee touched her knee, his right arm touched her left. Starkey didn't jerk away this time; she let the touch linger. She glanced at Pell, but Pell seemed lost in composing the message. Pictures flashed in her mind: *She touches his arm, their eyes lock, they kiss.* Her heart pounded, thinking about it. *She takes his hand, leads him to the bedroom, he sees her scars.*

Starkey felt sick to her stomach and eased away.

I'm not ready for this.

She stared at her pizza, but couldn't eat it.

Pell, oblivious, said, "What do you think?"

SUBJECT:	**Re: Truth or Consequences**
FROM:	**HOTLOAD**
MESSAGE-ID:	**>5521721.04 @ treenet<**

>>nobody shits Modex in the morning. Anybody got some for sale?<<

RDX is the best laxative! I might be willing to share for the right price. Ha ha yourself!

HOTLOAD

"It looks good."

Starkey glanced over and saw that he was rubbing his eyes and squinting.

"You okay?"

"Pretty soon I'm going to need reading glasses, then a cane."

"I have some drops, if you want."

"That's okay."

They posted the message.

"Anything else?"

"Just wait and see, I guess."

Pell closed the laptop.

"I don't want you to think I'm telling you what to do, but could I ask you to run another NLETS search on the RDX? See if we get a hit on anyone other than Tennant?"

"I already did, and we didn't. The only name that comes up is Tennant."

"We've already gotten what we're going to get from him."

"Maybe from Tennant, but not from Tennant's case."

"What does that mean?"

"I reread Mueller's case notes again. It's clear that he didn't need to find Tennant's shop or recover additional explosives to make his case, so he let a lot of stuff slide. His interview notes indicate that he didn't spend much time with Tennant's landlady or Tennant's employer. He had pictures of the three cars Tennant destroyed and the statement from the kid who stole the cars; that was all he needed. If he blew off the other wits, there still might be something to find."

"That's good thinking, Starkey. That could pay off."

Starkey realized that she was smiling at him, and that Pell was smiling back. The house was silent. With the computer off, Starkey was all the more aware that she and Pell were alone. She wondered if he felt that, too, and suddenly wished for other sounds: the television, the radio, a car on the street. But there was only the two of them, and she didn't know what to do with that.

She abruptly cleared the plates, taking them into the kitchen.

"Thanks again for the pizza. Next time has to be on me."

When the plates were in the sink, she returned to the dining room, but didn't go to her chair. She didn't offer more tonic, and hoped it was apparent that she wanted him to leave. Pell looked like he wanted to say something, but she didn't give him the chance. She wedged her hands in her pockets.

"So I guess we'll check back tomorrow. I'll call you about it."

Pell finally stood. She walked him to the door, then stepped well back from him.

"I'll see you, Pell. We'll catch this bastard."

"Good night, Starkey."

As soon as he stepped through the door, she shut it. Starkey didn't feel better with the door closed; she felt stupid and confused. She was still feeling that way when she went to bed, where she stared at the ceiling in the darkness and wondered why she felt so lost. All she had was the job. All she had was the investigation. That was her life these past three years. That was all it would ever be.

Pell

In his motel, Pell was staring at the computer when the monsters came. They floated up out of the keyboard like writhing segmented worms swarmed by fireflies. He closed his eyes, but still could see them, floating in the blackness. He stumbled into the bathroom for the ice and wet towels that were still in the lavatory, then lay on the bed, the cool towels on his face, his head aching from a pain so great that it left him gasping, and fearful.

He wanted to call Starkey.

He cursed himself for that and concentrated on the pain instead, on this place. He listened to the evening commuter traffic outside his window, the stop-and-go noise of people struggling upstream against the weight of the city; squealing brakes, revving engines, the rumble of overloaded trucks. It was like being on the edge of hell.

He was getting to know her, and that was bad. Every time they were together, he saw a deeper side of her, a surprising side, and his guilt was growing because of it. Pell was too good at reading people, at seeing the hidden face that all people secretly wear, their true face. Pell had learned long ago that everyone is really two people: the person they let you see and the secret person within. Pell had always been able to read the secret person, and the secret person within Starkey's tough-cookie exterior was a little girl who was trying hard to be brave. Inside the little girl was a warrior heart, trying to rebuild her life and career. He hadn't counted on liking her. He hadn't counted on her liking him. It ate at him. It was growing.

But there was nothing to be done for it.

After a time, the pain passed and his vision cleared. Pell glanced at the clock. An hour. Pell covered his face with his hands. Five minutes, maybe ten, but it couldn't have been an hour.

He climbed off the bed and went back to the computer. The flaming head stared out at him from the screen. Pell pushed the guilt he felt about Starkey to the side and opened the door into Claudius. Her name had been on the bomb. Mr. Red wanted her. He could work that.

Pell used a different screen name, one that Starkey didn't know, and began to write about her.

10

THE NEXT MORNING, Starkey was the first detective in the office as usual. She figured that Mueller probably didn't get into his office at six A.M., so she killed time with paperwork. Hooker arrived at five after seven, Marzik drifting in about twenty minutes later. Marzik had Starbucks.

Marzik was stowing her briefcase when she glanced over.

"How'd the big meeting with the A-chief go?"

"He told me to keep the case moving forward. That was his contribution."

Marzik dropped into her seat, sipping the coffee. Starkey smelled chocolate. Mocha.

"I hear Dick Leyton saved your ass in there."

Starkey frowned, wondering what Marzik had heard.

"What does that mean? What did you hear?"

Marzik pried the lid from her cup, blew to cool the coffee.

"Kelso told Giadonna. He said you floated some notion about Silver Lake being a copycat. I'm kinda curious when you were planning on telling me and Hooker about it."

Starkey was pissed off that Kelso would say anything, and pissed that Marzik thought she'd been keeping something from them. She explained about the Miami device and the difference she had found in the direction of the tape.

"It's not the big headline you're making it sound. I wanted to talk it over with you guys today. I didn't get a chance yesterday."

"Well, whatever. Maybe you were too busy thinking about Pell."

"What does that mean?"

"Hey, he's a good-looking guy. For a fed."

"I haven't noticed."

"He got you in on that Claudius thing, right? All I'm saying is when a guy does you a turn like that, you should think about paying him back. Give the man a blow job."

Hooker lurched to his feet and walked away. Marzik laughed.

"Jorge is such a goddamned tightass."

Starkey was irritated.

"No, Beth. He's a gentleman. You, you're trailer trash."

Marzik wheeled her chair closer and lowered her voice.

"Now I'm being serious, okay? It's pretty obvious you're attracted to him."

"Bullshit."

"Every time somebody mentions the guy, you look like you're scared to death. And it's not because he might take the case."

"Beth? When's the last time you were choked out?"

Marzik arched her eyebrows knowingly, then rolled her chair back to her desk.

Starkey went for more coffee, ignoring Marzik, who sat on her fat ass with a smugfuckingsmile. Hooker, still embarrassed by Marzik's remark, lingered on the far side of the squad room, too humiliated to meet Starkey's eye.

Starkey went back to her desk, scooped up the phone, and dialed Mueller. It was still early, but it was either call Mueller or shoot Marzik between the eyes.

When Mueller came on the line, he sounded rushed.

"I gotta get movin' here, Starkey. Some turd put a hand grenade in a mailbox."

"I just have a couple of questions, Sergeant. I spoke with Tennant, and now I need to follow up a few things with you."

"He's a real piece of work, ain't he? He loses any more fingers, pretty soon he'll be countin' on his toes."

Starkey didn't think it was funny.

"Tennant still denies that he had a shop."

Mueller interupted her, annoyed because she was wasting his time.

"Waitaminute. We talked about this, didn't we?"

"That's right."

"There's nothing new to cover. If he's got a shop, we couldn't find it. I been thinking about this since you called. I've got to tell you I think the guy is probably telling the truth. A pissant like this wouldn't have the balls to hold out when he could trade for time."

She didn't bother pointing out that for a pissant like Tennant, his shop would be the most important thing in the world.

Instead, she told him that she had reason to believe that Tennant had a shop and more RDX, also. This time when he spoke, his voice was stiff.

"What reason?"

"Tennant told us the same thing he told you, that he salvaged the RDX from a case of Raytheon GMX antipersonnel mines. That's six mines."

"Yeah. That's what I remember."

"Okay. I looked up the GMX in our spec book down here. It

says that each GMX carries a charge of 1.8 pounds of RDX, which means he would have had a little over ten pounds. Now, I'm looking at the pictures of these three cars you sent. They're fairly light-bodied vehicles, but most of the damage seems to be from fire. I ran an energy calc on the RDX, and it seems to me that if he had used a third of his load on each car, the damage would've been much greater than it is here."

Mueller didn't answer.

"Then I saw here in your interview notes with Robert Castillo that Tennant asked him to steal a fourth car. That implies to me that Tennant had more RDX."

When Mueller finally spoke, his tone was defensive.

"We searched that rathole he was living in. We searched every damned box and cubbyhole in the place. We had his car impounded for three months and even stripped the damned rocker panels. We searched the old lady's house, and her garage, and I even had the Feebs bring out a goddamned dog for the flower bed, so don't try to make out that I fucked up."

Starkey felt her voice harden and regretted it.

"I'm not trying to make out anything, Mueller. Only reason I called is that there aren't many notes here from your interviews with his landlady or employer."

"There was nothing to write. The old bat didn't want to talk to us. All she gave a shit about was us not tromping on her flower beds."

"What about his employer?"

"He said what they all say, how surprised he was, how Dallas was such a normal guy. We wear cowboy boots up here, Starkey, but we're not stupid. You just remember. That sonofabitch is sitting in Atascadero because of me. I made my case. When you make yours, call me again."

He hung up before she could answer, and Starkey slammed down her phone. When she looked up, Marzik was staring at her.

"Smooth."

"Fuck him."

"You're really pissed off today. What got up your ass?"

"Beth. Just leave it alone."

Starkey shuffled through the casework again. Tennant's land-lady had been an elderly woman named Estelle Reager. His employer had been a man named Bradley Ferman, owner of a hobby shop called Robbie's Hobbies. She found their phone numbers and called both, learning that Robbie's Hobbies was out of business. Estelle Reager agreed to speak with her.

Starkey gathered her purse, and stood.

"Come on, Beth. We're going up there to talk to this woman."

Marzik looked shocked.

"I don't want to go to Bakersfield. Take Hooker."

"Hooker's busy with the tapes."

"So am I. I'm still talking to the laundry people."

"Get your shit together and put your ass in the car. We're taking the drive."

Starkey left without waiting.

The Golden State Freeway ran north out of Los Angeles, splitting the state through the great, flat plain of the Central Valley. Starkey believed it to be the finest driving road in California, or anywhere; long, straight, wide, and flat. You could set the cruise control at eighty, put your brain on hold, and make San Francisco in five hours. Bakersfield was less than ninety minutes.

Marzik sulked, bound up tight on the passenger side with her arms and legs crossed like a pouting teenager. Starkey wasn't sure why she had made Marzik come, regretting it even as they left Spring Street. Neither of them spoke for the first half hour until they crested the Newhall Pass at the top of the San Fernando Valley, the great roller coasters and spires of the Magic Mountain amusement park appearing on their left.

Marzik shifted uncomfortably. It was Marzik who spoke first.

"My kids want to go to that place. I keep putting them off because it costs so much, but, Jesus, they see these damned commercials, these people on the roller coasters. The commercials never say how much it costs."

Starkey glanced over, expecting Marzik to look angry and resentful, but she didn't. She looked tired and miserable.

"Beth, I want to ask you something. What you said about me and Pell, is it really that obvious?"

Marzik shrugged.

"I don't know. I was just saying that."

"Okay."

"You never talk about your life. I just kinda figured you don't have one."

Marzik looked over at her.

"Now can I ask you something?"

Starkey felt uncomfortable with that, but told Marzik she could ask whatever she wanted.

"When's the last time you had a man?"

"That's a terrible thing to ask."

"You said I could ask. If you don't want to talk about it, fine."

Starkey realized that she was gripping the steering wheel so hard her knuckles were white. She took a breath, forcing herself to relax. She grudgingly admitted that she wanted to talk about this, even though she didn't know how. Maybe that was why she had made Marzik come with her.

"It's been a long time."

"What are you waiting for? You think you're getting younger? You think your ass is getting smaller?"

"I don't know."

"I don't know what you want because we never talk. Here we are, the only two women in the section, and we never talk about anything but the goddamned job. Here's what I'm saying, Carol, you do this damned job, but you need something else, because this job is shit. It takes, but it doesn't give you a goddamned thing. It's just shit."

Starkey glanced over. Marzik's eyes were wet and she was

blinking. Starkey realized that suddenly everything had turned; they were talking about Marzik, not Starkey.

"Well, I'll tell you what *I* want. I want to get married. I want someone to talk to who's taller than me. I want someone else in that house even if he spends all his time on the couch, and I have to bring him the beer and listen to him fart at three in the morning. I am sick of being alone, with no one for company but two kids eating crackers. Shit, I want to be married so bad they see me coming a mile away and run."

Starkey didn't know what to say.

"I'm sorry, Beth. You're dating, right? You'll find someone."

"You don't know shit about it. I hate this fucking job. I hate my rotten life. I hate these two kids. Isn't that the most horrible thing you've ever heard? I hate these two kids, and I don't know how I'm gonna get them up here to Magic Mountain."

Marzik ran out of gas and lapsed into silence. Starkey drove on, feeling uncomfortable. She thought that Marzik must want something for having said all that, but didn't know what. She felt that she was letting Marzik down.

"Beth, listen?"

Marzik shook her head, not looking over, clearly embarrassed. Starkey was embarrassed, too.

"I'm not very good at girl talk. I'm sorry."

They lapsed into silence then, each of them lost in her own thoughts as they followed the freeway down from the mountains into the great Central Valley. When Bakersfield appeared on the flat, empty plain, Marzik finally spoke again.

"I didn't mean that about my kids."

"I know."

They left the freeway a short time later, following directions that Estelle Reager had given until they came to a prewar stucco home between the railroad transfer station south of Bakersfield, and the airport. Mrs. Reager answered the door wearing jeans, a checked shirt, and work gloves. She bore the lined, leathery skin of a woman who had spent much of her life in the sun. Starkey guessed that Meuller had come in like a cowboy, thinking he could ride roughshod over the old woman, who had gotten her back up. Once up, she would be hard to win over.

Starkey introduced herself and Marzik.

Reager eyed them.

"A couple of women, huh? I guess none of the lazy men down there wanted to drive up."

Marzik laughed. When Starkey saw the twinkle that came to Estelle Reager's eye, she knew they were home free.

Mrs. Reager showed them through the house and out the back door to a small patio covered by a translucent green awning. The awning caught the sun, washing everything with a green glow. The driveway ran along the side of the house to a garage, behind which sat a small, neat guest house. A well-maintained vegetable garden filled the length of the yard between the patio and the guest house.

"We appreciate your seeing us like this, Mrs. Reager."

"Well, I'm happy to help. I don't know what I can tell you, though. Nothing I ain't already said before."

Marzik went to the edge of the patio to look at the guest house.

"Is that where he lived?"

"Oh, yes. He lived there for four years, and you couldn't ask for a better young man. I guess that sounds strange, considering what we know about him now, but Dallas was always very considerate and paid his rent on time."

"It looks empty. Is anyone living there now?"

"I had a young man last year, but he married a teacher and they needed a bigger place. It's so hard to find quality people in this price range, you know. May I ask what it is you're hoping to find?"

Starkey explained her belief that Tennant still had a store of bomb components.

"Well, you won't find anything like that here. The police searched high and low, let me tell you that. They were all in my garden. I was happy to help, but they weren't very nice about it."

Starkey knew that her guess about Mueller had been right.

"If you want to look through his things, you can help yourself. They're all right there in the garage."

Marzik turned back, glancing at Starkey.

"You've still got Tennant's things?"

"Well, he asked me to keep them, you know, since he was in jail."

Starkey looked at the garage, then at Mrs. Reager.

"These were things that were here when the police searched?"

"Oh, yes. I got'm in the garage, if you want to look."

She explained that Tennant had continued to pay rent on his guest house for the first year that he was in prison, but that he had finally written to her, apologizing that he would have to stop and asking if she would be willing to store his things. There weren't very many. Only a few boxes.

Starkey asked the older woman to excuse them, and walked with Marzik to the garage.

"If she says we can go into the garage, we're okay with that because it's her property. But if we go into his boxes and find anything, we could have a problem with that."

"You think we need a search warrant?"

"Of course we need a search warrant."

They would need a search warrant, but they were also out of their operating area, Los Angeles police in the city of Bakersfield. The easiest thing to do would be to call Mueller and have him come out with a request for a telephonic warrant.

Starkey went back to Mrs. Reager.

"Mrs. Reager, I want to be clear on something. These things in your garage, they are things that the police have already looked at?"

"Well, they were in the guest house when the police came. I would guess they looked."

"All right. Now, you said that Tennant asked you to store his things. Did you pack them?"

"That's right. He didn't have very much, just clothes and some of those adult movies. I didn't pack those. I threw them away when I found them. The furniture was mine. I rented it furnished in those days."

Starkey decided that there was nothing to be gained by searching the boxes. Her real hope was in identifying people with whom Tennant might have stored his components well before the time of his arrest.

"Did you know any of his friends or acquaintances?"

"No one ever came here, if that's what you're asking. Well, I take that back. One young man did come by a few times, but that was long before Dallas was arrested. They worked together, I think. At that hobby shop."

"How long before?"

"Oh, a long time. At least a year. I think they were watching those movies, you know?"

Marzik took out the three suspect sketches.

"Do any of these look like the man?"

"Oh, Lord, that was so long ago and I didn't pay attention. I don't think so."

Starkey let it go, thinking that she was probably right.

Marzik said, "That was Tennant's only job, the hobby shop?"

"That's right."

"Did he have any girlfriends?"

"No. None that I knew."

"What about family?"

"Well, all I knew of was his mother. I know she died, though. Tennant came into my house and told me that. He was heartbroken, you know. We had coffee, and the poor boy just cried."

Starkey wasn't thinking about the mother. Something about the boxes bothered her.

"Tennant continued paying rent to you for a year, even after he was in prison?"

"That's right. He thought he might be released, you know, and wanted to come back. He didn't want me to rent the house to anyone else."

Marzik raised her eyebrows.

"Imagine that. Is anyone renting it from you now?"

"No. I haven't had a guest in there since my last young man."

Starkey glanced over, and Marzik nodded. They were both thinking the same thing, wondering why Tennant didn't want to give up his apartment even when he had no use for it. If Tennant wasn't paying rent now and wasn't the occupant of record, they could legally enter and search the premises with the owner's permission.

"Mrs. Reager, would you give us permission to look inside?"

"I don't know why not."

The guest house was musty and hot, revealing one large main room, a kitchenette, bath, and bedroom. The furniture had long since been removed, except for a simple dinette table and chairs. The linoleum floor was discolored and dingy. Starkey couldn't remember the last time she had seen linoleum. Mrs. Reager stood in the open door, explaining that her husband had used the building as an office, while Starkey and Marzik went through the rooms, checking the flooring and baseboards for secret cubbyholes.

Mrs. Reager watched with mild amusement.

"You think he had a secret hiding place?"

"It's been known to happen."

"Those police who were here, they looked for that, too. They tried looking under the floor, but we're on a slab. There's no attic, either."

After ten minutes of poking and prodding, both Starkey and Marzik agreed that there was nothing to find. Starkey felt disappointed. It looked as if the drive up to Bakersfield was a waste, and her trail backwards to the RDX was at an end.

Marzik said, "You know, this is a pretty nice guest house, Mrs. Reager. You think I could send my two kids up here to live with you? We could put iron bars on the windows."

The older woman laughed.

Starkey said, "Beth, can you think of anything else?"

Marzik shook her head. They had covered everything.

Something about Tennant continuing to pay rent still bothered

Starkey, but she couldn't decide what. After thanking Mrs. Reager for her cooperation, Starkey and Marzik were walking through the gate when it came to her. She stopped at the gate.

Marzik said, "What?"

"Here's a guy who worked at a hobby shop. He couldn't have made very much money. How do you figure he could afford paying rent while he was in prison?"

They went back around the side of the house to the back door. When Mrs. Reager reappeared, they asked her that question.

"Well, I don't know. His mother died just the year before all that mess came up. Maybe he got a little money."

Starkey and Marzik went back to their car. Starkey started the engine, letting the air conditioner blow. She recalled that Mueller had noted that Tennant's parents were deceased, but nothing more had been written about it.

"Well, that was a bust."

"I don't know. I'm having a thought here, Beth."

"Uh-oh. Everyone stand back."

"No, listen. When Tennant's mother died, he could have inherited property, or used some of the money to rent another place."

"When my mother died, I didn't get shit."

"That's you, but say Tennant got something. I'll bet you ten dollars that Mueller didn't run a title search."

It would take a day or two to run the title check, but they could have a city prosecutor arrange it through the Bakersfield district attorney's office. If something was identified, Bakersfield would handle the warrant.

Starkey felt better as they drove back to Los Angeles, believing that she had something that kept her investigation alive. The A-chief had told her to keep the case moving forward; now, if Kelso asked, she could point to a direction. If she and Pell could turn a second lead through Claudius, fine, but now they didn't need it.

By the time they reached Spring Street, Starkey had decided to call Pell. She told herself that it was because she had to arrange a time for visiting Claudius tonight, but she finally realized that she wanted to apologize for the way she had acted last night. Then she thought, no, she didn't want to apologize, she wanted another chance to show him that she was human. Another chance at a life. Maybe talking with Marzik had helped, even though they had mostly talked about Marzik.

Starkey saw the manila envelope waiting on her desk all the way from the door. It was like a beacon there, hooking her eye and pulling her toward it. Giant letters on the mailing label read KROK-TV.

Starkey felt her stomach knot. She could tell by the way the envelope bulged that it was a videocassette. After ordering it, she had put it out of her mind. She had refused to think of it. Now, here it was.

Starkey tore open the envelope and lifted out the cassette. A date was written on the label. Nothing else, just the date three years ago on which she died. The noise of her breathing was loud and rasping, her skin cold, and getting colder.

"Carol?"

It took her forever to look over.

Marzik was next to her, her expression awkward. She must have seen the date, recognized it.

"Is that what I think it is?"

Starkey would have spoken, but couldn't find her voice.

"What are you going to do with it?"

Her voice came from a million miles away.

"I'm going to watch it."

Marzik touched her arm.

"Do you want someone with you?"

Starkey couldn't take her eyes from the cassette.

"No."

Driving home from Spring Street, the tape was a presence in Starkey's car. It sat on the passenger seat like a body brought back from the dead, breathing so deeply to fill long-empty lungs that it threatened to draw all the air from the car and suffocate her. When traffic forced her to stop, she looked at it. The tape seemed to be looking back. She covered it with her briefcase.

Starkey did not drive directly home. She stopped at a coffee shop, bought a large black coffee, and drank it leaning on a little counter that looked toward the street. Her neck and shoulders were wound tight as metal bands; her head ached so badly that her eyes felt as if they were being crushed. She thought about the bad stools at Barrigan's and how a double gin would ease the pressure on her eyes, but she refused to do that. She told herself no; she would see this tape sober. She would witness the events of that moment and her final time with Sugar Boudreaux sober. No matter how terribly it hurt, or how difficult it was. She was sober on that day. She would be sober now.

Starkey decided that the way to play it was not to race home and throw herself into the tape, but to act as if her life were normal. She would pace herself. She would be a mechanical woman feeling mechanical emotions. She was an investigator; this was the investigation of herself. She was a police detective; you do your job, leave it at the office, go home and live your life.

Starkey stopped at the Ralphs market. There was no food in the house, so she decided this was the time to stock up. She pushed the buggy up and down the aisles, filling it with things she had never eaten and probably would never eat. Canned salmon. Creamed corn. Brussels sprouts. Standing in the checkout line, she lost her appetite, but bought the food anyway. What in hell would she do with creamed corn?

Starkey fought an overpowering urge for a drink as soon as she stepped through the door. She told herself it was a habit, a learned pattern. You get home, you have a drink. In her case, several.

She said, "After."

Starkey brought her briefcase and three bags of groceries into the kitchen. She noticed that there were two messages on her answering machine. The first was from Pell, asking why he hadn't heard from her and leaving his pager number. She shut him out of her thoughts; she couldn't have him there now. The second call was from Marzik.

"Ah, Carol, it's me. Listen, ah, I was just, ah, calling to see if you were okay. Well. Okay. Ah, see ya."

Starkey listened to it twice, deeply moved. She and Beth Marzik had never been friends, or even had much to do with each other in a personal way. She thought that she might phone Marzik later and thank her. After.

Starkey set the cassette on the kitchen table, then went about putting away the groceries. She had a glass of water, eyeing the cassette as she drank, then washed the glass and put it on the counter. When the last of the groceries were away, she picked up the cassette, brought it into the living room, and put it into her VCR. Marzik's offer to be with her flashed through her head. She reconsidered, but knew this was just another ploy to avoid watching the tape.

She pressed the "play" button.

Color bars appeared on the screen.

Starkey sat cross-legged on the floor in front of her television. She was still wearing her suit; hadn't taken off the jacket or removed her shoes. Starkey had no recollection of when KROK arrived on the scene; when they had started taping or for how long. They might have gotten everything or they might only have the end. She recalled that the cameraman had been on top of their van. That was all. The camera was on top of the van and had a view of everything.

The tape began.

She was pulling the straps tight on Sugar's armor suit. She was already strapped in, except for the helmet. Buck Daggett and another sergeant-supervisor, Win Bryant, who was now retired, moved at the back of the truck, helping them. Starkey hadn't worn the suit since that day, but now felt the weight of it, the heavy density and the heat. As soon as you put the damned thing on, it turned your body's heat back at you, cooking you. Starkey, tall and athletic, had weighed one hundred thirty-five pounds; the suit weighed ninety-five pounds. It was a load. Starkey's first thought: *Why do I look so grim?* Her expression was somber, almost scowling; wearing her game face. Sugar, naturally, was smiling his movie star smile. Once, not long after they had begun sleeping together, she confessed to him that she was never scared when she was working a bomb. It sounded so much like macho horseshit that she had to work up her courage to say it, but it was true. She used to think that something was wrong with her because she felt that way. Sugar, in turn, had confessed that he was so terrified that as soon as they received a call out he would pop an Immodium so he wouldn't crap in the suit. Watching the tape, Starkey thought how relaxed Sugar looked, and that it was she who looked scared. Funny, how what you see isn't always what's there.

They were talking. Though the tape had sound, she could hear only the ambient noise around the microphone. Whatever she and Sugar were saying to each other was too far away for the mike to pick up. Sugar must have said something funny; she saw herself smile.

Daggett and Bryant helped them on with their helmets, then handed the Real Time to Sugar. Sugar smacked her helmet, she smacked his, then they lumbered toward the trailer like a couple of spacewalking astronauts.

The field of view gave her the full length of the trailer, the overhanging trees, and a prime view of the thick azaleas that made a thready, matted wall around the trailer. Sugar had cut away part of the bushes on an earlier trip out, leaving a bare spot to work through. As she now watched, they each pointed at different parts of the bush, deciding how to approach the device. The plan was for Starkey to hold the limbs aside so that Sugar could get the snaps with the Real Time.

Starkey watched the events with a sense of detachment she found surprising.

Sugar had less than thirty seconds to live.

She leaned into the bush first, using the weight of the suit to help her shove the limbs aside. She watched herself step away, then move in again for a better position. She didn't recall that, and marveled at it. In her memory, she had not made that second move. Sugar leaned past her with the Real Time, and that's when the camera bounced from the earthquake, not a big one, a pretty damned small one by L.A. standards, 3.2 centered just north of them in Newhall. The picture bounced, and she heard the cameraman mutter.

"Hey, was that—?"

The sound of the bomb going off covered his words. On television, it was a sharp *crack!* like a gunshot.

It happened so fast that all Starkey saw was a flash of light and the Real Time spinning lazily end around end through the air. She and Sugar were down. There were shouts and frantic cries from behind the camera.

"You gotta get this! Don't fuck up! Keep rolling!"

The picture was small and far away. It was like watching someone else.

Daggett and Bryant ran to them, Daggett to her, Bryant to Sugar, Buck dragging her away from the trailer. One of the things they drilled into you at Bomb School was to fear a secondary explosion. When there was one explosion, there might be another, so you had to clear the wounded from the area. Starkey had never known that she had been moved. She was dead when it happened.

The tape ran for another nine minutes as the paramedics raced forward, stripped away the armor suits, and worked to resuscitate them. In the dreams, Starkey was beneath a canopy of branches and leaves that covered her like lace, but now she saw that there was nothing above her. In the dreams, she was close enough to Sugar to reach out and touch him. Now, she saw that they were ten yards apart, crumpled like broken dolls, separated by a wall of sweating, cursing EMTs desperate to save them. There was no beauty in this moment. The tape ended abruptly as an ambulance was turning into the shot.

Starkey rewound the tape to a point where she and Sugar were both on the ground and pressed the "pause" button. She touched the screen where Sugar lay.

"You poor baby. You poor, poor baby."

After a while, she rewound the tape, ejected it from the VCR, then turned off her television.

Twice during the evening, the phone rang again. Both times the caller left a message. She didn't bother to check.

She went to bed without having a drink, slept deeply, and did not dream.

Manifest Destiny

"AND YOU ARE?"

"Alexander Waverly, attorney at law. I phoned about Dallas Tennant."

The guard inspected the California State Bar card and the driver's license, then handed them back, making a note in his log.

"Right. You're Tennant's new attorney."

"Yes, sir. I phoned to arrange the interview."

"Have you seen clients here at Atascadero before, Mr. Waverly?"

"No. I've never been to a facility like this before. My specialty is medical malpractice and psychiatric disorders."

The guard smiled.

"We call this 'facility' a prison. But it's more like a country club, if you ask me. You gonna talk to Tennant about why he's crazy?"

"Well, something like that, but I shouldn't discuss that with you, should I?"

"No, I guess not. Okay, what you do is sign here and here in the register. I'll have to inspect your briefcase, and then you come around here through the metal detector, okay?"

"All right."

"Do you have any weapons or metal objects on you?"

"Not today."

"A cell phone?"

"Yes. Can't I bring my cell phone?"

"No, sir. Your pager is okay, but not the cell. We'll have to hang on to it here. What about a tape recorder?"

"Yes. I have this little tape recorder. It's okay to have this, isn't it? I'm the worst at taking notes."

"The tape recorder's okay. I just need to look at it, is all."

"Well, all right, but about my phone. What if I'm paged and need to make a call? I have an associate in court."

"You let us know and we'll get you to a phone. Won't be a problem."

He signed the register where instructed, careful to use his own pen, careful not to touch the counter or logbook or anything else that might be successfully lasered for a fingerprint. He didn't bother to watch as the guard inspected his briefcase and tape recorder. Instead, he passed through the metal detector, smiling at the guard who waited on the other side. He traded the cell phone for the briefcase and recorder, then followed the second guard through double glass doors and along a sidewalk to another building. He was aware that a security camera had recorded him. The videotape would be studied and his picture reproduced, but he had a high level of confidence in his disguise. They would never be able to recognize his true self.

John Michael Fowles was delivered to a small interview room where Dallas Tennant was already waiting. Tennant was seated at a table, his good hand covering his damaged hand as if he was embarrassed by it. Tennant smiled shyly, then forgot himself and rested the good hand on a thick scrapbook.

The guard said, "You've got him for thirty minutes, Mr. Waverly. You need anything, I'll be at the desk down the hall. Just stick out your head and give a shout."

"That's fine. Thank you."

John waited until the door was closed, then set his briefcase on the table. He gave Tennant the big smile, spreading his hands.

"Tah-DAH! Mr. Red, at your service."

Tennant slowly stood.

"This is . . . an honor. That's what it is, an honor. There's no other way to describe it."

"I know. This world is an amazing place, isn't it, Dallas?"

Tennant offered his hand, but John didn't take it. He found Tennant's personal hygiene lacking.

"I don't shake hands, m'man. For all I know, you were just playing with your pecker, toying with your tool, commingling with your cockster, know what I mean?"

When Tennant realized that John wasn't going to shake hands, he pushed the heavy book across the table. His awkward, shuffling manner made John want to kick him.

"I'd like to show you my book. You're in here, you know?"

John ignored the book. He slipped off his suit coat, folded it over the back of the chair, then unbuckled his belt. He moved the chair with his toe.

"We'll get to the book, but first you have to tell me about the RDX."

Tennant watched John like a dog waiting for his master to spoon out the kibble.

"Did you bring it? What we talked about, did you bring it?"

"You don't have to stand there drooling, Dallas. You think I'm taking off my clothes because I want to flash my pecker?"

"No. No, I'm sorry."

"Mr. Red is a man of his word. You just remember that. I expect that you'll be a man of his word, too, Dallas. That's very important to me, and to our future relationship. You're not gonna get carried away and brag to anyone that Mr. Red came to see you, now, are you?"

"No. Oh, no, never."

"You do that, Dallas, and there'll be hell to pay. I'm just warning you, okay? I want that to be clear between us."

"I understand. If I told, then you couldn't come see me again."

"That's right."

John smiled, absolutely certain that Dallas Tennant couldn't go the week without telling someone of their encounter. John had planned for that.

"The police were already here, and, you know, they might come back. I don't want you to find out and think I told them anything. I can't help it that they came."

"That's fine, Dallas. Don't you worry about it."

"They came about the RDX. I didn't tell them anything."

"Good."

"One of them was a woman. Her name was Carol Starkey. She's in my book, too. She was a bomb technician."

Tennant pushed the book across the table, desperate for John to look.

"She wasn't alone. She brought an ATF agent named Pell or Tell or something like that."

"Jack Pell."

Tennant looked surprised.

"You know him?"

"You might say that."

"He was mean. He grabbed my hand. He hurt me."

"Well, you just forget about them. We got our own little business here, you and me."

John dropped his trousers, pulled down his shorts, and untaped two plastic bags from his groin. One contained a thin gray paste, the other a fine yellow powder. John placed them on top of Tennant's book.

"This oughta wake'm up out in the vegetable garden, you set it off."

Tennant massaged each bag, inspecting the contents through the clear plastic.

"What is it?"

"Right now, just a couple of chemicals in bags. You mix'm together with a little ammonia like I'm gonna tell ya, Dallas, and you're going to end up with what we in the trade call a very dangerous explosive: ammonium picrate."

Tennant held the two bags together as if he could imagine them mixing. John watched him closely, looking for signs that Tennant knew what he held in his hands. He figured that Tennant had heard of ammonium picrate, but probably had no experience with it. He was counting on that.

"Isn't that what they call Explosive D?"

"Yeah. Nice and stable, but powerful as hell. You ever work with D before?"

Dallas considered the chemicals again, then put the bags aside.

"No. How do I detonate it?"

John smiled widely, pleased with Tennant's ignorance.

"Easy as striking a match, Dallas. Believe me, you won't be disappointed."

"I won't tell where I got it. I promise. I won't tell."

"I ain't worried about that, Dallas. Not even a little bit. Now, you tell me who has the RDX, then I'll tell you how to mix these things."

"I won't forget this, Mr. Red. I'll help you out any way I can. I mean that."

"I know you do, Dallas. Now you just tell me about the RDX, and I am going to give you the power of life and death, right there in those little bags."

Dallas Tennant stuffed both bags down the front of his pants, then told Mr. Red who had the RDX.

*   *   *

Later, John took his time signing out, but once he was in his car and past the security gate, he pushed hard toward the freeway. He had made Tennant promise not to mix the components for at least two days, but he didn't trust in that any more than he trusted Tennant not to tell anyone about his visit. He knew that Dallas would mix the damned stuff as soon as possible; a goof like Tennant couldn't help himself. John was counting on that, too, because he had lied about what the chemicals were and how they would react.

They weren't Explosive D, and they were anything but stable.

It was the only way he had to make sure that Tennant kept his mouth shut.

11

STARKEY WOKE AT her usual early hour, but without the sense of anxiety she often felt. She made a cup of instant coffee, then sat smoking in the kitchen, trying to figure out how she felt about the tape. She knew she felt differently, but she wasn't sure how. There had been no revelations, no surprises, no hidden truths to be found. She had witnessed no mistakes on her part or Sugar's that would have sealed the curse of guilt, but also no heroic action that would remove it. Finally, it came to her. Every day for three years the trailer park had ridden her like a yoke, been immediate to her thoughts. Now the trailer park was farther away.

Starkey showered, put on the same suit that she had worn the day before, then went outside and positioned her car so that the headlights lit the white gardenia bush on the side of her house. She cut three flowers.

The Los Angeles National Cemetery in Westwood didn't open their gates until six A.M., but Starkey found a security guard, badged him, and told him she needed to go in. He was an older man, uncertain and insecure, but Starkey kept the flat cop eyes on him until he relented.

Starkey wasn't one for visiting the dead. She had trouble finding Sugar's grave, her flashlight darting over the uniform white grave markers like a lost dog trying to find her master. She walked past it twice, then doubled back, found it, and put the flowers beneath his name. Sugar had grown up with the scent of gardenias in Louisiana.

She wanted to tell him something about moving beyond it all, but didn't know that there was really anything to say. She knew that she would be saying it more for herself than him, anyway. Life was like that.

Finally, Starkey took a deep breath.

"We were something, Shug."

The old man watched her wordlessly from the gatehouse as she left the cemetery, driving away to start her day.

Starkey spent her first hour at Spring Street organizing her casebook, then made a list of things to cover with Marzik and Hooker. Hooker got there before Marzik, sidling up to her as if he expected her to spray the office with gunfire. Starkey could tell by his expression that Marzik had told him about the tape. She felt disappointed, but that was Marzik.

"Morning, Carol. Ah, how's it going?"

"I'm okay, Jorge. Thanks."

"You doing all right?"

"I saw the tape. I'm okay with it."

Hooker nodded nervously.

"Well, if there's anything I can do."

Starkey stood and kissed his cheek.

"You're a sweet man, Jorge. Thank you."

Hooker showed enormous white teeth.

"Now get out of my face and lemme get back to work."

Hooker laughed and went back to his desk. He was still laughing when Starkey's phone rang.

"Detective Starkey."

"It's Warren Mueller, up here in Bakersfield."

Starkey was surprised, and told him so. She asked why he was calling.

"Your people down there had our city attorney run a property check on Tennant's mother, a woman named Dorthea Tennant."

"That's right."

"You scored, Starkey. I wanted to be the one to tell you that. I'm standing outside the place right now. The old lady died owning a little duplex up here that's still in her name. Tennant must have never brought the issue to probate court."

Starkey felt a tremendous rush of energy. Marzik walked in as Mueller was saying it. Starkey waved her over, cupping the mouthpiece to tell her the news.

"It's Bakersfield. We got a hit, Beth. Tennant has property."

Marzik pumped her fist.

Mueller said, "What's that? I didn't hear you."

"I was telling the people here. Listen, Mueller, you need to have your Bomb Squad roll. There might be explosive materials on the site—"

Mueller cut her off.

"Throttle back, Detective. We're two jumps ahead of you. You didn't just score on the property; you got his shop. This is where he kept his goods, Starkey. Our bomb people are securing the location now."

Hooker and Marzik were both spreading their hands, wanting to know what was going on. She asked Mueller to hold on, told them what she knew, then got back to Mueller.

"Okay, Sergeant. I'm with you. What do you have?"

"This place his mother owned is a little duplex house. One's empty, but the other has people living in it."

"Jesus. Was his shop next door?"

Starkey was thinking this was how Tennant continued to pay rent on his own apartment even from prison.

"No, it wasn't like that. He's got a converted garage here in back of the place that he kept locked. That's where he kept the goods."

"You find the RDX?"

"Negative on the RDX, but we got some TNT and about twenty pounds of black powder."

"We're hoping that there might be evidence that links Tennant with his source for the RDX. This has a direct bearing on the Silver Lake investigation, Mueller. If you find anything like papers, correspondence, pictures, anything that gives us a trail, I want it secured. I'll drive up there to inspect it."

"Will do, but there's more. These people in the house said they had a prowler back here about a month ago."

"Wait. Someone went into the shop?"

"They didn't see him enter or leave the building. All they saw was some guy looking around. The old man who lives up at the house called out, but the guy takes off over the fence. My wit says it looked like he was carrying something."

"You're thinking the RDX?"

"Well, if there *was* RDX inside, he could have taken it."

"You get a description?"

"White male between forty and fifty, five ten to six feet, one-eighty, baseball cap, and sunglasses."

She cupped the phone to fill in Marzik and Hooker. The man in the baseball cap had them trading high fives.

"Sergeant, we have a similar suspect from Silver Lake. If we fax our likeness up there, would you run it past those people, see what they say?"

"You bet."

"Give me your fax."

Starkey passed the number along to Marzik, then got back to Mueller.

"One more thing. Was there any sign of forced entry? If the guy went in, did he have to break in?"

"I know what you meant. No. Tennant had the place locked up with a couple of heavy-duty Yale padlocks. We had to cut'm off with bolt cutters. They hadn't been forced. So if this guy went in there and took the RDX, he had a key."

Starkey couldn't think of anything else to ask.

"Mueller, I know you didn't have to make this call. It shows class."

"Well, you were right, Starkey. I might be a hardhead, but I'm also a gentleman."

"You are. This is good work, Sergeant. This is going to help us down here."

Mueller laughed.

"How about that? I guess me and you're just about the best two cops ever to strut the earth."

Starkey smiled as she hung up.

Marzik said, "Fuckin' A! Are we detectives or what?"

Starkey asked Hooker to see about getting them a look at the enhanced tape. She wanted to see it as quickly as possible because the similar description of the man in the baseball cap gave weight to their 911 caller as the bomber. She had a strong feeling that the man in the long-sleeved shirt would be on the tape. If Hooker was right about the three-hundred-sixty-degree view, he had to be. He had to be within the hundred-yard perimeter to detonate the bomb.

As Hooker set it up, Starkey filled in Kelso, then paged Jack Pell. She felt a powerful urge to share the news with him, which surprised her. She left her own pager number as the return.

The postproduction facility was a block south of Melrose, in an area saturated with Japanese tourists and used-clothing stores. Starkey and Santos drove over together where a thin young man named Miles Bennell met them in the lobby.

Starkey said, "Thanks for making the time for us."

Bennell shrugged.

"Well, you guys are trying to solve a crime. That's probably more important than editing a toilet paper commercial."

"Some days it is."

She was thinking that she would want Lester to see the tape, too, and probably Buck Daggett. She asked Bennell if they could have a copy when they left.

"You mean to play on a home machine?"

"That's right."

Bennell looked pained.

"Well, I can make a copy like that, but you're going to lose resolution. That's why you guys had to come here to see it. Do you know anything about how we do this?"

"I can't even program my VCR."

"A TV picture is made up of little dots called pixels. When we blow up the images on the tape, they get blurry because the pixels, which contain a set amount of information, expand and the information becomes diluted. What we do is take that pixel, break it into more pixels, then use the computer to extrapolate the missing content. It's kind of like making high-definition television in reverse."

"You mean the computer just colors in the space?"

"Well, not really. The computer measures the difference in lights and darks, determines where the shadow lines are, then makes the lights lighter and the darks darker. You end up with really sharp lines and concentrated colors."

Starkey didn't understand what he was saying and didn't care. All she cared about was whether or not it worked.

They walked along a hall past other editing bays, from which she could hear the voices of popular television series, and into a dark room with a console facing a bank of television monitors. The room smelled of daisies.

"How much tape do we have?"

"Eighteen minutes."

Starkey was surprised.

"Out of almost six hours, we got just eighteen minutes?"

Bennell sat at the console and pushed one of the green backlit buttons. The center TV monitor flashed with color bars.

"If the only people who were in the shot were the two Bomb Squad guys, we cut it. That was most of the tape. We only get to see bystanders when the cameras changed angles or the helicopters rotated out of position."

Starkey remembered that from when she viewed the tapes.

"Okay. So what are we going to see?"

"Short clips. Anytime an angle caught a view of the crowd, or the people hiding behind buildings, or things like that, we clipped them. That's what we enhanced. We got kinda lucky with the angles, too. Jorge said you guys wanted to see pretty much the entire perimeter."

"That's right."

"Between the different helicopters, I think we've got that. You're looking for a man in a baseball cap and sunglasses, right?"

"That's right, wearing a long-sleeved shirt."

Starkey put the likeness drawing on the console for Bennell to see.

"Hey, that looks like my roommate."

"Your roommate been to Miami recently?"

"Nah. He never gets out of bed."

Bennell continued adjusting his console.

"We've got a couple guys in caps, I can tell you that. Let's see what they look like. I can go as fast or slow as you like. We can freeze frame. When we freeze, it will appear to lose some clarity, but I can help that."

He pressed another button, and the tape started. There was a hyper-real quality to the image that Starkey thought made the objects in the picture look metallic. The blues were a brilliant blue; the grays almost glowed; the shadows were as sharply defined as the shadows on the moon.

Santos said, "It looks like a Maxfield Parrish painting."

Bennell grinned.

"You got it, dude. Okay, I left a few seconds lead on the camera swings to give our eyes time to keep up with the picture. See, right now there's no one but the cop—"

"His name is Riggio."

"Sorry, Officer Riggio. Now, watch, the camera is about to move."

The angle suddenly shifted, revealing several people clumped behind the cordon tape north of Sunset Boulevard by the Guatemalan market. Starkey recognized the landmarks she noted when she was pacing off distances. The people she was seeing were within that distance and therefore could have been the bomber.

The technician froze the tape, then tickled a joy stick to brighten the image.

Santos pointed at a figure.

"Here. Man here in a cap."

Starkey counted eight people in this slice of the crowd. The image quality was still indistinct, but far crisper than the images she'd seen on her television when she was half in the bag from too many gins. The man Santos pointed out was wearing a red or brown cap with the bill forward. Lester Ybarra had described a man in a blue cap, like a Dodgers cap, but Starkey had enough experience with eyewitnesses to know that this meant little. It was easy to misremember a color. Because of the angle, it was impossible to see if the man was wearing sunglasses or a long-sleeved shirt.

Starkey said, "Does the shot stay on these people for long?"

Bennell checked a clipboard with his notes.

"They're in the frame for sixteen seconds."

"Let's advance it and see what happens. I want a look at this guy's arms if we have it."

Bennell showed her a large dial on the console for controlling the frame advance.

"Here, you can advance it however fast or slow you want by twisting this dial. Clockwise is forward. You want to back up, turn it the other way."

Starkey turned it too much on her first try, making the tape blur forward. The technician brought it back and let her have the knob again. The second time went better. Twelve seconds into the shot, the man in the hat turned to look at the man behind him and could be seen wearing a short-sleeved shirt.

They worked back and forth through the tape for almost an hour, isolating on everyone within the perimeter. Finally, Santos had to pee. Starkey called a cigarette break and was standing in the parking lot, smoking, when her pager buzzed. She felt a jolt of excitement when she saw it was Pell. Santos stuck his head out the door.

"We're ready to go, Carol."

"Be there in a minute."

She called Pell from the front seat of her car and told him what Mueller had found in Tennant's shop. When she was done with that, there was a silence on the phone until she said, "Pell, listen, you got the pizza last time. I'll take care of dinner tonight."

She thought that he was going to say no or bring up what she'd said last night, but there was only a silence for a time that grew until he finally broke it.

"What time you want me over there?"

"How about seven?"

When they ended the call, Starkey asked herself what in hell was she doing. She hadn't intended to bring up dinner or get together with Pell or any of that; that she said those things had surprised her as much as they had probably surprised Pell.

Starkey finished her cigarette, then returned to the editing bay. Watching the eighteen minutes of enhanced tape took almost two hours. As they worked through the clips, Starkey charted the remaining perimeter landmarks, and, by the time they finished, was satisfied that they had a three-hundred-sixty-degree view of the scene, and a fairly complete picture of everyone within the maximum range of the radio transmitter.

But she was also disappointed because the man in the baseball cap was not to be found.

They finished on a wide shot that showed most of the area. Riggio was over the bomb in the instant before the detonation. Buck

Daggett was by the Suburban. The parking lot looked wide and empty. Starkey crossed her arms and considered that this particular search had come to nothing.

Santos looked crestfallen.

"I was sure he would be here. He had to be."

"He is, Jorge. Somewhere. If he took off his cap and rolled up his sleeves, he could be any of these people, and we wouldn't know it, but he has to be here somewhere."

Bennell seemed as disappointed as Santos. With all his work enhancing the film, he wanted to be a part of cracking the case.

"He could be on the other side of any of these buildings. He could be sitting on the sidewalk behind one of these cars, and we'd never see him."

Starkey shrugged, but she knew that wasn't likely. The representative from the radio-control manufacturer had said that the transmitter had to "see" the receiver, which meant that it had to have a clear line of sight.

Bennell said, "Do you still want a copy of the tape?"

"That would be good. Maybe I'll look at it again later."

"It won't be as sharp on your home machine."

"Right now, the sharpness isn't helping much."

Bennell made a copy for each of them.

Starkey and Santos drove back to Spring Street in silence, the enthusiasm of only three hours ago diminished, but not gone. Mr. Red had to be somewhere. The only question was . . . where?

Starkey's Mirror

JOHN MICHAEL FOWLES was liking the Beverly Hills Library just fine except for the Arabs. It didn't matter if they called themselves Arabs, Iranians, Persians (which was just another name for the goddamned Iranians), Iraqis, Saudis, sand niggers, dune coons, shade spades, or Kuwaitis; a raghead was a raghead. John hated the goddamned camel jockeys because they had such an easy time getting on the Ten Most Wanted List. You take an Arab, he farts sideways, and the feds put him on the list. A real American like John had to bust his ass to get there. Beverly Hills was crawling with Arabs.

John closed his eyes and meditated, trying to manage the stress. He pretended that the Arabs weren't swarming through the stacks like Guccied locusts. It wasn't easy being the world's most dangerous man walking free in open sunlight. You had to cope.

John knew where to find the remains of the RDX now and would soon recover it, though that would keep for a day or two. Tennant had been helpful that way, the creepy doof. John hated the socially disgusting, fingerless misfits like Dallas Tennant who inhabited his world. They gave the serious explosives hobbiest a bad name.

After John had learned what he needed to know about the RDX, he had enjoyed hearing about Carol Starkey. Tennant described her as a tough cookie, which John liked a lot. Tennant talked about her so much that John found himself asking questions, and even looking in Tennant's book just to see the articles on Starkey. After he had finished with Tennant, John had driven back to Los Angeles and here to the library. He spent several hours reading old newspaper stories about Starkey, searching for pictures of her, wondering if she was as good a bomb technician as the stories portrayed.

Tough break, that earthquake.

John had laughed aloud when he'd read that, causing a couple of Iranians to look. *Man*, John had thought, *if there is a God, He is one mean-spirited sonofabitch.*

A goddamned earthquake.

Only in California.

John was fascinated that Starkey had actually been killed by a bomb and had then returned from death. He marveled at the experience, and couldn't stop thinking about it. To have been so close to the blast, to have been washed by the energy, to feel it press over the totality of her body like some insane kiss, to be lifted and caressed that way.

He thought that he and Carol Starkey might be soul mates.

When he left the library, John returned to his room at the Bel Air Hotel, a lovely romantic bungalow renting for eight hundred dollars per night, thanks to his latest American Express Gold card and false identity. He signed on to Claudius. The past few days he had noticed an increased number of posts about himself, and about RDX. Several of the posters were even spreading the same rumor that Jester had said, that Mr. Red was behind Silver Lake. John didn't like that. Now that John knew Tennant had told Starkey and Pell about Claudius, he realized what was happening: Starkey thought that he had killed Riggio and was baiting him. She had fallen for the copycat's ploy. John was both annoyed and elated. He enjoyed the idea of Starkey thinking about him, of her trying to catch him.

John read through the new posts and found that they were no longer only about him. Many were about Starkey, some saying that the former bomb tech and poster girl of the bomb crank crowd was now in charge of the investigation. It was like she had her own cheering section.

John scrolled through the thread of posts until he came to the last one:

SUBJECT: **Showdown**
FROM: **KIA**
MESSAGE-ID: **136781.87 @ lippr**

They caught the Unabomber. They caught Hicks, and McVey, and the rest. If anyone can take Red down, it's Starkey. I heard he already tried to get her, and missed. Ha. You only get one shot.
Good-bye, Mr. Red.

John wondered what Kia had heard that made him think Mr. Red had tried to kill Starkey. Did these people shit rumors when they woke in the morning? John snapped off his computer and sulked. These people were out of their friggin' minds. Starkey was becoming the star and he was becoming . . . the other guy.

After he calmed down, John rebooted the iBook and dialed on to his site in Minnesota. When he had the software he wanted, he hacked into the local telephone company and downloaded Carol Starkey's address.

* * *

The bathroom window was louvered glass, dark green and pebbled, one of those narrow windows that go from the floor to the ceiling that you open to let out the steam from your bath. It had probably been in the house since the fifties. He used a shim to slip the latches on the screen, set it aside, then worked out the first piece of glass. The first was the hardest; he anchored the pane with a loose strip of electrician's tape so it wouldn't fall, then worked it free using a screwdriver and his fingertips. When the first was out, he reached inside, groped around until he found the lever, then opened the window. After that, the other panes came easily.

John Michael Fowles took out enough of the panes to make an opening about two feet high, then stepped through the window and was inside Carol Starkey's home.

He took a breath. He could smell her. Soap and cigarettes. He allowed himself a moment to enjoy the feeling of being here in her personal place. Here he was in her house, her home. Here he was, smelling her smells, breathing the air she breathed; it was like being inside her.

First thing John did was take a fast pass through the house, making sure there were no dogs, no guests, nothing that he hadn't foreseen. The air conditioner running made him edgy; he wouldn't be able to hear a car pull in, or hear a key slipping into a lock. He would have to hurry.

John unlocked the back door in case he had to leave fast, then returned to the bathroom. He pulled the screen back into place, latched it, then replaced the panes. That done, he gave himself a longer moment; he took a deeper breath. The bathroom counter was a clutter of jars and bottles: Alba Botanica lotion, cotton puffs in a glass jar, soap balls, a basket of dusty pinecones, a blue box of Tampax Super Plus, an LAPD coffee mug holding a toothbrush and a wilted tube of Crest. The mirror above the lavatory was spotted and streaked; the grout between the tile dark with fungus. Carol Starkey, John thought, had not paid attention in Home Ec. He found this disappointing.

John looked at himself in Starkey's mirror. He made a wide monkey smile, inspecting his teeth, then considered her toothbrush. He put it in his mouth, tasting the Crest. Mint. He worked it around his teeth and gums, brushed his tongue, then put it back in the jar.

He moved through the living room, shooting a quick peek out the window to check for her car. Clear. He sat on the couch, running the flat of his palms along the fabric. He imagined Starkey doing the same thing, their hands moving in unison. The living room was no cleaner than the bathroom. John was particular about his personal grooming and thought it reflected poorly on the character of people who weren't.

He found her computer on the kitchen table, its modem plugged into the phone line there. The computer was what he wanted, but he passed it now, moving through the kitchen to her bedroom. The bedroom was dark, and cooler than the rest of the house. He stood at the foot of the bed, which was unmade, the sheet and duvet mounded like a nest. This bitch lived like a pig. John knew it was crazy. He knew it was insane, that if she came home now, he would either have to kill her or pay a heavy price, but, Jesus Christ, man, here was her FUCK-ING BED. John took off his clothes. He rubbed his body over the sheets, his face into her pillow. He flapped his arms and legs like he was making a snow angel. He was hard, but he didn't want to take the time for that now. He climbed out of the bed, rearranged the mound as it had been, then dressed and returned to the kitchen.

John came prepared for both PC and Macintosh, but was still disappointed to find that she used a PC. It was like the sloppy house; it spoke poorly of her.

He booted the laptop, expecting the usual array of personal icons to appear on the screen, but was surprised to find only one. It hit him then, and John laughed out loud; Starkey didn't know a god-damned thing about computers. When Tennant told them about Claudius, Pell must have set her up through the feds. She probably didn't even know how to work the damned thing.

It only took moments after that. John hooked his zip drive to the laptop, installed the necessary software to copy her files, then uninstalled the software to remove all traces of what had happened. Later, at the hotel, he would open her files to confirm the screen name that she used on Claudius.

Now, he was inside her house. When he had her screen name, he would get inside her mind.

12

STARKEY DROPPED OFF Hooker at Spring Street, then turned toward home. She stopped at a Ralphs market, where she picked up a roasted chicken, mashed potatoes, and some diet soda. When she was waiting in line, it occurred to her that Pell might not drink soda, either, so she picked up a quart of milk, a bottle of merlot, then added a loaf of French bread. She couldn't remember the last time she'd had a dinner guest. When Dick Leyton dropped by that evening a year ago, he'd only stayed for a drink.

The traffic moving out of downtown was brutal. Starkey wallowed along in it, feeling stupid. She hadn't planned on asking Pell over and hadn't thought it through. The words had just spurted out, and now she felt obvious and embarrassed. Once, when Starkey was sixteen years old, a boy she barely knew named James Marsters had invited her to the junior-senior prom. On the day of the dance, Starkey had put on the gown she was borrowing from her older sister and thought herself so fat and ugly that she was convinced James Marsters would run screaming. Starkey had vomited twice and had been unable to eat anything all day. She felt like that now. Starkey could disarm a case of dynamite wired to a motion sensor, but things like this held a different potential for destruction.

She was late getting home. Pell was already there, parked on the street in front of her house. He got out as she pulled into her drive and walked over to meet her. When she saw the expression on his face, she wanted to reach for her Tagamet. He looked like he wasn't sure if he wanted to be here.

She got out with the bags.

"Hey."

"Help you with those?"

She gave him one of the two bags, telling him about Bakersfield as she let them into the house. When she told him that a man was seen at Tennant's shop who could have been the same man making the 911 call, Pell seemed interested, but when she described the suspect as a man in his forties, Pell shrugged.

"It's not our guy."

"How do you know it's not our guy?"

"Mr. Red is younger. This is Los Angeles; everyone here wears sunglasses and baseball caps."

"Maybe our guy isn't Mr. Red."

Pell's face darkened.

"It's Mr. Red."

"What if it isn't?"

"It is."

Starkey felt herself growing irritated at Pell's certainty, like he had inside information or something. She thought again of telling him about the joint tape, but she still wanted to wait for Janice Brockwell.

"Look, maybe we shouldn't talk about it. I think we've got something good here, and you're shitting on it."

"Then maybe we shouldn't talk about it."

They put the two bags on the counter near her sink. Starkey took a deep breath, then faced him, squaring off as if she was about to ask to see some identification. She decided that the only way to survive the evening was to get it out in the open.

"Tonight is a date."

She felt stupid. Here they were, standing in her kitchen, and she pops with that like it was a confession.

Pell looked so uncomfortable that Starkey wanted to crawl into the oven. He searched her eyes, then stared at the bags.

"I don't know about this, Carol."

Now she felt humiliated; three inches tall and kicking herself for being such an ass.

"I understand if you want to leave. I know this looks stupid. I've got to tell you, I *feel* really stupid right now, so if you think I'm as stupid as I'm thinking I am, I wish the hell you would leave."

"I don't want to leave."

"It's only a date, for Christ's sake. That's all it is."

She stared past him at the floor, thinking this was the biggest botch job anyone could imagine.

Pell started taking things from the bags.

"Why don't we put these things away and have dinner?"

He worked for several minutes while she stood there. Finally, she pitched in, taking the things from the bags, putting the milk in the refrigerator, taking freshly washed plates and silverware from the dishwasher. Some date. Nobody was saying anything.

Starkey put the chicken and mashed potatoes to one side, wondering what she should do with them. They looked pathetic in their foil and plastic containers.

"Maybe we should heat them."

Pell put his palm on the carton with the chicken.

"Feels warm enough."

Starkey got out plates and a knife to cut the chicken, thinking that she should have gotten stuff for a salad. She felt thoroughly dispirited, which Pell seemed to read. It made him look even more awkward.

He said, "Why don't I help? I'm a pretty good cook."

"I can't cook worth a shit."

"Well, since it's already cooked, you probably can't mess it up too badly. All we have to do is put it on plates."

Starkey laughed. Her body shook with it and she feared she might cry, but she refused to let herself. *You were always a tough girl.* Pell put down the food and came to her, but she held up a hand, stopping him. She knew that doors were opening. Maybe because of what had happened to Charlie Riggio; maybe because she had seen the tape of the events in the trailer park; but maybe just because it had been three years and she was ready. She thought, then, that it didn't matter why. It just was.

"I'm not very good at this, Pell. I'm trying to let myself feel something again, but it isn't easy."

Pell stared at the chicken.

"Damnit, why don't you say something? I feel like I'm stuck out here all alone and you're just watching me."

Pell stepped closer and put his arms around her. She tensed, but he did nothing more than hold her. She allowed it. Slowly, she relaxed, and when her arms went around him, he sighed. It was as if they were giving themselves over to each other. Part of her wanted it to grow into more, but she wasn't ready for that.

"I can't, Jack."

"Shh. This is good."

Later, they brought the food into the dining room and spoke of inconsequential things. She asked him about the ATF and the cases he had worked, but he often changed the subject or turned his answer into a question.

Later still, when the dishes were cleared and cleaned and put away, he stepped away from her, still awkward, and said, "I guess I should go."

She nodded, walking him to the front door.

"I hope it wasn't too awful."

"No. I hope we can do it again."

Starkey laughed.

"Man, you must be a glutton for punishment."

Pell stopped in the door and seemed to struggle with what he wanted to say. He had been struggling for all of their time together, and now she wondered why.

"I like you, Starkey."

She felt herself smile.

"Do you?"

"This isn't easy for me, either. For a lot of reasons."

She took heart in that.

"I like you, too, Pell. Thanks for coming by tonight. I'm sorry it got kinda weird."

Pell stepped through the door and was gone. Starkey listened as his car pulled away, thinking that maybe a little weirdness was good for people.

Starkey finished straightening the kitchen, then went back to her bedroom, thinking to get undressed and crawl into bed. She decided the bed was a mess, so she stripped the sheets and pillowcases, stuffed them in the wash, and put on fresh. Her whole damned house was a mess and needed to be scoured. She showered, instead.

After the shower, she checked her messages at work, and found that Warren Mueller had called. His was the only message.

"Hey, Starkey, it's Warren Mueller. I ran that crappy picture you faxed past the old man at Tennant's place. He couldn't tell one way or the other, but he thought they kinda looked alike, white guy around forty, the hat and the glasses. I'm gonna have our artist work with him, see if we can't refine the picture. We get anything, I'll fax it down. You take care."

Starkey deleted the message, then hung up, thinking that their picture might be crappy, but everyone was seeing someone who looked more or less like the same guy, and nothing like Mr. Red.

Starkey decided that she might as well check Claudius. She went back into the dining room, turned on the computer, and signed on. She reread the message boards, noting that AM7 had responded to their post about RDX with a long, meandering story about his time in the army. Several other people had responded also, though no one offered to buy or sell RDX or even hinted that they knew how. A lot of people were posting about her.

Starkey was reading when a message window appeared on her screen.

WILL YOU ACCEPT A MESSAGE FROM MR. RED?

A tingle of fear rippled up her back. Then she smiled because it had to be a joke, or some Internet weirdness that she had no chance of understanding.

The window hung there.

WILL YOU ACCEPT A MESSAGE FROM MR. RED?

Starkey opened the window.

MR. RED: **You've been looking for me.**

Starkey knew it had to be a joke.

HOTLOAD: **Who is this?**
MR. RED: **Mr. Red.**
HOTLOAD: **That isn't funny.**
MR. RED: **No. It is dangerous.**

Starkey went for her briefcase. She looked up Pell's hotel number and called him there. Getting no answer, she phoned his pager.

MR. RED: Are you calling for help, Carol Starkey?

She stared at the words, then checked the time and knew that it couldn't be Pell; he didn't have a computer. It must be Bergen. Bergen was probably a pervert, and he was the only other person besides Pell who knew about HOTLOAD.

HOTLOAD: Bergen, you asshole, is this you?
MR. RED: You doubt me.
HOTLOAD: I know exactly who you are, you ASS-
                   HOLE. I'm telling Pell about this. You'll
                   be lucky if the ATF doesn't fire your ass.
MR. RED: HAHAHAHAHA! Yes, tell Mr. Pell. Have
                   him fire me.
HOTLOAD: You won't be laughing tomorrow, you
                   prick.

Starkey stared at the message, irritated.

MR. RED: You do not know who ANYONE is, Carol
                   Starkey. I am not Bergen. I am Mr. Red.

Starkey's phone rang, Pell calling back.
She said, "I think we've got a problem with Bergen. I'm on Claudius. This window just pops up, and whoever it is knows that I'm Hotload. He says that he's Mr. Red."
"Blow him off, Carol. It must be Bergen. I'll see about him tomorrow."

MR. RED: Where are you, Carol Starkey?

When Starkey put down the phone, the message was hanging there, waiting. She stared at it, but made no move to respond.

MR. RED: Okay, Carol Starkey, you're not having

**any, so I will be gone. I will leave you
with the World According to Mr. Red.**

MR. RED: **I did not kill Charles Riggio.**

MR. RED: **I know who did.**

MR. RED: **My name is Vengeance.**

City Lights

John Michael Fowles signed off Claudius. He broke the cell phone connection through which he had signed on to the net and settled back, pushing the iBook aside. The moonlit shade felt good after the heat of the day, sitting there on the quiet street.

His car was parked just up the block from Starkey's house, in the dense shadows of an elm tree heavy with summer leaves. He could see her house from here. He could see the lights in her windows. He watched.

Brimstone

DALLAS TENNANT CARRIED the ammonia in a paper cup, pretending it was coffee. He blew on it and pretended to sip, the sharp fumes cutting into his nose, making his eyes water.

"Night, Mr. Riley."

"Good night, Dallas. I'll see you tomorrow."

Mr. Riley was still at his desk, finishing the day's paperwork. Dallas raised the cup to him.

"Is it all right if I take the coffee back to my cell?"

"Oh, sure. That's fine. Is there any more in the pot?"

Dallas looked pained, and held out the cup.

"This was the last, Mr. Riley. I'm sorry. I've washed the pot. Would you like me to make another before I go? Would you like this one?"

Riley waved him off and turned back to his work.

"That's all right. I'll be leaving soon enough. You enjoy it, Dallas."

Dallas bid Riley good night again, then let himself out. He hid the ammonia in a supply closet long enough to stop at the infirmary for his meds, then continued on to his room, walking more quickly because he was anxious to make the explosive. True, he had promised Mr. Red that he would wait for a few days, but Dallas would have mixed the Explosive D yesterday as soon as Mr. Red had gone, if he had had the ammonia and a detonation system. He didn't, so, earlier this morning when Mr. Riley was gone for lunch, Dallas had signed on to the Internet and printed out pornographic pictures from web sites in Amsterdam and Thailand. He had traded photographs of whores having sex with horses for the ammonia, and Asian women fisting each other for the match heads and cigarettes that he would use as a detonator. Once those things were in his possession, he had spent the rest of the day growing so anxious to mix his new toy that he was damn near running by the time he reached his cell.

Dallas waited long minutes by the door, making sure that no one was coming along the hall, then huddled at the foot of his bed with the two plastic bags and the cup of ammonia. Mr. Red's instructions were simple: Pour the ammonia in the bag with the powder, mix it well until the powder was dissolved, then pour that mixture into the bag with the paste. Mr. Red had warned him that this second bag would get warm as the two substances mixed, but that the mixture would stiffen to a tacky paste, sort of like plastique, and the explosive would then be active.

Dallas poured the ammonia into the first bag, zipped the top, and kneaded it to dissolve the powder. He planned to make the explosive, then spend the rest of the night fantasizing about setting it off in one of the metal garbage cans behind the commissary. Just thinking about the can coming apart, the crack of thunder that was going to snap across the yard, made him aroused.

When the powder was dissolved, Dallas was preparing to pour the solution into the second bag when he heard the guard approaching.

"Tennant? You get your meds okay?"

Dallas pushed the bags under his legs, bending like he was untying his shoes. The guard was staring in at him through the bars.

"Sure did, Mr. Winslow. You can check with'm, if you want. I went by there."

"No problem, Tennant. I'll see them later this evening. I just wanted to make sure you remembered."

"Yes, sir. Thank you."

The guard started away, then paused and frowned. Dallas's heart hammered; sweat sprouted over his back.

"You okay in there, Tennant?"

"Yes, sir. Why?"

"You're bent over all hunched."

"I have to poo."

The guard considered that, then nodded.

"Well, don't shit your pants, Dallas. You've got about an hour till lights out."

Dallas listened as the footsteps faded, then went to the door to peek up and down the hall before resuming his work. He opened the second bag, balanced it between his legs, then added the powder solution. He sealed the top and kneaded the second bag. Just as Mr. Red had told him, the bag grew warm.

What Mr. Red hadn't told him was that the contents would turn bright purple.

Tennant was excited, and concerned. Earlier that day, when he had finished downloading the pornography, he had web-searched a couple of explosives sites and read about ammonium picrate. He had learned that it was a strong, stable explosive, easy to store and use, and safe (as far as such things go) because of its stability. But both articles had also described ammonium picrate as a white, crystalline powder; not a purple paste.

The bag grew warmer.

Tennant stopped kneading. He looked at the paste in the bag. It was swelling the way yeasty bread dough swells, as if it was filling with tiny bubbles of gas.

Tennant opened the bag and sniffed. The smell was terrible.

Two thoughts flashed in Dallas Tennant's mind. One, that Mr. Red couldn't have been wrong; if he said this was ammonium picrate, then it must be ammonium picrate. Two, that some explosives don't require a detonator. Dallas had read about that once, about substances that explode just by being mixed together. There was a word for reactions like that, but Dallas couldn't remember it.

He was still trying to recall that word when the purple substance detonated, separating his arms and rocking Atascadero so deeply that all the alarms and water sprinklers went off.

The word was "hypergolic."

13

STARKEY TRIED TO ignore the way Marzik was staring at her. Marzik had finished interviewing the laundry people without finding anyone else who had seen the 911 caller and was supposed to be writing a report to that effect, but there she was, kicked back, arms crossed, squinting at Starkey. She had been watching Starkey for most of the morning, probably hoping that Starkey would ask why, but Starkey ignored her.

Finally, Marzik couldn't stand it anymore and wheeled her chair closer.

"I guess you're wondering why I'm looking at you."

"I hadn't noticed."

"Liar. I've been admiring that Mona Lisa smile you're sporting today."

"What are you talking about?"

"That smile right there beneath your nose, the one that says you bit the bullet and got yourself a fed-kabob."

"You always take something sweet and make it gross."

Marzik broke into a nasty grin.

"I WAS RIGHT!"

Every detective in the squad room looked. Starkey was mortified.

"You're not right. Nothing like that happened."

"Something must've happened. I haven't seen you this mellow since I've known you."

Starkey frowned.

"The change has come early. You should try it."

Marzik laughed, and pushed her chair back to her desk.

"I'd be willing to try whatever put that grin on your face. I'd try it *twice*."

Starkey's phone rang while Marzik was still smirking. It was Janice Brockwell, calling from the ATF lab in Rockville, Maryland.

"Hi, Detective. I'm phoning about the matter we discussed."

"Yes, ma'am."

"In the seven bombing events that we attribute to Mr. Red, we have six usable end caps, out of an estimated twenty-eight end caps used in the devices. I broke the six and determined that the joint tape was wrapped in a clockwise direction each time."

"They were all wrapped in the same direction?"

"Clockwise. That's right. You should know that the six end caps are from five different devices used in three cities. I consider this significant, Detective. We're going to include this as part of Mr. Red's signature in the National Repository and forward it along as an alert to our field offices. I'll copy my report to you via snail mail for your files."

Starkey's palms were cold, and her heart pounded. If Mr. Red wrapped the joint tape in the same direction every time, why had the Silver Lake bomb been wrapped in the *opposite* direction?

Starkey wanted to shout at Hooker and Marzik.

Brockwell said, "You did good, Detective Starkey. Thanks for the assist."

Starkey put down the phone, trying to decide what to do. She was excited, but she wanted to be careful and not overreact. A small thing like the direction in which that tape was wrapped might have meant nothing, but now meant everything. It did not fit within the pattern. It was a difference, and therefore it meant that the Silver Lake bomb was different.

Starkey paced to the coffee machine to burn off energy, then returned to her desk. Mr. Red was smart. He knew that his devices were recovered, that the analyses were shared. He knew that federal, state, and local bomb investigators would study these things and build profiles of him. Part of the thrill for him was believing that he was smarter than the men and women who were trying to catch him. That was why he etched the names, why he hunted bomb technicians, why he had left the false device in Miami. He would enjoy playing with their minds, and what better way to play than change a single small component of his signature just to create doubt, to make investigators like Carol Starkey *doubt*.

If the bomb was different, you had to ask *why*? And the most obvious answer to that was also the most terrible. *Because a different person had built it.*

Starkey wanted to think it through. She wanted to be absolutely certain before she brought it back to Kelso.

"Hey, Beth?"

Marzik glanced over.

"I've got to get out of here for a few minutes. I'm on pager, okay?"

"Whatever."

Starkey walked the few short blocks to Philippe's, smoking. She knew bombs, she knew bombers. She decided that Mr. Red would not change his profile, even to taunt the police. He was too much about being known; he didn't want them to doubt who they were dealing with; he wanted them to *know* it. The very fact of his signature screamed that he wanted the police to be absolutely certain with whom they were dealing. Mr. Red wanted his victory to be clear.

At Philippe's, Starkey bought a cup of coffee, sat alone at one of the long tables, and lit a fresh cigarette. It was illegal to smoke in the restaurant, but the customer load was light and no one said anything.

I did not kill Charles Riggio.

The feds had multiple suspect descriptions from the Miami library as well as earlier sightings, all of which described Red as a man in his late twenties. Yet Lester Ybarra had described a man in his forties, as had the old man in Tennant's duplex. If Mr. Red had not built this bomb, then someone else had built it, someone who had gone to great lengths to make the bomb appear to be Mr. Red's work. Starkey finally said the word to herself: *Copycat.*

Copycats were most common in serial killer and serial rapist crimes. Hearing frequent news coverage of such crimes could trigger the predisposed into thinking they could get away with a one-shot homicide, using the copycat crime to cover a motive that was far removed from an insane desire to kill or an overpowering rage against women. The perpetrator almost always believed that the cover of the other crimes would mask his true intent, which was typically revenge, money, or the elimination of a rival. In almost all cases, the copycat did not know the full details of the crimes because those details had not been released. All the copycat knew was what he or she had read in the papers, which was invariably wrong.

Yet this copycat knew all the details of how Mr. Red constructed his bombs except for the one thing that had never appeared in the bomb analysis reports: the direction in which Mr. Red had wrapped the plumber's tape.

Starkey watched the smoke drift off her cigarette in a lazy thread, uncomfortable with the direction of her thoughts. The pool of suspects who knew the exact components of Mr. Red's bombs, and how he put those components together, was small.

Cops.

Bomb cops.

Starkey sighed.

It was hard to think about. The person who murdered Charlie Riggio had been within one hundred yards. He had seen Riggio arrive at the scene, watched him strap into the armor, waited as Riggio approached the device. He knew who he was killing. In the two and a half years that she had served as a bomb investigator, she had made exactly twenty-eight cases, none of those against people with access to the details of Mr. Red's bombs or with the acumen to pull it off.

Starkey dropped her cigarette into the coffee, its life extinguished in a sharp hiss.

Starkey took out her cell phone. She caught Jack Pell at his motel.

"Pell? I need to see you."

"I was getting ready to call. I spoke with Bergen this morning."

They agreed to meet at Barrigan's. Starkey wanted to see him with an urgency that surprised her. It had occurred to her, late last night and again early this morning, that she might be falling in love with him, but she wasn't sure and wanted to be careful. The past three years had left an emptiness within her that longed to be filled. She told herself that it was important not to confuse that longing with love, and not to let that need distort friendship and kindness into something it wasn't.

The morning crowd at Barrigan's was the usual assortment of Wilshire detectives, sprinkled with drifters from the Rampart table and a clique of Secret Service agents who kept to themselves at the end of the bar. Even at ten in the morning, the place was loaded with cops. Starkey shoved through the door and, when she saw Pell sitting at the same table where they had sat before, felt a flush of warmth.

"Thanks. I really need to see you about this."

He flashed a smile, clearly pleased to see her. He looked happy. She hoped it was because he was seeing her.

"Jack, it's time for you to take the case."

He smiled the way somebody smiles when they think you're joking, but aren't sure.

"What are you talking about?"

It wasn't easy to say.

"I'm talking about you—the ATF—taking over the investigation into Charlie Riggio's murder. I cannot carry it forward, Jack. Not effectively. I now believe that what happened in Silver Lake to Charlie involves the Los Angeles Police Department."

He glanced toward the bar, probably to see if anyone was listening.

"You think one of your people is Mr. Red?"

"I don't think Mr. Red is behind this. I could go over Kelso's head to Parker, or go to IAG, but I am not prepared to do that until I have more evidence."

Pell leaned forward and took her hand. She felt encouraged. It was funny how you could draw strength from someone you cared about.

"Waitaminute. Hold on. I spoke with some people about Bergen this morning. Bergen was with other clients last night at exactly the time you called me. You had Mr. Red last night, Carol. We've got the bastard. We can use this to bring him in."

Pell was so excited she thought he was going to fall out of his chair.

"That can't be. He knew my name. He knew that Hotload is Carol Starkey. How could he know that?"

Pell answered slowly.

"I don't know."

"He told me that he didn't kill Riggio. He said that he knew who did."

Pell stared at her.

"Is that what this is about? He tells you he didn't kill Riggio, and you believe him?"

"He didn't build the Silver Lake bomb."

"Did he tell you that, too?"

"The ATF lab in Rockville, Maryland, told me that."

She told him about the call from Janice Brockwell, and how the

Silver Lake bomb differed from every other bomb that had been attributed to Mr. Red.

Pell grew irritated, staring at the Secret Service agents until she finished.

"It's just tape."

Pell's voice had taken on a note of impatience. Her own voice came out harder.

"Wrong, Jack, it is forensic evidence, and it shows that *this* bomb is different. It's different in the one way that no one knew about because it had never been in any of the bomb analysis reports. Every other component could have been copied from a police report. He cut Riggio's name in the bomb to make us think it was Mr. Red."

Pell stared at the bar again. With that one turn of his head, she felt a chill of loneliness that left her confused and frightened.

"It's Mr. Red. Trust me on this, Starkey, it's Mr. Red. Everything we're doing here is working. We're flushing out the sonofabitch. Don't get sidetracked. Keep your eye on the ball."

"The people in the Miami library described a man in his twenties. The other descriptions you had were also of men in their twenties. But here in L.A., we've got two descriptions of men in their forties."

"Mr. Red changes his appearance."

"Damnit, Pell, I need your help with this."

"Every investigation turns up contradictory evidence. I've never seen an investigation that didn't. You've grabbed onto a few small bits and now you're trying to turn the whole investigation. It's Mr. Red, Carol. That's who you need to have in your head. That's who we're going to catch. Mr. Red."

"You're not going to help me, are you?"

"I want to help you, but this is the wrong direction. It's Mr. Red. That's who did this. Please just trust me."

"You're so fixated on Mr. Red that you won't even look at the facts."

"It's Mr. Red. That's why I'm here, Starkey. That's what I'm about. Mr. Red."

The warm feelings that she had felt were gone. It should have helped, she later thought, that he seemed to be in as much pain as she, but it didn't.

She was alone with it. She told herself that was okay; she had been alone for three years.

"Pell, you're wrong."

Starkey walked out, and drove back to Spring Street.

"Hook, you have the casebook?"

Hooker looked up at her, eyes vague from his paperwork.

"I thought you were gone."

"I'm back. I need to see the casebook."

"Marzik had it. I think it's on her desk."

Starkey found the book on Marzik's desk and brought it to her own. One of the pages contained a list of all police officers at the Silver Lake parking lot on the day Riggio died. She felt surreal looking at the list. These people were friends and coworkers.

"You find it?"

Hooker was staring at her. She startled at his voice, closing the book, then tried to cover her embarrassment.

"Yeah. Thanks."

"Marzik had it, right?"

"It was on her desk. Thanks."

The book contained the names of those Bomb Squad officers present at the time of the call-out and also listed those officers who checked in on the scene after the event. Buck, Charlie, Dick Leyton, and five other members of the day-shift Bomb Squad. Eight out of the fourteen-person squad. Herself, Hooker, Marzik, and Kelso. The uniformed officers and detectives from Rampart. What the list could not say, and what she could not know for sure, was when those people had arrived or who else might have been at the scene, hidden by cover or disguise.

Starkey removed the page from the binder, made a copy of it, then returned the book to Marzik's desk.

The drive north to Glendale happened in slow motion. Starkey constantly questioned her actions and conclusions, both about Riggio and about Pell. She wasn't a homicide investigator, but she knew the first rule of any homicide investigation: Look for a link between the victim and the killer. She would have to look to Charlie Riggio and hope that something in his life would lead to who killed him. She felt sick about Pell. She wanted to call him; she wanted him to call her. She was certain that he felt something for her, but no longer trusted her certainty.

Starkey pulled into the police parking lot, but did not leave her car. She stared at the modern brick Bomb Squad building, the day bright and hot. The parking lot, the great dark Suburbans, the laughing techs in their black fatigues; everything was different. She was suddenly within the perception puzzle that Dana had described, one view giving her a picture of police officers, another the faces of suspects and murderers. Starkey stared at the building and wondered if she were out of her mind for thinking these things, but either she was right about what the plumber's tape meant or she was wrong. She hoped that she was wrong. She sat smoking in the car, staring at the building where she had felt most alive and at home, most a part of something, and knew that if she was wrong she had to prove it to herself.

"How're you holding up, kiddo?"

Starkey nearly jumped out of her skin.

"You scared me."

"I saw you sitting out here and thought you saw me. If you're coming in, you can walk with me."

Dick Leyton was smiling his kindly smile, the tall benevolent older brother. She got out and walked with him because she didn't know what else to do.

"Has Charlie's desk been cleared yet?"

"Buck came by and boxed it for the family. Charlie had two sisters. Did you know that?"

She didn't want to talk about Riggio's sisters or walk with Dick Leyton, who had come to see her every night when she was in the hospital.

"Ah, no, no, I didn't. Listen, Dick, are Charlie's things still here?"

Leyton didn't know, asking why she was interested. She was so embarrassed at the lie that she thought he must surely see it, but he didn't.

"I didn't know about the sisters. You work on something like this, you see the case, but you never see the man. I guess I was hoping to look at his things to get to know him a little better."

Leyton didn't answer. They walked together into the squad room where Russ Daigle pointed out the box of Riggio's things beneath his desk. Riggio's locker had been cleared also, his sweats and a change of clothes and toiletry items bagged and secured with the box. Waiting for his sisters.

Starkey carried the box into the suit room where she could be alone. Buck had been complete and careful in packing Riggio's things: Pens and pencils were bound together with a rubber band, then secured in the LAPD Bomb Squad coffee cup that had probably held them; two powerboat magazines and a James Patterson paperback were protecting a short stack of snapshots. Starkey examined the snapshots, one showing Riggio on a motorcycle, another of Riggio as a whitewalled Marine, three showing Riggio posing with a trophy deer. Starkey recalled that Riggio was a hunter, who often bragged of being a better shot than the two SWAT buddies with whom he hunted every year. She doubted that any of them concealed a motive for Charlie Riggio's death. The street clothes that Riggio had probably worn to work on the day he died were neatly folded and placed to cover everything else. A Motorola cell phone was wrapped in a black T-shirt to keep it safe. Starkey looked through the clothes for a wallet, didn't find it, and figured that Riggio had probably had the wallet in his fatigues when he died. The coroner's office either still had it or would release it directly to the next of kin. Starkey finished with the box in less than ten minutes. She was hoping for a desk calendar or day book that might give her an insight into his life over the past few months, but there wasn't anything like that. She was surprised at how little of a personal nature Riggio had brought to the job.

She brought the box back out to the squad room and stowed it beneath the now empty desk.

Russ Daigle nodded at her, his face tired.

"Pretty sad, isn't it?"

"Always, Russ. Has the family set a date for the funeral yet?"

"Well, you know, the coroner hasn't released the body."

She hadn't known. She'd been so busy with the investigation that she hadn't paid attention.

Daigle had turned back to his paperwork, his heavy shoulders hunched over the black desk. His gray hair was cropped short, the back of his neck was creased and stubbled. The oldest of the sergeant-supervisors, he had been on the squad longer than anyone. Last year an officer named Tim Whithers had transferred in from Metro, the elite uniform division. Whithers was a tough, cocky young guy, who insisted on calling Russ "Dad" even though Russ repeatedly asked him to stop. Whithers called him Dad until Russ Daigle coldcocked him one morning out in the parking lot. One punch below the ear. Knocked him out. Whithers went back to Metro.

"Hey, Russ?"

He glanced over.

"Were you at Silver Lake when it happened?"

"I was at home. Something like this happens, you always wish you had been there, though. You think you maybe could have done something. You feel that, too?"

"Yeah. I feel like that, too."

"Are you okay, Carol? You look like something's on your mind."

Starkey walked away without answering, feeling a sudden swell of panic as if she were trapped in a den of killers, and hated herself for it. Russ Daigle was happily married, had four adult children and nine grandchildren. Their pictures were a forest on his desk. To think he might have killed Charlie Riggio was absurd.

"Carol?"

She didn't look back.

14

STARKEY LEFT GLENDALE without knowing where she would go or what she would do. That was bad. Working an investigation was like working a bomb. You had to keep your focus. You had to have a clear objective and work to that end, even when you were drinking sweat and pissing blood.

If this were a normal investigation, Starkey would have questioned Riggio's coworkers about his friends and relationships, but now she couldn't do that. She considered contacting his two SWAT hunting buddies, but worried that word of it might get back to the Bomb Squad.

Leyton had said that Riggio had two sisters. Starkey decided to start there.

Every casebook included a page on the victim. Name, address, physical description, that kind of thing. On the night of Riggio's death, Starkey had assigned Hooker the task of gathering this information, and he had done his usual thorough job. She looked up the page and saw that Riggio was the middle child between two sisters, Angela Wellow and Marie Riggio. The older of the sisters, Angela, lived in Northridge, which wasn't far from Charlie's apartment in Canoga Park. The other sister lived south of Los Angeles in Torrance.

Starkey phoned Angela Wellow, identified herself, and expressed her condolences.

Angela's voice was clear, but tired. Jorge had listed her age as thirty-two.

"You worked with Charlie?"

Starkey explained that she had, but that now she was a bomb investigator with the Criminal Conspiracy Section.

"Ms. Wellow, there are some—"

"Angela. Please, I get enough of that missus from the kids. If you were a friend of Charlie's, I don't want you calling me missus."

"You live near Charlie's apartment, don't you, Angela?"

"That's right. It's just over here."

"Has anyone from the department talked to you?"

"No, not to me. Someone called our parents about Charlie, then Mom and Dad called me. They live in Scottsdale. I had to call my sister."

"Reason I'm calling now is because you live so close to Charlie's. We think that Charlie had some files that we need on two other cases. We think he brought them home. Now we need them back. Could you meet me at his apartment, and let me see if I can find them?"

"Charlie had files?"

"Bomb reports on older cases. Nothing to do with Silver Lake. Now we need them back."

A note of irritation crept into Angela's voice.

"I was already there. I've been there every day, trying to get his things packed. Oh, for God's sake."

Starkey made herself hard and detached, even though she felt like a dog for lying.

"I appreciate your feelings, Angela, but we really need those files."

"When do you have to do this?"

"I'm available right now. The sooner the better from our end."

They agreed to meet in an hour.

With the traffic, it took Starkey almost that long to get to Northridge, high in the San Fernando Valley. Riggio's apartment building was on a busy street three blocks south of the Cal State campus. It was a great cave of a building, an upscale stucco monster that had probably been rebuilt after the big earthquake in '94. Starkey left her car in a red zone, then went to the glass security doors where she and Angela had agreed to meet. Two young women on their way out with book bags held the door, but Starkey waved them off, telling them that she was meeting someone. Starkey watched them heading toward the campus and smiled. This was just the kind of place where Charlie Riggio would live. Inside, there would be a pool and Jacuzzi, probably a game room with a pool table, cookouts every night, and plenty of young women.

Now, a thin young woman with the harried look of a mother opened the glass door and looked out. She was carrying a little boy who couldn't have been more than four.

"Are you Detective Starkey?"

"Ms. Wellow? Sorry, Angela?"

"That's right."

Angela Wellow must have parked beneath the building and entered through the inside. Starkey showed her badge, then followed Angela through the central courtyard and up a flight of stairs to a second-floor apartment. The little boy's name was Todd.

"I hope this won't take long. My older boy gets home from school at three."

"It shouldn't, Angela. I appreciate your going to this trouble."

Riggio's apartment was nice, a two-bedroom loft with a high arched ceiling and an expensive big-screen television. A mounted deer head stared down at her from the wall. Starkey wondered if it was the same deer she'd seen in the pictures. The couch was lined with large boxes, and more boxes were in the kitchen. It would be a sad job, packing the belongings of the dead.

Angela put down her little boy, who ran to the television like it was a close and trusted friend.

"What do your files look like? Maybe I've seen them."

Starkey cringed at the lie.

"They look like three-ring binders. They're probably black."

Angela stared at the boxes as if she were trying to remember what was in them.

"Well, I don't think so. These are his clothes, mostly, and things from the kitchen. Charlie didn't keep anything like an office. There's his bedroom upstairs. He has one of those weight machines in the other bedroom."

"Do you mind if I look?"

"No, but I really don't have very long."

Starkey hoped that she would have Riggio's bedroom to herself, but Angela picked up the little boy and showed her up the stairs.

"It's this way, Detective."

"Were you and Charlie close?"

"He was probably closer to Marie, she's the youngest, but our family was a good one. Did you know him well?"

"Not as well as I would have liked. Something like this happens, you always wish you'd taken the time."

Angela didn't answer until they reached the top of the stairs.

"He was a good guy. He had a stupid sense of humor, but he was a good brother."

The bed had already been stripped of linen. More boxes waited on the floor, some empty, others partially filled. A dresser stood against one wall, a jumble of pictures wedged into the mirror frame. Most of the pictures were of an older couple that Starkey took to be his parents.

"Is this your sister?"

"That's Marie, yes. These here are our parents. We haven't taken down the pictures yet. It's just too hard."

The little boy upended a box and climbed inside. Angela sat on the bed, watching him.

"I guess you can look through these boxes. They're mostly clothes, but I remember some papers and books and things."

Starkey used her body to block Angela's view as she went through the boxes. Having Riggio's sister three feet behind her left her with the feeling that even if something was here, she would not find it. There was a heavy photo album that she wanted to look through, and a notepad, and, in the corner of the room, a Macintosh computer that might contain anything at all. There was too much, and here she was, going through it under false pretenses with the dead man's sister staring at her back. What a half-assed, pathetic way to conduct an investigation.

Angela said, "You were a bomb technician like Charlie?"

"I used to be. Now I'm a bomb investigator."

"Could I ask you something about that?"

Starkey said that she could.

"They won't release Charlie's body. They haven't even let us go see him. I keep seeing these pictures in my head, you see? About why they won't let us have him."

Starkey turned, feeling awkward with this woman's discomfort.

"Is Charlie, you know, in pieces?"

"It's not like that. You don't have to worry about Charlie being like that."

Angela nodded, then looked away.

"You think about these things, you know? They don't tell you anything, and you imagine all this stuff."

Starkey changed the subject.

"Did Charlie talk about his job?"

She laughed and wiped at her eyes.

"Oh, God, when didn't he talk about it? You couldn't shut him up. Every call out was either an atom bomb or a practical joke. He liked to tell about the time they rolled out on a suspicious package that someone had left outside a barber shop. Charlie looked inside and he sees that it's a human head, just this head. When Charlie's supervisor asks what's in the box, Charlie tells him it looks like the barber took too much off the top."

Starkey smiled. She had never heard that story, and thought that Riggio had probably made it up.

"Charlie loved working with the Bomb Squad. He loved the people. They were like a family, he said."

Starkey nodded, remembered that feeling, and the pang of loss that came with losing it. And now she suspected that family of murder.

Starkey finished with the boxes, then went through the dresser and the closet without finding anything helpful. She had lost confidence that, working alone, she could discover something that would suggest a motive for Riggio's death. Maybe there was nothing to be found, and never had been.

"Well, maybe I was wrong about those reports. It doesn't look like Charlie brought them home after all."

"I'm sorry."

Starkey couldn't think of anything else to say or ask and was ready to leave. Angela had been saying how she was in a hurry to get home for her son, but now she lingered on the bed.

"Detective, could I ask you something else?"

"Of course."

"Were you and Charlie girlfriend and boyfriend?"

"No. I didn't know Charlie had a girlfriend."

Starkey glanced at the pictures in the mirror: Riggio and his parents, Riggio with his sisters and nieces and nephews.

"He had a girlfriend, but he never brought her to meet us. Here's this nice Italian boy, you're supposed to be married and have a million kids. My parents were always after him, you know, when are you going to get married, when are you going to settle down, when do we get to meet this girl?"

"What did Charlie say?"

Angela seemed embarrassed again.

"Well, some of the things he said, I got the impression she was married."

"Oh."

Angela nodded.

"Yeah. *Oh.*"

"I'm sorry. I didn't mean it like that."

"No, I understand. But it happens, right? I think it was hard for Charlie. Here's this young, good-looking guy, but he was heartfelt. I think she was married to someone Charlie worked with."

Angela met Starkey's eyes as if she was waiting for a reaction, but then she looked away.

"I probably shouldn't have said that, but if it's not you, I thought you might know her. I'd like to talk to her. I wouldn't make a problem with her husband or anything like that. I just thought we could talk about Charlie. It might be good."

"I'm sorry. I don't know anything about that."

Starkey wondered if the photo album held pictures that Riggio had wanted to keep hidden, pictures of a woman who was married to someone else that he couldn't keep out on the mirror.

Angela suddenly glanced at her watch and jumped up.

"Oh, shit. Now I really am late. I'm sorry, but I have to go. My son will be home soon."

"It's all right. I understand."

Starkey followed Angela down, but now her mind was racing for a way to get a view of Riggio's photo album.

By the time they reached the door, Todd was squirming in his mother's arms. He was tired and cranky and overdue for his nap. When Starkey saw the time Angela was having with him at the door, Starkey took her keys.

"Here, I'll get the door. That boy's a handful."

"It's like trying to hold a fish."

Starkey held the door to let Angela through. She pretended to lock the door, but unlocked it, instead. She closed it, then rattled the knob as if checking to make sure it was secure. Angela's arms still filled with squirming child, Starkey placed the keys in Angela's purse.

"Thanks again for trying to help, Angela. I feel a little silly that I got you out here and couldn't find the files. I was sure Charlie brought them home."

"If they turn up, I'll call."

Angela saw Starkey to the glass doors and let her out. Starkey walked out to her car, climbed behind the wheel, but did not start her car. Her heart was hammering. She told herself that what she was about to do was insane. Worse, it was illegal. A D.A. out to make an example of her could press for breaking and entering.

Five minutes later, Angela Wellow appeared on the service drive at the side of the apartment building in a white Honda Accord, turned south, and drove away. Starkey flicked her cigarette out the window, then crossed back to the apartment building just as a young man with a book bag was wrestling a mountain bike through the glass door. Starkey held the door for him.

"Don't be late for class."

"I'm always late. I was born late."

Starkey walked calmly to the second floor, where she let herself into Charlie Riggio's apartment. She took the stairs two at a time, going directly to the box with the photo album. Now that she was thinking in terms of an illicit affair, she wanted Riggio's phone bills and charge receipts, but had no idea which box held those things and was too frightened to take the time to find them. Starkey smiled grimly; she might have been a fearless bomb technician, but she was a chickenshit crook. She found the photo album, but didn't dare look at it there. It was too thick, and held too many photographs.

She took the book, this time locking the door behind herself, and hurried down to her car. She drove straight home and brought the photo album inside under her jacket as if it were pornography.

She sat with the album at the dining room table, turning the pages slowly, telling herself that the odds were so long as to be unimaginable, that Angela Wellow was probably wrong, and that to-morrow she would be back to square one, all alone in her belief that someone other than Mr. Red was behind Charlie's death.

Page after page were pictures that charted Charlie Riggio's life: Charlie playing high school football, Charlie with his buddies, Charlie with pretty young girls who looked anything but like the wives of cops, Charlie hunting, Charlie at the Police Academy, Charlie with his family. They were happy pictures; the type of pictures that a man kept because they made him smile.

It was near the end of the book where she found a picture taken at last year's Bomb Squad Chili Cookoff. She found the second like it taken at the Christmas party, and then, two pages later, a third that had been taken at a CCS barbeque that Kelso had thrown on the Fourth of July.

Starkey peeled the pictures from the album and put them on the table side by side, asking herself if they could really mean what she thought they meant. She told herself they couldn't; she told herself she was wrong, and reading too much into them, but what Angela Wellow had said hung over her like an ax.

. . . she's married to someone he works with.

The pictures were all the same, a man and a woman, arms around each other, smiling, a little too close, a little too familiar, a little too friendly.

Charlie Riggio and Suzie Leyton.

Dick Leyton's wife.

Starkey poured a tall gin and tonic, drank most of it. She felt angry, and betrayed. Leyton being a suspect was too big to get her arms around. Just thinking about it wore her down. Starkey decided to deal with it as if Leyton were just another part of the investigation. There was no other way to see it.

She went to her own collection of pictures and found a shot of Leyton that she'd taken at an LAPD Summer Festival Youth Camp. It was a crisp shot, a close-up showing Leyton in civilian clothes and sunglasses. She brought it to Kinko's, made several copies, adjusting the contrast until she had one that showed the best detail, then returned home where she phoned Warren Mueller. She didn't expect him to be in his office, but she tried him anyway. To Starkey's surprise, she got him on the first ring.

"I've got a favor to ask, Sergeant. I have a photograph that I want you to show the old man who lives in Tennant's duplex."

"Is it the guy in the hat?"

"It could be. Here's the thing, I don't want anyone else to see the picture. I want this kept between me and you."

Mueller hesitated.

"I'm not liking the way this sounds."

"It's about tracing Tennant's RDX. I don't want to tell you any more than that, and I am asking you not to ask."

"All this makes me wonder who's in your picture."

"Look, Mueller, if this is too hard, I'll drive up there and do it myself."

"Now, hold on."

"It's someone who would be hurt badly by this if I'm wrong, and I might be wrong. I'm asking you for a favor here, goddamnit, so what's it going to be?"

"This guy in your picture, he's LAPD, isn't he?"

Starkey couldn't bring herself to speak.

"Okay. Okay, I'll take care of it. You know what you're doing down there, Starkey? You gonna be okay with this?"

"I'm okay."

"All right. You fax up your picture. I'll go wait by the machine. If you're expecting to use this ID in court, I'm gonna have to make up a six-pack."

The suspect picture was never shown to witnesses by itself; the courts ruled this to be leading. Detectives were required to show a spread of pictures, hoping that the witness would identify the right one.

"That's fine. Now, one more thing. If we get a confirmation from your wit, I'm going to want to see Tennant about this. I'd like to do that tomorrow."

Mueller cleared his throat, hesitating.

"Hell, Starkey, I guess you didn't hear. Tennant's dead. I called Atascadero today to set up a little interview about his shop, you know? The silly sonofabitch blew his damned arms off and bled to death."

Starkey didn't know what to say.

"He blew off his arms? His arms were separated?"

The energy it took to do that was tremendous.

"Yeah. Man I talked to over there said it was a real mess."

"What did he use, Mueller? Christ, you can't make anything like that out of cleaning products."

"Sheriff's EOD is running the analysis. Guess we'll know in a day or two. Whatever the case, you can forget about getting anything from Tennant. He's a memory."

Starkey was slow to answer.

"I'll fax that picture now. If it doesn't come through clear, call back and I'll try again."

She gave him her home phone.

"Owe you one, Sergeant. Thanks."

"I'll collect. You can bet your split-tail bottom on that."

"Mueller, you're the most charming man I know."

"Kinda grows on you, doesn't it?"

"Yeah. Like anal warts."

Starkey gave Mueller a minute, then put the photocopy of Leyton through her fax. She waited for his call, but after a few silent minutes had passed, she figured that the photo had gone through okay.

She didn't know what else to do. She could take the photo to Lester Ybarra, but if he told Marzik she would have to explain. She needed to put Leyton in Silver Lake at the time of the detonation, but that meant questioning more people who she couldn't question. She knew that Leyton was at the scene when she arrived, but had he been there in the moment when someone had triggered the device?

Starkey's eye kept going to the computer, waiting silently on her dining room table. She had not turned it on since she turned it off last night. Now it seemed to watch her.

I did not kill Charles Riggio.

I know who did.

Starkey lit a cigarette, then went into the kitchen and made herself another drink. Sobriety had lasted all of two days. She went back into the dining room, turned on the computer, and signed on to Claudius.

Mr. Red did not jump out at her. The chat room was empty. She sipped her drink, smoked, and read through the boards. There were new posts, but nothing beyond the mundane chitchat of defective personalities. She finished her second drink, then made another. She left the computer on with Claudius's flaming head like a painting on her wall. She smoked a second cigarette. Starkey walked through her house, once stepping out the back door, twice stepping out the front. She thought about Pell, and she thought that she might one day like a persimmon tree. She didn't know what persimmons were like, but that didn't stop her from wanting the tree. Outside, the eastern sky purpled and time passed.

Starkey floated like that for almost two hours as the purple dimmed to black, and then she was rewarded.

WILL YOU ACCEPT A MESSAGE FROM MR. RED?

She opened the window.

MR. RED: **Am I Bergen?**

She stared at the line, then typed her answer.

HOTLOAD: **No. You are Mr. Red.**
MR. RED: **THANK YOU!!! We're finally on the same
page.**
HOTLOAD: **Is that important to you? Us being on
the same page?**

Red's hesitation left her with a grim satisfaction.

MR. RED: **Are you alone?**

HOTLOAD: Room full of cops here, babe. It's a spectator sport.

MR. RED: Ah. Then you must be naked.

HOTLOAD: If you start talking trash, I'll go away.

MR. RED: No, you won't, Carol Starkey. You have questions.

She did. She drew deep on the cigarette, then typed her question.

HOTLOAD: Who killed Riggio?

MR. RED: Didn't I?

HOTLOAD: You said no.

MR. RED: If I tell you, it will spoil the surprise.

HOTLOAD: I already know. I just want to see if our answers match.

MR. RED: If you knew, you would have made an arrest. You might suspect, but you don't know. I would tell you if you and I were the only ones here . . . but not in front of a room filled with cops.

Starkey laughed at the way he wrapped the conversation around to force her admission.

HOTLOAD: They left. We're alone now.

He hesitated again, and she felt a stab of hope that he might actually tell her.

MR. RED: Are we? Are we really alone?

HOTLOAD: I wouldn't lie.

MR. RED: Then I will tell you a secret. Just between you and me.

HOTLOAD: What?

She waited, but nothing came back. She thought he might be typing a long reply, but the minutes stretched until she finally realized that he wanted her to beg. His need to manipulate and control was textbook.

> HOTLOAD: **What's the big secret, Crimson Boy? I'm on a timer here.**
> MR. RED: **It isn't about Riggio.**
> HOTLOAD: **Then what?**
> MR. RED: **It will scare you.**
> HOTLOAD: **WHAT?????**

He paused again, and then his message appeared.

> MR. RED: **Pell is not who he seems. He is using you, Carol Starkey. He has been playing us against each other.**

The statement struck her like a board. It came from nowhere, jolting her like a head-on collision.

> HOTLOAD: **What do you mean?**

He didn't answer.

> HOTLOAD: **What does that mean, Pell is not who he seems?**

No answer.

> HOTLOAD: **How do you know Pell?**

Nothing.

> HOTLOAD: **Answer me!**

No answers came back. The window hung there, unchanging. His statement that Pell was not who he seemed haunted her. Her first impulse was to phone Pell, but she felt caught between them like a ship between the ocean and a storm, Mr. Red on one side, Pell the other.

During the days when Starkey served on the Bomb Squad, the ATF had maintained a liaison agent with LAPD in an office housed with CCS. Three weeks after Starkey returned from Bomb School in Alabama, Sugar had introduced her to Regal Phillips, the ATF liaison agent. Phillips was a overweight man with a friendly smile, who had retired near the end of Starkey's first year; they had worked together only occasionally during that year, but Sugar loved the older man, and Starkey sensed then that the feelings had run deep both ways. Phillips had visited Starkey twice during her time in the hospital, both visits ending with Phillips weeping after recounting stories about Sugar's exploits on the squad.

That final visit had been the last time Starkey had seen Regal Phillips, almost three years ago. She hadn't phoned him after the hospital because she couldn't be with Regal without being with Sugar, and that hurt too much.

Now, after all this time, she felt embarrassed as she listened to his phone ring.

When Regal answered, she said, "Reege, it's Carol Starkey."

"Lord, girl, how are you? I had it in my head that you didn't talk to black people anymore."

He sounded like the same old Reege, the warm voice revealing only a hint of surprise.

"Pretty good. Working. I'm on with CCS now."

"I heard that. I still got friends over there. I'm keeping tabs on you."

He laughed softly when he said it, his voice so full of affection that she felt ashamed of herself.

"Reege, ah, listen, I'm really sorry I haven't stayed in touch. It's hard for me that way."

"Don't worry about it, Carol. Things changed for a lot of people that day in the trailer park."

"You know about Charlie Riggio?"

"What I see on the news. You working on that?"

"That's right. Reege, this is an awkward thing for me to ask."

"Ask it."

"I'm working with an ATF agent that I, ah, have my doubts about. I was wondering if you could look into him for me. You know what I mean?"

"No, Carol, I don't think that I do."

"I want to know who he is, Reege. I guess I'm asking you if I can trust him."

"What's his name?"

"Jack Pell."

Phillips told her that it might take a day or two, but that he would call back soon. Starkey thanked him, then hung up and doused the lights. She did not sleep. She didn't even get into bed. Starkey stayed on the couch in the dim light, waiting until morning, wondering how a man she now trusted so little could mean so much to her.

Pell

Earlier that day, when Pell left Barrigan's, he squinted against the nu-clear California sun. The light was so bright that it felt like an ax blade wedged between his eyes. Even the sunglasses didn't help.

Pell sat in his car, trying to figure out what to do. The look of hurt on her face had left him feeling like a dog. He knew that she was right: He was so obsessed by Mr. Red that he couldn't see anything else, but he had the fragment with her name on it. He had wanted to reach across the table and tell her everything, tell her the truth. He had wanted to open himself, because he had also been closed, and thought that she might be the only one who could understand, but he couldn't be sure. He had wanted to tell her of his growing feelings for her, but there was only Mr. Red. He no longer knew where Red ended and he began.

His head began to throb.

"Jesus. Not again."

Soft gray shapes floated up from the dashboard, from the windows, from the hood of his car.

It was happening more frequently now. It would only get worse.

15

STARKEY LEFT HER house well before dawn. She had had it with the emptiness of the quiet rooms, the conflicting thoughts about Pell and Dick Leyton and her shitty life. She told herself to get her head in the case, so she left the thoughts and emptiness, and made her way across town.

She needed to determine Dick Leyton's whereabouts at the time of the blast and thought that Hooker might have noted Leyton's TOA in the casebook. Starkey didn't bother to shower. She changed clothes, lit a fresh cigarette, and drove.

Spring Street was a tomb. Hers was the only car on the parking level. Not even the Fugitive Section had shown for work.

Starkey said fuck it and brought her cigarette into the office. She could always blame the cleaning crew.

The casebook was on Marzik's desk where she remembered it, but Hooker had made no note of Leyton's arrival time, just that he was present. Starkey pulled the box of videotapes from under Hooker's desk. She found the copy of the enhanced tape that Bennell had made for them, along with the news tape she remembered as having the widest angles, and brought them upstairs to the video room. She had watched those damned tapes so many times she knew them by heart, but she had always been looking for the man in the baseball cap; she had never looked at the cops.

The image quality of the enhanced tape was crappy on the VCR just as Bennell had warned, but she watched it anyway, searching the perimeter of the cordon for Dick Leyton. She remembered that he was wearing a polo shirt, that he looked as if he'd just come from home.

She watched the tape, then watched it again, but it was always the same: Riggio approached the box, the explosion, then Buck ran forward to strip away his partner's helmet. Starkey gave up trying to find Leyton in the moments prior to the explosion because the clips were too short and indistinct. She concentrated on that time after the blast, figuring that if Leyton were at the scene, he would have run forward to see about his man. She keyed the tape to the explosion, and watched again. *Bang!* For almost twelve seconds of real time after the blast, Buck and Charlie were alone in the frame. Then the paramedics' ambulance raced up beside them from the bottom of the picture. Two LAFD paramedics jumped out, taking Buck's place. Four seconds later, a single uniformed officer ran forward from the left side of the frame, and two more uniformed officers entered from the right. The officer from the left appeared to be trying to get Buck to sit down or move away, but Buck shook him off. Three more officers entered the frame from the bottom, turning back almost at once to head off two men in street clothes. Other men in street clothes entered from the right. Now a second ambulance moved into the frame, followed by more people on foot. Two of the figures appeared to be wearing polo shirts, but she didn't recognized them. Then the tape ended.

"Shit!"

Something about the tape bothered her, but she wasn't sure what. She was seeing something, yet not seeing it. The answer was in the tape. Starkey cursed the news station for not running the camera longer, then went back to CCS.

Starkey decided to ask Buck. She left CCS before the other detectives arrived and made her way to Glendale. She didn't know whether or not Buck had duty that day, so she stopped at a diner to wait until seven when the Bomb Squad receptionist, Louise Mendoza, arrived. Mendoza, who would know the duty roster, usually arrived before the bomb techs.

At five minutes before seven, Starkey phoned.

"Louise, it's Carol Starkey. Does Buck have duty today?"

"He's back in the shed. You want me to put you through?"

"I just wanted to know if he was there. I'm on my way over to see him."

"I'll let him know."

"One other thing, Louise. Ah, is Dick there?"

"Yeah, but if you want to talk to him you'd better let me put you through. He has to go down to Parker this morning."

"That's okay. It'll keep."

Starkey pulled into the Glendale PD parking lot ten minutes later. She found Buck and Russ Daigle in the shed, the brick building at the ass end of the parking lot where the squad practiced with the de-armer and the robots. They were standing over the Andrus robot, drinking coffee and frowning. Both men smiled when they saw her.

"Damn thing's pulling to the right. You try to make the damn thing go straight ahead, it veers off to the right. You got any idea what's wrong?"

"It's a Republican."

Daigle, a staunch Republican, laughed loudly.

"Buck? Could I see you for a moment?"

Buck joined her at the door, the two of them stepping outside.

She told him that she had come about the enhanced tape, that they were ready for him to take a look. That was her excuse for the conversation.

"I'll look if you want, but I didn't see anything in those other tapes. Jesus, I don't know if I can stomach it again, seeing Charlie like that."

She wanted to turn the conversation to Leyton.

"There's no rush. Maybe I should ask Dick if he saw anything. He might be able to pick out someone."

Daggett nodded.

"You might. He was back there behind the cordon."

Starkey felt sick. She told herself to be professional. This is why she was here. This is why she was a cop.

"When did he get on scene?"

"I dunno, maybe twenty minutes before Charlie went out, something like that."

"I'll talk to him about it."

Starkey walked back across the parking lot, feeling as if her legs were enormous stilts, pushing her to a height that left her dizzy. She could barely get into her car, taking forever to fold the stilts the way a mantis folds its legs. Nothing fit anymore. She stared at the Bomb Squad. Leyton's office was there. The box with Charlie Riggio's things was still beneath Daigle's desk. She thought of his cell phone there. If Riggio and Susan Leyton had been lovers, Starkey thought that he would probably have called her often. He would have snuck calls to her during the day when Dick was at work, and there would be the record of it in his phone bills. Starkey was surprised at how uninvolved she felt when that thought came to her. Maybe it was just another step along the case. It was as if nothing mattered very much except building the evidence that she could bring to Kelso, and prove Pell wrong.

She took out her own cell phone, and called Angela Wellow. This time she told her the truth.

* * *

Starkey sat with Angela Wellow in the quiet of her home, the two of them sitting on the edge of a tattered couch. Riggio's photo album was on the couch between them; Todd was sleeping facedown on the floor. Angela glanced at the album again and again, as if there were some explanation beyond what Starkey was giving. She rubbed her palm on her thigh.

"I don't know about this. I don't know what to think when someone says something like this. You're telling me that Charlie was murdered?"

"I'm investigating that possibility. That's why I need Charlie's phone bills, Angela. I need to see who he was calling."

Angela stared at her. Starkey knew what was coming. When Starkey gave back the album and explained that she had gone to Charlie's condo under false pretenses, Angela had listened to it all without saying a word. Now she was about to say it.

"Why did you have to lie to me yesterday? Why couldn't you just say?"

Starkey tried to look her in the eyes, but couldn't.

"I don't know what else to do. I'm sorry."

"Jesus."

Angela walked over to her little boy, stared down at him like she wasn't sure who he was.

"What do I tell my parents?"

Starkey ignored that. She didn't want to talk about the details of what was happening. She didn't want to get sidetracked. She wanted to keep moving forward until this thing was tied down, and she could bring it to Kelso.

"I need his phone bills, Angela. Can we please go look for his phone bills."

Angela said, "Todd? Todd, wake up, honey. We have to go out."

Angela lifted her sleeping boy onto her shoulder, then turned on Starkey with angry eyes.

"You can follow me over there. I don't want you going in Charlie's house again."

*   *   *

Starkey waited outside Riggio's building for almost an hour until Angela Wellow came out the glass doors with a handful of white envelopes.

"It took me forever to find them. I'm sorry."

"That's all right. I appreciate this, Angela."

"No, you don't. I don't know what you're doing or why, but you don't know me well enough to appreciate what I'm doing."

Angela left her with the envelopes, walking away without another word.

Starkey struck a cigarette, exhaling a cloud that settled in the car even with the windows open. She liked the taste of it, and the way smoking made her feel. She didn't see what all the whining was about. So what if you got cancer.

She opened Charlie Riggio's phone bills and there it was, so obvious that it jumped out at her. She didn't know the Leytons' home number, but she didn't need to know it. Charlie had called the same number in the same 323 area code two and three times every day, sometimes as many as six or seven calls, going back for months.

Starkey put the bills aside, finished her cigarette, then took out her own phone. She checked the number again, then dialed.

A familiar woman's voice.

"Hello?"

"Hello, Susan."

Starkey felt tired.

"I'm sorry. Who?"

Starkey paused.

"Susan?"

"I'm sorry. You have the wrong number."

Starkey looked at the number again, making sure she had dialed correctly. She had.

"This is Carol Starkey. I'm calling for Susan Leyton."

"Oh, hi, Detective Starkey. You dialed the wrong number. This is Natalie Daggett."

16

NATALIE DAGGETT SAID, "Are you still there? Hello?"

Starkey checked the phone numbers again. It was the same number; multiple calls every day for months.

"I'm here. I'm sorry, Natalie. I was expecting someone else. It's taking me a minute to switch gears."

Natalie laughed.

"That happens to me, too. I have these senior moments all the time."

"Are you going to be home for the next hour or so?"

"Buck isn't home. He went back to work."

"I know. I'll be stopping by to see you. It won't take long."

"What do you want to see me about?"

"It won't take long, Natalie. I'll see you in a few minutes."

"What is this about?"

"It's about Buck. I'm working on a little surprise for him. Because of what happened to Charlie. Sort of a welcome back party."

"Is that why you were calling Susan?"

"That's right. Dick is the one who suggested it."

"Oh. Oh, okay. I guess so."

"I'll see you in a few minutes."

"Okay."

Starkey closed her phone, then put it aside. Not Dick, but Buck Daggett. She had searched the tapes for the killer again and again, and he was right there in plain sight every time, hiding in open view, waiting for his partner to get over the bomb. Starkey thought about Dana again, and the perception puzzle. It was all in how you looked at it. Now she realized what had bothered her about the tape. Buck hadn't cleared the area for a secondary device. He should have pulled Riggio away from the scene before stripping off his armor, just as he had pulled Carol away from the trailer; she'd seen that on the tape of her own death, but he hadn't pulled Riggio. All bomb techs were trained to clear the area for a secondary, but Buck knew there wasn't a secondary. It was always there, glaring at her, and she'd missed it.

Starkey made the long drive to Monterey Park in good time. She didn't hurry. Starkey was confident that Natalie did not know that her husband had murdered her lover. Buck had planned the murder far too carefully to risk confessing to his wife, even if to punish her.

Starkey was still relieved when she pulled into the Daggetts' drive and saw that Buck's Toyota 4-Runner wasn't home. She put on her best cop face before she went to the door, the same face that she had used when she confronted the father in Venice with his little girl's thumb.

Starkey rang the bell.

Natalie looked drawn when she answered the door. Starkey thought that she probably hadn't been sleeping.

"Hi, Natalie. Thanks for seeing me."

Starkey followed her into a small dining room, where they sat at a bare table. The Lawn-Boy mower was still sitting in the backyard. Buck had never mowed the lawn. Natalie didn't offer something to drink, just as she hadn't offered anything the last time Starkey was there.

"What kind of surprise did you have in mind?"

Starkey took the phone bills from her purse and put them on the table. Natalie glanced at them without comprehension.

"Natalie, I'm sorry, but I'm not here about a party. I went through Charlie's things and found some things I need to ask you about."

Starkey could see the fear rise when she mentioned Charlie's name.

"I thought this was about Buck?"

Starkey pushed the bills across the table, turning them so that Natalie could read them.

"These are Charlie's cell phone bills. You see your number there? You see how many calls he made? Now, I already know the answer to this, but I need to hear you say it, Natalie. Were you and Charlie having an affair?"

Natalie stared at the pages without touching them. She sat absolutely still as her nose turned red and tears bled from her eyes.

"Natalie, were you? Were you and Charlie in love?"

Natalie nodded. She looked twelve years old, and Starkey's heart filled with an embarrassing ache, and shame.

"How long were you involved?"

"Since last year."

"Please speak up."

"Since last year."

"Does Buck know?"

"Of course not. He would be so hurt."

Starkey took back the telephone bills and returned them to her jacket.

"Okay. I'm sorry I had to ask, but there it is."

"Are you going to tell Buck?"

Starkey stared at the woman, then lied.

"No, Natalie. This isn't something I'm going to tell Buck. You don't have to worry about that."

"I just made a mistake with Charlie. That's what it was, a mistake. Everybody's entitled to a mistake."

Starkey left her like that, walking out to her car in the fierce heat, then driving away to Spring Street.

Buck

Buck Daggett didn't like it that Starkey had been spending so much time in Glendale. Her asking so many questions about that bastard, Riggio, made him nervous. Especially when he'd heard about her wanting to get to know Riggio now that Riggio was dead. What in hell was that about? Starkey had never given a damn about Riggio or anyone else since that fucking bomb in the trailer park. She had turned into a lush and a has-been, and now she was supposed to be Ms. Maudlin?

Buck had been proud of himself that he'd built in the connection between Mr. Red and Starkey. He had wanted to keep the investigation as far from Riggio as possible, but just his rotten luck the only piece of her name that had been found was the goddamned S, letting them think it was part of Charles. Still, he'd thought everything was going to be fine when the feds rolled in and everyone started chasing their tails about Mr. Red, but now it looked as if that bitch, Starkey, had tumbled to the truth anyway. Or at least suspected it.

Buck Daggett had still been fucking around with the Andrus robot when Natalie called. The stupid bim couldn't help telling him that Starkey was coming by because they were going to toss a surprise party for him. To cheer him up. Ha. Buck had hung up and barely made it to the toilet before he'd puked up his guts, then he'd raced home to see for himself.

As Starkey drove away from his house, Buck crouched in his neighbor's yard, watching her. He didn't know how much she had on him yet, but he knew she suspected him, and that was enough.

Buck decided to kill her.

17

STARKEY PHONED MUELLER from her car, trying to catch him at his office, but he was gone. She left word on his voice mail that the man in the photo was no longer a suspect, and that she would be faxing up a new image. She phoned Beth Marzik next.

"Beth, I want you to get together a six-pack and meet me at the flower shop. Call Lester and make sure he's there. If he's on a delivery, tell them to have him come back."

"I was just getting ready to go to lunch."

"Damnit, Beth, lunch will keep. I want a mix of Anglos and

Latins in their forties, just as Lester described. Don't tell anyone, Beth. Just get it together and meet me at Lester's."

"Listen, you can't just drop this on me. Who am I putting together the six-pack for? Do you have a suspect?"

"Yes."

Starkey hung up before Marzik could ask who. Time was now a factor. She could not trust that Natalie wouldn't tell Buck about her visit, or about her interest in Charlie Riggio. She didn't fear that Buck would flee; her concern was that he would move to destroy evidence that might be necessary in the case against him.

She drove faster now, swinging past her house for a snapshot of Buck Daggett before turning toward Silver Lake. Like the shot of Dick Leyton, it was a picture of Buck in civilian clothes. When she reached the flowershop, Marzik and Lester were talking together on the sidewalk. Marzik left Lester, and walked over as Starkey got out of her car. She had the six-pack sheet in a manila envelope.

"You want to tell me what's going on here? That kid's old man is raising nine kinds of hell."

"Let me see the sheet."

The six-pack was a paper sandwich with places for six photographs like a page from a photo album. Detective bureaus kept files of them based on age, race, and type, most of the pictures being file photos of police officers. Starkey pulled out one of the six pictures, then fitted in the picture of Buck Daggett.

Marzik gripped Starkey's arm.

"Tell me you're joking."

"I'm not joking, Beth."

Starkey brought the sheet to Lester. She explained that she wanted him to look at each picture carefully before making his decision, then asked if any of the men pictured here was the man that Lester saw using the telephone. Marzik watched Lester so closely that Lester asked her what was wrong.

"Nothing, pal. Just look at the pictures."

"None of these guys are wearing hats."

"Look at their faces, Lester. Think back to the guy you saw on the phone. Could any of these men be him?"

"I think it's him."

Lester pointed out Buck Daggett.

Marzik walked away.

"Is she okay?"

"She's fine, Lester. Thanks."

"Did I pick the right one?"

"None of the answers are right, Lester. Some are just more wrong than others."

Marzik was staring at the sidewalk when Starkey joined her.

"You going to tell me now?"

Starkey laid it out, and then they called Kelso, telling him that they were on their way in. Starkey asked if he would have Hooker meet them. Kelso demanded to know why Starkey wanted to see them together.

"I have some additional evidence in the case, Barry. I need your advice on how to proceed with it."

The ploy of asking for his guidance worked. Kelso told her that he and Santos would be waiting.

Marzik was still leaning against her car when Starkey got off the phone.

Marzik said, "This is going to sound stupid, Carol, but can we take one car? I don't want to ride back alone."

"It doesn't sound stupid."

When they reached Spring Street, Starkey didn't bother wrestling her car in the parking garage. They left it in the red zone out front and used the elevator.

For the first time that she could remember, Kelso's computer was turned off. He was waiting behind his desk with his fingers steepled, as if he had been like that since she called. Santos was on his couch, looking like a kid who'd been called in to see the principal. Carol thought he looked tired. They probably all looked tired.

Kelso said, "What is it, Carol?"

"It isn't Mr. Red, Barry. It was never Mr. Red."

Kelso raised his hands, shaking his head even as she spoke.

"We covered that, didn't we? The signatures are identical—"

Marzik snapped, "Barry, just *listen*."

Santos arched his eyebrows, surprised. Kelso stared at her, then spread his hands.

"I'm listening."

Starkey went on.

"Barry, the signatures are *not* identical. Almost, but *not*. If you don't believe me, call Rockville yourself and ask the ATF."

Santos said, "What will they tell him?"

"That the Silver Lake bomb is *different*. They will *suggest* that the person who built the Silver Lake device was working from an ATF bomb analysis because the one deviation from the other devices was an element that was *not* included in those reports."

Starkey took it one step at a time, never mentioning Buck Daggett until the end. She went through the difference in the bomb devices, then the similarities, and that the builder would need to find a source of RDX in order to mix the Modex Hybrid that Mr. Red favored.

"RDX is the hardest of the components to find, Barry. The only person in this area in recent history who's had any was Dallas Tennant. If you were looking to find some, you would go to him. Beth and I found Tennant's shop. A man similar in description to the individual who made our 911 report was seen there about a month ago. I believe he went there for Tennant's RDX. I don't know how this man learned of Tennant's shop. I don't know if he discovered it the way Beth and I did, through a property search, or if he made a deal of some kind with Tennant. We can't ask Tennant because Tennant is now dead."

"What man?"

Starkey plowed on without answering. She believed that if she accused Buck Daggett before laying out the supporting evidence, the meeting would become a shouting match.

Starkey held up the six-pack, but didn't yet give it to him.

"We showed this six-pack to Lester Ybarra. Lester identified one of these men as the man who placed the call. We'll have to show a similar six-pack to the witness up in Bakersfield to see if they confirm."

She handed the sheet to Kelso and pointed out Buck Daggett's picture.

"Lester identified that man."

Kelso shook his head and looked up.

"He made a mistake. That's all there is to it."

Starkey put Riggio's phone bills on top of the six-pack.

"These are Charlie Riggio's cell phone bills. Look at every phone number I've marked. That's Buck Daggett's home phone number. Riggio and Natalie Daggett were involved. Natalie Daggett confirmed this involvement to me less than an hour ago. I believe that Buck found out, and murdered Charlie because of it."

Hooker sighed loudly.

"Oh, my Lord."

Kelso's jaw flexed. He went to the window, looked out, then came back and leaned against his desk with his arms crossed.

"Who else knows this, Carol?"

"Only the people in this room."

"Did you tell Natalie that you suspect Buck of the murder?"

"No."

Kelso sighed again, then went back behind his desk.

"Okay, we can't let this sit. If Buck has explanations for these things, he can make them and clear this up."

Marzik grunted, and Kelso's eyes flashed angrily.

"You think this is easy, Detective? *I've known this man for ten years*. This isn't just some fucking collar."

Starkey had never heard Barry Kelso swear.

Jorge said, "No, sir. It's not."

Kelso glanced at Santos, then took another breath and leaned back.

"I'll have to notify Assistant Chief Morgan. Starkey, I'll want you with me. He might want to see us, and I'm damned well sure he'll have questions. This is goddamned terrible, a Los Angeles police officer involved in something like this. We'll have to bring in Dick Leyton. We're not going to roll over there and arrest one of his people without telling him what's happening. As soon as I talk to Morgan and Leyton, we'll get this done."

Starkey found herself liking Barry Kelso. She wanted to say something.

"Lieutanant, I'm sorry."

Kelso rubbed at his face.

"Carol, you don't have anything to be sorry for. I want to tell you that this is good work, but it doesn't seem like the thing to say."

"Yes, sir. I understand."

Penance

BUCK DIDN'T GO back to Glendale. He phoned Dick Leyton to tell him that he'd left early for the day and wouldn't be back. The real reason for the call was to get a sense of what Leyton knew. If Leyton considered Buck a suspect, Buck was going to hire the best damned attorney he could find and ride it out straight down the middle. But Leyton was relaxed and friendly, and Buck was willing to bet the farm that Starkey had kept her suspicions to herself.

And that's what he was doing, betting the farm.

Buck still had almost seven pounds of Modex Hybrid, plus

components left over from copycatting Mr. Red's bomb. He convinced himself that Starkey hadn't yet gathered enough evidence to make her move, which gave him hope. If he acted fast enough and took her out before she could develop her case, he might still get out of this.

After he spoke with Leyton, Buck concocted an elaborate list of errands to get Natalie out of the house, then went home. She seemed strained, probably from Starkey's visit and questions, but he pretended not to notice. He gave her the list, kicked her out, then forced himself to calm down and think it through again. He was desperate, and scared; he knew that desperate and scared men make mistakes.

When Buck felt composed, and absolutely convinced that killing Starkey was the only way out, he said, "Well, get to it, then."

Buck kept the Modex Hybrid and the remaining components in a large Igloo cooler out in the garage. He backed his 4-Runner out to give himself room, then shut the overhead door so no one could see him from the street. He opened the side door that let onto his backyard for air and turned on a utility fan; the Modex sublimated vapors that were toxic.

Buck pulled the cooler from the high shelf where it was out of Natalie's reach and brought it to his workbench. The remaining Modex was in a large, nonreactive glass jar. It was dark gray in color and looked like window putty. He wore vinyl gloves as he laid out the components so as not to leave fingerprints, but also to avoid getting the Modex on his skin. The shit could kill you dead as lead just from handling it.

The sudden voice in Buck's backyard damn near made him piss his pants.

"Yo yo yo, whasup, whasup? Anybody home?"

Buck threw a towel over his bench, and went to the door. He had thought it was a black guy from the voice, but this kid was white.

"What do you want?"

"Be lookin' to earn a little extra bank, my man. Saw the yard was in, shall we say, disarray? Thought I'd offer my landscaping services."

"I'll mow it myself, thanks anyway. Now I've got to get back to work."

"Looks like that ain't exactly on your immediate agenda, if you see what I'm sayin'. Help a brother who wants to earn a living instead of do crime."

Buck's head began to throb. Now that he looked at him, this kid wasn't a kid. He looked to be in his late twenties.

"Help yourself by getting out of here, asshole. I said I was busy."

The kid took a step back, but didn't look scared.

"Yowza! Guess you be handin' out walkin' papers. Feets, do yo stuff!"

"Are you fuckin' crazy?"

"Nah, Mr. Daggett, I'm just tryin' to have a good time. Sorry I bothered you."

Buck caught the name right away.

"How'd you know my name?"

"Chinaman across the street told me. I tried to cut his place first, but he told me to come over here. He said your place always looks like shit."

"Well, fuck him, too. Now let me get back to work."

Buck watched the kid walk away, then went back into his garage, hating the Chinaman across the street. Buck didn't see the kid come back, didn't see the hard thing that knocked him to his knees. Even if he had seen it coming, it would not have mattered. It was already too late.

Buck was never fully unconscious. He knew that something had hit him, and that he was hit twice more after he went down. He saw the kid over him, but he couldn't raise his arms to protect himself. The kid handcuffed him to the workbench, then disappeared from view.

Buck tried to speak, but his mouth didn't work any better than his arms and legs. Buck grew frightened that he was paralyzed, and cried.

After a while, the kid came back and shook him.

"You awake?"

The kid looked into his eyes, then slapped him. The kid had a

thin, gaunt face like a ferret. Buck noticed now for the first time that
his scalp was very pale; he hadn't been bald for long.

"You awake? C'mon, I know I didn't hit you hard enough to kill
you. Get your fuckin' act together."

"I don't have any money."

"I don't want your money, dumbass. You should be so lucky, I
only wanted your money."

Buck's ears were ringing, a steady high-pitched sound that did
not diminish. Once, during a high school baseball game, he had col-
lided with another player and gotten a concussion. He remembered it
feeling like this.

"Then what do you want? You want the truck, the keys are in
my pocket. Take it."

"What I'm going to *take* is the rest of this Modex. What I *want*
is to teach you a lesson."

Buck wasn't thinking at his best. It surprised him that this kid
made up like some kind of black rapper would know about the Modex,
or even what it was.

"I don't understand."

The kid took Buck's face in his hands and leaned close.

"You stole my fucking work, you cocksucker. You *pretended* to
be me. Can you spell . . . *error in judgment*?"

"I don't know what in hell you're talking about."

"Maybe this will help you understand."

The kid went to the other end of the bench. When he came
back, he had one of the pipes. Wires led into an open end; the other
end had been capped. He waved it under Buck's nose to let Buck
catch the sharp smell of the Modex inside, and in that moment, Buck
grew scared.

"*Now* do you know who I am?"

Buck knew, and felt so scared in that moment of knowing that
the urine ran out of him in a rush of warmth.

"Please don't kill me. Please. Take the fucking Modex and go.
Please don't kill me. I'm sorry I pretended I was you but you see I had
to kill that motherfucker who was fucking my wife and—"

Mr. Red put a hand over Buck's mouth.

"Chill. Just be cool. Relax."

Buck nodded.

"You okay now?"

Buck nodded.

"Okay. Now listen."

Mr. Red sat cross-legged on the hard concrete in front of him, holding the bomb in his lap as if it was a playful kitten.

"You listening?"

"Yes."

"I'm not going to kid you about this, I am seriously pissed off you tried to make everyone think it was me who killed that guy, but here's your shot. You got one shot, and here it is."

Buck waited, but Mr. Red was waiting for him to ask.

"What? What's my shot?"

"Tell me what Carol Starkey knows."

John walked out to the stolen car he'd left on the street. The Chinaman was nowhere to be seen. He had left Buck at his bench, very much alive, but unconscious. John had splashed some water on Daggett and slapped his face to bring him around. When he saw that Buck was waking up, he left.

John climbed behind the wheel, started his car, and shook his head. It was a hot day on a crappy street in the middle of Shitsville, U.S.A. How could people live like this? John let his car creep down the street as he counted to a hundred. When he reached one hundred, he figured Buck was fully awake.

That's when he pressed the silver button.

Spring Street

Marzik and Santos phoned their homes, Santos telling his wife and Marzik her mother that they would be late. Starkey could tell from

Marzik's reaction that her mother wasn't happy about it. After those calls, the three detectives sat at their desks, alone with their thoughts. At one point, Jorge asked if anyone wanted a fresh pot of coffee, but neither Starkey nor Marzik answered. He did not make the coffee.

Marzik was the first one bored with the wait, and expressed her annoyance.

"What in hell is taking so long? We don't need Parker Center to rubber-stamp this thing. Let's just go pick up the sonofabitch."

Santos frowned at her.

"He wants Morgan to sign off, is all. It's politics."

"Kelso's such a chickenshit."

"Maybe Morgan isn't there. Maybe he can't reach Lieutenant Leyton."

"Oh, screw that."

Starkey had decided to head for the stairwell with a cigarette when Reege Phillips called. The tone of his voice was careful and measured, which immediately put her on edge. She didn't want Hooker and Marzik to hear.

Starkey said, "I don't know that I can talk right now, Reege. Will this keep?"

"I don't think so, Carol. You got a problem on your hands."

"Ah, can I call you right back?"

"You want to change phones?"

"That's right. I've got your number."

"Okay. I'm right here."

Starkey hung up, told Santos and Marzik she was going for a smoke, and brought her purse. When she was in the stairwell, she called Phillips on her cell phone. Just pressing the numbers left her feeling sick.

"What do you mean, that I have a problem?"

"Jack Pell isn't an ATF agent. He used to be, but not anymore."

"That can't be right. Pell had bomb analysis reports from Rockville. He had a spook at Cal Tech doing work for us."

"Just listen. Pell was an ATF field agent working for the Violent Crime Task Force, attached to the Organized Crime Division of the Justice Department. Twenty months ago, he was in a warehouse in Newark, New Jersey, trying to get the goods on some Chinese AKs coming up from Cuba. You read those reports he gave you?"

"Yes."

"Think Newark."

"Mr. Red's first bomb."

"Pell was in that warehouse when it went off. The concussion caused something in his eyes called commotio retinae. You catch it in time, you can fix it with the laser. Pell's didn't show up until later, and then it was too late."

"What does that mean, too late?"

"He's going blind. Way the man explained it is that the retinas are pulling away from his optic nerves, and there's nothing they can do to stop it. So the Bureau retired him. Now you're telling me he's acting like he's still on the job. You got a rogue agent on your hands, Carol. He's hunting down the bastard who took his eyes. You call the FO and get them in on this before Pell hurts somebody."

Starkey leaned against the wall, feeling numb.

"Carol? You there?"

"I'll take care of it, Reege. Thank you."

"You want me to get the office on this?"

"No. No, I'll do it. Listen, I've gotta go, Reege. We have something here."

"You watch out for that guy, Carol. He's looking to kill that sonofabitch. No tellin' what he might do. He might even kill you."

After she ended the call, Starkey finished her cigarette, then went back into the squad room. She must have looked odd.

Marzik said, "What's wrong with you?"

"Nothing."

Finally, Kelso's door opened and Kelso stepped out. Starkey could see that something was wrong with him, but Marzik was already halfway to the stairs, muttering.

"It's about goddamned time."

"Beth, wait."

Kelso stared at them. He didn't speak; he didn't move for the longest time.

Santos said, "What is it, Lieutenant?"

Kelso cleared his throat. His jaw worked as if he were trying to make spit.

"Detectives, the San Gabriel police were notified that an explosion occurred at Buck's home. He was pronounced dead at the scene."

18

BY THE TIME they reached Daggett's home, the San Gabriel Fire Department had the fire out. The garage and the back side of the house were still venting steam, but the Sheriff's bomb investigators were already walking the scene. Starkey wanted to walk with them, but the commander of the Sheriff's Bomb Squad refused to clear her onto the site until the body had been removed. Only Kelso was allowed in the rear. Dick Leyton had arrived a few minutes before them.

Starkey, Marzik, and Santos stood in a tight knot in the front yard, Santos talking to burn off the nervous energy.

"Do you think he killed himself? That's what happens when you get close, you know?"

"I don't know."

"You hear that a lot with officers. They realize they're about to take the fall, bang, they kill themselves."

Starkey, feeling bad enough, walked away.

"I wonder if he killed his wife, too."

Marzik put a hand on his shoulder.

"Jorge? Shut the fuck up."

Starkey's first thought had also been suicide, but that was something they might never know unless Daggett left a note. If he didn't, the rubble would be sifted, the frag collected, the device reconstructed as with any other bomb. They would try to place the moment of detonation and determine if it had been accidental, or by design. Starkey knew it would all be a matter of guesswork.

Waiting there on the street, Starkey's thoughts drifted back to Pell. She considered paging him, but didn't know what she would say if he returned her call. She put it out of her head. She was getting good at that, putting things out of her head.

After a while, Kelso came up the drive past Buck's 4-Runner and waved them to join him.

"How many bodies?"

"Just Buck. It looks like Natalie wasn't home. We don't yet know if she left before it happened or after, but her car is missing."

Starkey felt some of her tension ease, though not much. She had been worried that Buck and Natalie had gone together.

Kelso looked at Starkey.

"The thinking now is that it was a suicide. I want you to be ready for that, Carol. We can't be sure yet, but that's what it looks like."

Marzik said, "Why?"

"He wrote something on the wall above his workbench. The spray paint is still tacky. We can't be sure it's a suicide note, but it could be."

Starkey took a deep breath.

"Does it mention me?"

"No. All it says is, 'the truth hurts.' That's all it says."

The San Gabriel coroner investigators wheeled a gurney bearing a blue plastic body bag to their van. The bag was misshapen and wet.

Kelso started back down the drive.

"Come on. We can go back now. I want to warn you all that it's a mess. His body was badly dislocated. Also, I want you to remember that this is not our crime scene. The Sheriff's investigators are talking to Dick Leyton now, and they will want to talk to us. Stay close."

Santos looked sad.

"So Carol was right."

Marzik frowned at him.

"Of course she was right, you idiot."

"I was hoping that . . . even with everything we know, I guess I was hoping she was wrong."

Marzik stopped, and waved them on.

"Screw it. I don't want to see all that blood. I'm going to stay out here."

They walked back along the drive past the firemen and the San Gabriel Bomb Squad. Under other circumstances, at another crime scene, Starkey would have talked to these people, but she ignored them. Dick Leyton was in the backyard with a couple of San Gabriel suits that Starkey took to be Sheriff's investigators. Kelso and Santos joined them, leaving Starkey alone. She was glad for that. She didn't want to look at these things, and think the things that she was thinking, and have to talk to anyone. She wished she hadn't heard all that crap about suicide because now she was feeling guilty about it.

The drive and the buildings were wet. The firemen were cranking in their hoses, moving in teams around Buck's 4-Runner and away from the garage. Starkey stepped off the drive to make way for them and felt the water squish up around her shoes. The aluminum garage door had been pulled out of its frame by the fire department. Starkey could see that it had been down at the time of the detonation by the way the aluminum panels were bowed outward. The firemen would have wanted to raise it to get water on the flames, but couldn't; they had probably set grappling hooks to pull it away. Inside the garage, the Sheriff's bomb investigators were sifting and photographing the debris exactly as Starkey and her people had done in Silver Lake. The air in the garage was damp, and heavy with the scent of burned wood.

The spray-painted words were above his bench.

THE TRUTH HURTS

They were red.

"You one of the L.A. people?"

Starkey showed her badge.

"Yeah. CCS. You mind if I look?"

"Just tell us before you touch anything, okay?"

Starkey nodded.

A half-moon shape like a jagged crown of splinters was blown out of Buck's workbench. Wooden shrapnel sprouted from the inner garage walls like porcupine quills. Much of the bench was charred from the fire, but not the area shattered by the blast. Something had hit the far wall and left a red smear. Starkey concentrated on the painted words. THE TRUTH HURTS. It could mean anything or nothing. What truth? The truth that was about to come out? The truth that his wife loved another man? That Pell had lied to Starkey, and used her?

Starkey said, "How do you call the scene?"

"Too early for that."

"I know it's too early, but I haven't seen the body. You have, so you probably have an idea."

The investigator didn't stop what he was doing to offer his opinion. Like any investigator, he wanted to finish his work and get the hell out.

"Judging from the way he came apart, I'd say he was right on top of it, there at his bench. His lower extremities are fine except for the wood frag they caught. Most of the damage was in his chest and abdomen. He was damn near eviscerated, which suggests he had the device against his stomach when it went off. If it was a suicide, well, I guess he figured tucking it into his stomach was the way to go. If it was accidental, he was probably setting the leg wires into the detonator and he caught a spark. That would be my guess."

Starkey tried to picture Buck Daggett stupid enough to wire a charge with the batteries connected, but couldn't. Of course, she also couldn't picture Buck building bombs to murder someone.

Starkey walked back out onto the drive to consider the scene. She tried to get a sense of the pressure release. The garage door had been bowed, the side door blown out, and Buck Daggett seriously injured, but the structural damage was minor. She guessed the energy released was about as much as two hand grenades. Big enough, but not on the order of what killed Charlie Riggio or what Tennant was using to blow apart cars.

Kelso called out to her.

"Starkey, come over here."

"Just a minute."

The side door had been blown off its hinges and cracked by the pressure change, which meant the door had been closed. She could understand that Buck would want the garage door closed so that his neighbors couldn't see what he was doing, but it didn't make sense that he would close the side door. She knew that he was working either with Modex or RDX, and either one threw some pretty nasty fumes.

Starkey went back inside to the investigator.

"Your Bomb Squad recover any undetonated explosive?"

"Nope. What was here is what went up. They ran a dog through, too, before they let in the coroner's people. You just missed him. Those dogs are something to see."

"What about his hands?"

"You mean the injuries?"

"Yeah."

"They were intact. We noted some lacerations and tissue loss, but they were still on. I know what you're thinking, that the hands should've gone, but if he was hunched over it, it kinda depends what he was doing when the charge let go."

Starkey couldn't see it. If Buck had committed suicide, she

thought that he would have been gripping the bomb, holding it tight against his body to make sure he died quickly. His hands would have been gone. If he was seating a detonator in the charge and the explosive had set off accidentally, his hands would still be gone.

"Starkey."

Starkey had an uneasy feeling as she joined Kelso and the others in the yard. She kept thinking about the red paint, and that Mr. Red claimed to know who had imitated him. How could Mr. Red know that? From Tennant?

The two suits were Sheriff's homicide detectives named Connelly and Gerald. Connelly was a large, serious man; Gerald had the empty eyes of a man who had been on the job too long. Starkey didn't like being around him.

After the introductions, Kelso told Starkey that Connelly and Gerald wanted to interview her. They exchanged cards, Connelly saying that they would be in contact sometime within the next few days.

Gerald said, "Maybe there's something you can help us with right now."

"If I can."

"Did you see Sergeant Daggett earlier today?"

"Not today. I saw him yesterday."

"You see any bruises or contusions on his face or head?"

Starkey glanced at Kelso, who was staring at her.

"I didn't see anything like that. I can't say about today, but there was nothing like that yesterday."

Gerald touched the left side of his forehead.

"Daggett has a lump here that shows edema and bruising. We're wondering when he got it."

"I don't know."

She wasn't liking this. First Tennant blows up, now Daggett blows himself up. Mr. Red claims he knows the copycat, and how could he know except through Tennant?

Starkey looked back at the garage.

"It wasn't a very big charge."

Gerald made a grin like a nasty shark.

"You didn't see the body. It blew that poor fucker to shit."

Starkey forgot about Gerald and spoke to Kelso.

"I got a description from the bomb investigator in there, Barry. Daggett shows the injuries because of his proximity, but I don't think it was much of a blast. I can't know for sure how much RDX Tennant had, but it was more than this."

Kelso squinted at her.

"Are you saying that some explosive is missing?"

"I don't know."

Starkey walked back to the street to smoke. Everything had come to an end that wasn't really an ending. She kept thinking about the contusion on Buck's head, and about his hands. His hands should be gone. She found herself wondering what Tennant had used to blow himself up, and how he had gotten it. It took enormous energy to blow a man's arms off. She didn't like the little questions that had no answers. They were like reconstructing a bomb, only to find that there are wires that lead nowhere. You couldn't pretend they didn't exist. Wires always led somewhere. When you were dealing with bombs, wires always led to someplace bad. She thought about Pell.

Marzik came up, shaking her head.

"Was it bad?"

"Not too bad. We've both seen worse."

"It must have been pretty goddamned bad. You're crying."

Starkey turned away.

Marzik cleared her throat, embarrassed.

"I didn't want to see all that mess. I've got enough mess to last me into my next life. Let me have a cigarette."

Starkey looked at her, surprised.

"You don't smoke."

"I haven't smoked in six years. Are you going to give me one of those things or do I have to buy it from you?"

Starkey gave her the pack.

They heard Natalie's screams before they saw her, coming from the cordon at the end of the street. Natalie tried to push past the officers, struggling to get to her home. An older woman, probably a neighbor, wrapped Natalie in her arms as Dick Leyton ran to her from the front of the house. Later, Starkey knew, a San Gabriel detective would question her, asking about the explosives, asking if Buck had talked about suicide. Starkey was relieved that she would not have to ask those questions, and guilty for feeling that relief.

Marzik shook her head.

"Could this get any worse?"

Starkey knew that it could. She crushed out her cigarette.

"Beth, get a ride back with Kelso, okay? I'm taking the car."

"Where are you going?"

Starkey walked faster.

All the small, odd things about Pell made sense now; the shitty motel, him needing her to run the NLETS search and the evidence transfer, the way he had lost it with Tennant. Driving to his motel, Starkey tried to put herself into the same mind-set that she used when she was de-arming bombs. It had always felt to her, then, as a kind of separation. As if she was in some other dimension, safe and secure, from where she used her body to handle the bomb like a flesh-and-bone robot, devoid of feelings. She tried to get to that place, but failed. It wasn't so easy to separate herself from her feelings anymore.

Starkey parked outside the motel, used her cell phone to call him. The phone rang ten times before the hotel operator, a tired male voice, asked if she'd like to leave a message. Starkey hung up, then went inside, walking past the lobby as if she knew where she was going. She knew Pell's room number from calling him there, found the room, then searched the halls until she found a housekeeper. Starkey tried to make herself look pleasant, an expression she didn't trust herself to pull off.

"Hi, I'm Mrs. Pell, in 112. My husband has both keys, and he's not here right now. Could you let me in?"

"Wass you name?"

"Pell. P-e-l-l. It's room 112."

The housekeeper, a young Latina, looked up the room on her clipboard.

"Shoe. I let you in."

The housekeeper keyed the lock, then stepped out of the way as Starkey entered. Mr. Red's words echoed in her brain.

He is using you, Carol Starkey. He has been playing us against each other.

The computer was sitting on a spindly desk against the wall. Identical to her computer. The same. She turned it on. The same icons on the screen. She opened them. The same doorway to Claudius.

Starkey turned to the bed. It was rumpled, and smelled of sweat. A thought came: *I would have slept in that bed.* Words lost like a whisper on a breeze.

She searched the room. She did not know what she was looking for, nor what she might find, but she went through the bathroom, the chest and desk, and his suitcase without finding anything more. Again in the center of the room, she tried to decide if she should wait or go. She was walking to the door when she turned to the closet, and searched the pockets of his clothes there. A plastic Ziploc baggie was in the inner pocket of his leather jacket. A piece of frag. She unzipped the plastic, dropped the fragment into her palm, and saw the letters:

TARKEY

Her hands and forearms tingled as if the blood had been cut off. It didn't matter that it was Buck Daggett who had etched her name to mislead them; Pell had thought that Mr. Red had built the bomb. Sitting in Barrigan's, he had *known.* That night in her house, holding her, he had believed that she was the target. And he had hidden that from her. He had used her.

"What are you doing here?"

Pell stood in the door. His face was pale, cut with hollows. He looked like a hundred-year-old man waiting for his second stroke. Now that she understood that he was a victim just as she was a victim, some deep part of her felt the urge to soothe him. She called herself a fool.

"You bastard."

She didn't slap him. She used her fist. She hit him hard in the mouth, making him bleed.

Starkey held up the bit of black metal.

"Where did you get this? The medical examiner? The *first* goddamned day you were here?"

Pell didn't move. He didn't even seem to feel the blow.

"Carol, I'm sorry."

"What was I, Jack? Bait? All along you thought he was after me, and you didn't warn me?" She pointed at the computer. "You've been on that damned thing trying to make him come for me, *and you didn't warn me!*"

He shook his head, his silence making her even more angry.

"*IT WASN'T MR. RED!* Buck Daggett killed Riggio, and now Buck is dead!"

"It's Mr. Red."

She hit him again.

"STOP SAYING THAT."

The housekeeper appeared in the hall, staring with wide eyes. Starkey forced herself to calm.

"Charlie was having an affair with Buck's wife, so Buck killed him. An eyewitness in Bakersfield put Buck at Tennant's shop. That's where Buck got the materials to make the bomb. We were on our way to arrest Buck when he was killed in his own garage with those same materials. *IT WASN'T MR. RED.*"

Pell moved past her to sit on the edge of his bed.

"Is that why you came here? To tell me that?"

"No. I know that you're not on active duty anymore, and I know why. I'm sorry about your eyes. I really am, Jack, but you're already blind. You can't even see that we're killing people."

"What are you talking about?"

"Dallas Tennant. Buck Daggett. If they didn't do it to themselves, then someone did it to them. What if we drew Mr. Red here, and they're dead because of us?"

"If he's here, then we can catch him."

Starkey felt sad for him.

"Not you, Jack. That part of it is over. I'm going to tell Barry. He's going to call the ATF field office. What you do about that is up to you. I wanted you to know it was coming."

Pell started toward her, but Starkey shook her head.

"Don't."

"I wasn't going to ask you not to."

"It doesn't matter what you were going to do. What matters is what you did. I have tried for so long to feel nothing, but I opened myself to you, and you used me. Three years, I finally take a step, and it was a lie."

"That isn't true."

"Don't say that. It doesn't matter if you felt something for me. Don't tell me if you did, because that will just make this harder."

To his credit, he nodded.

"I know."

It was harder than Starkey thought it would be, to tell him these things. More difficult because she had expected that he would argue with her, or be defensive, but he wasn't. He seemed hurt and confused.

"I believe that everyone has a secret heart, a heart deep down inside where we keep our secret selves. I think our secret hearts see things that our eyes can't. Maybe mine saw that you had been hurt the way I had been hurt. Like we were kindred spirits. Maybe that's why I let myself feel again. I only wish mine could have seen that you were lying to me."

When she looked at him again, tears had filled his eyes. She had to turn away from him. All of this was so much harder than it should have been.

"That's what I came here to say. Good-bye, Jack."

Starkey put the fragment bearing her name on the desk, then walked out.

* * *

Starkey signed on to Claudius as soon as she reached home. The chat room occupancy counter showed four people, none of whom were Mr. Red. She didn't bother to read what they were writing. She typed three words.

HOTLOAD: **Talk to me.**

The others responded, but no message from him appeared.

HOTLOAD: **I know you're there. TALK TO ME!**

The window appeared. He was waiting for her.

WILL YOU ACCEPT MESSAGES FROM MR. RED?

Starkey slapped the mouse to open the message window. The conversation would be between only them. Private.

MR. RED: **Hello, Carol Starkey. I have been waiting for you.**

Starkey closed her eyes to calm herself. She waited until she was ready.

HOTLOAD: **Did you kill him?**
MR. RED: **I have smoked much ass in my time. Be specific.**
HOTLOAD: **You know who I mean, you fuck. Daggett.**
MR. RED: **Oooo. I like it when you talk dirty.**
HOTLOAD: **DID YOU KILL HIM?**
MR. RED: **Now she's shouting. If I shout back, you won't like it, babe. My voice is EXPLOSIVE.**

Starkey went into the kitchen, mixed a tall drink. She downed two Tagamet, telling herself that she had to stay calm and control the conversation.

She returned to the computer.

HOTLOAD: **Did you kill him?**

MR. RED: **Do you want the truth, Carol Starkey? Or do you want me to tell you what you want to hear?**

HOTLOAD: **The truth.**

MR. RED: **The truth is real. Real things are a commodity. If I answer this question for you, you must answer a question for me. Do you agree?**

HOTLOAD: **Yes.**

MR. RED: **The truth hurts.**

She knew that he had given his answer. He had written that on Buck Daggett's wall. *The truth hurts.*

Calmly, she typed.

HOTLOAD: **Fuck you.**

MR. RED: **In my dreams, you do.**

HOTLOAD: **Why did you do this?**

MR. RED: **He took my name in vain, CS. You're smart enough to know that he murdered Riggio, aren't you?**

HOTLOAD: **I know what he did.**

MR. RED: **Do you know this? He was building a second bomb when I found him. He was going to do to you exactly what he had done to Riggio.**

HOTLOAD: **You can't know that.**

MR. RED: **He gave his confession. Moments before I**

knocked him out, laid him across the device he had built, and set it off.

The screen blurred through Starkey's tears. She had more of the drink, then wiped her eyes.

HOTLOAD: **Is this my fault?**
MR. RED: **Do I detect the faint aroma of . . . guilt?**
HOTLOAD: **Was it because of me and Pell? Did we draw you here?**
MR. RED: **You've had your question. Now it's time for mine.**

Starkey composed herself.

HOTLOAD: **All right.**
MR. RED: **By now, you must know that Pell is not who he claims. You know that he is one of my first victims. You know that he is outside the law.**
HOTLOAD: **I know.**
MR. RED: **You know he was using you.**

It took Starkey a moment to compose herself.

HOTLOAD: **Get to your question.**

He let her wait. Starkey knew that he wanted her to ask again, but she didn't. She decided that she would sit there the rest of her life and not ask him. She was tired of being manipulated.

Finally, he couldn't stand it anymore.

MR. RED: **How does it feel to be used by a man you love?**

Starkey read the question and felt nothing. She knew that he wanted a reaction, but she would not give him the satisfaction.

HOTLOAD: **I am going to arrest you.**
MR. RED: **I am laughing. Ha ha.**
HOTLOAD: **Laugh now, cry later.**
MR. RED: **My work here is done, Carol Starkey. I have enjoyed you. Good-bye.**

Starkey knew that there would be no more messages that night. She turned off the computer, then sat in her silent house, smoking. She went to her answering machine and played the messages that Pell had left. She played them over and over, listening to his voice. It hurt.

19

STARKEY DRANK FOR most of the night, smoking an endless chain of cigarettes that left her home cloudy and gray. She fell asleep twice, both times dreaming of Sugar again and the day in the trailer park. The sleep was anguished, only lasting for a few minutes at a time. Once, she woke seeing the trailer with red words painted on its side: THE TRUTH HURTS. That was the end of the sleep.

She decided that she would tell Kelso first thing in the morning. There wasn't anything else to do. The investigation had to turn back to

Mr. Red, and it had to turn quickly if they were to have any chance of catching him. She thought she knew how.

At ten minutes after five that morning, she paged Warren Mueller. She was too drunk to give a damn about the time. Her phone rang twelve minutes later, a groggy voice on the other end of the line.

"Damn, Mueller, I didn't expect you to call until later. I guess you sleep with your pager right there by your bed."

"Starkey? Do you know what time it is?"

"Listen, I know how Tennant got the explosives that he blew himself up with. He got them from Mr. Red. Red went in there to see him."

She could hear Mueller clearing his throat.

"How do you know that?"

"He told me."

"Tennant?"

"No, Warren, Mr. Red. There's two things you need to do. First, you want to check the video record for whoever went in there to see him in the past couple of days. And here's the other thing, and this is important. You know Tennant's scrapbook?"

"I don't know what in hell you're talking about."

"You never went to see Tennant there?"

"Why in the hell would I go see him?"

"He had a scrapbook, Mueller. A collection of clippings and junk about bomb incidents. Anyone who went in there to see him had to look at that damned book. Get the book. Have it printed and run every print you find. There's no way Red went to see him and didn't touch that book."

She described the book in detail, giving Mueller the rest of the facts. After that, she showered, dressed, and packed up the computer. She would need it when she explained to Kelso about Claudius. The last things she did before leaving were fill her flask and drop a fresh pack of Tagamet into her purse.

Starkey timed her arrival at Spring Street so that Kelso would be in his office. She didn't want to get into the office first and have to make conversation with Marzik and Hooker. She wedged her car into the parking lot next to Marzik's, gathered up the computer, and brought it with her.

Hooker was at his desk.

"Hey, Hook. Is Kelso in?"

"Yeah."

"Where's Beth?"

"The ladies' room."

Starkey loved Jorge. He was the last man in America who called it the ladies' room.

Starkey went out to the bathroom, where she found Marzik smoking. Marzik fanned the air before she realized it was Starkey, and looked guilty.

"This is your fault."

"Why don't you just go in the stairwell?"

"I don't want anyone to know. Six years I've been off these damned things."

"Throw it away and come inside. I've got to see Kelso, and I want you and Hooker with me."

"Jesus, I just lit the damned thing."

"For God's sake, Beth, please."

Even when Starkey was loving Marzik, she hated her.

Starkey didn't wait for Hooker and Marzik to get themselves together; she didn't want the three of them trooping into his office like a bunch of ducks in a row. She knocked on the door, then pushed her way inside with the computer. Kelso eyed it because he knew that Starkey didn't own a computer and knew nothing about them.

"Barry, I need to see you."

"You and I have a meeting with Chief Morgan later. He wants to be briefed before the press conference. He also wants to congratulate you, Carol. He told me that. Everyone except you was running off half-cocked about Mr. Red, and you broke this case. I think he's going to bump you to D-3."

Starkey put the computer on his desk. Both Marzik and Hooker came in behind her.

"Okay, Barry, we can do that. But I have to tell you some things first, and I want Beth and Jorge to hear it, too. Buck didn't kill himself. It wasn't an accident. Mr. Red killed him."

Kelso glanced at Marzik and Santos, then frowned at Starkey.

"Maybe I'm confused. Weren't you the one who said that Mr. Red wasn't involved here?"

"Mr. Red did not kill Charlie Riggio. That was Buck. Buck copycatted Red's M.O. to cover the murder, just like we proved."

"Then what in hell are you talking about?"

"Mr. Red didn't like someone pretending to be him. He came here to find that person. He did."

Santos said, "Carol, how do you know that?"

Starkey pointed at the computer.

"He admitted it to me on that through Claudius. Mr. Red and I have been in personal contact now for almost a week."

Kelso's face closed into an unreadable scowl as she told them about the entire avenue of the investigation that she had held secret, and how, through Claudius, it had led to her contact with Mr. Red. Kelso only stopped her once, when she was telling them about Jack Pell.

"How long have you known that Pell is not a representative of the ATF?"

"Since yesterday. I confronted him about it last night."

"You are sure about this? You are *positive* that this man is functioning without authority?"

"Yes."

Kelso's jaw flexed. His nostrils flared as he drew a deep breath. When Starkey glanced at Hooker and Marzik, they both stared at the floor.

She said, "Barry, I'm sorry. I was wrong for playing it this way, and I apologize. But we still have a shot at Mr. Red. Buck had more Modex. I'm sure he had more, and I think Red took it."

"Did Red tell you this?"

"We don't have conversations. It's not like we tell each other secrets; he taunts me, he teases me. We have this, I don't know what you would call it, a relationship. That's why Pell and I went on-line like this, to try to bring him out. I'm sure I can contact him again. We can work him, Barry. We can catch the sonofabitch."

Kelso nodded, but he wasn't nodding agreement. She could see that in his face. He was angry, and probably nodding to something he had thought.

"We look like fools."

Starkey took a breath.

"You don't, Barry. I do."

"That's where you're wrong, Detective. I'm going to call Morgan. I want you to wait outside. Don't go anywhere. Don't do anything. Marzik, Santos, that's you, too."

They nodded.

"Did either of you know about this?"

Starkey said, "No."

"Goddamnit, I'm not asking you."

Marzik said, "No, sir."

"No, sir."

"Wait outside."

As Starkey was walking out, Kelso stopped her.

"One more thing. At any time during your, I don't know what to call them, conversations? At any time when you were talking to that murderer, did you impart or reveal any, and I mean anything at all, information about this investigation?"

"No, Barry, I did not."

"Starkey. Never call me by my first name again."

Outside, Starkey apologized to Santos and Marzik. Santos nodded glumly, then went to his desk and lapsed into silence. Marzik was livid and didn't try to hide it.

"If you cost me a promotion, I'm going to kick your drunken ass. I knew you were fucking that bastard."

Starkey didn't bother to argue. She sat at her desk and waited.

Kelso's door remained closed for almost forty-five minutes. When it opened, Starkey, Marzik, and Santos all rose, but Kelso froze Marzik and Santos with a glance.

"Not you. Starkey, inside."

When she went in, he closed the door. She had never seen him as angry as he was right now.

He said, "You're finished. You are suspended immediately, and you will be brought up on professional-conduct charges, as well as charges of compromising this investigation. I have already spoken to

334 * ROBERT CRAIS

IAG. They will contact you directly, and you will be subject to their administrative orders. If any criminal charges arise from the subsequent investigation, you will be prosecuted to the full extent of the law. I would advise you to contact a lawyer today."

Starkey went numb.

"Barry, I know I fucked up, but Mr. Red is still out there. He has more Modex. We can't just stop; we can't just end it like this."

"The only thing at an end is you. You're done. The rest of us are going to continue doing our jobs."

"Damnit, I *am* the investigation. *I can get to him*, Barry. You want to fire me, fine, fire me after we get the sonofabitch!"

Kelso slowly crossed his arms, considering her.

"*You* are the investigation? That's the most arrogant, self-centered statement I've ever heard from a detective on this department."

"Barry, I didn't mean it like that. You know I didn't mean it like that."

"I *know* you took it upon yourself to conduct an investigation independent of my office. I know—because you told me so—that you secretly set about baiting the murderer we were all supposed to be trying to find. Maybe, if you had come to me, we would have done that anyway, but we don't *know* that. And now, according to you, I know that Buck Daggett is dead by that man's hand. How does that feel, Carol, knowing that you may have cost Buck his life?"

Starkey blinked hard, trying to stop the tears that filled her eyes. *The truth hurts*. But there it was.

"It feels just like you think it feels. Please don't, Barry. Please let me stay and help you catch this guy. I need to."

Kelso took a deep breath, stood, then went behind his desk and took his seat.

"You're dismissed."

Starkey moved for the computer. She needed the computer to get to Mr. Red.

"That stays."

Starkey left the computer on his desk and walked out.

20

MARZIK WAS AT her desk; Santos wasn't in the squad room. Starkey thought about telling Marzik what had happened, but decided to hell with it. Later, when everyone had calmed, she thought she might call.

"Good-bye, Beth."

Marzik didn't respond. So far as Starkey could tell, she didn't even look.

Starkey worked her car out of the parking garage and drove out into the city with no idea of what to do or where to go. She had expected that Kelso would punish her, that there would be a suspension and loss of pay, but she never thought that he would jerk her from the investigation. She was too much a part of it, had too much of herself invested in it. Everything she had was invested in it. In Mr. Red. Thinking that, she felt the tears, and angrily fought them back. Pell was probably telling himself the same thing.

Starkey fished her flask from beneath the seat, propped it between her legs. She lit a cigarette, blowing a geyser of smoke out the window. The flask was real. She wanted the drink. She squeezed the flask hard between her legs and thought, *Oh, for Christ's sake.* She shoved it back under the seat.

She drove to the top of Griffith Park. The place was crawling with tourists. It was hot; the smog was so thick it hung like a mist, hiding the buildings. Starkey watched the tourists trying to see the city through the curtain of crap in the air. They probably couldn't see more than two or three miles out into the basin. It was like staring at lung cancer. Starkey thought, *Here, here's some more.* She lit a fresh cigarette.

She told herself to stop it. She was acting like an ass. She knew that it was Buck Daggett. Whatever Buck had done, it was eating her up that she might have played a role in his death. It was Pell, because the rotten prick had meant something to her, even more than she cared to admit.

Starkey bought a Diet Coke at the concession stand and was walking to the top of the observatory when her pager buzzed. She recognized Mueller's number by the area code. When she reached the top, she called him.

"It's Starkey."

"You're gonna be the FBI's cover girl."

"The book?"

"Oh, baby. Was that a call, or was that a call? We got a clean set, eight out of ten digits, both thumbs. You know the bastard went in there posing as Tennant's attorney? Can you believe the balls?"

"Warren? Is there a surveillance tape?"

"Yeah. We've got that, too. The SLO field office is all over this thing. Starkey, the feds up here are creaming their pants. We got his ID. Listen to this, John Michael Fowles, age twenty-eight. No criminal record of any kind. Had his prints in the federal casket because he enlisted in the Navy when he was eighteen, but washed out as unsuitable for service. He used to start fires in the goddamned barracks."

Starkey was breathing hard, like a horse wanting to get into the race.

"Warren, listen, I want you to call CCS down here and give them this information, okay? I'm off the investigation."

"What in hell are you talking about?"

"I fucked up. It's my fault. I would tell you about it, but I just can't right now. Would you call them, please? They're going to need this."

"Listen, Starkey, whatever you did, they gotta be crazy. I just want you to know that. You're a top cop."

"Will you call them?"

Starkey felt as if the world was shifting away beneath her feet, sliding out to sea and leaving her behind.

"Yeah. Yeah, sure, I'll do that."

"I'll talk to you later about it."

"Starkey?"

"What?"

"Look, you just take care of yourself, okay?"

"Good-bye, Sergeant."

Starkey closed her phone and watched the tourists putting dimes into the telescopes so they could get a better view of the smog. John Michael Fowles. She saw John Michael hunched over his computer, waiting for Hotload to sign on. She saw him building his bomb with Buck Daggett's leftover Modex. She saw him targeting another bomb technician and waiting to punch the button that would tear someone apart. She wanted to be on that computer with him. She wanted to finish the job she had started, but Kelso had cut her out of it.

No.

There was another way.

She opened her phone again, and called Pell.

Pell

Pell left the motel. He knew that once the local ATF field office was informed that an agent was illegally prosecuting a case, they would act quickly to investigate. He assumed that Starkey would identify his hotel, so he moved. He didn't know what he would do or where he would go, but he was certain that his pursuit of Mr. Red was at its end. Now that he was found out, the local field offices around the country would be notified, as well as the bomb units of every police force in America. He was done.

He decided not to run. His retinas would soon detach completely, and irreparably—and that would be that. He thought he might wait a day or two, hoping that Starkey and the L.A. cops could bag Mr. Red, and then he would turn himself in. Fuck it. There ain't no prize for second place.

He felt no loss at missing Mr. Red. That part of it surprised him. For almost two years, his private pursuit had been his consuming passion. Now, well, it just didn't matter. The loss he felt was for Starkey. The regret he felt was for the pain he had caused her.

Pell checked into a different hotel, then drove aimlessly until he found himself at a diner on the water in Santa Monica. He had gone there to see the ocean. He thought that he should probably try to see as many things as possible while he was still able, but once there he hadn't even bothered to get a table facing outward. He sat at the counter, thinking that he might try to stay in Los Angeles. At least long enough to try to make peace with Starkey. Maybe he could apologize. If he couldn't make it right, maybe he could make her hate him less.

When his pager vibrated, he recognized her number, and

thought that she might be calling to tell him to turn himself in. He thought that he might do that.

He returned her call.

"You calling to arrest me?"

What she said surprised him.

"No. I'm calling to give you one last chance to catch this bastard."

Starkey found him at a rathole diner, waiting in a booth. Her heart felt heavy when she saw him, but she pushed that aside.

"You might as well know. You're not the only one on the wrong side of the law."

"What does that mean?"

She told him what had happened. She kept it short. She was uneasy being around him.

"Here's the deal, Pell, and you have to agree to it. If we get this guy, we are not going to kill him, we are going to arrest him. This is no longer your personal vendetta. Agreed?"

"Yes."

"If we get this set up, we are going back to Kelso. I am not a goddamned cowboy like you. I want to do this the right way, and I want to make sure it works."

"You want to save your job."

"Yes, Pell, I want to save my job. They might fire me anyway, but I want to go out as the police officer I am, and not some half-cocked asshole who got Buck Daggett killed."

Pell stared out the window. She thought he was trying to memorize whatever he saw out there.

"If I go in with you, I might be taken into custody."

"You don't have to go. Come if you want, or not. I'm just telling you how it has to be played."

Pell nodded again. She knew that was hard for him. He would be taking himself out of the play.

"Then what do you need me for?"

"Mr. Red waits for me. He's got this . . . fixation. I can use that. But I need your computer to get back on Claudius. Kelso took mine."

Pell glanced away again.

"I should have told you what I was doing. I'm sorry I didn't."

"Stop. I don't want to hear it."

"I've been living with one thing in my life for a long time. You get used to doing things a certain way."

"Is this what you've been doing for two years, Pell? Bullshitting your way from city to city after this guy?"

Pell shrugged, as if it embarrassed him.

"I have a badge and an ID number. I know the procedure, and I have friends. Most people don't question the badge. Cops never question it."

"Look, I don't care, and I don't want to talk about it. You want to do this or not?"

He looked at her.

"I want to do it."

"Then let's go."

She started to slide out of the booth. He took her arm, stopping her.

"Carol?"

"What? Don't touch me like that, Pell. I don't like it."

"I fell in love with you."

She hit him again, so fast that she didn't even know she was doing it. The people at the surrounding tables looked at them.

"Don't you say that."

Pell felt his face.

"Jesus, Starkey, that's three."

"Don't you say that."

He shoved himself out of the booth.

"The computer is in my car."

They went to her place.

It was hard looking at Pell. It was difficult being in the same room with him, but she told herself to be strong. They had brought themselves down this road together. There was no other way to play it, but she was uncomfortably aware of the feelings she'd had when they'd been in this position before.

They set up the computer at the dining room table, and Starkey signed on as before. It was earlier than the previous times she'd had contact with Mr. Red, but she couldn't just sit. When the flaming head stared out at her, she entered the chat room, which was empty.

Pell said, "What are you going to say?"

"This."

HOTLOAD: **John Michael Fowles.**

"Who's John Michael Fowles?"

"Mr. Red. Warren Mueller got his prints off Tennant's book. I knew that if Red had gone in there, Tennant would have made him look at that damned book."

Pell stared at the screen. Starkey saw his lips move, as if he were reading the name silently to himself, branding it into his cells.

Starkey didn't expect Fowles to be waiting for her, not this early in the day. He might come anytime, or no time; they might have a long wait. She struck a cigarette, and told Pell that if he wanted anything in the kitchen, he could find it for himself. Neither of them left the computer.

Fowles was there almost at once.

WILL YOU ACCEPT A MESSAGE FROM MR. RED?

Starkey smiled. Pell shifted forward, Starkey thinking he might fall into the computer.

"Fast."

"He's been waiting."

She opened the window.

MR. RED: **Excellent, Detective Starkey. You rock.**

HOTLOAD:	Your praise makes me blush.
MR. RED:	How did you learn my name?
HOTLOAD:	Ah . . . a question. Do you want the truth, or do you want me to tell you what you want to hear?
MR. RED:	I am laughing, Carol Starkey. Well done.

Starkey did not answer.

Pell said, "Why aren't you answering him?"

"Let him wait. It's a game he plays."

Finally, another message appeared.

MR. RED:	The truth is a commodity. What will you want in return?
HOTLOAD:	You will have to answer a question of mine. Do you agree?
MR. RED:	Within reason. I will not tell you my whereabouts or answer questions of that nature. All else is fair game.
HOTLOAD:	Agreed.
MR. RED:	Agreed.
HOTLOAD:	Tennant's book. When I realized that you had seen him, I knew he would have made you look at the book.

Fowles again fell silent. It was several moments before he replied.

MR. RED:	Fuck.
HOTLOAD:	Only in your dreams.

"Christ, Starkey, how close *are* you two?"

"Shut up."

MR. RED: **Do you know why I looked at his book, Carol Starkey?**

HOTLOAD: **To read the articles about yourself?**

MR. RED: **To read the articles about you.**

Pell shifted again. Starkey watched the screen, thinking, then typed:

HOTLOAD: **Now, my question.**

MR. RED: **Yes.**

Starkey hesitated. Her fingers trembled, and she thought of the flask again. She lit a fresh cigarette.

Pell saw the tremble.

"You okay?"

She didn't answer him.

HOTLOAD: **I ask you again: Would you have come to Los Angeles if we had not baited you?**

MR. RED: **The truth, or what you want to hear?**

HOTLOAD: **Answer my question.**

Fowles paused again.

"What's he doing?"

"He's thinking. He wants something. He's trying to figure out how to get it."

"What does he want?"

"Pay attention, Pell. He wants me."

MR. RED: **I will answer your question in person. Give me your phone number.**

HOTLOAD: **You must be nuts.**

MR. RED: **I AM MR. RED! OF *COURSE*, I'M NUTS!**

HOTLOAD:	Don't have a cow, John.
MR. RED:	Don't call me John. I am Mr. Red.
HOTLOAD:	I still won't give you my number. That is farther than I'm willing to go.
MR. RED:	I've had more than a few fantasies about you going all the way, Carol Starkey.
HOTLOAD:	Remember the ground rules, John. You get graphic, I'm gonna sign off and go take a cold shower.
MR. RED:	What's in it for you is . . . the truth.
HOTLOAD:	The truth hurts.
MR. RED:	The truth can also set you free.

She leaned back, letting it sit. She needed to think. She knew that they would have only one shot to bring him in; if he figured out what she was trying to do, her chance would be gone, and so would he.

Pell said, "Be weak."

Starkey glanced over and found Pell watching her.

He said, "He's male. If you want him, need him. Let him take care of you."

"That isn't me."

"Pretend."

She turned back to the keyboard.

HOTLOAD:	I am afraid.
MR. RED:	Of the truth?
HOTLOAD:	You want to be in the Ten Most Wanted. I am afraid you will use me to get there.
MR. RED:	There are things I want more than being on that list.
HOTLOAD:	Like what?
MR. RED:	I want to hear your voice, Carol Starkey. I want to have a conversation. Not like this. I want to see your expressions. I want to hear your inflections.

HOTLOAD: Do you see how weird this is? I am a
police officer. You are Mr. Red.

MR. RED: We are both in Tennant's book.

She didn't respond.

MR. RED: We are the same.

She hesitated again. She knew what she wanted, but she could
not suggest it. He had to suggest it. It had to be his idea or he would
never go for it.

HOTLOAD: I will not give you my phone number.

MR. RED: Then I will give you a number.

HOTLOAD: I am laughing. If you give me a number, I
will know your location.

MR. RED: Perhaps that is my idea. Perhaps I would
like you to, ah, cum.

HOTLOAD: Don't be crude.

MR. RED: Crude, but not stupid. Let us do this:
Sign on to Claudius later today at exactly
three p.m. I will be here. I will give you
a phone number. If my phone doesn't
ring in fifteen seconds, I will leave, and
you will never hear from me again. If you
call, we will talk for exactly five minutes,
and I will answer your question. No more
than five minutes. I would like a longer
conversation, but we both know what
you'll be doing.

HOTLOAD: Yes. I will be tracing the call.

MR. RED: Perhaps. But perhaps I can convince
you that we were meant for better
things.

HOTLOAD: Don't count on it.

MR. RED: **Fair enough. I will beat you at that, you know. You won't catch me.**

HOTLOAD: **We'll see.**

"You've got him, Starkey."

"Maybe."

She had what she needed to go back to Kelso, but everything depended on Mr. Red. A large part of her was scared that if he signed off now, he would not return. He would not be there at three o'clock. She knew better than to type this, but something in her wanted to know. She told herself that if she brought him to this point, he would be hers. He would not vanish, he would not disappear. He would return to her, and she would catch him.

It was such an intimate thing that she felt embarrassed writing it in front of Pell.

HOTLOAD: **When you're having your fantasies of me, what do you think about?**

He hesitated so long that she grew scared that he had gone. When his answer came, she regretted having asked.

MR. RED: **Death.**

Starkey did not reply. She signed off Claudius, then turned off the machine.

Pell was staring at her.

She said, "Stop looking at me like that. We've got a lot to do."

Mr. Red

JOHN MICHAEL FOWLES was parked less than two blocks up the street from Starkey's house. He closed the iBook and smiled.

"DAMN, I'm good! I am so fucking good that somebody should tattoo 'Mr. Irresistible' on both cheeks of my ass."

He pushed the iBook aside and patted the jar of Modex. He liked having it with him, the gray explosive in its jar like a big glob of toothpaste. It was better than having a goldfish. You didn't have to feed it.

He waited until Starkey and Pell left, then drove back to his hotel to work on the new bomb. He was building a different kind of bomb this time, one just for Carol Starkey. He didn't have much time.

21

STARKEY WANTED TO maneuver John Michael Fowles into revealing his location so that she could bag him. To do that, she needed phone traps in place in the event they spoke on a land line, and the cell companies standing by for a triangulation in the more likely event that his number linked to a cell phone. Once his position was fixed, she needed bodies to close the perimeter. Since the target was John Michael Fowles, AKA Mr. Red, she feared that he would have explosives on his person, which required a call-out from the Bomb Squad. All of this meant that she needed Kelso's help.

She phoned Dick Leyton.

When he came on the line, he sounded distant, but concerned. She knew from his tone that he'd heard the news.

"Dick, I need your help."

"I don't know that I'm in a position to give it. I spoke with Barry. What in hell were you thinking, Carol?"

"Did Barry tell you that I was in contact with Mr. Red?"

"Of course, he told me. You're in serious trouble because of this. Serious. I don't think you'll get off with just a suspension."

"Dick, I know I'm in trouble. Please listen to me. I am *still* in contact with Mr. Red. I was just on-line with him."

"Damnit, Carol, you're only making it worse for yourself. You need to—"

Starkey interrupted him.

"I *know* Barry fired me, I *know* that I'm not part of the team, but I can get this guy, Dick. I have a relationship with him whether Barry likes it or not, and we can use that to bag this mutt. I have him set up, Dick. I have the guy set up."

Leyton didn't say anything. She knew he was thinking, so she pressed ahead to convince him.

"At exactly three o'clock, he's going to be on-line again. He's going to give me a phone number to call. I will call it. Dick, I think I can arrange a face-to-face. If I can't, maybe we can still trap the call. This is Mr. Red, for God's sake, do you think we should walk away from an opportunity like this? Take me to Barry, Dick. Please."

They spoke about it for another ten minutes, Leyton asking questions, Starkey answering. They both knew that Leyton would have to call Morgan. He needed to convince the A-chief before Kelso would go for it. They would also need Morgan's horsepower to get everything set up in time. Starkey immediately regretted agreeing with Fowles to do this today; she kicked herself for not putting him off until tomorrow, but it was too late for that now. Leyton finally said that he would do it, telling Starkey to meet him at Spring Street by two o'clock.

When she hung up, she looked at Pell.

"You heard."

"We're on."

"If Morgan goes for it, I would guess that he's going to alert the ATF and the Feebs. They might be there."

"They probably will. Those boys don't like to sit out the dance."

"Maybe you shouldn't come."

"I didn't come this far to quit, Starkey."

"Well, let's go. You want to get something to eat?"

"I don't think I could."

"You want some Tagamet?"

Pell laughed.

She brought him back to the diner for his car, and then they went their separate ways.

Starkey put her car in the red zone outside Spring Street at five minutes before two, and went up with the second computer. Leyton was already present, as were Morgan and two of his Men in Black. Pell hadn't yet arrived. Starkey found herself hoping that he would change his mind about coming. Kelso was outside his office with two suits who Starkey took to be federal agents. Marzik was talking up one of the Men in Black and ignored her.

Everyone in the room stopped what they were doing and looked at her.

Dick said, "Carol, why don't we go into Barry's office."

Starkey followed them into Kelso's office, where Morgan nodded politely.

"Looks like you're in some trouble, Detective."

"Yes, sir."

"Well, let's see how this turns out."

Kelso wasn't happy about any of it, but he wasn't stupid, either. He wanted Mr. Red, and if this was their best shot, he was game to take it. Three representatives from the phone company had set up a computer of their own, feeding into Barry's phone jack.

Leyton said, "Carol, I sketched out our discussion both to Chief Morgan and to Lieutenant Kelso. They're on board with this. The dispatch office is standing by with secure communication to the patrol division. SWAT has been alerted, and the Bomb Squad is, as always, ready to roll."

Starkey nodded, smiling at the "as always."

"All right."

Secure communication meant that all directions to patrol units would be transmitted through the computers in the black and whites. No one wanted to use radio calls because those could be intercepted by the media and private citizens.

"Where do you want to do this?"

Kelso said, "Here in my office. Do you need anything special for the computer?"

"Just a phone line. I'll use my cell phone to make the voice call."

One of the Men in Black said, "Shouldn't she use a hard line for the trap?"

One of the phone company people said, "Negative. He's providing the number. We'll work the address from that unless he's on a cell. If he's mobile, it doesn't matter what she's on."

Kelso cleared his desk so that Starkey could set up the computer. She caught a glimpse of Pell out in the squad room, talking with the federal suits.

At ten minutes before three, Starkey was waiting to sign on with an audience crowded around her. Leyton came up behind her and rubbed her shoulders.

"We've still got a few minutes. Get a cup of coffee."

Starkey left for the squad room, glad for the break. Pell was still with the two suits, but he wasn't in handcuffs. She didn't go for a cup of coffee. She went over to Pell.

"Are these people with the ATF?"

The shorter of the two introduced himself as Assistant Special Agent-in-Charge Wally Coombs and the taller as Special Agent Burton Armus, both of the Los Angeles field office.

"Is Mr. Pell under arrest?"

"Not at this time. We'd like to ask you a few questions about all this."

"You'll have to ask me later."

"We understand that."

"I will need Mr. Pell's assistance in the other room."

The two agents traded a look, then Coombs shrugged.

"Sure."

Pell followed her back to Kelso's, walking very close behind her.

"Thanks."

At two fifty-nine, Starkey was again in front of the computer.

She said, "Are we ready?"

Morgan met the eyes of the section leaders and the phone company people. One of the phone people murmured something into his private line, then gave a thumbs-up. Morgan nodded at her.

"Go."

Starkey opened the door into Claudius. Almost at once, the words appeared.

WILL YOU ACCEPT A MESSAGE FROM MR. RED?

Kelso said, "Jesus."

Morgan frowned.

"No talking."

When the window appeared, it wasn't what any of them expected.

MR. RED: **Sorry, babe. Changed my mind.**

Kelso said, "Damnit!"

Morgan shushed him. He nodded to Starkey, encouraging.

"Play it as you would, Detective Starkey. You know what they say, shit happens."

Starkey glanced up at him, and the Man in Black smiled.

Starkey typed.

HOTLOAD: **You're an asshole.**

MR. RED: I have been thinking.

HOTLOAD: Don't bruise yourself.

MR. RED: A conversation isn't going to be enough for me. I am a man of LARGE appetites, if you catch my drift.

HOTLOAD: We had a deal.

MR. RED: Your point?

HOTLOAD: You said you would answer my question.

MR. RED: What I said was, I will answer your question in person. I will still do that.

HOTLOAD: I think you're jerking me around. You know I won't meet you. No way am I going to do that.

Kelso said, "Ah, Carol—"

Pell said, "She knows what she's doing."

MR. RED: Then you will never know why Buck Daggett died.

Starkey leaned back, waiting. She could feel Kelso, Leyton, and the others shifting behind her, and didn't like it.

MR. RED: Meet me, Carol Starkey. I will not hurt you.

HOTLOAD: Where?

MR. RED: Don't say it if you don't mean it.

HOTLOAD: Where?

MR. RED: Echo Park. You know the big fountain.

Morgan quietly told his assistants to have plainclothes units position themselves around Echo Park. She heard Dick Leyton speaking softly into his cell phone, alerting the Bomb Squad. She ignored them.

HOTLOAD: Yes.

MR. RED: **Park on the south side of the pond and walk toward the concession stand. Walk all the way to the concession stand, and only from that direction. I will be watching you. If you come alone, we will meet. If not, I will think less of you.**

HOTLOAD: **You're a fool.**

MR. RED: **Am I, Carol Starkey? I am Mr. Red. The truth is out there.**

They set it up on the roll, coordinating SWAT and the Bomb Squad to meet in a parking lot six blocks east of Echo Park. Plainclothes spotters of Latin descent were posted on the streets surrounding the park, equipped with radios. All uniformed officers and black and white radio cars were pulled.

The phone people wrapped a wire on Starkey there in Kelso's office, even as the orders were being given. Starkey was to drive to the park in her own car and do exactly as John Michael Fowles had instructed. Once in the park, if and when he approached her and identified himself, the area would be sealed. Snipers would be in position if needed.

Pell said, "You okay with this?"

It was happening so fast that she wanted to throw up.

"Sure."

They hustled her out to her car less than eight minutes after the computer was off.

Starkey drove to Echo Park, pretending that none of this was happening. She knew that this was the best approach. Forget about all the activity in support of her, just like approaching a bomb. Do it that way, and she wouldn't be caught looking for the snipers or the plainclothes people, and give herself away.

The drive from Spring Street to Echo Park took twelve minutes. She parked on the south side like he said, fighting the urge to throw up. He wouldn't be standing there with a grin and a hot dog in his hand. He was Mr. Red. There would be a surprise.

"Radio check."

"One two three, three two one."

"You're clear."

"I'm pulling the plug."

"Rog."

She took the plug from her ear. If he saw it, he would know she was wired. The mike taped between her breasts would pick up her voice. If she said, "Hello, Mr. Red," they would hear.

The plan was simple. Point him out, hit the ground, let everyone else do their jobs.

Starkey locked her car and walked toward the concession stand. It was a weekday summer afternoon. The park was jammed with families, kids with balloons, bladers and boarders and plenty of ice cream. It was so hot that the tarmac beneath her feet was soft. Starkey hoped that it wouldn't get hotter.

A long line waited at the concession stand. She had to cover about sixty yards, which she did slowly so that she could search each face in the area. She didn't care if Fowles thought she was being careful, but she didn't want him to think she was stalling to give other officers a chance to set up.

When she reached the concession stand, she stopped. No one approached her, and no one even looked like they could be Mr. Red. The crowd was mostly Latin, with a smattering of blacks and Asians. She was one of the few Anglos that she could see.

Starkey shook out a cigarette and lit up. The minutes stretched. He could be anywhere, he could be nowhere. She wondered if he had changed his mind again.

A short, squat woman and her children joined the line. She reminded Starkey of the women she had seen from Dana's window, the women trying to catch their bus. This woman had four children, small ones, all boys, all short, squat, and brown like their mother. The oldest boy stood close by his mother's side, but the other three ran pell-mell in circles, chasing each other and screaming. Starkey wished that they would shut the hell up. All the screaming was getting on her nerves. The two smallest boys raced behind the concession stand, came out from around the other side, and skidded to a stop. They had found the bag. At first, Starkey wasn't sure what they were doing or what they had, but then the earth heaved up against her feet and she knew.

The two smallest boys looked in the bag. Their older brother joined them. A plain paper shopping bag that someone had left at the corner of the concession stand.

Starkey wished she had eaten more Tagamet.

"Get away from there."

She didn't shriek or rush forward. This was Mr. Red. He would have a remote. He was watching, and he could fire the charge whenever the fucking hell he wanted.

Starkey dropped her cigarette and crushed it. She had to get those kids away from there.

She walked toward the bag.

"We have a possible device. I say again, possible device. I gotta get these kids away."

When she was closer, she raised her voice, made it sharp and angry.

"Hey!"

The boys looked. They probably spoke no English.

"Get the fuck away from that."

The boys knew she was talking to them, but stared at her without comprehension. Their mother said something in Spanish.

Starkey said, "Tell them to get away from that."

The mother was chattering in Spanish when Starkey reached the bag and saw the pipes.

"BOMB!"

She grabbed two of the boys, she could only get two, and lunged backwards, screaming, "BOMBBOMBBOMB! POLICE OFFICER, CLEAR THE AREA, MOVE MOVE MOVE!"

The boys screamed, their mother lit into Starkey like a mama cat, the people in the line milled in confusion. Starkey pushed and shoved, trying to get the people to move even as police units bucked over the curb and roared toward her across the park—

—and nothing happened.

*   *   *

Russ Daigle, wet with sweat, his face drawn in the way a person's face can be drawn only when they work a bomb, said, "There's no charge in the pipes."

Starkey had guessed that forty minutes ago. If Mr. Red had wanted to blow it, he would have blown it when she was standing there. Now she was sitting in the back of Daigle's Suburban, just as she used to sit when she was on the squad, and winding down from de-arming a device. Daigle had sent the Andrus robot forward with the de-armer to blow the pipes apart.

"There was a note."

Daigle handed her the red 3 x 5 index card. Dick Leyton and Morgan had walked over with him.

The note said: *Check the list.*

Starkey looked at them.

"What the fuck does this mean?"

Leyton squeezed her arm.

"He's on the Ten Most Wanted List. As soon as the Feebs had his identity, they added him."

Starkey laughed.

"I'm sorry, Carol. It was a good try. It was a really good try."

They were done. Any relationship she'd had with Mr. Red was history. He would've seen what they had tried to do. Wherever he was, he was no doubt laughing his ass off. She might sign on to Claudius again, and he might be there, but any hope of baiting him into a trap was gone. He had what he wanted.

Kelso came over and told her pretty much the same thing. He even managed to look embarrassed.

"Listen, Carol, we're still going to have to deal with what happened, but, well, maybe we can work out something to keep you on the job. You won't be able to stay with CCS, but we'll see."

"Thanks, Barry."

"You can even call me by my first name."

Starkey smiled.

The two ATF agents hovered around Pell like his personal guards. Starkey caught Pell's eye. Pell spoke to the agents, then walked over.

"How you doing?"

"Been better. But I've been worse, too. You hear they put him on the list?"

"Yeah. Maybe he'll retire. The sonofabitch."

Starkey nodded. She didn't know what to think about that. Would Mr. Red stay in Los Angeles? Would he continue to kill, or would he simply vanish? She thought about the Zodiac Killer up in San Francisco, who had murdered a string of people, and then simply stopped.

She looked at the two feds.

"What's going to happen with your friends?"

"They're not going to drag me away in chains. They want me to come in to the FO for an interview, but they advised me of my rights, and told me to get an attorney. What does that tell you?"

"That you're fucked?"

"You have such a way with words."

Starkey smiled, even though she didn't feel much like smiling.

"That's a nice smile."

"Don't."

"I need to talk to you, Carol. We have to talk about this."

Starkey shoved off the back of the Suburban.

"I don't want to talk. I just want to go somewhere and heal."

"I don't mean talk about what's going to happen to me. I mean talk about us."

"I know what you meant. Good-bye, Jack. If I can help you when they interview me, I will."

Starkey looked deeply into the two dimming eyes, then walked away so that he could not see how very much she wanted that time with him.

22

STARKEY DID NOT drive back to Spring Street. The summer sun was still high in the west, but the air was clear, and the heat felt good. She drove with the windows down.

Starkey stopped at an A.M./P.M. minimart, bought a jumbo iced tea, then took a turn through Rampart Division. She watched the citizens and enjoyed the play of traffic. Every time she saw a black and white, she tipped her head at them. The pager at her waste vibrated once, but she turned it off without checking the number. Pell, she figured. Or Kelso. Either way, it didn't matter. She was done with the bombs. She could walk away and live without working the bombs or being a bomb investigator and get along just fine. She was heartened by what Kelso had said. She thought that she might like working Homicide, but most detectives wanted Homicide. It was a tough billet to get, and she hadn't done all that well at CCS. When word got out that she had withheld information from her own detectives, she'd be lucky to find a spot in Property Crimes.

Starkey thought about these things until she realized that she was doing it so she wouldn't think about Pell, and then she couldn't get him out of her head. The tea was suddenly bitter, and the knowledge of how Red had played her was a jagged pill that cut at her throat. She threw away the tea, popped two Tagamet, then turned for home, feeling empty, but not so empty that she wanted to fill that lost place with gin.

That was something, and, she guessed, maybe she had Pell to thank for it, though she was in no mood to do so.

By the time Starkey reached her house, she was hoping that she would find Pell waiting in the drive, but she didn't. Just as well, she thought, but in that same moment her chest filled with an ache of loss that she hadn't known since Sugar had died. Realizing that did not improve her spirits, but she forced the thought of it and what it meant away. She was better now. She had grown. She would spend the rest of her day trying to save her job, or deciding how best to leave it and the memory of Jack Pell behind.

Starkey shut her engine and let herself into her home. The message light was blinking by the front phone, but she did not see it, nor would it have mattered if she had.

The first and only thing she saw, the thing that caught her eye as if it had reached out with claws, was the device on her coffee table. An unexpected visual jolt of twin galvanized pipes duct-taped to a small black box, red and blue and yellow wires neatly folded along its length. Alien and mechanical, stark and obvious as it rested on a stack of *Glamour* and *American Crime Scene*; everything about it screaming BOMB in a way that flushed acid through Starkey's soul in the same moment her world exploded in a white fury.

* * *

"Can you hear me?"

His voice was surprisingly mellow. She could barely understand him over the shrill ringing in her ears.

"I can see your eyes moving, Carol Starkey."

She heard footsteps, heavy heels on hard floor, then smelled the overripe odor of what she thought was gasoline. The footsteps moved away.

"You smell that? That's charcoal starter fluid I found in your pantry. If you don't wake up, I'm going to set your leg on fire."

She felt the wet on her leg, the nice Donna Karan pants and the Bruno Magli shoes.

The sharp throb behind her right ear was a swelling spike that made her eyes water. She could feel her heart beating there, strong and horrible. When she opened her eyes, she saw double.

"Are you okay, Carol Starkey? Can you see me?"

She looked toward his voice.

He smiled when their eyes met. A black metal rod about eighteen inches long sprouted from his right hand. He'd found her Asp in the closet. He spread his hands, gesturing wide and presenting himself.

"I'm Mr. Red."

She was seated on the hearth, arms spread wide, handcuffed to the metal frame surrounding her fireplace. Her legs were straight out before her, making her feel like a child. Her hands were numb.

"Congratulations, John. You finally made the list."

He laughed. He had beautiful even teeth, and didn't look anything like she'd imagined or anything like the grainy photos that she'd seen. He looked younger than his twenty-eight years, but in no way the shabby misfit that most bombers were. He was a good-looking man; he had all his fingers.

"Well, now that I'm there, it ain't so much, you know? I've got bigger fish to fry."

She thought to keep him talking. As long as he was talking, her odds of survival increased. The device was no longer on the coffee table. Now, the device was sitting on the floor inches beyond her feet.

She tried not to look at it.

"Look at it, Carol Starkey."

Reading her mind.

He came over and sat cross-legged on the floor, patting the device like a friend.

"The last of Daggett's Modex Hybrid. It's not the mix I prefer, but it'll get the job done." He stroked the device, proud of it. "And this one really is for you. Got your name on it and everything."

She looked at it just to watch his hand; the fingers were long and slender and precise. In another life, they could have belonged to a surgeon or watchmaker. She looked at the bomb. The two pipes were the same, but the black box was different. A switch topped the box, with two fine wires leading to a battery pack. This bomb was different. This bomb was not radio-controlled.

She said, "Timer."

"Yeah. I gotta be somewhere else when this one goes off. Celebrating my ascension to the Ten. Isn't this cool, Carol Starkey? They wouldn't put me on the list until they knew my name, and you're the one who identified me. You made my dream come true."

"Lucky me."

Without another word, he reached to the black box, pressed the side, and a green LED timer appeared, counting down from fifteen minutes. He grinned.

"Kinda hokey, I know, but I couldn't resist. I wanted you to watch the damned thing."

"You're insane, Fowles."

"Of course, but couldn't you be more original than that?"

He patted her leg, then went to her couch and came back with a wide roll of duct tape.

"Look, don't do anything chicken and close your eyes, okay? I mean, why waste the moment? This is my gift to you, Carol Starkey. You're going to see the actual instant of your destruction. Just watch the seconds trickle down until that final second when you cease. Don't sweat being wounded or anything like that. You'll reach death as we know it in less than a thousandth of a second. Oblivion."

"Fuck you."

He tore off a strip of tape, but stopped on his knees and smiled.

"In a way, that's what I'm doing to you."

"I want the truth about something."

"The truth is a commodity."

"Answer me, you bastard. Did all of this happen . . . did Buck die because I brought you here?"

He settled back on his heels to consider her, then smiled.

"Do you want the truth?"

"Yes."

"You'll have to answer one of mine."

"I'll tell you whatever you want."

"All right. Then here's the truth. Spend your guilt on other matters, Detective Starkey. I learned about the Silver Lake bomb on the NLETS system before you and Pell ever started playing your little game. Daggett brought me here, not you."

Starkey felt a huge wedge of tension ease.

"Now you answer mine."

"What?"

"How did it feel?"

"How did what feel? Being used?"

He leaned closer, like a child peering into an aquarium.

"No, no, no. The trailer park. You were right on top of it. Even though it was just black powder and dynamite, it had to hit you with an overpressure of almost sixty thousand pounds."

His eyes were alive with it. She knew then that this was what he wanted, to be the person in that moment, to feel the force of it. Not just control it, but feel it, to take it into himself and be consumed by it.

"Fowles. It felt like . . . nothing. I lost consciousness. I didn't feel anything until later."

He stared at her as if he was still waiting for her answer, and she felt her anger rage. It had been the same with everyone since the day it had happened; friends, strangers, cops, now even this maniac. Starkey had had enough of it.

"What, Fowles? Do you think a window opens so that you see God? It's a fucking explosion, you moron. It happens so fast you don't have time even to know it's happening. It's about as mystical as you hitting me when I walked through that door."

Fowles stared without blinking. She wondered if he was in a fugue state.

"Fowles?"

He frowned, irritated.

"That's because you had nothing but a low-end piece of bull-shit, Starkey. Homemade crap thrown together by some ignoramus. Now you're dealing with Mr. Red. Two kilos of Modex boiling out at twenty-eight K. The pressure wave is going to sweep up your legs in one ten-thousandth of a second, smashing the blood up into your torso just like a steamroller driving right up to your hips. The hydrostatic shock is going to blow out every capillary in your brain in about a thousandth of a second. Instant brain death at just about the same time as your lower legs separate. You'll be dead, though, so you won't feel it."

"You should stay and enjoy the show. You could sit on my lap."

Fowles grinned.

"I like you, Starkey. Too bad I didn't know you when you worked the bombs. I would've gotten it right the first time."

He grabbed her hair with his left hand, forced her head back, and pressed the tape over her mouth. She tried to twist away, but he pressed the tape down hard, then added a second piece. She opened her mouth as far as she could, letting the skin pull. She felt the tape loosen, but it didn't pull free.

The timer was down to thirteen minutes and forty-two seconds. Fowles checked his watch.

"Perfect."

She tried to tell him to fuck himself, but it came out a mumble.

John Michael Fowles squatted beside her and gently touched her head.

"Save a place in hell for me, Carol Starkey."

He stood then and went to the door, but she did not see him. She watched the timer, the green LED numbers spinning down toward eternity.

Pell

Coombs and Armus were gentlemen about it. They could have brought him in like just another mutt, but they played it straight. They wanted his gun and his badge, which he had left in his motel, and they wanted to talk to him. He asked if he could meet them at the field office, and they said fine. It helped that Dick Leyton told them that Pell had been instrumental in getting them this close to Mr. Red.

Pell drove back to his motel, got the ID and the big Smith 10, then checked out. He sat in his car for a long time, listening to his heart beat and feeling sweat run down his chest. He did not think about John Michael Fowles, or about Armus and Coombs; he thought about Starkey.

Pell cranked his car and went after her, having no idea what he would say or do, only knowing that he could not let her go this easily. Coombs and Armus could wait.

Pell parked on the street in front of her house, relieved when he saw her car in the drive. Funny, he thought, that his heart beat now with the same kind of intensity as when he was facing a mutt in a life-or-death situation.

When Starkey didn't answer, his first thought was that she'd seen him approach, and was ignoring him.

He knocked, and called through the door.

"Carol, please. I want to talk."

He tried to see through the little panes of glass that ran vertically beside her door, but they were crusted with dust. He rubbed at them, looked harder. He thought that she was sitting at the fireplace, but then he saw the tape, and her wrists and the handcuffs. Then he saw the device at her feet.

Pell slammed the door with his foot, and then he was in, going through the door when something heavy hit him from behind and the world blurred. He stumbled forward, seeing flashing bursts of light. Starkey's eyes were wild. Something exploded brilliantly in his head. A man was behind him, hitting him. The man was screaming.

"You fuck! You fuck!"

Pell clawed out his Smith as he was hit again. He could feel consciousness slipping away, but the Smith came out and the safety went off and he fired up into the shadow above him even as the light bled into darkness.

When Pell came to the door, Starkey tried to call through the tape, whipping her head from side to side. She kicked at the floor with her heels, trying to warn him with the noise. She raked her face on her shoulders, tearing at the tape, and jerked at the handcuffs, letting them cut into her wrists.

Fowles jumped behind the door with the Asp just as Pell crashed through. Pell saw only her, and even as Starkey tried to warn Pell with her eyes, Fowles nailed him with the Asp. Fowles hit him again and again, the hard weight of the Asp crashing down like a cinder block.

Pell went down, woozy and blank. Starkey saw him reach out his gun, that monster ugly autoloader, and then he was shooting, shooting up into Fowles, who flipped back and sideways, then crawled toward her couch.

Starkey raked her face against her shoulders, feeling the tape work free, even as she watched the timer. It was winding down so fast the numbers blurred.

Fowles tried to rise, but couldn't.

Pell moaned.

Starkey worked at the tape, stretching her jaw and raking her face until finally one end of the tape came free and she found her voice.

Starkey screamed, "Pell! Pell, get up!"

6:48.47.46.

"Pell. Get up and get the keys! Wake up, Pell, goddamnit!"

Pell pushed himself onto his back. He stared straight up at the ceiling, blinking his eyes again and again as if he were seeing the most amazing thing.

"Damnit, Pell, we've got six minutes, this thing is gonna explode! Come over here."

Pell pushed onto his side and blinked some more, then rubbed at his face.

"I can't see you. I can't see anymore. There's nothing left but light and shadows."

Starkey's blood drained. She knew what had happened. The fight had finished the work on his eyes, caused the damaged retinas to separate and fold away, severing their final fragile connection to the optic nerves.

She felt herself hyperventilating and forced herself to hold her breath, to stop breathing just long enough to get herself under control.

"You can't see, Jack? How about up close? Can you see your hand?"

He held his hand in front of his face.

"I see a shadow. That's all I see. Who hit me? Was it him?"

"You shot him. He's on the couch."

"Is he dead?"

"I don't know if he's dead or not, Jack, but forget him! This bomb is on a timer. The goddamned timer is running down, you understand?"

"How much time do we have?"

"Six minutes, ten seconds."

Not enough time for the police to respond. She knew it was the first thing he would think.

"I can't see, Carol. I'm sorry."

"Goddamnit, Jack, I'm handcuffed to this fucking fireplace. You get me loose and I can de-arm that bomb!"

"I CAN'T SEE!"

She could see the sweat leaking from his short hair down his face. He rolled onto his side and pushed himself up onto his hands and knees. Facing away from her. Across the room, Fowles tried to rise once more, failed, and whatever life was left seemed to drain from him.

"Jack."

Pell turned.

She forced her breathing to even out. When you work the bomb, you stay calm. Panic kills.

"Jack, quick now, okay? Turn toward my voice."

"This is pathetic."

But he did it.

6:07.06.05.

"Straight ahead of you is twelve o'clock. Fowles is at eight o'-clock, right? Just across the room. Maybe fourteen feet. He's on a couch behind the coffee table, and I think he's dead. The keys might be in his pockets."

She could see the hope flicker on his face.

"MOVE, damnit!"

He crawled, two knees and a hand, the other feeling ahead for the table.

"That's it, Jack. Almost at the table and he's right behind it."

When Pell reached the table, he shoved it aside. He found the couch before Fowles's leg, then walked his hands up the legs to the pockets. Fowles's shirt was wet, and the blood had soaked down along his thighs. Pell's hands grew red as he worked.

4:59.58.57.

"Find it, Jack! GET THE DAMNED KEYS!"

"They're not here! They're not in his pockets!"

"You missed them!"

"THEY'RE NOT HERE!"

She watched him dig in both pants pockets and the back pock-ets, then run his fingers around Fowles's waist just as he'd frisk a suspect.

"The socks! Check his socks and shoes!"

She searched the room with her eyes, thinking maybe Fowles

had tossed the keys. You didn't need keys to lock handcuffs, only to remove them. He had never intended to remove them. She didn't see them, and it would only be wasting time for him to feel his way around the room searching for something so small.

"I CAN'T FIND THEM!"

Fowles moaned once, and shifted.

"He's still alive!"

3:53.52.51.

Her eyes went back to the flashing timer and watched the seconds trickle away.

"Is he armed? Does he have a gun?"

"No, no gun."

"Then forget him! Five o'clock now. Come around to five o'clock."

Pell continued ripping at Fowles's clothes.

"JACK GODDAMNIT DO IT! FIVE O'CLOCK!"

Pell turned toward her voice.

3:30.29.28.

"The door's at five o'clock. Get out of here."

"No."

"Romantic, Jack. Very romantic."

"I'M NOT LEAVING YOU!"

He crawled toward her, covering the ground without concern for obstacles, veering far to the right—

"Here."

Changing course to find her foot, barely missing the device, then walking his hands up her legs.

"Talk to me, Carol. You're handcuffed to what?"

"An iron fire grate. The frame is set into the bricks."

His hands slid across her body, jumped to her arms and found her right hand, felt over the cuffs and her wrist to the iron frame. He gripped the frame with both hands and pulled, his face going red. He swung around and wedged his feet against the wall and pulled even harder until the veins bulged huge and swollen in his face.

"It's solid, Jack. The bolts are set deep."

He crabbed across her and tried the other bar. She found herself, strangely, growing calm. She wondered what Dana would say about that. Acceptance? Resignation.

Pell's voice was frantic.

"A lever. Maybe I can pry it out. There's gotta be something I can use."

"The Asp."

The Asp had rolled against the far wall. They lost almost a minute as she directed him to it, then back. He wedged it behind the rail and pulled.

The Asp bent at its joint, useless, and fell free.

"It broke."

Pell threw it aside.

"Something stronger, then! A fireplace poker! A log!"

"I DON'T HAVE ANY OF THAT, PELL!! THERE'S NOTHING IN MY GODDAMNED HOUSE!!! I'M A ROTTEN HOMEMAKER!! NOW GET OUT OF HERE!"

He stopped then, and looked toward her face with eyes so gentle and open that she felt sure he could see.

"Where's the door, Carol?"

She didn't hesitate, and loved him for going, loved him for sparing her the final three minutes of guilt that she had caused his death, too.

"Behind you, seven o'clock."

He touched her face, and let his fingers linger.

"I did you wrong, Carol. I'm sorry about that."

"Forget it, Jack. I absolve you. Hell, I friggin' love you. Now please go."

He followed her leg down to the device, cradled it under his arm, and began navigating toward the door.

Starkey realized what he was doing and screamed in a rage.

"GODDAMNIT, NO!!! PELL, DON'T YOU DO THAT!!! DON'T YOU KILL YOURSELF FOR ME!!"

He crawled for the door, carrying the device under his left arm, moving well right of the door as he'd lost his bearings.

"You're doing me a favor, Starkey. I get to go out a hero. I get to die for the woman I love. That's the most a guy like me can ever hope to do."

He bumped into the nester tables, lost his balance, and dropped the bomb. She could see the lights in the timer blurring.

As he fumbled to pick it up, Starkey knew that he was going to do it. He was going to carry the damned thing outside and blow himself to hell and leave her in here to carry the weight of it just as she'd done with Sugar, and then, only then, her eyes filled and the only possible way to save them both came to her.

"Pell, listen."

He had the bomb again and was feeling for the door.

"Pell, LISTEN! We can de-arm the bomb. I know how to de-arm the fuckin' bomb!"

He paused, and looked at her.

"How much time?"

"I can't see it. Turn it to the right and put it on its side."

2:44.13.12.

"Bring it over here, Jack. Let me look close at it, and I'll tell you what to do."

"That's bullshit, Starkey. You just want to die."

"I want to live, Pell! Goddamn you, I want to live and I want you to live, too, and you're wasting time! We can do this!"

"I CAN'T SEE!"

"I CAN TALK YOU THROUGH IT! Pell, I'm serious. We've still got a little time, but we're losing it. Bring it over here."

"Shit!"

Pell followed her directions until he was next to her, breathing hard and sweating so much that his shirt was wet.

"Put it on the floor. Next to me. A little farther away."

He did as she said.

"Now rotate it. C'mon. I want to see the time."

1:56.55.54.

"How long?"

"We're doing great."

She once more forced herself to hold her breath. It reminded her of the first time she had walked a bomb, and then she remembered that it had been Buck Daggett who'd been her supervisor that day, and who had told her the trick of holding her breath as they had buttoned her into the suit.

"Okay. Now turn it over. Lemme look at the bottom."

"I got no clippers. I got no pliers. I think I have a knife."

"Shut up and let me think."

You make choices. The choices can haunt you forever, or they can set you free.

"Tell me what you see, Carol. Describe it."

"We've got a black Radio Shack timer fastened on top of a translucent Tupperware food storage container. Looks like he melted holes in the lid to drop the leg wires. Typical Mr. Red . . . the works are hidden."

"Battery pack?"

"Gotta be inside with everything else. The top isn't taped. It's just snapped on."

She watched his fingers feel lightly over the timer, then around the edges of the lid. She knew that he would be thinking exactly what she was thinking: that Red could've built a contact connection into the lid that would automatically trigger the explosive if the lid were removed.

You make choices. The choices can haunt you forever, or they can set you free.

"Open it, Jack. From the corners. Just pop up the corners. Slow."

She could feel the sweat creep down from her hair.

Pell was blinking at the Tupperware, trying to see it, but then he wet his lips and nodded. He was thinking it, too. Thinking that this could be it, but that, if it were, neither of them would know it. A ten-thousandth of a second was too fast to know much of anything.

1:51.50.49.

Pell opened the lid.

"Loose all four corners, but don't lift the lid away from the container. I want you to lift it just enough to test the tension on the wires."

She watched him do as she instructed, sweat now running into her own eyes so that she had to twist her face into her shoulders to wipe it away. She was blinking almost as much as Pell.

"I can feel the wires pull against whatever's inside."

"That's the explosive and the initiator. Is there play in the wire?"

He lifted the top a few inches away from the container.

"Yeah."

"Lift the top until you feel the wire pull."

He did.

1:26.25.24.

"Okay. Now tilt the container toward me. I want to see inside."

When Pell tilted the Tupperware, she saw the contents slide, which was good. That meant it wasn't fastened to the container and could be removed.

A squat, quart-sized metal cylinder that looked like a paint can sat inside with the end plug of an electric detonator sticking up through the top. Red and white leg wires ran from the end plug to a shunt, from which another set of wires sprouted up through the lid to the timer, and off to the left to a couple of AA batteries that were taped to the side of the can. A purple wire ran directly from the batteries to the timer, bypassing the shunt, but connecting through a small red box that sprouted yet another wire that led back to the detonator. She didn't like that part. Everything else was simple and direct and she'd seen it a hundred times before . . . but not the red box, not the white wire leading back to the detonator. She found herself staring at these things. She found herself scared.

"Tell me what to do, Carol."

"Just hang on, Pell. I'm thinking. Lift it out, okay? It looks like everything is taped together in there, so you don't have to worry about it falling apart. Just cup it with your hands, support it from the bottom, and lift it out. Put it on the floor."

He did as she instructed, handling it as gently as a lace egg.

"Can you see it okay?"

"Fine."

1:01.00.

0:59.

"How're we doing with the time?"

"All the time in the world, Pell."

"Are we going to be able to do this?"

"No sweat."

"You don't lie worth shit, Starkey."

With the bomb sitting openly on the floor, she could see the connections and wiring more clearly, but she still did not know the purpose of the tiny red box. She thought it might be a surge monitor, and that scared her. A surge monitor would sense if the batteries had been disconnected or the wiring cut and bypass the shunt and the timer. It would be a built-in defense trigger to prevent de-arming the bomb. If they cut the wires or pulled the timer, the shunt would automatically fire the detonator.

Her heart rate increased. She had to twist her head again to wipe away the sweat.

"Is there a problem, Carol?"

She could hear the strain in his voice.

"No way, Pell. I live for this stuff."

Pell laughed.

"Jesus Christ."

"Wish He was here, pal."

Pell laughed again, but then the laugh faded.

"What do I do, Carol? Don't lose it on me, babe."

She guessed that he could hear the strain in her, too.

"Okay, Pell, here's what we're looking at. I think there's a surge monitor cut into the circuit. You know what that is?"

"Yeah. Auto-destruct."

"We try to disconnect anything, it'll sense a change in something called the impedance and detonate the bomb. The timer won't matter."

"So what do we do?"

"Take a big chance, buddy. Put your fingers on the timer, then find the wires that lead down through the lid. I want you to be on the bottom side of the lid, okay, so you're closest to the device."

He did it.

"Okay."

"There are five wires coming through the lid. Take one. Any one."

He took the red wire.

"Okay, that's not the one we want, so separate it from the others, and take another."

Purely by chance, he took the purple.

"That's it, babe. That's the one. Now follow it and you'll come to a little box."

She watched the gentle way his fingers moved along the wire, and thought that he would have been equally gentle as his fingers moved along her scars.

"I'm there. Two wires lead out the other side."

"Right, but don't worry about it. Before we can de-arm the timer, we've got to de-arm this thing, and I don't know how to do that. I'm telling you the truth now, Jack. I don't know what we're dealing with, so all I can do is guess."

He nodded without saying anything.

"Real easy now, because I don't want you to accidentally pull loose a wire, I want you to separate the surge monitor from the rest of the device. Just kinda pull the wires to the side so that the box is off by itself and put it on the floor."

"What do you want me to do with it?"

"You're going to stomp on it."

He didn't bat an eye or tell her she was crazy.

"Okay."

As he did that, she said, "It could detonate, Jack. I'm sorry, but it could just fucking let go."

"It's going to go anyway."

"Yes."

"We've both been through it before, Carol."

"Sure, Pell. No sweat to people like us."

When he had the monitor on the floor away from the other wires, he kept one hand on the surge monitor, then crabbed around into a squat to position his heel over the monitor.

"Am I lined up over the damned thing?"

"Do it, Pell."

One ten-thousandth of a second.

Pell brought his heel down hard.

Starkey felt her breath hiss out as if her chest had been wrapped in iron bands.

Nothing happened.

When Pell lifted his foot, the plastic square was in pieces. And they were still alive.

"I crushed it, right, Starkey? Did I get it?"

She stared at the broken pieces. A set of small silver keys were in the debris. The handcuff keys. That bastard had put the keys in the bomb.

"Starkey?"

She glanced at the timer.

0:36.35.34.

Something inside her screamed for him to scoop up the keys, unhook her, and let them both run. But she knew he couldn't. He could never find the keys and fumble to the cuffs and unlock her in time. There wasn't nearly enough time.

"What do I do? Talk to me, Carol. *Tell me what to do!*"

She didn't want him thinking about the keys. She didn't want him distracted.

"Find the batteries."

His fingers traced over the device until they found the little 9-volt taped to the side of the paint can.

"Got it."

"Feel the wires coming off the top? They're attached by a little snap at the top of the battery."

"Got it. Now what?"

If she was working this bomb in a call-out, she would be in the armor and would've set up the de-armer and blown the bomb apart from the safety of the Suburban sixty yards away. They wouldn't be handling the bomb because you never knew what might set them off, or how stable they were, or what the builder might have rigged. Safety was in distance. Safety was in playing it safe, and taking no chances and thinking everything through before you did it.

"Take it off."

Pell didn't move.

"Just take it off?"

0:18.17.16.

"Yes, take it off. Just unsnap the damned thing. That's all we can do. We have to break the circuit, and we don't have any other way to do it, so we're going to cut the battery out of the loop and pray there won't be a backcharge that fires the detonator. Maybe this sonofabitch didn't build in a second surge monitor that we can't even see. Maybe it won't go off."

He didn't say anything for a while.

0:10.09.08.

"I guess this is it, then, right?"

"Pull it off in one clean move. Don't let the contacts brush together again after you separate them."

"Sure."

"Don't let it be halfway, Pell. One clean move. Cut the connection like your life depends on it."

"How much time?"

"Six seconds."

He tilted his head toward her, his eyes looking too much to the right.

He smiled.

"Thanks, Starkey."

"You, too, Pell. Now pull off the damned cap."

He pulled.

0:05.04.03.

The timer continued reeling down.

"Is it safe, Starkey?"

The timer continued spinning, and Starkey felt her eyes well. She thought, *Oh, goddamnnit*, but she said nothing.

"I'm sorry, Jack."

0:02.01.

She closed her eyes and tensed for something she would never feel.

"Starkey? Are we okay, Starkey?"

She opened her eyes. The timer showed 00:00, but there was no explosion.

Pell said, "I think we're still alive."

John Michael Fowles did not want to die. His head grew light, even as his chest seemed to swell. He heard Starkey's voice, and Pell's. He realized that they were working to de-arm the bomb, and, in that moment, wanted to laugh, but he was bleeding to death. He could feel the blood filling his lungs. He passed out again, then once more heard their voices. He lifted his head just enough to see them. He saw the bomb. They had done it. They had de-armed it. John Michael Fowles laughed then, blowing red bubbles from his mouth and nose. They thought they had saved themselves. They didn't know that they were wrong.

Fowles summoned all of his strength to rise.

"Pell, my hands hurt."

Pell was holding her. He had crawled to her when the moment had passed, put his arms around her, and held her close. Now, he pushed up onto to his knees.

"Tell me how to get to the phone. I'll call 911."

"Get the keys first and unhook me. There were keys in the surge monitor. I think they probably go to the handcuffs."

Pell sat back on his heels.

"There were keys, and you didn't tell me?"

"We didn't have time, Jack."

Pell sighed deeply, as if all of the tension was only then flooding out of him. He followed her directions to the keys, then back to her. When her hands were free, Starkey rubbed her wrists. Her hands burned as the circulation returned.

Beyond Jack, from the couch, Fowles made a sound like a wet gurgle, then rolled off the couch onto the floor.

Pell lurched around.

"What was that?"

Starkey felt no sense of alarm. Fowles was as limp as a wet sheet.

"It's Fowles. He fell off the couch."

Starkey called to him.

"Fowles? Can you hear me?"

Fowles reached a hand toward her dining room. His legs slowly worked as if he was trying to crawl away, but he couldn't bring his knees beneath himself.

"What's he doing, Carol?"

"I'll call 911 and get an ambulance. He's still alive."

Starkey rose, then helped Pell to his feet. Across the room, Fowles inched past the end of the coffee table, leaving a red trail.

Starkey said, "Just lay there, Fowles. I'm getting help."

She left Pell by the front door, then went back to Fowles just as he edged to the far end of the couch.

Starkey came abreast of him as he reached behind the end of the couch, his back to her.

"Fowles?"

Fowles slowly teetered onto his back, once more facing her. What Starkey saw then made all of her training as a bomb technician come screaming back at her: *Secondary! Always clear for a secondary!*

She should have cleared the area for a secondary, just as Buck Daggett had always preached.

Fowles was clutching a second device to his chest. He looked up at Starkey with a blood-stained smile.

"The truth hurts."

Starkey pushed away from him, shoving hard against a floor that tried to anchor her, trapped in a nightmare moment with legs that refused to move, her heart echoing thunder in her ears as she rushed in a painful, panicked, horrible lunge for Pell and the door as—

John Michael Fowles gazed up through the red lens of his own blood at a crimson world, then pressed the silver button that set him free.

After

STARKEY STOOD IN the open front door of the house they were renting, smoking as she watched the house across the street. The people who lived there, whose name she didn't know, had a black Chihuahua. It was fat and, Starkey thought, ugly. It would sit in their front yard, barking at anyone or anything that passed, and stand in the middle of the street, barking at cars. The cars would blow their horns, but the damned Chihuahua wouldn't move, forcing the cars to creep around it in a wide berth. Starkey had thought that was funny until two days ago when the Chihuahua came over and shit on her driveway.

She'd tried to chase it back across the street, but the dog had just stood there, barking. Now she hated the mean little sonofabitch.

"Where are you?"

"Smoking."

"You're going to get cancer."

She smiled.

"You say the most romantic things."

Starkey couldn't wait to move back to her own house, though the repairs would take another month, what with the foundation work, the new floor, two new shear walls, and all the doors and windows being replaced. Not one window or door was square after the blast because of the overpressure. It could have been worse. Starkey had reached Pell in the doorway when the device detonated. The pressure wave had washed over her like a supersonic tidal wave, kicking her into Pell and both of them through the door. That's what saved them. Kicked out the door, off the porch, and into the yard. They had both been cut by glass and wood splinters, and neither of them could hear for a week, but it could have been worse.

Starkey finished the cigarette, then flicked the butt into the yard. She tried not to smoke in the house because it irritated his eyes. She had been twenty-three days without a drink. When she was done with that, maybe she would try to kick the smokes. Change wasn't just possible, it was necessary.

They weren't going to prosecute a blind man. The Bureau of Alcohol, Tobacco, and Firearms had made a lot of noise about it at first, but Starkey and Pell had gotten Mr. Red, and that counted for a lot. They even let Jack keep the medical; no one would take health benefits from a guy who'd lost his eyes on the job.

Starkey was still waiting to hear about herself. She had a good Fraternal Order of Police lawyer and Morgan's support, so she would do all right. She had the month off, and then the hearing. Morgan had told her that he would take care of it, and she trusted him. Barry Kelso called from time to time, asking after her. She found that she liked hearing from him. Beth Marzik never called.

Pell said, "Come here. I want you to see this."

He always said things like that, as if by her seeing something, he could enjoy it. She found that she liked that, too. She liked it very much.

Jack had placed candles around the bedroom. He had them in little stubby candleholders and on saucers and plates, twinkling on the dresser and the chest and the two nightstands. She watched as he set the last one, tracing the wick with his fingers, lighting it with one of her Bic lighters, dripping the wax that he aimed so carefully with his fingers onto a plate, setting the butt of the candle into it. He never asked for help with anything. She would offer, time to time, but she never pushed it. He even cooked. He scared the shit out of her when he cooked.

"What do you think?"

"They're beautiful, Jack."

"They're for you."

"Thank you."

"Don't move."

"I'm here."

He followed her voice, edging around the bed to her. He would have missed her by a couple of feet, so she touched his arm.

Pell had been living with her since he left the hospital. His eyes were gone. That was it. Neither of them knew if his staying here would be permanent, but you never know.

Starkey pulled him close and kissed him.

"Get in the bed, Jack."

He smiled as he eased himself into the bed. She went around, pulling the shades. It was still light out, but with the shades down, the candles cast them in a copper glow. Sometimes, after they had made love, she would make shadow creatures in the candlelight and describe them to him.

Starkey took off her clothes, dropping them to the floor, and moved into his arms. She allowed his hands to move over her body. His fingers brushed her old scars, and the new scars. He touched her in places where she liked being touched. She had been frightened, their first time together, even in the dark. He saw with his hands.

"You're beautiful, Carol."

"So you say."

"Let me prove it."

She gasped at his touch, and at the things he did for her. Starkey had come a long way; there was farther still to go. Getting there would be a better thing with Pell in her life.